The Bishop's Daughter

By Ray Russell

The Summerfield Saga

PRINCESS PAMELA

THE BISHOP'S DAUGHTER

THE MOUNTEBANK'S MISTRESS (*forthcoming*)

Other Novels

THE CASE AGAINST SATAN

THE COLONY

INCUBUS

Story Collections

SARDONICUS

SAGITTARIUS

UNHOLY TRINITY

THE BOOK OF HELL

THE DEVIL'S MIRROR

Nonfiction

HOLY HORATIO!

THE LITTLE LEXICON OF LOVE

THE SECOND VOLUME OF THE SUMMERFIELD SAGA

The Bishop's Daughter

A CHRONICLE
of Certain Personal Events
written by
Miss MELISSA WORTHING
of Hans Town, London
to Mollify her Mind
and Chasten her Spirit
in a time of
GREAT TRIBULATION

Edited, with an Afterword, by
RAY RUSSELL

HOUGHTON MIFFLIN COMPANY BOSTON
1981

Printed in the United States of America

S 10 9 8 7 6 5 4 3 2 1

Library of Congress Cataloging in Publication Data

Russell, Ray.
The Bishop's daughter.

(The Summerfield saga / Ray Russell; v. 2)
I. Title. II. Series: Russell, Ray.
Summerfield saga; v. 2.

PS3568.U77B5 813'.54 81-4467
ISBN 0-395-31562-X AACR2

Note

The division of this chronicle into books and chapters is entirely my own. I also devised the title this volume bears, as I devised the title of a later narrative, that of Melissa's daughter, brought out in 1979 as *Princess Pamela*. It was somewhat after the publication of that book that I found one morning in my mail the present manuscript, leather bound in early Nineteenth Century album style. No letter accompanied it; the ragged wrapping bore no return address; and the postmark had been in large part effaced by the rigors of transatlantic travel (the stamps were English). The album reached me in poor condition, with both covers and several leaves damaged, not recently, by fire and/or water. Some few passages — happily, they are indeed few, most of them in the chronicle's opening and closing pages — are illegible or only partly legible due to this damage, and these I have presumptuously endeavored to reconstruct, to the best of my ability and intuition. All such reconstructions are enclosed in [brackets] for immediate identification, and I hold myself fully accountable for any criticism they may provoke. I have kept my footnotes to the barest minimum, reserving most of my editorial commentary for the Afterword that appears at the end of the book.

R. R.

Contents

BOOK ONE

Queen

Grim Companions — First Impressions — A Gentleman from Suffolk — Marvels of Science — Not a Hottentot — Riding St. George — Venus Crucifixa — Vanity, Vanity — Hangman's Wages — Tipping the Velvet — Masked Marauders — Inequities and Iniquities — More Woman Than Girl — Toujours de l'Audace! — Thou Shalt Commit Adultery — Smoke — Ice — The Gypsy's Bride — The Queen of Love — Sic Transit Gloria Percy — Ungrateful Rabble — Total Tittle-Tattle — Country Matters — Arts and Farces — The St. Arthur's Day Mystery

I

Grim Companions

I have lied and I have killed. I have committed unspeakable grossness in the name of love. And yet I am not repentant, for it is I who am the victim — the abused plaything of a cruel despot.

What lies ahead for me? What further punishment is in store? Igno[miny, at the] very least. Agony, without a doubt; and not alone the figurative agony of the mind, but grisly torture of the flesh; even to the extremity of rending, ripping death, perhaps, my bleeding body split apart as if by horses. I dare not think upon it, and I give thanks — to that same harsh God who tested Job with affliction — that the future is a landscape hidden from the sight of mo[st mo]rtals.

With me always now are my grim companions: memories by day and dreams by ni[ght; lu]rid images of those horrors which have brought me low; those horrors which I have shared with nobody in their worst particulars; for so ghastly were they, so gory and repugnant, that I could never tell Mamma or Esmie or Freddy or my most dearly beloved one or — least of all — Papa.

My father i[s a good ma]n — and as I write those words, "a good man," I know full well that they have fallen into loose employment, for in these days they can offer a deal of meanings: A good man, in the City, means no more than a rich man; at St. Giles's or at Hockley, an expert boxer; in an ale-house, a proficient tosspot; in the ba[gnios of Covent

Ga]rden, a fornicator *par excellence*. On rare occasions, it is used to mean a man of purity and virtue. That is the use to which I put the words when I say that my father is a good man. How should he be else, seeing that he is a bishop? This goodness of his is in harmonious alloy with strict morality, observance of form, and an inclination to preach, none of which is inappropriate to a clergyman of high rank.

Thus it has followed that he has admonished me to — in his words — "Desist in this stiff-necked behaviour. Break your s[ilence. It i]s prideful and stubborn. I might indeed deem it sinful; or, if it is not an actual sin, then surely it is wayward and impious. It displeases me. It displeases God — to Whom you must pray on your knees for guidance. I have no doubt that He will command you to tell me all."

And then, yielding to the softer part of his nature, he added, "Must I assure you yet again, my dear, that I do not blame *you* in this lamentable matter? You are my own precious jewel, and I wear you close to my heart. Saving God Himself, I love you as I love no other being. I would give my very life for you. I wish only to protect you. That is why I entreat you to place your trust in me and gather me into your confidence."

Alas, I could not; and so he left my sitting-room, mere moments ago, with a furrowed brow and in a state of mind closely resembling anger. He came very near to slamming the door.

His wrath notwithstanding, nothing will shake me from my decision to carry this secret to the grave. I am certain it is best that no-one but I ever know it — I and the pages of this discreet album, into which I will drain off the ruminations and reveries that will occupy me in the anxious weeks to come.

The future holding nought but darkness, I will turn away from it to contemplate the brighter past and those events which fetched me to this unhappy period of my life.

II

First Impressions

Were these pages meant to be an autobiography, I should be obliged to disgorge a cataract of trivialities, beginning with my birth — or possibly even *before* my birth, providing detailed accounts of my parents' early lives — and tediously recording every thing that has happened to me between that time and this. Happily, I have no intention of doing so.

It is enough to say that I was born in the same year as Wilhelm Grimm of the enchanting fairy-tales, and the composer Weber. Frederick the Great died in that year, as did our superb master cabinet-maker, Mr. Hepplewhite. In the same year, Mont Blanc was scaled by Messieurs Balmat and Peccard; and in Vienna, Mozart's *Marriage of Figaro* was performed for the first time.

If I add that in the year prior to my birth, the *Times* was started (although it was known as the *Daily Universal Register* for the first three years of its life), and that Papa's friend and ecclesiastical colleague, the Reverend James Wilmot of Warwickshire, positively identified Francis Bacon as the true author of the plays attributed to Shakespeare; and that in the year following my birth, the Marylebone Cricket Club was founded, then the precise extent of my age easily may be reckoned.*

I have always been grateful that, like many another female offspring of the clergy, I was schooled here at home by Papa and Eadward rather than by a governess or at a boarding-school. Thanks to their teaching, I am far better educated than most other young ladies I know.

Eadward — whom I call Teddy — is my elder brother, a husband and father now, living in his own house. And a handsome house it is, designed by his own hand, for he is a much

* In other words, Melissa was born in 1786. — R. R.

respected member of the architect's profession. I have also a twin brother, Aelfred — Freddy — who still abides under this roof; and a sister, Esmeralda, who is the eldest of my parents' living children, already a widow and residing again here with us ever since the violent and shocking death of her husband. I shall have more to say later of these dear siblings — each of them so different from the others and from myself — so different and yet in some respects so much alike.

Esmeralda and I were taught by Mamma to play the harpsichord, but Esmie has always been better at it than have I. More to my liking is the clarinet, which Papa taught me, for he is a veritable amateur virtuoso of that instrument. We have several of them in our house: one of the old crescent-shaped sort; and the later model, which is sharply bent, forming almost a right angle; as well as the newer straight variety, which is my favourite. I like its singing sound; the feel of it; even the taste of the reed. I dearly love to set up my music-stand before me, and to open the printed sheets of notes; and then to take up my clarinet in my fingers, delicately, by its wooden shaft; to put its beak into my mouth and moisten with my spittle the thin piece of cane that is its reed; and then to coax from out that rigid stick the most supple, creamy tones — ah, that is true enjoyment! I often play to Esmie's accompaniment on the harpsichord; but my keenest pleasure is to play, alone, such heart-melting airs as "Greensleeves," which is said to have been written by King Henry VIII. (Can he really have written it? Can such a dread decapitator of women have had such sweet melodies in him?)

Our house — the episcopal residence, as it is called officially — is placed in a delightful situation in Hans Town, close to the market-gardens and orchards of Brompton and not far from the village of Chelsea, where there are coffee-houses, taverns, and other means of diversion. It is such a pity that Ranelagh Gardens in Chelsea, a favourite haunt of the *beau monde,* closed down six years ago; but Vauxhall Gardens, across the river, is still very much with us, with its masquerade nights, its gardens illuminated by a thousand lamps all taking fire together, its long avenues of trees, its fountains, its cascades, and Mr. Roubiliac's statue of Mr. Handel.

This year, Marylebone Park reverted to the Crown, releasing several hundred acres for building north of the New Road.

There is a public house there, The Jew's Harp, which Freddy frequents, with a bowling-green, a skittle-alley, and all manner of merry-making.

Hans Town is one of the newer estates north of the river, built by Mr. Henry Holland some half-dozen years before my birth, and called after Sir Hans Sloane, the original landowner. Our best parlour is one of the finest to be seen hereabout, with its black-boarded floor covered with a Lisbon mat, the handsome heirloom timepiece over the fire-place, an embroidered silk fire-screen, the tortoise-shell cabinet filled with china, the kidney-shaped writing table, cherry-wood arm-chairs, and mezzotints in black Brazilian frames, curtained to protect them from flies. We have also, of course, a coach-house on the grounds, which shelters the grand episcopal carriage, as well as the family coach, the horses, and Tuttle, the coachman.

No-one could wish for a finer house, nor for finer family members to dwell amongst. I have been happy here; but soon it will be the scene of my downfall.

When may my present misfortune be said truly to have begun? I speak not of the harrowing event in specific, but of the circumstances that carried me along in their inexorable current to that terrible day. Surely it all began quite early in the year, when I first met, however briefly, Teddy's brewer friend.

I mind that time well. It had been quite late *last* year — November, if I recollect aright — that the King's mind had decayed into a distemper so hopeless that the poor old man had to be laced into a strait-waistcoat and kept in that cruel restraint for the whole of eleven days. Fashionable ladies, as if by way of contrast, began to leave *off* their strait-waistcoats (by which I mean to say their corsets) at about the same time, permitting the fullness of their figures to flourish untrammelled under the thin fabrics of their frocks. The King being in no condition to rule, his son, the Prince of Wales, was appointed Regent early in January of the present year.* He began to put *on* the corsets the ladies had taken off, so to speak, to contain his ever-increasing corpulence. Thus, father and son were confined in their own strait-waistcoats, although for different reasons.

Another event of this year was the anonymous publication

* 1811. So Melissa's age at the time of this writing is twenty-five. — R. R.

of the first book by my friend Eliza's sister-in-law. That lady — daughter of the Rector of Steventon — is an even better example than am I of home-schooling in a clergyman's house, for she is an artist of consummate skill. So heartily did I enjoy her book that when I met her in the house of her brother Henry (he and Eliza live not far from us, in Sloane Street), I told her that she must write another at once.

"I have, in point of fact, done so," she replied, "some time since, and am encouraged by the profit from my first published book to revise the draught of the earlier one for publication. Indeed, I shall be forced to do so if prices continue to rise any more. Can you believe it when I tell you that in a linen-draper's shop to which I went for checked muslin, I was obliged to give seven shillings a yard? At such prices, even the hundred and forty pounds I received from my book will soon be gone!"

"What is the title of the new book?" I asked her.

"First Impressions. Would you like to read the manuscript, Miss Worthing? I should value *your* first impressions."

"Oh! Indeed I should be honoured to read it!"

"Then so you shall."

And so I did. I found it to be even better than her first book — deliciously, delicately witty — and as I returned the manuscript to her when she came to tea here some days later, I told her that I could criticise nothing but the title.

"You think it to be a bad title, then?" she enquired.

"No — only that it has been already used, by Mrs. Holford, ten years ago."

"You are right. I had quite forgotten that. How very tiresome. What would you suggest by way of replacement?"

"I have been thinking of that," I told her. "Do you remember a novel by Fanny Burney called *Cecilia?"*

"I most certainly do. An interesting book, in its way . . . but you are surely not advising me to entitle my book *Cecilia?"*

"Oh, no. However . . ." I took down *Cecilia* from the shelf. "If I may read a short passage from the conclusion?"

"Pray do so."

I read aloud:

" 'The whole of this unfortunate business,' said Dr. Lyster, 'has been the result of pride and prejudice. Yet this, however, remember: if to pride and prejudice you owe your miseries, so wonderfully is good and evil balanced, that to pride and prejudice you will also owe their termination.' "

Putting aside *Cecilia,* I said, "*First Impressions* is also a story of pride and prejudice. Why not call it so? That title would have the additional benefit of agreeably echoing the form and alliteration of your first book's title, *Sense and Sensibility.*"

She tapped a finger to her chin, murmuring, "*Pride and Prejudice.* Yes. I quite like it. You are a treasure, my dear, truly a treasure."

"Thank you, Miss Austen."

"It is I who must thank *you.* And please call me Jane. I shall call you Melissa, if I may."

Miss Austen — Jane — is a lady some ten or a dozen years my elder. In person she is very attractive. Her figure is tall and slender, her step light and firm, and her whole appearance one of health and animation. In complexion she is a clear brunette with a rich colour, and with brown hair forming natural curls around her face. She has full, round cheeks; both her mouth and nose are small and well formed. But most distinctive amongst her attractions are the intelligence and mischief which fairly *sizzle* in those bright hazel eyes.

III

A Gentleman from Suffolk

Not many weeks after that occasion on which I helped Miss Austen to title her second book, we met again, this time at the house of my elder brother, Teddy. His wife, Luisa, is well regarded hereabout as a superior hostess, and indeed it was a grand party, with over sixty guests, who filled the back drawing-room and overflowed into the passage. Papa, Mamma, Freddy, Esmie, and I were the first to arrive, at seven. At half past that hour, the musicians appeared, two hackney-coaches of them, and by eight o'clock, the remainder of the guests began to flow into the house.

Amongst them was that interesting Mr. Charles Lamb, who

always preserves a cheerfulness and ebullience of spirit despite the blows that life has dealt him. How gruesome it must have been when his sister, Mary, driven mad, they say, by attention to needlework by day and to their mother by night, stabbed the old woman through the heart and killed her. Mr. Lamb's sister was put into an asylum at Hoxton, and would have remained there for ever had not he secured her release on the condition that he would assume full responsibility for her behaviour. What a cross for him to bear, and surely it must be chief amongst the reasons that he has remained unmarried (I know that he has an appreciative eye for the members of my sex).

He smiled when he caught sight of me; and, after an exchange of greetings, I asked him about his friend, poor Mr. Coleridge.

Mr. Lamb shook his head and replied, in that porridge of impediment and Cockney accent that serves him for speech: "Alas, Miss Worthing, Sam is in 'orrible cyse. 'Is annuity from Mr. Josiah Wedgwood 'as been withdrawn. An' you know that 'is wife left 'im some five years since. Well, 'oo could blyme 'er? The opium 'as brought 'im low. When last I saw 'im, 'e said: 'The poet is dead in me, Charles. My imaginytion lies like cold snuff on a brass candlestick, wivout even a stink o' tallow to remind you that hit was once clothed an' mitred wiv flyme.' " Mr. Lamb sighed. "Sad, innit?" he added. I agreed that it was.

Miss Austen, with her brother and his wife, entered at that moment. She was speaking animatedly of the terrible murders which this year have put London into a panic. "I am amazed," she said, "that you London folk appear to *prefer* such horrors to any organised peace-keeping force by public authority."

"For my part," said her brother, "I favour the formation of private groups for security, but a public force? . . ." He shook his head.

"I am of the same mind," said Teddy. "I had rather that half-a-dozen throats be cut every three or four years than be subject to domiciliary visits, spies, and all the rest of it. This isn't France, after all!"

"But," Miss Austen objected, "London is prey to the most unscrupulous villains. There are thieves, pickpockets, footpads, highwaymen, confidence tricksters everywhere. At night, one can not travel beyond the turnpike at Hyde Park Corner through Knightsbridge without taking one's life in one's hands."

"An' yet, dear lydy," said Mr. Lamb, "you 'ave no idea 'ow much I love this London o' mine."

"Indeed?" she said, incredulously.

"Oh, yuss! The crowds, the very dirt an' the mud, the sun shinin' upon 'ouses an' pyvements; the print-shops, the ould bookstalls and pantomimes — why, London hitself is a right pantomime! — all o' vese fings work themselves into my mind an' feed me. Streets, streets, streets! Theatres, churches, shops sparklin' wiv the pretty fyces of industrious milliners an' neat sempstresses! What could be more charmin', I arsk you? An' then the lamps lighted at night, the noise o' coaches, the drowsy cry o' mechanic watchmen, wiv bucks reelin' 'ome in their altitudes — drunk, that is — all the bustle an' wickedness about Covent Garden, the very women o' the town, the drunken scenes an' rattles . . . these are the sights an' sounds that move me, Miss Austen."

"Upon my word, sir," she replied when she had been finally afforded an opportunity, "those emotions are strange to me."

"I might sigh the syme," he countered, "of your rural emotions."

"Chacun à son goût," Miss Austen commented, and Mr. Lamb responded with an amiable shrug.

"Touching on things rural," said Teddy, "I should like all of you to meet my friend just in from Suffolk, Mr. Wilfrid Summerfield."

This new arrival, I have no hesitation in declaring, was — if not, perhaps, the handsomest — the most compellingly attractive and virile gentleman I had ever seen in my life. His masculinity crackled from him. He was tall, well set-up, with a head of thick brown hair, and strongly defined facial features. Possibly his nose was a jot *too* classic for perfect beauty — that is to say, large and arched — but it suited his brilliant eyes and full-lipped mouth. Introductions were traded all round, and Mr. Summerfield's bright brown eyes lingered on mine, or so it pleased me to suppose.

Teddy said, "Mr. Summerfield and I first met when he came to me to discuss the building of a house."

"But, alas," said Mr. Summerfield, "my father overruled your brother's plans, in favour of those submitted by James Wyatt, and the job of work went to him."

"He is an excellent architect," Teddy said, diplomatically.

"But the house is rather a monster," Mr. Summerfield replied.

"It is finished, then?" I asked.

"Just. It is all very Gothic and all very grand. A bit too grand for my taste, but there's nothing like it to be seen in our part of Suffolk."

Papa had come our way, and had been included in the introductions. "Suffolk?" he said. "How is it now in your corner of the country, Summerfield? I have heard much outcry about an upstart gentry, or gentry so-called, displacing the good old aristocracy."

"My father might be one of those upstarts, your lordship," replied Mr. Summerfield with an easy smile, "for he is a brewer; and, in his steps, so am I."

"Take no offence, my boy," said Papa. "I did not have honest brewers of good ale in mind — where would England be without them? I meant, rather, moneyed men from the town, profiteers, usurers, stock-jobbers from 'Change Alley — sons of Moses, some of them, no doubt — buying up the estates of the old native gentry and supplanting the true gentlemen of England, of which you and your father are numbered, I feel sure."

"Well, your lordship," said Mr. Summerfield, "nothing remains the same for ever."

"Hincludin' the brewin' of beer, so I've 'eard," put in Mr. Lamb. "Thy sigh hit's all done by machines now. His that true?"

"Not entirely," said Mr. Summerfield. "But in our new London branch, just opened in Southwark, we indeed use the latest methods, such as a steam engine."

"A steam engine!" I exclaimed. "I should admire to see such a thing in action."

"And I should admire to shew it you," said Mr. Summerfield, "whenever you wish." He turned to Papa. "With your father's approval, of course, and accompanied by such others of your family who share your curiosity."

"The duties of my office leave me little time for diversions," said Papa, and Mamma admitted to an antipathy to the odour of beer, whilst Teddy said that he had already seen the Summerfield brewery.

"Never fear, Mel," Freddy said to me; "I'll brave the den of malt and hops with you."

"To-morrow morning, then?" said Mr. Summerfield. "I shall call for you, if I may."

"Agreed," said Freddy.

I said nothing. I only smiled at the handsome brewer, and he returned my smile.

IV

Marvels of Science

Mr. Summerfield was as good as his word. At precisely ten o'clock the next morning, he drove up to our house in an elegant stanhope as high as a first-storey window, drawn by sleek and spirited steeds.

After Freddy and I had settled ourselves into that magnificent conveyance, and Mr. Summerfield had ordered his coachman to drive to Southwark, I remarked upon the grandeur of his vehicle.

"Yes," he said with a chuckle of pleasure, "it *is* rather magnificent, is it not? I enjoy riding about the town in it. I had my choice of curricles, tilburies, tandems, timwhiskies, and all other sorts, but I chose this. However, I must confess that it is not mine. I've hired it only for the duration of my stay here."

Freddy asked, "You didn't travel from Suffolk in it, then?"

"No, I came by stage-coach."

"A rough ride, surely?" said Freddy.

"Some might think it so, but I'm partial to it. The coaches themselves are quite good, you know; strong and clean and built well. And the horses, beautiful creatures, flecked with lather, snorting and prancing, impatient to be off. The inside of the coach filled with passengers — and even the outside covered in every part with men, women, children, boxes, bundles, bags. The coachman takes the reins in one hand and his whip in the other, gives a signal with his foot, and away we go! At the rate of seven miles an hour!"

"Heavens!" I said. "I fear that such an experience would be too exciting for me."

"Not in the least, Miss Worthing," he assured me. "You would love it. As the stage-coach drives through a town, it draws every eye to it, and its sound fills every window. Children take off their hats and shout as it passes. And there are the jolly coaching-inns along the way, with good food and drink, and accommodating ostlers, yard-boys, waiters, and chamber-maids . . ."

"Accommodating chamber-maids?" remarked Freddy. "I say, that *is* jolly!" I slapped his hand in reproof.

Mr. Summerfield laughed. "My words were meant chastely," he said. "I'm not unmindful that my companions are the children of a bishop."

"I hope," I said, "that the thought of our parentage does not place too much constraint upon you."

"Do you think me too constrained, Miss Worthing?"

"I mean only to tell you that, in our company, you need not comport yourself as if you were in church."

"No fear of that," he said.

Barnaby Summerfield & Son, in Southwark, is a fascinating place, in its way, although the odour of its product can be overwhelming. We saw more than twenty thousand quarts of beer being boiled and cooked in four huge vats before being run off into barrels.

"Our brewery is bigger than Whitbread's," said Mr. Summerfield proudly, "and even Barclay's."

"I have never been inside them," I said, "but I can well believe it. Papa detests Mr. Whitbread."

"Because of his beer?"

"No, because he is such a very Radical Whig. And favourably disposed towards Bonaparte — or so Papa says."

"Look at those dray-horses!" Freddy exclaimed, pointing to the enormous animals used for delivering the beer. "They're the size of elephants!"

"You always exaggerate," I said severely.

"They *are* large," Mr. Summerfield conceded, "but they *must* be, you know, to pull such heavy loads. I can not bear to see poor wretched ill-fed nags pulling weight far too much for them: lame, broken-winded, galled by friction, under a burning sun, suffocated with hot dust . . ."

"You have a tender heart, Mr. Summerfield," I observed, as we entered his private office, where there was blessed relief from the noise and odour.

He coloured, as if ashamed of his tender heart, and remarked, "It has been truly said, Miss Worthing, that England is a paradise for ladies, a purgatory for servants, and a hell for horses."

"And what is she for gentlemen?" I enquired of him.

"Ah," he rejoined, "a gentleman makes his own life into a paradise, a purgatory, or a hell, according to his taste, his will, and, of course, his opportunity. One mustn't neglect to seize opportunity." His eyes dallied with mine as he said this.

His clerk, a man with spectacles and a severe expression, opened the door and said, "Mr. Heathman requires a moment with you, sir."

"Send him in, Cavendish."

A young man entered the office deferentially. He had dull grey eyes like gooseberries, and a shock of straight dark hair that fell over one side of his forehead. He muttered something to Mr. Summerfield, who replied, "Yes, John, and bring glasses for my guests." Turning to us, he explained, "My foreman, Mr. Heathman, has asked me to taste this batch which we've just finished brewing. Actually, he's more than capable of judging its quality himself, but it's a family custom to let no batch go to market unless it's been tasted by a Summerfield."

"None for me, thank you," I said.

"I'll gladly join you," Freddy declared.

"Just two glasses, then, John," said Mr. Summerfield, and the young man hurried away. Resuming his discourse on the brewery, he said to us, "Yes, we do things on a vast scale here. Everything is machinery, all made to run by a single steam engine, as you've seen."

"Is not something lost, as well as gained?" I asked.

"I think not. But that's for you to judge — or, rather, your brother, when he tastes our brew. We are living, after all, in a modern age. This is no longer the Eighteenth Century. We are nearly a dozen years into an exciting *new* century. Don't you agree, Worthing?" he said, speaking directly to Freddy.

Freddy merely nodded, somewhat bemused.

"I mean to say," Mr. Summerfield went on, "we must move with the times, as they are doing in Germany. Consider this fellow Krupp, who opened that enormous munitions works last year at Essen. And there's another German chap, just this year, who's found a way of preserving food over long spans —"

"In glass jars," I said. "I've heard of it."

"And in containers made of tin, as well," he added.

"Tin!" Freddy responded, unbelievingly. "I say, Summerfield, will you be putting up your beer in tin jars one day?"

Our host laughed. "I hardly think that likely," he replied, "but science is moving along marvellously. Look at the gas-lamps that were installed along Pall Mall just three or four years ago. What an improvement over the old kind — and yet how violently they were opposed by the whale-oil industry, and for what obvious reasons of self-interest."

"I agree that they are an improvement," I said, "and yet I resist the use of gas-light indoors: gas is lethal when inhaled, and thousands might die in their sleep."

"Not if reasonable precautions and good sense are used," said Mr. Summerfield. "And even the lethal qualities of gas might one day be put to humane use . . ."

"Humane! —"

"Why, yes, in the execution of criminals. Put a condemned prisoner in a sealed room, pump in the gas, and *presto!* — he's gone to his Maker."

"What a ghastly idea!"

"Much better than being throttled by a noose or decapitated by the guillotine, don't you think? Science fascinates me, Miss Worthing: it is always coming up with the most astonishing ideas. This Frenchman Lamarck, for instance, a year or two ago put forth the notion that living forms evolve, so to speak, in an ever-ascending scale of perfection."

"Living forms?" I said. "By that you mean beasts, I suppose, like those colossal dray-horses of yours?"

"Not only horses, Miss Worthing, at least according to Monsieur Lamarck. He argues that, through a combination of unconscious striving, the physiological effects of use and disuse, the influence of the environment, and the inheritance of acquired characteristics, anatomical parts — this little hand of yours, for instance — slowly became modified."

"Sacrilege," I said, reclaiming my hand.

"Too deep for me," confessed Freddy.

"Why do you call it sacrilege, Miss Worthing?"

"Because if human beings have been changing through the ages, it follows that you and I would bear very little resemblance to Adam and Eve."

"Perhaps we do not."

"But they were made in the image of God."

"I am sure that they were. But where in Scripture does it say that God looks like *us?*"

"Are you saying that Adam and Eve may have been covered with hair like that woolly mammoth that was found in the ice in Siberia some years ago?"

"Well . . ."

"And that God, Who made them in His image, is also covered with hair? You are saying, if I grasp your meaning, that you and I are *improved* editions of Adam and Eve — which is simply another way of saying that we are improved editions of God. That is why I call the notion sacrilege. I hope you are not a disbeliever, Mr. Summerfield?"

"I?" He held up his right hand, as if swearing a vow. "Solid Church of England."

The young foreman returned, bearing a tray with two glasses. "Thank you, John," said Mr. Summerfield, handing a glass to Freddy, and adding, "Your very good health." They drank, Freddy quaffing half the tumbler in one breath; Mr. Summerfield taking only a small taste before returning his glass to the tray.

"Bang-up stuff!" Freddy pronounced the brew.

"It passes inspection," Mr. Summerfield told his assistant. "Send it off to market." The foreman, with a curt nod, left us.

"But you've barely touched it," Freddy observed.

"A touch is enough to judge its character," said Mr. Summerfield. "For, truth to tell, I'm not keen on my family's stock-in-trade. When I'm thirsty, I prefer Adam's ale."

"Water?" I said. "You, a brewer, are an abstainer?"

"Oh, never that," he replied. "I like a good claret, a fine brandy with a cigar, a noble port after dinner. It's just beer that's not to my taste, Miss Worthing, strange as that may seem. Perhaps it's due to my being so close to it all my life. I admit that I'm susceptible to most of the other temptations this world offers."

"I never doubted it, Mr. Summerfield," I said.

V

Not a Hottentot

On our way home, Freddy engaged Mr. Summerfield in a discussion of cricket.

"Papa deplores cricket," I said.

"But why, pray?" asked Mr. Summerfield. "Surely it is a healthful and innocent pastime."

"Papa says it brings gentlemen together with men of low station; clergy and barristers mingling with butchers and cobblers and all sorts. It also draws large numbers of people away from their employments, and openly encourages gambling."

"Your father is a bit hard on us, I think. Lesser men, who are not of his exalted calling, can not be expected to share his rectitude."

When the stanhope pulled up in front of our house, Mr. Summerfield expressed the hope that he might be permitted to call before he returned to Suffolk.

"We are at home every Thursday," I told him. "But will you not be required to live always in London, now that your brewery has opened a branch here?"

"I shall probably be removing to London for good and all before the year is much older. I rather fancy the town. In the mean time, my foreman is more than capable of looking after things."

"And tasting the brew? Is that not the prerogative of the Summerfields?"

The brewer laughed. Winking, and touching a finger to his

nose, he said, "I've made him an honorary Summerfield. Thursdays, you say?" With a jaunty wave at us, he tapped his stick authoritatively, and the stanhope pulled away.

"Not a bad chap," Freddy remarked.

Inside our house, I found Esmie in the library, absorbed with her pack of *tarot* cards. "And what does our mystic fortune-teller prophesy?" I sallied, a jot too flippantly, I fear, for she replied:

"You needn't mock me or my late husband."

"Dear Esmie, you know I don't mean to," I said in apology, and kissed her cheek. "I was always fond of Mr. Cooper."

"True," she conceded. "You were the only member of this family who did not look down upon him."

"That's not so. Freddy liked him, and so did Mamma."

"Teddy took a superior attitude towards him."

"That was only to please Luisa. And Luisa is not family, to my way of thinking. She is only an 'in-law.' "

"So was my husband."

"Yes, but . . . well, he was so much more agreeable than Luisa."

"And then there was Papa," said Esmie. " 'Touched with the tar-brush,' Papa called him. 'Scarcely better than a heathen Hottentot.' "

"That was before you married him," I reminded her. "Papa was merely upset, and had not come to know him."

"He was neither a heathen nor a Hottentot. He was a fine Christian man." Esmie handled the *tarot* pack with veneration. "These were his cards," she said softly, "and his mother's before him."

"Do they say that I will fall in love with a handsome stranger?"

"They are not to be trifled with, nor used for silliness or nonsense."

"You are so *stern,* Esmie."

She smiled. "Forgive me, Lissa dear. I am melancholy today, remembering my poor dead love."

I took her hand and stroked it. "Shall you ever marry again?" I asked her.

She shook her head. "I am too old."

"You are not yet forty-four!"

"Where should I find a man like Mr. Cooper? No, Lissa, I consider that he is still my husband, and will always be, and that he is waiting for me on that distant shore. When my life is over, I will join him and we will be together again, for all the time that is to come." She gripped my hand. "I believe that. I must believe it. You believe it, too, do you not?"

I fought back the tears that were stinging my eyes. "Oh, yes, I do, I *do!*"

We kissed and embraced each other.

I felt in need of a hot bath, and went up immediately to my rooms to ring for Abigail, my maid. As I entered my sitting-room, however, I heard the most peculiar sounds emanating from the adjoining bedroom. I am happy to say that I have never seen or heard a pig being stuck, but if ever the simile "squealing like a stuck pig" were appropriate, it was at that moment.

I quickly opened my bedroom door, to discover Abigail, bent forward on my bed, her skirts up, her under-garments down, and the division of her pearly fundament being plumbed in a rapid, rhythmic *presto con brio* by my scapegrace of a twin brother. She squealed with each of his thrusts, but howled with horror when she saw me enter the room.

"There, Mister Aelfred!" she wailed. "I *told* you that Miss Melissa might walk in at any moment!"

"Freddy! Abigail! For shame!" I cried.

They disengaged and covered themselves, hastily. "I say, most frightfully sorry, Mel," Freddy mumbled. "Thought you were in solemn conclave with Esmie."

"Abigail, fetch the water for my bath," I said sharply. "Freddy, leave my rooms, please."

Whining and snivelling, Abigail went off to do as she had been told, and Freddy, shrugging his wistful apology, made for the door.

"Best do up your breeches first," I advised him.

"Good girl! Thanks, Mel!" he said, fastening his buttons before quitting my rooms.

As I undressed before stepping into the bath, I said to Abigail, "How *could* you?"

"It weren't my fault, Miss," she said, snuffling. "I was just smoothin' down your bed, when in walks Mister Aelfred, bold as you please, throws up me skirts, and has at me!"

"Pour a little of that Cologne water into the tub. That's enough. Are you saying that he raped you?"

"Not exactly, Miss. He ain't a bad lad, really."

" 'Isn't.' "

"Yes, Miss."

I stepped into the tub. "Wash my back, please." As she did so, I said, "Then you admit that he had his way with you entirely with your compliance."

"Beg pardon, Miss?"

"You did not object."

"I didn't like to disappoint the young gentleman."

"Did you enjoy it?"

"What! *There,* Miss? Of course not!"

"Then why did you —"

"Well, Miss, he *wanted* it the other way, but what would have become of me if I'd got in the family way, I ask you? Dismissed! Sent packin'! That's what! So I made him go round to the after passage. Very obligin' he was, I must say."

"So were you, Abigail. Altogether *too* obliging! Be sure that it does not happen again!"

"Please, Miss, you won't tell his lordship, will you?"

"Tell Papa? Heavens! I shouldn't be able to find the words!"

VI

Riding St. George

Papa has been a bishop for very nearly four decades now, having been consecrated in 1772, at the age of thirty, the youngest age at which an Anglican priest can be made a bishop. He and Mamma had then been married for six years, and Esmie was five years old. "And yet, I swear that I can remember it," she claims. "Mamma held me up so that I could see. I remember Papa kneeling before the King and placing his hands between his. Papa then said some words — I learnt much later that it was the oath of temporal allegiance — and then he kissed the King's hands."

That King was our same George III. He had been on the throne for only a dozen years, and was a young man of thirty-four at the time. At any rate, ever since that day, Papa has been a spiritual peer, with a rank immediately above that of baron, and a seat in the House of Lords — of which, however, he has never made actual use. As a bishop, he can administer the rite of confirmation, can ordain priests and deacons, and can exercise certain powers of dispensation. In addition, he has many other administrative, as well as spiritual, duties; is much in demand as a speaker; and therefore leads a busy and useful life.

Freddy, who — as I have already shewn — is an incorrigibly naughty young man, once told me, when we were younger, that Papa's parents must have been "riding St. George" before he was born, because "that's the way to get a bishop, you know."

" 'Get a bishop'?"

"Give birth to a son who'll become a bishop," he patiently explained.

"Fudge!" I responded, scornfully; and then asked, "What is 'riding St. George'?"

"You're too young to know."

"I am exactly as old as you are. Five minutes older, in fact. Tell!"

"Oh, very well. It means, when a man and a woman are shagging —"

" 'Shagging'?"

"— *she's* astride *him,* riding up and down on his pego —"

" 'Pego'?"

"— and *that,* they say, is the way to get a bishop."

"Fudge!" I retorted again.

Whether or not my paternal grandmamma rode St. George, she did get a bishop, who is a fine and respected gentleman, as well as dear and loveable. One might not think it, to look at him in all his episcopal solemnity, but he is often given to the sweetest and most touching sentiments, such as the writing of charming verses to his children on their birthdays. On the twenty-first anniversary of Esmie's birth, he actually

wrote a sonnet, quite a good one (albeit here and
cryptic, as all the best poems are), which she has
amongst her treasures and has shewn to me from t
And yet, despite such fond endearments in his r
that I may have painted too severe a picture of him in earlier pages. This I must endeavour to correct.

His strictures against cricket may have seemed stern to Mr. Summerfield, but if that game indeed gives rise to gambling and idleness, surely Papa is right to condemn it? As for his attitude towards Esmie's husband, it was merely the natural distrust of an exotic race with strange customs, its own language, and a reputation not remarkable for industrious or even honest ways.

Also, his passing reference to "sons of Moses," which I have recorded, must not be misunderstood. Many persons believe that the Jews murder Christian children to obtain their blood; Papa knows that this is not so. Some say that one can tell a Jew by the fact that he has always one eye smaller than the other, or because he has a distinctive odour, or that his skin is indelibly speckled with filth; others aver that every Jew has a mark of blood on one shoulder and a malignant blackness under his eyes. Papa does not believe these absurdities.

Neither does he believe that the Jews are a cause of pestilence. Seven years ago, when a deadly fever broke out in Gibraltar, a letter was written to the *St. James's Chronicle,* suggesting that the filth of the Jews was its cause. From the beginning of time, argued the anonymous correspondent, the Jews have been a dirty race. They were driven out of Egypt on account of a contagious distemper, which, by means of their filthiness, was always amongst them. The Romans, continued the letter, would not allow them to dwell in Rome, and so forth, and anybody who ventured into the Jewish districts of London would discover the followers of Moses to be the most nasty and filthy people under the canopy of Heaven. The letter concluded with the thought that if the Jews did not reform themselves, they should be shut up in a *ghetto,* as in Rome or Venice, and made to wear a badge when they come into the city. Many people are in thorough agreement with such ideas, but not Papa, for, although he is a Tory, he is an enlightened peer of liberal beliefs.

He is simply opposed, on soundly religious principles, to

the naturalisation of Jews, which misguided if well-meaning folk advocate, and as was actually attempted some half-dozen decades ago by a defeated Bill.* "To naturalise them," he has said to me, "would be to defy the Will of Providence. Did not God cast them out of their native land in punishment for their wickedness, and disperse them throughout the world? How can England, then, take them in and naturalise them? We should be flying in the face of Scripture, challenging the decrees of the Almighty. The Jews, my dear, having murdered Jesus, are perpetually marked as aliens wherever in the world that they wander — and it is just and proper that this should be so. They are an outcast, outlawed people, an ally of the Antichrist. The essence of their 'religion,' so called, is an avowed contempt of Christ, an implacable hatred of Christians, and an impious detestation of Christianity. How, then, can it ever be thought that England, or any Christian state, should allow such professed enemies to be admitted into its privileges, much less to be on the same footing with its own natural-born subjects?"

"But, Papa," I asked him once, "what of those Jews who have converted to our faith? I believe that they can be naturalised, can they not?"

He snorted, and replied, "Unfortunately, they can. But it takes more than a splash of water from the baptismal font to wash away the stain of Jewishness. Once a Jew, for ever a Jew."

How clear it all is, I said to myself, when he explains it.

VII

Venus Crucifixa

Papa's views, for reason of the fact that they are so sensible, are seldom contradicted — and certainly are *never* contradicted

* The "Jew Bill" of 1753. — R. R.

by members of this family. On rare occasions, however, some guest of ours, more wilful than respectful, has been known to offer opposition to a statement of Papa's, and this never fails to take him by surprise. At such times, the expression on his face is one of astonishment, and he seems to be saying: "You contradict me? *Me?* The Right Reverend Ambrose Worthing? That is like contradicting natural law; like saying that day is night or black is white. You must be bereft of your reason: that can be the only explanation."

On the Thursday following my visit to the Summerfield brewery, during our at-home, a pronouncement of Papa's was challenged by a friend of Freddy's, the young Mr. Shelley, who was in London, briefly, on holiday (or, perhaps, on French leave) from Oxford.

Papa had been saying that it was the responsibility of the middle classes to set an example for the lower orders in all things, but most particularly in regard to restraint in sexual behaviour. "Else," he pointed out with unassailable logic, "numbers will outstrip subsistence, and there will be an inevitable decline in living standards all round. The Reverend Malthus has shewn this conclusively."

Every one of our guests nodded agreement, except Percy Shelley: "Restraint, you say? You are very hard, your lordship, to rob the poor of the single alleviation of their sufferings and scorns. They have not the reading of poetry to divert them, nor theatre shows, nor operas, nor race-courses. They have not even cricket, for I have heard you would deny them that, as well. They are cold and hungry and in despair, and it is only the soothing, elevating, and harmonious gentleness of the sexual congress that lends a humanising charity to their domestic lives."

Papa bristled. "How old are you, Master Shelley?"

"Nineteen."

"Perhaps your views may be excused by your youth, but I am not sure that they are fit for the ears of my unmarried daughter."

"You brought up the subject, your lordship," Mr. Shelley reminded him.

"So I did," said Papa, "but not in order to sing the praises of carnality, as you have done. I spoke of the need to wage war upon profligate breeding; the need for self-control if a poor family is to survive the battle of life."

Mr. Shelley laughed, which infuriated Papa even more. " 'Wage war' . . . 'the battle of life' . . . such *martial* metaphors, your lordship! Such great artillery you amass against the sweetest of the passions!"

His praise of that sweet passion is of no wonder, in light of a later event of this year, which I will write about in its proper — or improper — place. But I will note now that before Mamma and Papa joined us that Thursday afternoon, I saw a curious ornament hanging from Mr. Shelley's watch-chain. It was a small crucifix of gold, and its use as a decoration struck me as shockingly irreverent. Sensing my disapproval, he said:

"Look closer, Miss Worthing, and you will see that it is no ordinary crucifix. I had it made up especially, to my design."

Taking it in my hand, I then saw that the figure hanging from the cross was not the Saviour, but a naked woman! She was full-bodied, voluptuous, unequivocably female, and not even a breech clout shielded her beauty from the eye. In all other respects, the attitude was the same as the Saviour's: the face sad and full of suffering, the head drooping forlornly to one side, the arms outstretched, the legs bent gracefully at the knees. Two nails pierced her hands, and a third pierced both of her feet.

"She is Venus," Mr. Shelley explained, rubbing his thumb sensuously over the tiny golden breasts of the figure. "*Venus Crucifixa*. It represents the cruel manner in which you followers of Jesus have nailed the goddess of love to your Christian cross and killed her. Rather clever, is it not?"

"Too clever by half, Mr. Shelley," I replied. "Pray be sure that my father does not see it."

Laughing, he hid it in his waistcoat pocket. I will add here that his freethinking ways were not so well known to us at that time as they would be some weeks later — else Papa should not have allowed him entry to this house. Another friend of Freddy's who was our guest that day, Mr. Brummel, was tolerated by Papa (just!) only because he had made himself so charming to Mamma, and possibly because he was known to be well liked by the Prince who will one day be our King.

Further contention between Papa and Mr. Shelley was averted when that same Mr. Brummel said: "The sweet passion — as you call it, Percy — isn't the only entertainment that the poor enjoy. Blue Ruin is cheap — I've heard that they can get drunk for a penny and dead drunk for tuppence. Presumably," he added, "they can get half-drunk for a ha'penny. Speaking of which, I was accosted by a beggar in the street t'other day. The pathetic shabbaroon asked me for alms, 'even if only a ha'penny.' I said to him, 'My poor fellow, I believe that I have *heard* of such a small coin, but I assure you that I never have possessed one.' I gave him a shilling."

All of us laughed at that; and I asked, "But what is Blue Ruin?"

Freddy said, "You know: jackey — max — diddle — drain — lightning — heart's-ease — rag water — frog's wine — Madame Geneva — strip-me-naked . . ."

"Aelfred!" Mamma scolded. "Such language!"

"Your brother means gin, Miss Worthing," Mr. Shelley explained, with an enchanting smile.

"And beer is even cheaper," added Freddy, "but it doesn't make you as drunk — am I right, Summerfield?"

For, indeed, Mr. Summerfield had arrived at that moment. "Gin is evil stuff," he said, "but good beer and ale are healthful foods. Liquid bread, I call them."

Introductions were made to those of our guests who did not already know Mr. Summerfield. Approval of the new arrival's clothing was expressed by Mr. Brummel, after he appraised it with his small grey scrutinising eye. "Some people from the outlands have no idea of how to dress in the town," he elucidated. "My brother, for example. I saw him in the street yesterday, and I cut him directly. He was wearing country clothes! In London! My *dear!*"

"Welcome to this house, Mr. Summerfield," said Mamma.

"Thank you, ma'am: I am mindful of the congeniality of this company, for I am come straightway from an unpleasant visit in Queen Anne Street. Number Twenty-three, to be precise."

"Who resides there," I asked, "and why was the encounter unpleasant?"

"It is the house of the painter Mr. Turner," he replied, "and a more disagreeable man I have never met. I went there, thinking to buy a painting to take back with me for our new house in Suffolk. I found him to be secretive, sharp of tongue, mean with money, and with not the least faculty for friendship or even civility. If this be an artist, give me a good honest joiner!"

"He *looks* rather like a joiner, for the matter of that," commented Mr. Brummel. "Or possibly a master carpenter. Lobster-red face, staring eyes. Wears a blue coat with brass buttons, I swear it! And turned-up boots! He makes no attempt to look like a gentleman."

"Or to behave like one," added Mr. Summerfield.

"And he bargains worse than a Jew."

"Forgive me, Mr. Brummel," said my sister, Esmie, "but when you say that he bargains worse than a Jew, do you not mean that he bargains *better* than one? I have been told that they are masters of that difficult and subtle art. At least, they enjoy that reputation. Do you mean that Mr. Turner is not such a master? — that he bargains badly, ineptly, foolishly? Or do you mean that he is a greater master than even a Jew? I require elucidation."

Esmie was being very naughty, of course, and I could see that Mr. Summerfield was enjoying her persecution of poor Mr. Brummel, but I came to his rescue by saying, "Whether he is a greater or a lesser master of *bargaining,* I can not tell, but his pictures are thought to be exquisite." Of Mr. Summerfield, I enquired, "Did you buy one of them?"

"I did not! He may go hang, for all I care!"

"On the subject of hanging," said Mr. Brummel, "there's to be a public one at Newgate to-morrow morning. Every window overlooking the prison has been booked by this time, naturally, but Wales has invited me and my guests to share his window. Percy, would you care to join us?"

"Depends upon who's being hanged," replied Mr. Shelley. "There are one or two Members of Parliament I should like to see dangling."

Mr. Brummel, laughing, responded, "No, it's just some poor wretch who strangled his doxy in a drunken fit."

"Then I respectfully decline, George, with thanks for your gracious invitation. Besides, I must hie me back to Oxford before I am missed."

"Freddy? Miss Worthing? Summerfield?"

"I return to Suffolk in the morning," said the brewer.

"It does sound exciting," admitted Freddy. "Still, I don't know . . ."

"Do come, my dear chap," Mr. Brummel urged. "All the young bloods will be there, to say nothing of sober tradesmen and their bulbous wives."

"All right, I will."

Mr. Brummel turned to me. "And you, Miss Worthing?"

A hanging! The thought of it froze my blood. And yet, I must in truth allow that a part of me was fascinated — the worst part, I expect. "Are ladies permitted to attend?" I asked.

"Permitted?" Mr. Brummel laughed. "Wild horses can't keep them away. You would be amongst company of the highest *ton,* I assure you."

I turned to Papa, my eyebrows raised inquisitively. He said, "It is a grim spectacle, no doubt, but we must keep in mind that it is also a process of justice, quite legal and extremely necessary. I approve of the publicity of hangings — they provide a salutary example to potential wrong-doers. I see nothing wrong, Melissa, in your attendance, should you wish to go."

"Come, Miss Worthing," Mr. Brummel urged. "It promises to be the best show in town."

"You're going along, Freddy?" I asked.

"Yes. As Papa says, there's nothing wrong in it."

"Very well, Mr. Brummel, I will accompany you."

"Good! We shall make a day of it."

Mr. Brummel is a tall, handsome, impeccably groomed young man not too much past thirty years of age, I should judge: perhaps thirty-two or -three. Freddy describes him as "a flash cove"; others call him a strutting coxcomb; he is often referred to as the Beau. His grandfather, they say, was a valet ("And a damned good one," according to Mr. Brummel). I have heard that Harriette Wilson, one of the demi-reputables of his acquaintance, has pronounced him cold, heartless, and satirical. He was at Eton; and had a coronetcy in the Prince of Wales's regiment, the 10th Hussars, until the Hussars were ordered to Manchester to suppress a riot in the cotton mills. Rather than go, he resigned his commission. "Out of sympathy for the mill-workers?" I once heard Lord Byron ask him.

"Don't be tiresome," Mr. Brummel had replied. "I simply couldn't tolerate the thought of being exiled to a provincial town. Manchester — now *really.*"

I shewed Mr. Summerfield some of our finer things: our tables and chairs by Sheraton, with the heavier pieces resting on feet done in the likeness of paws and claws of beasts and birds. I shewed him our pedestal tables and cerule chairs with gilded animals as supporters. "The piece that always delights our foreign visitors most," I said, "is this arm-chair. They think it quite the novelty."

"Why, it delights me, too," he said brightly, "and I am no foreigner." He sat down in it and pronounced it "Marvellous comfortable. I feel quite at home in it."

"I hope you shall always feel at home — when we are 'at home.' "

He laughed at my pleasantry, and I felt emboldened enough to ask "Must you truly leave London to-morrow?"

"I'm afraid so. And I shall miss it." His eyes said that he would miss *me,* I divined, although his words were, of necessity, impersonal.

"I have fallen over head and ears in love," he said, rising from the arm-chair, "with the glass-makers of Whitefriars, the enamel-works of Battersea, and the Chelsea china-factories; not to mention the clock-makers of Clerkenwell, the jewellers and goldsmiths of Hatton Garden . . ."

Would his litany of mercantile zeal go on, I wondered, to include the brick-kilns and lead-factories at Islington, the market-gardeners at Brompton, Kennington, Lambeth Walk, and Earls Court, the barley- and wheat-farming in Fulham and Hammersmith, the very cows that graze in the meadows off Kensington High Street, the dairy farms of Belsize Park, as well as all the glove-makers, stay-makers, fishmongers, greengrocers, pastry cooks, and street-sellers of gingerbread, oysters, and cats' meat who vend their wares in London? But no, he got only as far as "the gunsmiths in the Strand . . ." when Mr. Brummel strolled by and interrupted him:

"Ah, do not speak of the Strand, my dear Summerfield," he said with distaste. "Fashionable gentlemen seldom are seen there now-a-days. Why, bless me, not a week since, I actually encountered Dick Sheridan in the Strand, and was forced to assume that he had *lost his way* by straying so far east of Piccadilly."

And what were *you* doing there, I wanted to ask him, but Mr. Summerfield merely said, "I shall try to remember that." To me, he added, "And I shall try to return very soon."

"Will you call on us," I shamelessly asked, "the very first Thursday after your return?"

"I may not even wait till Thursday," he replied.

VIII

Vanity, Vanity

I must set down here something touching upon Mr. Sheridan, mentioned in passing above.

He is, of course, Richard Brinsley Sheridan, the noted playwright. He and his second wife live in Bruton Street. She is the daughter of the Dean of Winchester. They receive guests on occasion, but I fear that he, like Mr. Coleridge, is in decline (although, thank God, not addicted to opium). He is a man of sixty now. His two great comedies, *The Rivals* and *The School for Scandal,* are far behind him, for they were first staged more than thirty years ago.

He has been active in political life for many years as a Member of Parliament; was appointed treasurer of the Navy when the Whigs came to power in '06; and became a member of the Privy Council. Throughout his parliamentary career, he has been a close companion of the Prince of Wales; and when the Prince was appointed Regent this year, one would have thought that Mr. Sheridan's fortunes should have risen, too. But he has been plagued by debt and disappointment, poor man.

Two years ago, his Drury Lane Theatre burnt to the ground. (Theatres *for ever* seem to be burning to the ground: Covent Garden went up the year before!) Mr. Sheridan sat at a tavern near by, with a glass of Rhenish in his hand, watching

Drury Lane blaze away. "Why not?" he said, when my elder brother, Teddy, expressed amazement at seeing him there at such a time. "Can't a man take a glass of wine at his own fireside?"

Not long after, during a visit to this house, he told me that all of his troubles and triumphs have been the result of vanity. He quoted the Book of Ecclesiastes on the subject, and then added: "They talk of avarice, lust, ambition, as great passions — and I have been afflicted by at least two of them, I warrant you — but it is a mistake, Miss Worthing; they are little passions. Vanity is the great commanding passion of all. Not only is it the ruling force in the lives of men like Brummel, but it also produces the great and heroic deeds — Nelson at Trafalgar, and so on — or impels us to the most dreadful crimes. Save me from but this passion, and I can defy the others. They are mere urchins, but vanity is a giant."

Perhaps it was the Jerusalem Chambers (as I have heard them called) of money-lenders that drew Mr. Sheridan to the Strand. And Mr. Brummel, as well, for the matter of that.

IX

Hangman's Wages

In the pale chill dawn of the following morning, Freddy and I went with Mr. Brummel to the hanging.

Outside Newgate Prison — or "City College," as Freddy waggishly called it — a restless rabble had gathered overnight. We saw street vendors, crippled soldiers and sailors, painted prostitutes and their pimps, chimney-sweeps and their climbing boys, ballad-singers, pickpockets: all of them pressed up against the barrier in front of the scaffold. I was unpleasantly reminded of the mobs that flocked to the guillotine in France, and I said as much to Mr. Brummel.

"Quite," he agreed, fanning himself with a scented handkerchief. "Or of a Roman carnival? An example, perhaps, of history repeating itself. *Plus ça change,* and all that."

The rabble grew thicker and more suffocating with every passing minute, it seemed to me, and it was a relief to reach the sanctuary of the rooms which the Prince Regent had booked for himself and his friends. The windows looked down upon the yard of the castellated prison, affording a clear prospect of the gallows and of the mob below. They were becoming still more excited, more vicious, and more ribald, their noise nearly drowning out the sound of the clock on St. Sepulchre's Church as it chimed the hour.

"George!" cried the Prince with delight, on espying Mr. Brummel. He was standing with a company of gentlemen and ladies, dressed in the latest fashion. The gentlemen, all with their necks encased in high starchers, had exchanged their former breeches for trousers; and their female companions all looked like pages out of *The Lady's Magazine* or *La Belle Assemblée,* having forsaken strait-lacing for high busts and loosely flowing gowns of veritably transparent muslin. I could see their rosebud nipples quite plainly, and so could Freddy. The towering feathered hats and high-piled *coiffures* that had, until but recently, been fashionable had given way to bonnets and fringes, or bunches of corkscrew ringlets.

"Your Royal Highness," said Mr. Brummel, "may I present to you Miss Melissa Worthing and her brother Aelfred."

"Charming," said the Prince, as he looked me over. "I am honoured. And Mr. Worthing: so pleased."

I said, after curtseying, "Your Highness does not remember me, but that is not surprising. I was a child when last we met, in my father's house."

He knitted his brows. "Worthing, Worthing . . . surely not his lordship, the right reverend bishop?"

"Yes, sir."

"Of course! You were a little bit of a thing. But you have grown admirably — and, if I may say it, amply!"

"So have you, my dear Wales," observed Mr. Brummel.

The Prince laughed. "This rogue is for ever twitting me about my *embonpoint,*" he said with a pout. "Am I become *too* ample since our last meeting, do you think, Miss Worthing?"

"Your Royal Highness is every inch a — a Regent," I replied.

"Well said!" Winking at Mr. Brummel, he added, "Not only lovely, but a diplomat, as well. Truly, George, I swear that I have not put on another ounce of flesh in the past six months. Only yesterday I weighed myself in Berry's shop in St. James's Street. They have enormous scales, Miss Worthing, to weigh huge bags of coffee and tea and tobacco."

"All of the fashionables weigh themselves there," Mr. Brummel explained. "The Prince, Lord Petersham, Lord Alvanley, even I. In boots and out of boots. Occasionally in only my stockings. And a frock, of course."

"Come have some cherry brandy," said the Prince, "and meet my other friends . . ."

However, as he said this, a great cry went up from the crowd outside, and all of us buzzed to the windows like flies to manure. Those thousands of faces down in the courtyard were directed towards the grim black door of the prison, which had opened. How ugly those faces were! — brutal, scowling, grinning, necks stretched with craning — but were *our* faces any prettier, I wondered?

The dark-attired hangman appeared, and was greeted with vulgar applause, as if he were an actor. With him was the condemned man, in chains. I could not see his face, for he kept his eyes fixed on the ground. The hangman and his victim slowly mounted the steps of the scaffold. The mob strained forward, like one immense monster, all crushed together into a singularity of many limbs and eyes and gaping, laughing, jeering mouths.

I said, to nobody in particular: "There are trades which I have always thought to be distressingly loathly, although necessary: the slaughter-house-worker, who kills animals for our tables; physicians, who must deal with disease . . . but to be a hangman! To strangle poor souls to death . . ."

"There is no strangling, Miss Worthing," the Prince assured me. "The neck breaks like *that*" — he snapped his fingers — "and death comes at once."

"Still," I said, "to work at such a trade . . . to be *paid* for it . . ."

"Thirteen pence ha'penny," said Mr. Brummel. "A shilling for the executioner and three ha'pence for the rope. Those are a hangman's wages."

"You are behind the times, George," said the Prince. "Hangmen of these days, like other tradesmen, have raised their prices."

"What is his name?" Freddy asked in a small voice.

"The hangman?" enquired Mr. Brummel. "Jack Ketch, they're usually called."

"No, the — the other one."

"Hanged if I know," he replied, causing the Prince to laugh, and me to wonder how Mr. Brummel had ever acquired his reputation as a wit.

Now the doomed man's chains were struck off, and this act provoked a great chorus of howls from the rabble. Were they howls of pleasure, of disapproval, of eager expectation? It was impossible to tell. It was the roar of a beast — loud and ferocious and powerful, but without mind or character.

The noose of hemp was placed over the victim's head. The noise of the crowd swelled. I closed my eyes, for I could not bear to watch the dreadful moment, now that it had arrived.

But all noise suddenly ceased. There was a profound hush, total silence, and this was so surprising to me that I opened my eyes — just in time to see that wretched man kicking his feet and dangling by his neck as the trap-door sprang open beneath him.

I tried to close my eyes again, but I could not. They were fixed to the sight of that unfortunate creature — kicking, twitching, strangling — for seconds that seemed like hours. I was appalled, but I could not turn away. His eyes bulged; his tongue protruded from his mouth. I had thought that the noose was merciful, providing instant death; but this was a foul display of torture, a barbaric and disgusting spectacle, and oh! how the audience — including those in the room with me — relished it.

Still the poor man writhed and twisted at the rope's end. Would he never die? I moved my lips in silent prayer: Dear God, please end his suffering.

Now the hangman crept beneath the scaffold. He seized his victim's jerking ankles with his hands and pulled down with one strong sudden tug. We all heard, even up in that room, the sharp *crack* of the breaking neck, like a pistol-shot. The twitching stopped; the body hung limp and quiet, dead at last. The mob cheered.

"Is it . . . over?" asked Freddy, and I turned to see that his eyes, unlike mine, were shut tight, and his face the colour of whey.

"Yes," I said softly, "all over."

He opened his eyes. He was trembling. "If I may . . . be excused, Your . . . Highness," he managed to mutter as he dashed towards the door of the room. Then I heard him, on the landing, being exorbitantly sick.

I was proud of him.

X

Tipping the Velvet

Papa was never very proud of Freddy. Indeed, each of his sons had been a disappointment to him in some sense, for neither had taken holy orders, as Papa had wished. He had come to look with favour upon Teddy, however, because of Teddy's high reputation as an architect, his harmonious family life, and his unblemished respectability.

But Freddy, to Papa's way of thinking, left much to be desired. His friends were people like Shelley and Brummel: dandies and radicals and libertines, Papa called them. Freddy's idea of an occupation was strolling about with such fellows in St. James's or Piccadilly; or going to Watier's or White's to play at whist, faro, and hazard. He was even observed in the green glades of Hyde Park at five o'clock, that fashionable hour when the most well-bred ladies of *ton* drive out to be seen — as well as the demi-reputables whose affections are sold for a fee, and quite a high fee, I am told, when they are in great demand, like the notorious Harriette Wilson. I fear that Freddy spent his money on them from time to time. At least, I know that he was remarked amongst their plumed and painted company at the Royal Italian Opera in Haymarket, and Freddy not being a lover of opera, one drew certain conclusions.

"Dash it, Mel," he said to me one afternoon when we were playing at backgammon in the drawing-room, "can you really imagine your twin brother in the lawn sleeves of a bishop? Preaching sermons? Quoting Scripture? I believe in God and all that — I'm no atheist like Percy — but I simply have never been able to understand what's wrong with a game of cricket or tipping the velvet with a pretty girl. I mean to say, Sodom and Gomorrah must have been jolly places, don't you think? A bit like Margate or Vauxhall Gardens. One might have had quite a good time there. Rather awful of the Almighty to have smitten them as He did. And consider the way He treated poor old Job. Or His own Son, for the matter of that. I've often thought that God would not be a very pleasant chap to have for a friend. One could never completely trust Him, don't you know. You could never be sure that He wouldn't trip you up with His stick, just for a laugh, or fling a cupful of punch in your face for no good reason."

"It's a good job that Papa isn't in the room to hear you say that."

"You won't tell him, will you?"

"Of course I won't . . . if you tell *me* what you meant by 'tipping the velvet.'"

"Oh, that's just a way of talking."

"But what does it mean, precisely? Is it *very* naughty?"

"No, not very. It refers to kissing."

"That's all? Just kissing?"

"A certain kind of kissing."

"*What* kind?"

"Well . . . it's difficult to explain . . ."

"Then shew me."

"Oh, very well," he said, and, leaning over the backgammon board, he put his lips to mine, then slipped his tongue between them.

"Is that all there is to it?" I asked. He nodded. "But I see nothing very exceptional in it. It's not even nasty. Well, just a little, perhaps. There is surely nothing pleasurable about it."

"That's because I'm your brother."

"Being my brother has nothing to do with it."

"It has everything to do with it. I find nothing pleasurable about it, either — when I do it with you. But with a prime article . . ."

"A what?"

"A jolly girl."

"I'm not jolly enough for you, is that the way of it?"

"No, that's *not* the way of it," he said, exasperated. "It's just that there's no sport in it when one does it with one's sister."

"Do it again."

"No."

"Just once again, Freddy, please." I crossed over to his side of the table, and sat on his lap. "Or I'll tell Papa what you did to Abigail."

"You wouldn't dare!"

And then he tipped the velvet with me again. This time, it took a bit longer, and our tongues touched, lingeringly. I felt a tingle deep in my body.

When it was over, I reflected on my own feelings. "Well," I admitted, "it *was* rather pleasant that time. Was it pleasant for you — even though I'm your sister?"

He shrugged. "Not bad."

"Shall we do it again?"

"No."

I smiled at him. "Do you remember, Fweddikins —"

"Don't use that silly name."

"Do you remember, when we were both of us *quite* little, and Nurse would bathe us?"

"What about it?"

"And, when she wasn't looking, how I would play with you?"

"Oh, see here, Mel . . ."

"And tickle your twiddle-diddles?"

"I say!"

"Why, Fweddikins, you've gone red as a beetroot!" I kissed him chastely on the cheek. "Oh, I *do* love you, you young rake," I said with deep affection. "But what are we to do about you? What is to become of you? Papa is quite right, you know — you can't spend your life *just* playing cricket and whist and tipping the velvet, as pleasing as those things are. You must make something of yourself. If not a clergyman like Papa, then *some*thing."

"Yes, but what? There's the rub."

"The Army, perhaps?"

"Freddy Worthing? Rattling sabres? Marching on parade?"

"You would look ever so delicious in uniform."

"No, thank you very much."

"The Navy, then?"

He tapped his stomach. "I get sea-sick too easily."

"Perhaps you should take to writing, like your friend Percy."

He laughed, ruefully. "Just writing a *letter* ties my poor brain into knots." He rubbed his chin thoughtfully. "But, do you know, from time to time I've thought . . ."

"Thought about what, dear?"

"Well, I'm not a bad-looking cove . . ."

"You're an Adonis!"

"And we *are* on speaking terms with Dick Sheridan, after all. And perhaps he could put me in touch with somebody like Mrs. Siddons . . ."

"Freddy!" I said, aghast. "Are you seriously suggesting that you should become an *actor?"*

"Well . . ."

"A *mummer?* A *mountebank?* Paint your face like a demi-rep and prance about on a stage? What would Papa say?"

"Quite a lot, I'm afraid, and all of it disapproving. But damn it, Mel, in these days some actors can be deuced respectable. Look at Kemble. And the better ones make good money."

"And tip the velvet with the most prime articles."

He positively *smirked*. "Well, yes, I must admit there is that about it, too!"

I read from an imaginary broadsheet: " 'Mr. Aelfred Worthing, in *The Tragedy of* HAMLET, *Prince of Denmark!'* "

"Oh, I say," he objected, "not the big bow-wow stuff like that. Comedies like Sheridan's or Murphy's or Cholmondeley-Cockburn's or Goldsmith's. I fancy myself as Marlow in *She Stoops to Conquer."*

"And so do I," I said, decisively. "I can fairly see you in it." I slipped into the voice of Miss Hardcastle: " 'The ladies, I should hope, sir, have employed some part of your addresses?' "

Freddy instantly assumed the shy, stammering, stuttering manner of young Charles Marlow: " 'P-P-Pardon me, m-m-m-madam, I — I — I as yet have studied — only — to — d-d-deserve them.' "

We both laughed. Embracing him, I said, "Then it's settled. Our Freddy must needs be a votary of Thespis, and tread the boards as Captain Absolute and Sir Giles Overreach — and why not Romeo? You're handsome enough. 'O Romeo, Romeo! wherefore art thou Romeo? Deny thy father, and refuse thy name —' "

Freddy nodded, tight-lipped. " 'Deny thy father' is right enough, at that," he said. "Papa will be in an apoplexy. You won't tattle to him, just yet, about these acting notions of mine?"

I locked my lips in pantomime and replied, "Not a word." Then I proceeded to trounce him at backgammon.

XI

Masked Marauders

Before Mr. Summerfield returned to Suffolk, he asked me to write to him, "if that is not too bold a request."

I hit upon the notion of sending him by the post a copy of Hannah More's new tract, *Practical Piety*, published this year, enclosing my letter in the packet.

He did not respond immediately, but when he did, he wrote:

"My dear Miss Worthing, —

"Thank you for the religious tract, which I read with interest. You must allow me to say, however, that I side with my friend Will Cobbett, who holds that the purpose of such tracts is simply to teach people to starve without making a noise; keeping the poor from cutting the throats of the rich. You may, however, consider Will to be a criminal, for since last year he has been sitting in prison by reason of his denouncing the flogging of mutineers. I am afraid that he is an unrepentant Radical, and continues to publish his *Political Register* every week, even from his cell. I hope I do not offend. My family are all Tories, I assure you, and as members of the upper classes, we have no wish to have *our* throats cut!

"This brings me to the subject of these 'Luddites' in Nottingham, of whom you ask in your welcome letter. I will tell you all that I know, which is precious little. They are, I have heard, a band of night marauders, and they go about in masks, smashing machines such as stocking- and lace-frames, looms, *et cetera.* Such violent destruction of property can not be excused, but one can understand their feelings. The installation of machines in the textile mills has caused dismissal of those handicraftsmen hitherto employed in that work. Even amongst those few who have not been dismissed, there have been distressing reductions in their wages. To their credit, the Luddites never have shed blood in their riots; and yet one of the mill-owners, Mr. Horsfall, is threatening to instruct soldiers to fire upon them, should they attack his mill again. Let us pray that it will not come to that.

"No, the Luddites have not as yet reached Suffolk, thanks for large mercies, and I fervently hope they never will, for if poor innocent looms inflame these zealots, shall brewers' vats escape their wrath? Their name, about which you enquire, is said to derive from the will-o'-the-wisp who directs their activities, a certain 'Ned Lud' or 'General Lud' or 'King Lud' of Sherwood Forest — surely an imaginary figure of no more substance than Robin Hood. Less, no doubt!

"You know, I think, that there has been other unrest amongst the workers of the North. I have heard that they march through their towns bearing placards with the words NO REGENT! The cause of this, it is said, is resentment of the extra taxation made necessary by the Prince's enormous debts. Jacobinism walks in our midst, if not outright revolution. I have seen pamphlets directed against the Prince, saying, 'If His Royal Highness would have us hate Republicans like those of France, let him teach us first to love our Princes. Let Jacobinical vices be opposed by royal virtues.' This is distressing, but one can not deny that there is some truth behind it.

"I look forward to my return to London. Until then, I hope that you will convey my greetings to the members of your family.

"I remain
"Your most obedient
"Wilfrid Summerfield"

In a part of my reply to him, I wrote:

". . . But surely your friend Mr. Cobbett is wrong to denounce the flogging of mutineers? Such villains are no better than traitors. Flogging is considered to be quite the thing in the Army, so why object to its maritime use? Wellington has had fifty men flogged all at one time, I have heard. I can not, however, approve of his flogging of women, as he is said to have done in Spain to camp-followers. You will accuse me of bias in favour of my own sex, but it is simply that we are not so strong as men, and our skins are too soft; therefore a woman flogged suffers an inequitably greater punishment than does a man under the same lash . . ."

I was a little troubled by his comments on Hannah More's tract. They sounded a touch atheistical to me. I hoped I was wrong. Had he not, after all, assured me — that day in the brewery when we had been discussing the theories of Lamarck — that he was "solid Church of England"?

XII

Inequities and Iniquities

Mr. Summerfield's views would have been of little concern to me had he not been the first man I had ever met who had stirred thoughts of marriage in my mind. For, although the prospect of marriage had never been repugnant to me, there were always its inequities to be considered. As part of the wedding ceremony, the man declares to the woman: "With all my worldly goods I thee endow." But the opposite is true. The customary marriage settlement bestows the bride's money upon the bridegroom, to have and to hold from that day forward. She may no longer call it her own, nor command the use of it. Indeed, she may not call her own person her own, for she is owned by her husband as part of his goods and chattels. In such a state of affairs, the marriage bed assumes the function of a sacrificial altar.

Its appearance, as well, is often that of a grotesque altar. Look at my parents' bed, for example. Those two tall square posts at its head, rising seven or eight feet high; that pair of huge projecting scrolls, three quarters of the way up; the tester, with its heavy moulding on top and lighter on the bottom, like a cornice. That front panel, with its crockets and pendant drops like huge acorns; the whole curved like a wavy bow. That dark velvet curtain falling from the back of the tester — drawn at night to keep Mamma and Papa from draughts, looped back and held in place by those heavily tasselled cords by day. Head-board and foot-board alike bedizened with such a quantity of curlicued scrolls and *paterae:* the whole bedstead, in sum, a riot of jarring styles — the half-tester, a survival of mediæval times; strap-work, courtesy of the Elizabethan era; curves, scrolls, and curlicues, baroque; *paterae,* neo-classical in the school of the last century. To say nothing of the bell-flower in decorated Gothic. It is all so intimidating, and (as I have said) so altar-like, as if to warn the occupants that this massive receptacle is not a place for plain sleeping, certainly no place for snoring, and most assuredly not a sporting-field to accommodate the gambols of light-hearted nymphs and satyrs: No, no, it says, this is A Solemn Instrument for Procreation.

Indeed, it does make one sober to look upon that bed and know that here, all of my parents' children were conceived and those same children born. A massive engine of regeneration it is, manufacturing human merchandise, like a mill.

My own bed is so much nicer and not as portentous: it has a single iron-framed half-tester of much less height than theirs, with attractive *papier-mâché* head- and foot-boards. The tester is a half-circle, with valance, back curtain, and straight-hanging side curtains of green silk with gold trimmings. Quite simple.

On the subject of simplicity, or perhaps the proper word is abstemiousness, Papa delivered a speech earlier this year at a dinner of notable gentlemen and peers. It concerned the problem of hunger among the poor, a thing which deeply troubles him. His speech drew merited applause from the gathering. I will not copy it down entire, but will content myself with an extract, from Papa's draught:

"While the poorer orders of society labour under great difficulty to provide the daily sustenence for themselves and their families, it is the sacred duty of every *paterfamilias* to do his utmost not to aggravate this grievous condition in his own household . . . In my household, I have given instructions that all possible economy be used in the consumption of every article of food."

That is true; and I can add nothing to those sentiments, so I will merely append, without comment, the menu which Papa brought home from the dinner:

Turtle soup and iced punch
Salmon, turbot, fried fish
A sideboard of petites pâtés

Chickens, capons, turkey poults, larded; hams and tongues, ornamented; ribs lamb, raised ornamented pies, lobster salads, prawns, Chantilly biscuits, ornamented trifles, noyeau *and* maraschino *jellies, pine, strawberry and Italian creams; Genevoise pastry, Swiss and Venetian* meringues, *Chantilly tartlets, creamed tarts, Nesselrode puddings, plovers' eggs.*

Haunch mutton, chine mutton, sirloin beef, currant jelly; ducklings, goslings, leverets, pea fowl.

Dessert: Hot-house grapes, apples, strawberries, oranges, pears, dried fruits, Savoy and almond cakes, mixed cakes,

brandied cherries, preserved ginger.
Ices: Raspberry, strawberry, orange,
millefruit.

The world in which we live appears to have been designed to confuse me. We are taught one thing, and our eyes and ears tell us quite another. Is all of life a disguise, a masquerade, like those plants and insects which Nature paints to resemble things other than themselves? Is it even thus in our more exalted human sphere? Does iniquity wear the mask of virtue — and virtue, that of iniquity? Do the just and good always prevail, as we would wish, or do not unjust men too often attain high peaks of power and position?

XIII

More Woman Than Girl

I would not call the Prince of Wales an unjust man, although as Regent he has indeed attained those aforementioned peaks of p. and p. — and when his poor old royal father dies and he becomes our King, he will be even more powerful.

Some call him dissolute. They point to his many mistresses; they are shocked by his marriage to Princess Caroline of Brunswick-Wolfenbüttel, his first cousin. They ridicule his silhouette, which has become bloated by reason of his fondness for food and drink. As a young man, he was famous for his good looks: for, although they say he had always his high colour, it was then the ruddiness of health and youth, which complemented his bright blue eyes, elegant figure, and shapely legs. Even to-day, although he is immense and nearing fifty, he exudes a disquieting virility. When he was fifteen, one of his tutors (Papa's friend, Bishop Hurd) said, "He will be either the most polished gentleman or the most accomplished blackguard in Europe — possibly both." He has turned out to be neither, but none can tell what the future will bring, of course.

When we met at the hanging, he was princely, indeed, in every particular of his dress and manner, all of which he owed to the guidance and tutelage of Mr. Brummel. I sensed, however, a beginning coolness between the two men, as if overmuch familiarity had bred contempt; and I could not but be reminded of how the jolliest companion of Prince Hal's riotous youth, merry old Sir John Falstaff, was cruelly renounced when the Prince became King. The Prince of Wales was not, and is not, yet King, but upon becoming Regent, I expect that he proceeded to put certain of his former companions behind him.

And yet he is not an unkind man: when Freddy was sick, the Prince shewed great solicitude and understanding. "Your brother is of tender years, Miss Worthing," he said. "He has not yet grown calluses on his sensibilities. It is no discredit to him."

"My years are as tender as his, Your Royal Highness, for he and I are twins — and yet I watched the hanging callously."

"Callously? Never! Bravely. Twins, you say: and yet you seem to be, I will not say older, but more a woman than a girl, and he seems to be still a boy. In any case, those of your sex have stronger stomachs than men do. The weakness and faintings for which ladies are known are mere affectation."

"I will not deny that we are often less delicate than we pretend."

"And yet, Miss Worthing," said the Prince, "if 'delicate' be used in its sense of 'fine,' or 'exquisite,' to describe rare grace and beauty, then I must deem you delicate indeed."

"Your Highness is most kind."

"It is you who are kind, dear lady, to join my company today, and delight our eyes with your presence. When may we hope to see you again?"

"Does Your Highness use 'we' in its princely sense, to mean himself; or is the general meaning intended?"

The Prince chuckled, and waggled a finger at me, as if he were a pedagogue and I an unruly pupil. "I see I must speak by the book," he said. "You may take the 'we' in either sense, my dear, provided that you answer my question."

"Then you and I will meet again," I replied, "whenever it pleases Your Highness to command it."

" 'Command' — so hard a word from such soft lips! But if command I must, command I will, Miss Worthing. You may rely upon it. 'We' — in any of its senses — will meet again, I promise you."

I attempted to curtsey, but he stopped me, and kissed my hand instead.

"Brother," said an approaching voice behind me, "will you not present me to your charming friend?"

I turned to see a very tall, gaunt gentleman with a tangled beard, a fierce scar, and a chilling dead eye. More chilling still was his living eye, which snapped back and forth from the Prince to me, and seemed to peer quite through my clothes to my naked flesh. These attributes, and his unsavoury reputation, were well known; and I guessed who he was, even before the Prince said:

"That, my dear Ernest, would be like presenting a great spider to a pretty little fly. However: this is Miss Melissa Worthing, daughter of the bishop of that name. Miss Worthing, the Duke of Cumberland."

The Duke took my hand. "Flies are disgusting creatures," he said. "*I* would not compare you to one, Miss Worthing. May I ask to hear your impressions of the hanging?"

"It was educational, Your Grace," I replied. "I should not wish to repeat the lesson, however."

"Nor should I," said the Duke. "Pallid stuff. Milk-and-water. Nothing like the way they despatched that fellow Damiens in Paris, some fifty years ago or so. Wish I'd seen it. The ladies loved it, so I'm told; watched it all from windows, just as we did to-day. They tore him apart with four horses, in the Place de Grève. And before that, they did all manner of other things to him: ripped off his flesh with hot pincers, poured molten lead into —"

"Was his crime so great," I interrupted, "that such cruelties were justified?"

"I should think so!" replied the Duke. "The blackguard tried to assassinate the King!"

"Only *tried?*"

The Prince of Wales explained: "Louis the Fifteenth came away with a *piqûre d'épingle.*"

"A mere pin-prick?" I rejoined. "And yet they did much more to poor Monsieur Damiens than only prick him with a pin!"

The Prince said, "It was the punishment prescribed by French law for regicides."

"But he did not commit regicide. He failed. Had he succeeded in his attempt, could his punishment have been any harsher?"

The Duke of Cumberland stroked his beard. "Oh, I dare say. If *I'd* had the sentencing of him, I warrant you I'd have thought of a few embellishments that would have made the death he died seem, in comparison, a pleasant afternoon's tea. And as for this minuet that was danced for us down there on the scaffold this morning — I call it insipid. We English have grown lax in meting out punishments. It will be our undoing."

On our way home in Mr. Brummel's carriage, Freddy — still pale, but recovered — said to his friend, "Do you really think it wise, George, to poke fun at the Prince's paunch as you did?"

"He's getting fat as a hog," snapped Mr. Brummel.

"Even so —" Freddy began to respond, but Mr. Brummel did not allow him to finish:

"I made him what he is," he said. "And I can unmake him."

Pride goeth before destruction; and an haughty spirit before a fall.

XIV

Toujours de l'Audace!

"I talked to Dick Sheridan," Freddy told me not long after our discussion of his theatrical ambitions. "He wrote me a letter of introduction to Mrs. Siddons, and I went to see her to-day at her house in Upper Baker Street. I had no idea she was so old. Half-way between fifty and sixty, I should think."

"Sarah Siddons past fifty?" I marvelled. "I should not have thought it, to see her on the stage."

"She was rather decent to me, I must say, but very much in the grand manner. Imperious is the word. I expect it's all part of being an actress. *'SIT DOWN, YOUNG MAN, AND TAKE SOME TEA,'* she said — and, upon my word, it was like a church organ! I mean to say, what a voice!

" 'So you wish to become an actor,' she went on. I was tongue-tied, and I simply nodded. 'Mr. Sheridan speaks well of you. Have you had experience of the stage?' I shook my head. 'What makes you think you have the gift?'

" 'Well, ma'am,' I said, 'I have the desire.'

" 'If desire were all,' she came right back, 'every pretty young man with a saucy smile would be on the stage. And you *are* pretty, I must allow. Rather arrogant, too, I expect, like most good-looking young men. You think that your profile will open every door and win every heart. You believe that all the playwrights and managers in London — yes, and all the young actresses, too — must needs shower you with their attentions.' "

"Oh, dear," I interjected. "What did you reply?"

"Mel," Freddy said, "I can not tell you what possessed me. I think I was inspired. Without in the least planning it, I answered her by slipping into the very bit of dialogue that you and I were playing about with t'other day — do you remember?"

"From *She Stoops to Conquer."*

"That's right. When she accused me of thinking that everybody in the London theatre must shower me with attentions, I said: 'P-P-Pardon me, m-m-m-madam, I — I — I as yet have studied — only — to — d-d-d-d-d-d-d-deserve them.' "

"You didn't!"

"I did."

"And she — ?"

"At first she looked at me as if she were frozen into ice. I prayed to die there on the spot. And then the old girl threw back her head and *roared* with laughter! I thought that she would never stop. Finally, she dabbed at her eyes with a lace handkerchief and smiled at me. 'You may have the makings in you, at that,' she said.

" 'You mean — I was good?' I asked.

" 'Good? *Good?* Of course not. You were wretched. Too broad, too calculated, too pleased with yourself, altogether overdone. But you have an ear and a voice. And you have shewn audacity. That, sir, is an indispensable quality if one wishes to be an actor. Let your motto be the words of Monsieur Danton: *"Il nous faut de l'audace, encore de l'audace, TOUJOURS DE L'AUDACE!"* '

"Then she looked me over, and tapped a finger to her chin, and said, 'Yes. Young Honeywood, perhaps, in that other piece of Goldsmith's, *The Good Natur'd Man.* Not yet, of course. You are too raw, too undisciplined. But one day . . .'

"She sent a servant to fetch pen and paper. 'I shall give you a note to my brother,' she said."

I clutched Freddy's hand. "Not Mr. Kemble?"

"John Philip K., no less," he said in confirmation. "After writing the letter, she said, 'Pray allow me to give you a piece of advice, Mr. Worthing. Audacity is a necessary ingredient, as I have said, but do not be *too* audacious when you see my brother. He is a good man and a fair man, and needless to say he is a *great* artist — but, and I tell you this in strictest confidence, he has a fear of young actors. Particularly if they are good. And audacious. So: use all gently, as Hamlet says. If you do not frighten him with your impetuosity and your youth, he may grant you an opportunity to shew what you can do. Small *rôles* only, at first. But do not overwhelm him, as you overwhelmed me. There is a young strolling player whom he fears. Fiery, crude, full of excesses, not too many cuts above the juggler he recently was — but brilliant. He played a very small part with me six years ago in Belfast, when he was only sixteen, and he was impressive even then. He has set his sights on London, drawing nearer and nearer in ever-smaller circles, like a hawk. His name is Kean. So let discretion be your guide,' she said, and handed me the letter."

"Oh, Freddy, how truly wonderful!" I kissed him.

"I haven't seen Kemble yet, of course," he said. "And he may not fancy me at all."

"He will; I know he will!"

"But not a word to Papa and Mamma as yet."

"My lips are sealed."

"Perhaps when they see me as Honeywood or Absolute . . ."

"With all of London at your feet and the press hailing you as the new Garrick . . ."

"Well, hardly that."

"Why not? You must aim high. *TOUJOURS DE L'AUDACE!*"

XV

Thou Shalt Commit Adultery

Audacity of another stripe was displayed by me one day some years ago when I was no longer a child and not yet quite a woman. At dinner I surprised my family and our servants by suddenly asking, "Papa, does the Bible condone adultery?"

He dropped his fork and stared at me. I asked another question: "Did Adam and Eve wear breeches? Like Teddy?"

Mamma hastily said, "For shame, Melissa, what foolish, naughty questions!"

Papa continued to stare at me. "*Any* interest in Scripture is welcome from you, Melissa," he said, "albeit somewhat sur prising. I had not known that you, or, indeed, any of my children — saving Esmeralda — gave much thought to Holy Writ. But what prompts these particular, and I may say *peculiar,* questions, pray?"

"One of the Bibles in your library, Papa, gives the Seventh Commandment as 'Thou shalt commit adultery.' And another says that Adam and Eve wore breeches."

"I see." He picked up his fork and resumed eating. "After dinner," he said, "come into the library with me and I will explain it."

It was on that evening that I learned of Papa's famous collection of erroneous Bibles, most of them very old. "The errors are not deliberate," he told me, "but the result of bungled printing. To me they aptly illustrate the thought 'To err is human'; and they serve to remind us that perfection is not to be found in this world, among mortals, even when those mortals be well-meaning men, printing the Word of God." He then spent several hours shewing me his collection and pointing out the various errata, holding the books close to his eyes, for Papa is almost as near-sighted as was Dr. Johnson. It was one of the most pleasant evenings I had ever spent with Papa, and I remember it fondly.

First he took down from the shelf the edition that seemed not only to condone adultery but to command it. That Bible, the handiwork of a pair of printers named Barker and Lucas, was published in 1631. It is a handsome volume, as well it should be, for Messrs. B. and L. were the King's printers — but it has one little flaw. A three-letter word — "not" — is missing from the Seventh Commandment. The careless printers of the book that became notorious amongst bibliophiles as The Wicked Bible were fined three hundred pounds, "which effectively put them out of business," said Papa.

Ten times that amount was the fine imposed on another firm of printers, during the reign of Charles I, for perpetrating what has come to be known as The Fool Bible, also in Papa's collection. Their slip-of-the-type occurred in Psalm XIV, which came out reading, "The fool hath said in his heart, There is a God" — instead of "There is no God."

At Cambridge in 1653 was printed the justly nicknamed Unrighteous Bible. It is marred by two errata, both concerning righteousness. In I Corinthians, it asks the question: "Know ye not that the unrighteous shall inherit the Kingdom of God?" Obviously, a "not" is missing from between "shall" and "inherit" — probably dropped on the print-house floor by the same mischievous imps who lost the Barker-and-Lucas "not" twenty-two years before. As if that were not evil enough, in this edition's version of Romans may be seen, "Neither yield ye your members as instruments of righteousness unto sin." Of course, "*un*righteousness" is the correct word — another absent negative.

Absent negatives appear to be the single most prevalent kind of error in Papa's collection, and they always succeed in completely reversing the Scriptural meaning. "And there was no more sea," we are told in Revelation — except in a certain 1641 edition, which says, "And there was more sea."

Nor was it Jesus who, in the garden of Gethsemane, told His disciples to "Sit ye here, while I go and pray yonder." It was Judas — at least according to an edition of 1611.

Eight thousand copies of one Bible were printed and bound in Ireland in 1716, Papa told me, before it was discovered that the command, in John, to "sin no more" had come out as "sin on more," a directive with somewhat more appeal to chronic sinners, I should think.

"The Parable of the Vinegar" (instead of "Vineyard") appears in a chapter heading of Luke in a 1717 Oxford printing. Philip, rather than Peter, is singled out as the apostle who will deny Jesus, in Luke of a 1792 Bible. Unlucky Luke again is blemished in a Bible of 1638, where "Her sins, which are many, are forgotten" may be seen, rather than the correct "forgiven." "If any man come to me, and hate not his father and mother . . . yea, and his own wife also . . ." So begins another passage in long-suffering Luke, as given in the so-called Wife-Hater Bible of 1810. Here, one letter is the culprit — *w*. It should be *l,* and the phrase should read "and his own life also . . ."

An edition organised by Archbishop Matthew Parker, and known affectionately as The Bishops' Bible, made its first appearance in 1568, and was gratifyingly popular, Papa says. Its third edition, however, published in 1572, did not fare as well. Nothing was amiss with the words, but the decorations left much to be desired. The printer used highly ornamental initial letters, quite huge, at the beginnings of several books of this Bible. "That would have been a splendid idea," said Papa, "if the letters had not been left over from printings of Ovid's *Metamorphoses* and other classics of pagan literature." The greatest offender is the emphatically pictorial letter that meets the eye at the beginning of the Book of Hebrews: a vivid depiction of the god Zeus, disguised as a swan, offering his amorous attentions to a naked lady known as Leda.

Eccentric translations, rather than printing errors, make armfuls of other Bibles on Papa's shelves worthy of note. There are, for example, two Bug Bibles. Miles Coverdale's Bible of 1535 has earned that curious *sobriquet;* and so has a

Bible printed in Antwerp two years later. In both of these, a passage in Psalm XCI is presented as "Thou shalt not nede to be afrayed for eny bugges by night." In most other English-language Bibles, it is "the terror by night."

To-day, the thought of Adam and Eve wearing breeches may provoke us to laughter, because the word conjures up images of dandies like Mr. Brummel strolling through Piccadilly in skin-tights, but in The Geneva Bible of 1562 the appropriate passage in Genesis is given as: "And they sewed figge-tree leaves together, and made themselves breeches." The same word is used in other early Bibles; and in all of them, Papa assured me, "They were almost certainly meant in the sense of 'aprons' — *not* the sort of garment your brothers wear."

Translations have played havoc with the well-known "balm in Gilead," too. The phrase, which occurs in Jeremiah, is rendered in the 1609 Douai Bible as "Is there noe rosin in Galaad?" If one prefers treacle to rosin, both The Bishops' Bible and Coverdale's Bible provide *that*.

But printers, more often than translators, have been to blame for the curiosities in Papa's collection, so it is only simple poetic justice that they should have pointed the accusing finger at themselves in an edition published about 1702. In that version's Psalm CXIX, David, instead of complaining that "Princes have persecuted me without a cause," says, "Printers have persecuted me . . ."

I have said that I fondly remember that evening with Papa and his collection, and I think it is because it shewed me a side of him that I had seldom seen before. The old dear tried to pretend that his interest in those Bibles rested merely in the example they gave us of the imperfection of Man. But I am certain that the true reason he likes them is that they are often so funny.

Of course, I did not say that to *him*.

XVI

Smoke

Years after that pleasant evening, the subject of humour in the Bible came up in another connexion, and led to an unhappy outburst.

The family had been gathered in the drawing-room, and Papa had been going on about what a wealth of poetry, drama, and wisdom were to be found in Holy Writ, when Freddy said, "Yes, but there's nothing comical in it, is there? I mean to say, poetry and wisdom are all very well, but a chap likes a bit of a laugh now and again."

Papa replied, "In point of fact, I have always thought that the conversation between Abraham and the Lord, in Genesis, Chapter Eighteen, was amusing, and intended as such. You know the passage. The Lord tells Abraham that He will destroy Sodom, and Abraham asks Him, 'Wilt Thou also destroy the righteous with the wicked? Peradventure there be fifty righteous within the city.' The Lord replies, 'If I find in Sodom fifty righteous within the city, then I will spare all the place for their sakes.' "

"I'm sorry," said Freddy, "but my sides are not bursting with laughter."

Papa frowned. "Pray permit me to finish. Abraham is not satisfied, you see. 'Peradventure there shall lack five of the fifty righteous: wilt Thou destroy all the city for lack of five?' And the Lord says, 'If I find there forty and five, I will not destroy it.' But still Abraham is not satisfied, and he asks the Lord if He will spare the city for the sake of *forty* righteous, and the Lord assures him that He will."

A smile began to brighten Papa's face. "Abraham is persistent, but he knows that he has gone beyond the bounds, and so he is trembling in his boots when he says, 'Oh let not the Lord be angry, and I will speak: Peradventure there shall be thirty found there.' And the Lord says, 'I will not do it, if I find thirty there.'

"Does this silence Abraham?" said Papa, chuckling. "Not a bit of it! 'Peradventure there shall be twenty found there,' he offers. The Lord replies, 'I will not destroy it for twenty's sake.' Any other man would have known when he was well-off, but not Abraham. He says, 'Oh let not the Lord be angry, and I will speak but this once: Peradventure *ten* shall be found there.' And the Lord — rather wearily, I think, just to be rid of him — says, 'I will not destroy it for ten's sake.' "

Papa's whole frame was shaking with mirth by this time. "From fifty, to forty-five, to forty, to thirty, to twenty, to ten! Abraham had the unmitigated gall to *bargain* with the Lord, to actually *Jew Him down,* as we say to-day, all the way from fifty to ten! There we see the shrewdness and cunning of the race, demonstrated in the first Jew of all. And they have never changed. Ask anybody who has had dealings with them. They will always get the better of you in any bargain. It is in the very marrow of their bones, in their hearts, in the depths of their larcenous souls . . ."

"Papa!"

It was my sister who spoke, in a voice of outrage. All of us turned to her. She had risen from her chair. Her face was white. "I am grown accustomed to hear such words from fools and wastrels like Beau Brummel. They speak derisively of the 'Jerusalem Chambers,' where they borrow money to conduct their spendthrift lives withal. They sneer at the 'Father Abrahams' with whom they do their business. But such words from a man of God? For shame, Papa; they are unworthy of you! I can not sit in this room and listen to such stuff any longer!"

She rushed, weeping, from the drawing-room, and ran upstairs.

"I say," muttered Freddy, "what's got into old Esmie?"

"Do not take it to heart, Ambrose," Mamma said soothingly to Papa. "We must make allowances for her. She has not been the same since the death of her husband."

Papa snorted. "From the way she behaved, one would think he'd been a Jew."

A tumble and a *thump!* told us that Esmie had fallen. We all scrambled from the drawing-room to find her sprawled halfway up the staircase, moaning softly.

"Dear God," Papa uttered fervently, his face stamped with the guilt he was feeling. "Esmeralda . . . *Esmie!* . . . speak to me!"

Her eyelids fluttered and opened. "I'm quite all right, Papa," she said in a faint voice. "Please forgive me."

"Forgive you?" Papa said with a groan. "Oh, my child, it is I who must beg *your* forgiveness!"

"Do not upset yourself," she said, as Papa helped her to her feet. "I merely felt faint for a moment. I could not catch my breath. I expect it was the smoke. But I feel much better now."

Mamma said, "Come, my dear, I will take you to your rooms."

"Yes, I should like to lie down."

Papa accompanied them upstairs. Freddy and I returned to the drawing-room. After a moment, Freddy said, "Smoke? What did she mean by smoke? No fires have been laid today — it's too warm. And neither Papa nor I have been puffing on our pipes . . ."

I shook my head. "Poor Esmie. She's muddled in her mind," I said.

It was the first, but far from the last, time that my sister fell ill because of smoke — smoke that nobody else could either see or smell.

XVII

Ice

After fainting in the staircase, Esmie spent the remainder of that day and all of the next in her bed, boiling with fever and racked by delirium. Mamma and I took turns sitting at her side during that time. "It was this ailment of hers, no doubt," said Mamma, "that honed her nerves so keen and caused that extraordinary response to Papa's harmless remarks."

Mr. Julian Cargrave, a young physician of Freddy's acquaintance, was called in. He was not bad-looking, with hair yellow as flax and a fine moustache to match. He saw no need to bleed Esmie. The younger physicians, I have observed, place less reliance on bleeding than do their older colleagues.

"Her indisposition is temporary," he told us. "She must remain abed until it has passed. 'Time and rest will physick her best.' No food or stimulating drink. If she thirsts, give her barley-water. It is an effective demulcent, and will serve to soothe her."

"She fainted earlier to-day," Mamma reminded him. "What if she should do so again?"

"I expect that you have some hartshorn in the house?" he asked. Mamma nodded. "Let her inhale its vapours, and send word to me at once." To Papa, Mr. Cargrave said with a smile, "How clever God is, your lordship, to arrange this world of His in such a way as to provide medicine everywhere to ease our ills. The poppy nullifies our pain. A simple decoction of pearl barley gives us a lenitive beverage. From the powdered horn of the hart, we extract ammonia, one sniff of which will rouse us from the deepest faint." Turning to Mamma again, he added, "But I do not expect that she will faint again."

He was right: she did not. But she remained delirious for a day and a half. In the second day of her illness, as I sat by her, she was seized by a profound chill. Her whole body trembled with it, and her teeth chattered. I piled more bed-clothes upon her, but still she shook with cold, although the day was warm. I gave orders for a fire to be laid, even though it made her bedroom stifling to me and I streamed with sweat under my frock.

She babbled nonsense as she shivered: "Thames . . . frozen over . . ." she said. I assured her that the weather was far too warm for any such a thing, but she shook her head and insisted upon it. "From London Bridge . . . as far as Blackfriars Bridge . . . see! . . . ice! . . . all ice! . . ."

"Why am I sweating like a horse, if it is so cold?" I said, thinking to calm her.

"Affair," she seemed to say.

I sought to amuse her: "Why, Esmie dear, do you suggest that I am conducting an *affaire?* With whom, pray?"

"Fair . . . a fair . . . on the ice," she went on, in her fevered imaginings. "Do you see? . . . booths . . . booths under tents . . ."

It was no use contradicting her, so I pretended to see her fairy booths and tents on the frozen river.

"Selling things . . ." she ranted. "Hot loaves . . . meat . . . pigs and oxen roasting . . ."

Meat roasting on the ice? How wild the mind becomes in time of fever!

Now she laughed with delight, like a child. "See Punch and Judy, Lissa? And look, there are book-shops . . . and skittle-alleys . . ."

Skittle-alleys and book-stalls in the middle of the Thames! And even a Punch and Judy show! Her poor afflicted mind was wandering willy-nilly in that frigid dream, whilst her body continued to shake and mine continued to perspire.

"Look at all the people," she whispered. "Pedlars . . . pie-men . . . oyster-girls . . . all on the ice . . . the ice . . ."*

Then her chill subsided. She became calmer, and sank into a restful sleep. I ordered the fire put out, and soon I was asleep, too, in the chair at her bedside.

XVIII

The Gypsy's Bride

My sister is a beautiful woman, to my way of thinking, but she has always been thought, even by herself, to be plain. Her beauty is quiet, restrained, without extravagance; a glow, rather than a blinding brilliance. Moreover, she has not ever cultivated those artful feminine wiles of coyness and beguile-

* All these people and things (and more, such as a printing press) were part of a fair set up on the solidly frozen Thames during a great frost — which, however, was not to grip London until the winter of 1813–1814, some time after Esmie's delirium. — R. R.

ment which the other sex requires of us — which very Nature, it may be, requires of us. Thus it was that she remained unmarried somewhat past the time of life when most women marry. Papa and Mamma were beginning to be worried for her sake — and for mine, as well, because, as the younger daughter, I could not marry until she did.

One summer, all of us save Papa went to Margate for a week's holiday. Margate is an extremely popular place because of its proximity to London, as well as its well-ordered and respectable pleasures (not at *all* like Sodom or Gomorrah, no matter *what* Freddy may say!). Its rules of conduct for the Assembly Rooms are patterned after the decrees of Beau Nash at the Bath Pump Room. Dancing, which begins at eight o'clock in the evening, must end sharply at midnight. No ladies are admitted in riding habits; no gentlemen in swords or boots, unless they be military officers. Papa does not disapprove of the place (if he did, he would not have allowed us to go); but he did not deem it suitable for a bishop to be seen there. "If you wish to take the children thither for a holiday," he said to Mamma, "I will not object, but I do not understand its attraction. Surely London offers many of the same diversions?"

"Oh, Margate is much more lively than London," said Mamma.

Papa sniffed. "Indeed? So is a cheese full of mites more lively than a sound one." Still, he did let us go.

And it was at Margate that Esmie met Mr. Cooper. He was a man of middling height, quiet and unassuming; dressed well; and tawny-skinned — but not more so than many Spanish or French or Italian gentlemen. Freddy first made his acquaintance at the punch bowl:

"Hullo. My name's Worthing."

"Cooper."

"Deuced good punch, what?"

"Quite refreshing. Like all punch, it is a strange harmony of contradictions."

"I don't follow."

"Each ingredient contradicts the other. Spirits to make it strong, water to make it weak, lemons to make it sour, sugar to make it sweet."

Freddy laughed. "I say, that's rather good!"

"It was my mother's old family recipe."

"Come, Cooper old man, you must dance with my sisters."

"I should be honoured."

Now, it is *I* who have always been acknowledged to be the beauty of this family, but when Freddy presented his new friend to us, Mr. Cooper was no more than cordial to me, whereas Esmie — elder, "plain" Esmie — drew his dark eyes as if they were nail-heads and she a lodestone. Indeed, there was a moment of embarrassment and confusion when Mr. Cooper asked Mamma for permission to dance with her daughter and all of us naturally had assumed that he'd meant *me,* whereas it was Esmie to whom he had referred. But all came out right in the end, and I was pleased that Esmie had found an admirer.

When our holiday was over, Mr. Cooper told Mamma that he frequently came to London on affairs of business, and could he be so bold as to enquire . . . ? Mamma gave him the address of our house and told him that we were at home on Thursdays.

One day, quite soon after we had returned to Hans Town, the three women of the family were in the drawing-room at our needlework, when Esmie asked a very curious question. "Mamma, was there anything unusual about my birth?"

"Unusual? What on earth do you mean?"

"Simply that. Anything that you have never told me?"

Mamma shook her head (and coloured a bit, I thought). "Nothing. Why do you ask?"

Esmie put aside her needlework. "Mamma, was I born in a caul?"

Now it was the turn of Mamma to put down her needlework. "In point of fact, you were."

"Why did you never tell me?"

"It was of not the slightest importance. I had forgotten it until now. Does a woman tell her children all the indelicate details of their coming into the world? Birth is a disagreeable thing of pain and blood and offal. It is hardly a fit subject for pleasant conversation. However, in view of the fact that you have asked: yes, when you were born, your head was covered with a kind of sack, or membrane. The midwife referred to it as a caul."

"What else did she say of it?"

"Nothing that I can remember. She asked if she might keep

it. I told her yes, for it was of no earthly use to me. I later heard that she'd sold it for a few pennies to the sort of gullible person who prizes such things. She said something about it being a sign of good fortune. Superstition, of course, so I paid no attention."

Esmie was excited by now, and her eyes were alight with a fire I had never seen in them before. "It is more than a sign of good fortune," she said. "A child born with a caul is said to possess . . . certain powers . . ."

I said, "What kind of powers, Esmie?"

"Powers of prophecy."

Mamma, taking up her needlework again, asked wryly, "And have you ever shewn evidence of prophetic powers?"

Esmie cast down her eyes. "No, Mamma."

"What *I* should like to know," said Mamma, "is how you learned of this caul."

"Mr. Cooper told me."

"I beg your pardon? Mister who?"

"You remember, Mamma; that gentleman who danced with me at Margate."

"Oh, yes, to be sure." Mamma set aside her needlework again. "But how did *he* —"

"Whilst we were dancing, he said to me: 'I knew at once, the first moment I saw you.' I said, 'You knew what, Mr. Cooper?' He replied, 'Two things. First, that you were born in a caul.' "

"Extraordinary!" exclaimed Mamma.

"I had never even heard the word before, and I had to ask him what it was. He explained it to me, and told me that children so born are favoured with the gift of what he called 'seeing clear.' "

"In the French, *clairvoyance,*" I said. "And what was the other thing he knew when he saw you?"

"That was the next question I asked him. And he replied: 'That I love you, and will love you to the very end of time.' "

"Impertinence!" said Mamma.

"Oh, Esmie, how wonderful!" I cried. "I am so happy for you! But . . . how in the world could Mr. Cooper have known about the caul?"

Esmie replied, "I am sure I don't know. Do you think it

could be for reason that he is — that is to say, his mother was — a gypsy?"

"*That* explains his swarthy complexion," said Mamma.

I only said, "Oh, dear," because I knew that there was trouble in store — trouble with Papa.

Some time, perhaps, when I am not so vexed by my own uncertainties and terrors, I will set down the story of my sister's marriage in full. Here, let me say only that Mr. Cooper called and courted — was coldly received by Papa — but Mamma proceeded to convince him that the gypsy gentleman was Esmie's last chance for happiness and marriage — and I, for Esmie's sake and for my own selfish reasons, added my own suasions to hers — until, at length, an engagement was announced and a wedding took place, here in this house, with Papa performing the service.

Soon after the wedding, Esmie and her husband left London to live in his family home in the Cotswolds. I think that Papa was relieved that many miles would now separate him from a son-in-law who was "touched with the tar-brush."

Esmie became with child soon after, and all of us — even Papa — rejoiced to learn of her condition. Her marriage continued happily until a black day when she and Mr. Cooper were traveling to London to visit us, and stopping for the night at an inn. A tipsy regimental serjeant made suggestive remarks to her, and Mr. Cooper quietly rebuked him.

"Why, what is she to you?" the serjeant asked.

"The lady is my wife," said Mr. Cooper.

"And what of that? You're nothing but a damned gypsy. I can smell one of your sort in the dark. 'Wife,' forsooth! Don't give yourself a white man's airs. You lot 'marry' by leaping over a broomstick, I believe. I don't call that a marriage. I shall talk to this woman as I please, and I'll thank you to keep your gypsy nose out of it."

Mr. Cooper spoke with a soft and level voice, Esmie told us; soft and level and chilling: "Before this month is over," he told the serjeant, "you will be in pieces, sliced into strips like jerked beef hung up to cure."

"No dirty gypsy talks to me like that!" the drunken soldier roared; and drawing his sabre, he plunged it through Mr. Cooper's heart. He died at once.

My sister says it was as if that sabre pierced her own body, for, in the same instant, she was smitten by deep pain and was brought to bed of her child, before its time, there in that inn. The baby lived not an hour, and afterwards my sister was pronounced for ever barren. That soldier had despatched two lives with one thrust of his blade.

He was court-martialled and sentenced to be flogged. "Only flogged?" Freddy cried indignantly when he heard. "He skewers our Esmie's husband with his damned cheese-toaster, and gets off with a flogging? The blackguard should be hanged!"

Hanging would have been more merciful. The sentence was for three hundred lashes, but the full measure was not given. He was dead before the two-hundredth stroke — sliced into strips like jerked beef hung up to cure.

Esmie watched and counted every single lash — she demanded to be present at his punishment, threatening the regiment with the fact that her father was a member of the House of Lords. "There were a hundred and eighty-nine lashes in all," she said, "but I suspect that the last dozen or so were laid upon a lifeless body. He was stoic and made no cry through the fifty-third of them; but with the fifty-fourth he began to whimper; then beg for mercy; then call out for God's forgiveness; then curse; then scream like a woman at each stroke; until he became too weak to utter more than pitiable shuddering gasps."

"It was what he deserved," said Freddy.

"No man deserves that," she replied.

When the bleeding carcass was cut down, she uttered a prayer for the serjeant's soul, and then took herself back here to Hans Town and the protection of our roof, where she has remained ever since.

XIX

The Queen of Love

Mr. Cooper himself had been born in a caul, Esmie told me much later. "That, and his half-gypsy blood," she said, "gave him especial faculties which other men do not possess. To most of us, the future is a dark path, hidden from our eyes by deep, black night. I am not saying that it was all bright sun for him. It was not. It was shadowed to his eyes, too — but on rare occasions that path would be bleached by lightning, just for a moment, and the way ahead would be etched with vivid clarity. Then all would be dark once more."

I asked her, "Did he not see his own death and the death of your child — as well as the way the serjeant would die?"

"If he did, it was only in that last moment before the serjeant killed him," Esmie said. "He could not command the power; it would come to him unbidden, and suddenly depart. He said that I had the power, as well, but I have never beheld prophetic visions. 'You will, my love,' he told me, 'for I saw that caul upon your head as surely and clearly as it had been a cap, there in the Assembly Room at Margate. Your gift will be nurtured by your marriage to me, for in the sweet congress of our love, when we are one flesh, when I probe deep within you and imbue you with my substance, those powers now asleep in you will stir, and rouse, and come awake . . . in time, in God's good time.'

" 'Is it truly God who has granted you this gift?' I asked him. 'Is not prophecy forbidden? Scripture tells us to give no thought to the morrow. "Sufficient unto the day is the evil thereof." '

"But he smiled and kissed me, and said, 'Is not the Bible full of prophets, and are they not esteemed and venerated above all men?' "

(In the *Inferno* of Dante, I thought but did not say, those who had sought to foretell the future were condemned to walk for ever with their heads facing backwards, so their tears rolled down their backs and between their buttocks.)

Hesitantly, I asked Esmie about that "sweet congress" of love, for I deemed it ironic that I, the beauty of the family, had never tasted those sweets, whereas "plain" Esmie had partaken of them to the full.

"Ah, Lissa, there is nothing like it in the world," she replied, with rapture. "At least it was so for me, in the arms of Mr. Cooper. I bestowed myself upon him without hindrance. Whatsoever he wanted of me I gave him, willingly, ardently! Wheresoever he chose to spend himself, I received him there with welcome. No part of me did I deny him; no pleasure or caress did I gainsay. Shame, modesty, restraint, I cast aside; and so must you, my dear, when you give yourself in marriage to a man. Revel in your flesh, and in his. Seek out new ways to fondle and delight him; explore him like a new-discovered land, and open up yourself to exploration, conquest! Proffer your body, as it were tribute to a mighty king — for king in very deed he'll be to you, and with a royal sceptre to represent his majesty withal. Worship and revere that representative, Lissa — adulate and praise it, touch it, press it to your lips, weigh its regal power in your hands. Abolish pride and swear yourself his bondmaid. For if you do, such is the paradox of love that he, the monarch, will be your happy and devoted slave; his sceptre, but your toy — and you, although yet his subject, will become his queen, and he will worship at your feet.

"Always regard yourself as a queen, my dear, and know that you wield great power. Do not be cruel with that power, but do not be foolishly free of your largesse, either. Your woman's body is a beautiful palace; below is the canopied entrance to that palace, locked to all but one by the portcullis of your maidenhood. Inside that palace you reign supreme, the Queen of Love; whilst, outside, all men kneel to you and pay you homage, hoping for your queenly favour, and dreading your disdain. Many will come with battering-rams to break through the portcullis and claim the palace as their own, but you must resist them until your own true love appears; and then you must surrender to his might, and make him welcome inside the palace, and rule side by side with him, crowned with joy, for the rest of your days."

She took my hands in hers, and looked long into my eyes. "My time with Mr. Cooper was short," she said, "cruelly short, and I miss him every hour; but so great was our love that it will last me all my life. I pray to God that you will find such a man, and such a love."

"Oh, Esmie," I cried, "can this little world hold two such men? And will I ever know that dear abandonment, that blissful and abject surrender?"

"You will," she said. "I know it. I see it."

XX

Sic Transit Gloria Percy

"Percy's bolted!" cried Freddy, one day not long after that occasion on which Mr. Shelley had angered Papa with his views on the amatory habits of the poor.

"Bolted?" I said. Freddy, flushed and excited, had just returned to the house after a day in Marylebone Park.

"I heard it at The Jew's Harp," he told me. "I was playing skittles there with Tom Hogg — you know that Tom and Percy have been flung out of Oxford?"

I nodded. All of our circle had heard of it. An anonymous "little syllabus" entitled *The Necessity of Atheism* had been circulated at Oxford, and the college authorities, suspecting Mr. Shelley, had summoned him before them and required him to state whether he had written it. He refused to answer either yes or no. Next, his close friend and confidant, Mr. Hogg, was asked the same question. He, too, declined to answer. As a consequence of their stubbornness, both young men had been sent down. (Privately, to his friends, Mr. Shelley had proudly admitted his authorship of the offending pamphlet.)

Freddy continued: "Well, Tom told me that Percy's run off with a sixteen-year-old girl named Harriet."

Shocked, I cried, "His cousin Harriet Grove! He's been courting her openly, shamelessly!"

Freddy shook his head. "No, no, this is another Harriet. Pour me out a brandy, will you, there's a good girl." As I did so, he explained: "Name of Harriet Westbrook. A little schoolmate of his sisters'. Deuced fetching, Tom says."

Freddy gulped down half the tumbler of brandy and went on:

"Daughter of a Methodist hotel-keeper. Now, you know how Percy is; that turn he has for arguing and moralising . . ."

"*Im*moralising."

"Point taken. What better audience could he hope for than this pretty little Methodist? As soon as he laid his eyes upon her, he set about 'enlightening' her and converting her to his doctrine of anti-Christianity. Well, of course, the poor girl was bowled over like a ninepin. Fell over head and ears in love with him. Began parrotting Percy's atheistical humbug here, there, and everywhere. Her Methodist papa found no joy in that, as you may well imagine, so he set about packing her off to school — but the saucy little wench rebelled, and told Percy that she was putting herself *under his protection,* if you please, and that they must fly away together." Freddy swallowed the rest of the brandy. "Neither of them has been seen since."

I was outraged. "Your friend Percy is a disgraceful young man!" I declared.

"I dare say. But you have never thought him disgraceful at our Thursdays when he was busying himself paying compliments to *you.*"

"I own that I was once flattered by his attentions. But they were harmless. This latest adventure is not. He has corrupted a sixteen-year-old girl, turned her away from God, and debauched her into the bargain, I have no doubt!"

"Oh, no doubt at all," Freddy agreed. "One doesn't kick over the traces and run off with a girl merely to preach the gospel of godlessness to her. Percy is very susceptible, *very* susceptible *indeed,* to the charms of young ladies. His cousin, that other Harriet you spoke of; and that schoolmistress in Hurstpierpoint, Elizabeth something-or-other . . . I expect it's all due to his being a writer."

"You shall not make excuses for him on that account!" I rejoined. "For one thing, his writing is rubbish!"

"I don't know that I agree," Freddy responded with an offended air. "That romance he published last year — I thought it was bang-up stuff."

"If you had ever read Ann Radcliffe or 'Monk' Lewis — or even Rosa Matilda — you would know that *Zastrozzi* is no more than an aping of what they have done much better."

"That book of poems of his —" Freddy started to say.

"*His?* It was written with the help of his sister."

"Well, hang it all, Mel, he's only nineteen. Give him time."

"My dear Aelfred," I said solemnly —

"Aelfred, am I, indeed? Oh-dear-oh-dear-oh-*dear!* Whither hath poor Freddy flown?"

"My dear Freddy: the quality of his writings is neither here nor there. Were they glorious, sublime, infused with genius, they would not excuse his immorality and misconduct."

"I expect you're right," he mumbled. "But, damn it, he can be jolly good company. I shall feel quite lost without him."

"Never mind, Fweddikins. Likely, he'll tire of her in a month or two, and he'll be playing skittles with you and Tom at The Jew's Harp again."

Later, we heard that Percy and little Harriet had been married in Edinburgh, with all the rites of the Scottish Church.

"What price atheism now?" I asked Freddy.

He merely sighed and said, "One more bachelor caught in the double yoke. And so young! *Sic transit gloria Percy.*"

XXI

Ungrateful Rabble

I will now write of Freddy's visit to John Philip Kemble, at Covent Garden Theatre in Bow Street, as Freddy told it me:

"He's a bit younger than his sister," said Freddy, "although not much. And what a sober-sided cove he is! Perhaps that's from his having studied for the priesthood — his father was a papist, you know — but, at any rate, there's nothing bright or jolly about him.

"He read Mrs. Siddons's letter carefully, folded it again, and ceremoniously handed it back to me. 'My dear Mr. — Worthing, is it? You wish to enter the life of the theatre. No doubt you think it to be a life of gaiety and larks — one great long party, so to speak. Let me dispel that notion from your mind at once. It is a hard life, sir, hard and heart-breaking, even for the greatest of us. For those of lesser gift, it can mean long hours, short sleeps, wretched accommodation at provincial inns, and many a missed meal. Thin actors are more commonly seen than fat ones.'

"We were standing on the theatre's stage," Freddy continued, "and Kemble extended his arm in a great sweeping gesture, as if inviting me to gaze at the building. Gaze I did, whilst he kept on talking: 'The hardships are many,' he said. 'Just three years since, all that you see before you was burnt to the very foundations. Three-and-twenty firemen lost their lives. *I* lost one hundred and fifty thousand pounds — of which but a third was recovered from the insurance. Can you imagine my discomfiture? And yet I persevered; I sold shares; I raised the money to rebuild; and rebuild I did, as you can see. My architect, Mr. Smirke, modelled this new theatre after the Temple of Minerva at the Acropolis. The statuary that you see is by Mr. Flaxman.'

"I allowed that it was all splendid stuff, and he said, 'I am glad that you appreciate it. The public do not. The public are ungrateful dogs, sir. When we opened again, almost a year to the day after the holocaust — with an admirable programme, *Macbeth* and *The Quaker,* two most effective pieces — I naturally was obliged to raise the prices because of the great expense I had incurred by the restoration of the theatre. But I had not even begun to speak the prologue, when pandemonium broke out — cries of "Old prices! Old prices!" went up from the spectators. A riot ensued, soldiers were called in, the Riot Act was read to that rabble, but nothing would stop them. The rioting went on, sir, for all of sixty-one nights! No doubt you remember that vulgar *furor* . . .' "

Freddy chuckled. "Indeed I did!" he confided. "I was part of the rabble, as he called us, and I shouted 'Old prices!' as loudly as the rest. But, of course, I said nothing of that to Kemble. 'Why, the whole of London took sides,' the old boy went on. 'Men wore the letters O.P. on their hats and waistcoats; even women wore medals with those letters upon them. They did not even respect my private lodgings, for ruffians gathered outside my house in Great Russell Street and smashed my parlour windows! What could I do? I was forced to surrender to the demands of the mob. *I,* John Philip Kemble!

" 'No, my dear sir, it is not an easy life. I do not mind

saying to you that I look to my retirement with eager expectation.'

"Well, Mel, I expected him to maunder on for ever in that fashion, unburdening himself of his troubles, so I said: 'Your sister, Mrs. Siddons —'

" 'Ah, to be sure,' he said. 'Dear Sarah. My sister appears to be of the opinion that you would be suited to comedy. No doubt she is correct in this. I value her judgments in such things. And yet, sir, although I shall ever consider her to be one of the best comic singers of the day, I must tell you that she has never made a mark in comedies. She is a *great* tragic actress, the greatest of all living, it may be — I mind the words which one critic wrote of her: "Power is seated on her brow; tragedy emanates from her breast as from a shrine" — but she has been wise in eschewing comedy and cleaving to heroic *rôles*. I, too, am no brilliant comedian, sir. Indeed, only Mr. Charles Lamb has commended me in such fare. A certain stateliness in my very nature; a formality, as it were, has made me unfit for that side of our art . . .'

"I began to wonder when he would get to his point," said Freddy, "when he got to it all too soon. 'In few, my dear young sir, comedy is not my *métier,* neither as an actor nor as a manager. I present very little of it here at Covent Garden. To please my sister, I could allow you to hold a spear in *Coriolanus,* let us say, or to play the sailor who hands Horatio the letter from Hamlet — but these parts are not what you seek. Will you allow me to offer you a suggestion — that is to say, a pair of suggestions?'

" 'Of course, sir,' I said.

" 'The first of them is this: forget this vain ambition of yours. My sister writes that you are the son of a bishop. Surely a life in the clergy is more suited to you? If I had my life to live over, I would continue my clerical studies at Douai, as my father wished, and be a priest to-day — a bishop, perhaps, like your father, albeit of the Roman persuasion.'

" 'And what is your second suggestion, Mr. Kemble? — for I am bound to tell you that I must ignore your first.'

"He sighed. 'I suggest that you go to the Proteus Theatre and address yourself to Cholmondeley-Cockburn. Comedy is by way of being a speciality of his, I am told, and he is always in need of young men and women to take parts in his burlettas. I can not give you a letter of introduction to him, for he and I are not acquainted. His is not a Patent House, like Covent Garden or Drury Lane. I know his work only by its reputation.' And then Kemble held out his hand to me and said, 'Good luck to you, my boy.' "

XXII

Total Tittle-Tattle

"And when will you see Mr. Cholmondeley-Cockburn?" I asked of Freddy. (I will interject here that the gentleman's name is pronounced "Chumley-Coburn," although spelt as I have given it above.)

Freddy shrugged. "I don't know," he said.

"Why not to-day?"

He shook his head. "The truth of the matter, if you must know, is that I'm frightened out of my wits."

"Of Cholmondeley-Cockburn?"

Freddy nodded, somewhat shamefaced.

"But, Freddy, you have bearded Mr. Sheridan, Mr. Kemble, and Mrs. Siddons in their dens — and they are all more eminent than he!"

"Yes," he admitted, "but Dick Sheridan is a friend of our family and has been a guest in our house. He smoothed the path for me with that letter to Sarah Siddons, and she smoothed yet another path by her letter to Kemble. I have no such introduction to Cholmondeley-Cockburn, and so I tremble at the thought of facing him."

"What nonsense!" I said severely. "Have you forgotten so soon what Mrs. Siddons said? *'TOUJOURS DE —'* "

"That's all very well, but I don't *feel* audacious. Mel — will you go to the Proteus with me?"

"I will not!" I replied. "It is not *I* who am seeking a life on the stage."

"I don't mean you to go inside the theatre with me," he said. "Just come along, and wait for me in the coach."

"You are being as silly as a child."

"But will you come?"

"Oh, *very* well, you great baby."

And so it was that my trembling twin and I directed Tuttle, the coachman, to drive us to the Proteus Theatre. It had not the grandeur of Covent Garden, nor had its proprietor, Mr. Humphrey Cholmondeley-Cockburn, the acting repute of Mr. Kemble — but one must start somewhere. I have always thought our system of Patent Houses to be cruelly unjust. Only two theatres in all of London are permitted to perform proper plays — Drury Lane and Covent Garden. In the summer, when they are closed, the Lord Chamberlain grudgingly licenses the Haymarket to take their place, but no other theatres may present plays, *per se,* at any time of the year. The minor theatres — Sadler's Wells, the Surrey, the Pantheon, the Olympic, the Proteus — may do only pantomimes, ballets, equestrian shows, burlettas, and the like. The Proteus, I had been given to understand, obeyed the letter of this unfair law but roguishly violated its spirit by calling its comedies "lampoons," "pasquinades," *et cetera,* and seasoning them with songs, dances, and acrobatic turns between the acts.

"I hope I shan't have to juggle oranges," Freddy muttered.

"Courage," I said to him as he stepped out of the coach and into the play-house.

Whilst he was inside, I occupied myself by the reading of *The Vicar of Wakefield,* which Papa had recommended to my attention. So absorbed was I in its pages that I had read all the way through to Chapter V before I was aware of Freddy's long absence. "Whatever can be keeping him?" I said aloud.

Tuttle, who was pacing on the pavement, heard me and said, "Theatres is fearsome places, Miss."

"Do not say such foolish things, Tuttle."

"Beg pardon, Miss, but dens of ink-witty I've heard 'em called."

"The word is 'iniquity,' and it is Puritan nonsense. We are not living in the time of Cromwell, thank Heaven."

"Many a good, God-fearin' soul has been lost in 'em — so I've heard, Miss."

"Pray go inside and tell Mr. Aelfred that I am growing impatient."

"Me, Miss? Go inside there? Why, Miss, I'd be set upon by bawds!"

"That's ridiculous, Tuttle."

"Yes, Miss."

"It's absurd."

"Yes, Miss."

"It's unmitigated twaddle."

"Yes, Miss."

"It's total tittle-tattle, Tuttle!"

"If you say so, Miss."

"I do say so, and I say that you shall go inside that theatre and seek out Mr. Aelfred."

"Yes, Miss. But I do it under protest."

"Oh, *very* well, never mind. You needn't go in if you are so set against it."

"Thank you, Miss."

"What an old Roundhead you are!"

"Yes, Miss."

"You men! You can not say Boh to a goose. Very well, then: *I* shall go in."

"You, Miss? Oh, no, Miss!"

I turned a deaf ear to his protestations, stepped out of the coach, and boldly walked through the front door of the Proteus Theatre.

It was dark within its walls, for no ray of the outside sunlight was allowed to penetrate. Gradually, my eyes grew accustomed to the gloom, aided by the dim light of a candle on a table in a far corner of the vestibule. A figure was seated at that table. It arose, carrying the candlestick, and walked towards me, throwing a wavering shadow on the wall behind it; and I soon saw that it was a tall, somewhat portly man of about fifty. His large face was dominated by a magnificently iridescent malmsey-nose that veritably twinkled and glittered in the candlelight, enormous and red, generously pimpled with the rich rubies and carbuncles of its grog-blossoms. He spoke to me in the deep, plummy voice of an actor:

"And what may I do for you, little lady?"

"Are you Mr. Cholmondeley-Cockburn?" I enquired.

He bowed, causing the candle flame to flutter and his

shadow to dance wildly on the far wall. "The same," he said. "And may I ask your purpose here, my sweeting?"

I did not fancy being called a sweeting by this person, but I replied, "I have come here looking for —"

"A career in the theatre," he cut in. "Well, and why not? Why not, indeed? Pretty young faces are always required, and pretty young figures, too. You are blest with both. There is a well-stocked apple-dumpling-shop inside that bodice, I'll be bound. And you have sparkling eyes, as well!"

"Mr. Ch——"

" 'Mister'? No such formality is required here. This is Liberty Hall! You may call me what everybody calls me: Chum." He took my arm. "Come, then, step with me inside my private office . . ."

I withdrew my arm. "Why should I do that?"

"So that we may discuss our business," he said, with a predatory grin. "Such serious intercourse as ours may not take place in draughty vestibules. You will find my office warm and comfortable. The cushions are soft, the couches commodious. And the claret is of a fine year. Or perhaps you prefer sherry?"

"I prefer neither, thank you very much," I rejoined with spirit. "I see that I have made a mistake." And I turned on my heel to leave.

"Please yourself," I heard him say, coldly. "One cunt is much like another."

The unfamiliar word caught in my ear like a fish-hook. I turned to him again. "I beg your pardon? One *what?"*

He chuckled softly and nastily. "I cry you mercy, gracious lady. I perceive that I am in the presence of dewy innocence, and you are not a wagtail, as I thought you to be. I beg leave to be excused, then, for virgins do not interest me overmuch. They require too long a time in the breaking-in, and I am a busy man. Good day to you." He bowed again, mockingly, causing his shadow to gambol again extravagantly on the wall, and he began to walk away.

I called after him: "I am looking for Mr. Aelfred Worthing!"

He stopped and turned. "Ah, *his* bit of crackling, are you? Why didn't you say so? Lucky young devil. He left by way of the stage-door, not a moment before you walked in."

I quickly left the theatre (thinking that Tuttle had not been wrong!), to discover Freddy, standing at our coach and looking bewildered.

"Ah, there you are," he said.

"And here *you* are," I rejoined. "Did you have a satisfactory interview with Mr. Cholmondeley-Cockburn?"

"Yes. He gave me a part. I begin rehearsals to-morrow."

"So your fear of him was unfounded?"

"Quite." We climbed into the coach and ordered Tuttle to take us home. "It all went easily," said Freddy; and then he added, "Perhaps too easily . . ."

"What do you mean?"

"Well, old Chum took a liking to me at once. I hope that doesn't mean that he plays at back gammon."

"What if he does? You're rather good at the game."

"No, no, not backgammon. Back — gammon. I mean to say, I hope he's not one of those coves who fancy boys."

"I don't think you need worry about *that,*" I assured him.

XXIII

Country Matters

I thought it best to say nothing of "old Chum's" indecent advances to me: for if I had, Freddy would have been obliged to rebuke him, and there would have been an end of his theatrical career. So I kept mum about it.

Back in our house, safely ensconced in my rooms, I bade him tell me exactly how the interview had been conducted.

"Well, for a start, he looked at me. And then he asked me to stroll about. 'I shall have to teach you how to walk,' he said. 'But no matter. Now read this —' He handed me a sheaf of pages with words written on them in his own fair hand. 'A comedy of my own,' he said it was, *'The Dandy's Deception*. I'm presenting it in a fortnight. Read from the part of Sir Malcolm Malfeasance — no, better yet, read the part of young

Reggie Rakehell.' I read for quite a time, and then he said, 'A good voice, a good figure. You'll do. Come back to-morrow.' But as I turned to go, he said, 'Ah, one moment, Worthing. I am forgetting the financial terms.'

"Needless to say, I was so pleased at his ready acceptance of me that I would have played in his company for nothing at all, but I thought it more prudent to say 'Yes, sir. What will you pay me?'

" 'Pay *you?*' he roared. 'You come to me, a raw recruit, an unlicked bear-whelp, in need of training, in need of my expert teaching, and you require that *I* shall pay *you?* I call that impudence!'

" 'Are you saying, Mr. Cholmondeley-Cockburn, that it is *I* who must pay *you?*'

" 'Of course!' he replied. 'It needn't be much. I am not a greedy man. A quid a week.'

"Well, that simply wasn't on, and I told him so. 'I have had my fill of schooling,' I said, 'and I believe that acting is considered to be one of the professions. If I am to be an apprentice, earning small wages whilst I learn the ropes, well and good. But I shall not pay *you,* sir, and you may jolly well forget about that.'

" 'How much do you want?' he asked.

" 'Three pounds a week,' I told him, which I thought was damned small.

"He laughed. 'What a hope! Why, you can't even walk properly! I'll give you one.'

" 'Two.'

"He looked at me sternly and delivered a miniature sermon: 'Dr. Johnson wrote that an annual income of fifty pounds is a sum on which families are supported above the fear of want. You are a single man, and I offer you two quid *more* than that per annum, and still you cavil.'

"I reminded him that Dr. Johnson lived in another time.

" 'But under the same King who wears the crown to-day,' he replied, 'George the Third, God bless him, dotty though he now be.'

" 'And that same King,' I said, 'granted Dr. Johnson an annual pension of three hundred pounds.' I'd heard that from Papa, you see.

" 'Do you dare to put yourself on the level of the great Johnson?' he said with a frown. 'And do you think my resources to be as overflowing as the royal coffers?'

" 'No to both questions,' I replied; then I pointed out that a quid per week doesn't necessarily add up to fifty-two quid a year because the London theatrical season doesn't last the whole year through. He answered:

" 'Members of my company eat the year round — when the season here is ended, we take to the provinces. Next year, we may even go to America. Come, sir, one pound, take it!'

" 'One pound ten,' I said.

" 'One pound five,' he countered.

" 'Agreed,' I said. 'As a beginning wage.'

"He laughed again. 'You young rascal, you bargain like a Jew, but I like you! Now get you gone — and commit Reggie's lines to your memory by to-morrow!' "

We spent what remained of that afternoon fixing the *rôle* of Reggie Rakehell in Freddy's mind. It was not a large part, but by the time we had finished, we sank exhausted onto my bed, our arms around each other, as when we were children in the nursery.

Before I closed my eyes, I thought of that short word which Cholmondeley-Cockburn had used, and which was new to my ears. Freddy is my walking lexicon of low language; and so, without telling him where I had heard it, I asked him what it meant.

"Why, surely you know, Mel — it refers to a woman's notch — her madge — her bun — her quim — her cauliflower — her crinkum-crankum — her tuzzy-muzzy — her mantrap — her water-mill — her ware — her commodity, as some call it — her black joke or brown madam — her bite — her bottomless pit —" He yawned widely, and continued: "Cock Alley or Cock Lane I've heard it called, and Miss Laycock, and the mother of all saints, as well . . ."

Even before he drifted into a nap, I divined that all of those ridiculous expressions referred to a woman's privities, and I marvelled that those parts had even more nicknames than had gin (a dubious honour, to be sure).

For some years, I had known of Mr. John Cleland's variations on that theme — ever since I had discovered Freddy's hidden copy of that writer's *Memoirs of a Woman of Pleasure* and read it avidly behind the door of my bedroom when I was thought to be asleep. Mr. Cleland's heroine, Fanny Hill, in the course of her escapades, encountered the terms Main Spot, Main Avenue, Tender Cleft, Beggar's Wallet, Favourite Quarters, Centre of Attraction, Treasury of Love, Genial Seat of Pleasure, Delicate Glutton, Nether-Mouth, Soft Laboratory of Love, Pleasure-Thirsty Channel, Theatre, Cockpit, Stronghold of Virtue, and probably more. But these I can not think to have had common currency, and are more likely to have been his inventions — as surely were his imposing string of synonyms for the male counterpart: Machine, Engine, Instrument (these often preceded by the adjectives "wonderful," "terrible," "enormous" or "plenipotentiary"), Nail, Truncheon, Maypole, Affair, Weapon of Pleasure, Object of Enjoyment, Battering-Ram, Conduit Pipe, Dear Morsel, Piece of Furniture, Red-Headed Champion, That Capital Part of Man, Sinew, Gristle, Blind Favourite, Wedge, Whitestaff, Master Member of the Revels, Standard of Distinction, Label of Manhood, Master-Tool, Stake, Handle, IT — in capital letters! — and Sensitive Plant (in full: "the true, the genuine sensitive plant, which, instead of shrinking from the touch, joys to meet it, and swells and vegetates under it").

In regard to that particular monosyllable employed by Mr. Cholmondeley-Cockburn, I must say that I think it to be a hard, cold, cutting word, unsuitable to the soft, warm, accommodating part it professes to name. Its use by men shews a contempt for womanhood, I believe, and I applaud Mr. Cleland's avoidance of it in favour of his prodigiously inventive and delightful substitutions. I realise — just now, in this moment of writing — that Shakespeare must have used that harsh monosyllable in clever disguises. Consider, for example, this exchange of dialogue in *Hamlet:*

HAMLET: Lady, shall I lie in your lap?
OPHELIA: No, my lord.
HAMLET: I mean, my head upon your lap?
OPHELIA: Ay, my lord.
HAMLET: Do you think I meant *count*ry matters?

In *Twelfth Night,* he spelt it out, I am certain. I refer to that scene wherein Malvolio, picking up a letter from the ground and thinking that he recognises Maria's writing, says: "By my life, this is my lady's hand! these be her very *C*'s, her *U*'s and her *T*'s; and thus makes she her great *P*'s."

Here, I think we must assume that the Elizabethan actor entrusted with the *rôle* of Malvolio was directed to pronounce the "and" that separates "her *U*'s" from "her *T*'s" not as *and,* but as a broadly emphasised *'n'* — and, to make sure that the point was made, naughty Shakespeare immediately followed it with the "*P*'s" reference, the intent of which is plain; and in the event that the groundlings and other dullards in the Globe Theatre *still* did not take his meaning, he had Sir Andrew Aguecheek respond in a veritable echo: "Her *C*'s, her *U*'s, *'n'* her *T*'s: why that?"

Such an old word, and yet so newly come within my ken. I was to hear it again, under different circumstances, a fortnight later.

XXIV

Arts and Farces

The Dandy's Deception; or, An Exquisite Unmask'd is not a farce of the first rank, but it is constructed with a skill for theatrical *coups* and with a knowledge of what will best please an audience not overly critical. The dandy of the title is the largest *rôle,* designed to display the talents of the author, Mr. Cholmondeley-Cockburn. The story is too silly and too complicated to recount here, for it is a knotted skein of mistaken identities, botched intentions, divers deliberate duplicities, and disguises. Freddy, as the dandy's companion, young Reggie Rakehell, was required in one scene to wear a lady's frock and a curled blond wig, thus to pass himself off as a girl, for a dramaturgical reason too convoluted to describe.

It took all of our ingenuity, Freddy's and mine, to get him letter-perfect in the part before the night of the comedy's opening, and to do so without any other members of our family being the wiser.

Further ingenuity was required to devise an intrigue

whereby I might see him in the play; for Freddy had no wish for our parents to see him in what he called "my *maiden* voyage" (an allusion to the feminine costume he was obliged to wear in that scene).

Our stratagem required the enlisting of Mr. Brummel's aid. He would ask Papa's permission to escort Esmie and me to the theatre, a task he was pleased to perform (but neither he nor Esmie had been let in on the secret of Freddy's involvement in the play — that they would learn only at the last moment, if at all; and Freddy's true name was, by his wishes, not printed in the play-bill).

Papa gave his permission, after some coaxing. Mr. Brummel called for us in his carriage, and we were off to the Proteus Theatre.

"I can't think why you should desire to go to the Proteus, Mrs. Cooper," said Mr. Brummel to my sister. "Its shows are inferior to others which London offers, or so I have heard."

Esmie replied, "Our brother Freddy tells us that Mr. Cholmondeley-Cockburn excels in such fare."

"Then why isn't Freddy with us to-night?" he enquired.

"He *will* be," I said; and quickly added, "He . . . will join us later."

"Good," he said, as we rode along the streets to the theatre. "I want to tell him that Byron is back. I saw him briefly before he rushed off to Newstead to visit his ailing mother."

"He has been gone from England for a very long time," I observed.

"The deuce of a long time," said Mr. Brummel. "He has been in Lisbon, and Malta — where he tarried with that charming Mrs. Spencer Smith — and some place called Albania, wherever the devil *that* may be — and Athens, Marathon, Constantinople — bless me, where else? Did I tell you that he swam the Hellespont, reckless lad?" (I shook my head.) "Well, I told it to *some*body, I can't think who, Harriette Wilson, perhaps. At any rate, he's back in England . . . if you can call Newstead England."

There was a good crowd already assembled inside the Proteus when we arrived. Mr. Brummel, on our way to the box he had reserved, nodded to an enormous variety of ladies and gentlemen of his acquaintance. After we had seated ourselves in the box, he bought us ices.

The show began with a group of comic songs, sung before the curtains by a plump woman of middle age. Her offerings were greeted by desultory applause and a few hoots.

When she had left the stage, Mr. Cholmondeley-Cockburn appeared, and was roundly welcomed by the audience. Bowing and smiling, he held up his hand for silence, and commenced to speak his prologue:

> "To-night, dear friends, 'tis our delightful task
> A devil of a Dandy to unmask,
> And, by his own fell treachery, to shew
> The true, unpainted visage of that Beau . . ."

Mr. Brummel's whole body stiffened. I guessed his fear, and I whispered assurance to him that the comedy contained no satire aimed at him (as, indeed, it did not; for all of its characters were of an extravagance so great as to be unrecognisable as human beings). But Mr. Brummel pretended not to know what I meant: he merely sniffed, and replied:

"Tut, Miss Worthing, I only felt a chill. Deuced draughty theatre, this."

Following the recitation of the prologue, which was of some dozen lines or so, the curtains parted on the first act. After a few minutes of conversation amongst a number of ladies, a pair of gentlemen entered the scene. One of them was Cholmondeley-Cockburn, and the other was Freddy, in the character and costume of Reggie Rakehell. I recognised him at once, of course, despite his altered appearance and unaccustomed walk and manner. Mr. Brummel obviously did not.

However, Esmie suddenly leant forward and peered at Reggie Rakehell through her opera-glasses. Whether it was her vaunted *clairvoyance,* or merely her long familiarity with a young man whom she had known since his infancy, I can not tell, but she saw through Reggie to Freddy at once, and turned to me with an expression of astonishment upon her face. I touched a finger to my lips, as if to say "Betray him not!"

A quarter of an hour into the first act, the ladies, having used all of their wiles upon young Reggie, were lightly rebuked by him when he said, with a tinkle of artificial laughter,

"Upon my soul, you shall not hoodwink *me,* dear ladies, for all your arts and farces."

That is to say, Freddy *should* have spoken those words. He had said them without fail in my sitting-room at home; and I have no doubt that he uttered them correctly in the rehearsals. But, owing presumably to the presence of the audience and the nervousness of the first night, he committed a metathesis or transposition of initial sounds, unwittingly plucking the *f* from "farces" and moving it to the front of "arts."

"Upon my soul," was what he actually said, "you shall not hoodwink *me,* dear ladies, for all your farts and arses."

Some of the spectators tittered, but I was covered with goose-flesh from head to foot, knowing what awful embarrassment Freddy was feeling.

His *faux pas* might have gone unnoticed by the larger part of the audience, had he not tried disastrously to *correct* it, saying, "That is — your arses and farts!"

And this time, a great howling of laughter went up from the whole house. I wanted to sink into the carpeting, such sympathy was I feeling for my brother. The entire theatre was rocking with laughter — and Freddy's fellow-players, of both sexes, were likewise made helpless by their vain attempts to suppress their own giggling. Cholmondeley-Cockburn, however, did not appear to be amused; and I could see, by Freddy's unpainted neck and ears, that he was blushing with humiliation.

"Low stuff," Mr. Brummel said; and I understood by this that he thought the mistake to be the character's, not the actor's, written into the text deliberately.

The hilarity subsided at last, and the play went on. No further mishaps occurred — until the final act. This was the act in which Reggie Rakehell donned a lady's frock and high, curled wig, in order to disguise himself and thus escape his creditors. Freddy made rather a fetching girl, I thought, and he mimicked the piping voice of some of my sex quite creditably. His skill as an actor, I told myself, could not be denied.

Reggie's creditors were a tailor called Benjamin Hunt and a wine-merchant with the name of Michael Dover. "You two gentlemen, I think, are not acquainted?" simpered Freddy as the bewigged and befrocked Reggie. "We do not stand on ceremony here, dear sirs — no 'misters' or 'miladies' — it is all

Christian names and fellowship. Permit me to present you to each other —" And then, instead of saying, "Mike Dover, Ben Hunt," Freddy transposed their Christian names and said, "Mike Hunt, Ben Dover."

The slip was innocuous, and so small that it was scarcely noticed, but once more Freddy in vain attempted to repair the damage. He laughed hysterically and said, "Excuse me — so silly — I meant to say — " His voice rose to a higher pitch and he pronounced his "correction" distinctly and loudly: *"Ben Dover, Mike Hunt."*

This time, the audience fairly fell from their chairs. The dialogue on the stage was completely drowned by the tide of laughter rolling from the spectators. I did not grasp the cause of their riotous amusement — merely mixing up the names of the two creditors was the palest, most insipid provocation to laughter — until I repeated the names, silently, in my mind, not as names, but as sounds: ben dover, mike hunt, ben dover mike hunt, bend over my cunt . . .

The laughter continued to swell. The play was stopped in its tracks. The actors, all save Freddy, had collapsed with laughing. And he, my poor dear brother, was completely bereft of all the skills of deportment and demeanour which Cholmondeley-Cockburn had taught him. Despite the feminine frock, despite the blond wig, he stood there, looking for all the world precisely what he was: a thoroughly chagrined, ashamed, discomfited young man.

"Bless me!" suddenly shouted Mr. Brummel. *"It's Freddy!"*

Fortunately, that scene was very near to the end of the play; and the text in any case required Reggie to leave the stage immediately after presenting the two creditors to each other. Five minutes more, and the curtains closed, to thunderous applause, and opened again to allow the players, led by Cholmondeley-Cockburn, to take their bows. All did — with the single exception of Freddy.

His absence impressed me as ominous. The cries of the spectators swelled. Fear and concern seized me. Turning to my sister and Mr. Brummel, I said, "Come quickly. We must rescue Freddy." As we rose from our chairs and left the box, Cholmondeley-Cockburn was smiling and blowing kisses to his noisy customers.

We found Freddy in the common dressing-room shared by

the company's minor players. He was alone, still wearing the frilly frock and wig, and he was soaked with sweat, reeking with fear. He sat on a stool, shaking. As we entered, he looked up, terrified. "Oh, God," he groaned. "I've made an utter ass of myself. Old Chum will *kill* me. I must leave London for ever . . . I can never shew my face in town again . . ."

Esmie and I were without words to comfort him. We merely cooed and crooned and stroked his shoulders. Mr. Brummel drawled frostily, "Rubbish, my dear fellow. I thought you were rather good . . ."

Just then, Cholmondeley-Cockburn burst into the room. "Worthing!" he boomed, ignoring the rest of us. "Come out of this, damn you!"

"Let him alone!" I cried.

"Mind your own business!" Chum growled at me, and turned again to the trembling Freddy. "Do you hear me, Worthing? Come out upon the stage where you belong! Take your bows!"

Freddy shook his head. "I can't . . ."

"You *will,* by God!"

"No . . . I'll never step out on a stage again, as long as I live . . ."

"You must!" Chum insisted. "They're calling for you — do you not hear them?"

And, indeed, the roaring chorus from the house had taken the raucous form of "Reggie! Reggie! Bring out Reggie!"

"I'll give you a rise in your wages," said the manager. "One pound ten." But Freddy continued to shake his head. "All right, then, damn your eyes — two quid! *Now* will you shew yourself to your public?"

Freddy looked up at his employer. "My . . . my public?" he said softly.

"Yes, lad! Your admiring, your adoring public! Listen to them out there, stamping and clapping and shouting for you! Will you come? And mark this, my boy: we shall for evermore play this piece with your improvisations written into it. They were brilliant, inspired!"

"But I — that is, I didn't —"

"*Will* you come out, sir?! For if you do not, I swear that they will tear the theatre down!"

"Five pounds," said Freddy.

Cholmondeley-Cockburn howled in anguish. "Oh, you Shylock! You'll ruin me! Three."

"Four."

"Never! I'll go no higher than three — plus one per cent of the nightly profits."

"Two per cent."

"One and a half."

"My own dressing-room?"

"Granted."

"Done," said Freddy, rising from the stool. His manager seized him by the arm and fairly dragged him from the room. In a moment, we heard a great earthquake of approval from Freddy's public.

XXV

The St. Arthur's Day Mystery

The reliving of these past scenes, so many of them happy or amusing, has been, as I had hoped, like balm of Gilead (not rosin or treacle!) to my sorely vexed spirit. Here in my sitting-room, with this album's pages spread open before me and my pen in my hand, I have been able to put my troubles aside, in great part, and dwell in that land of other days.

From time to time, however, I am jolted forward into this horrid present by Papa, who continues his insistence. He wishes me to marry, of course. That is why he demands to know the name of the creature who, some weeks since, took me against my will, despite my struggles, by main force; who, in plain words, ravaged me, planting his seed in my all-too-fertile garden.

I am not, in point of fact, being stiff-necked (as Papa says) by refusing to marry that personage. Marriage to him not only would have been repugnant to me in the extreme; it is an absolute impossibility; and yet, I can not tell Papa the *reason* it is an impossibility, lest I also reveal the other horror that weighs upon my heart so heavily.

And so it is that Papa looks with consuming suspicion upon every man whom I have known, no matter in how casual a way. Under his especial scrutiny fall those gentlemen whose reputations are not remarkable for propriety:

"Was it Brummel?" he snapped at me this morning during breakfast, after Esmie and Freddy had left the table and the servants were out of earshot.

"Ambrose," said Mamma, "let the poor child eat her porridge."

"Well, was it?" he persisted. "That insufferable coxcomb respects nothing but his own cravats! Was it your one-time admirer Wellington? — no, he has been out of the country far too long. But Byron has returned to England after a long absence! Was it he? Melissa, please tell me that it was not *that* outrageous libertine."

"Dear Papa," I said, deferentially and calmly, "you must excuse me if I decline to play at this game of eliminations. If I were to tell you who it was *not,* you would soon entrap me into disclosing who it *was;* and that, I say again, I am resolved to do only on St. Arthur's Day."

"You would do well to eschew flippancy, my girl," he said firmly. "You know as well as I that there is no St. Arthur."

"It is only a manner of speaking, Papa. All the young gentlemen use that expression. I heard it from Mr. Shelley. It means 'never.'"

"If that is your meaning, it were wiser to speak it plainly and without recourse to catch-phrases more suited to an alehouse."

"I'm sorry, Papa," I said submissively.

"Shelley!" he suddenly barked. "Yes, of course, how could I have not guessed it before? That impudent, atheistical young pup! He has the morals of a tom cat! *Was* it he? Or Walter Scott? Or Sheridan? — old enough to be your father, and an M.P. into the bargain — ought to know better, have some sense of what is decent, but what can one expect of a man who defended the French Revolution? This is the end to which all that confounded writing of bawdy farces leads . . . *The School for Scandal,* indeed!"

Suddenly Papa stopped. "Merciful Heaven preserve us," he

whispered. *"Was it the Regent himself?* You must not be afraid to tell me so, my dear. His rank shall not protect him. Royal blood or no, he shall have *me* to contend with. I know you had a private audience with him at Carlton House, and he gave you that costly necklace — *why* did he give it you, eh? By Heaven, for once the Prince of Wales has gone too far! Mark me, child, he shall answer for it, or — "

"But Papa — "

"He holds no fear for *me,* the crapulous jackanapes!"

Thus it went — and thus it has been going — every day since the truth of my condition became known to my parents. Mamma has been less insistent than Papa, but she, too, has tried to guess the culprit's identity:

"As regards Mr. Summerfield, I need not tell you that your father and I find him most agreeable. I know that you have told us he is not the man who — but if he *had* been — if, in the course of a natural affection and warmth of feeling — he — by which I mean you and he — that is to say . . . But you must not think that I am prying, dear. It is only that . . . well, you must consider your father. You would remove a great cross from his shoulders if you were to . . ." *Et cetera.*

So it is that I have come to a pass for which no woman could have wished, and none can envy. As I have said, I am a pathetic plaything, the battered toy of a cruel despot, that icy-hearted tyrant known as Life. I see ahead for me disgrace, humiliation, shame; the racking pain of child-birth; the risk of death during that birth — all for a child I never wanted, forced upon me, into me, by a man I loathed.

And what of dear Papa? His position as a bishop of the Church of England will be stained with a filthy, indelible blot flung at him all unwittingly by his loving daughter. I would do anything to avert that; but I am powerless to prevent the scandal that must come.

However, I am getting ahead of the story. Let me return to my account of the pleasures and pains that led me to my present misfortune.

BOOK TWO

King

What's in a Name? — A Vile Bounder — A Man Made of Moonbeams — Enter Olivia — In the Dark Walk — Lord Byron's Curse — Chum's Last Tragedy — The Lost Cripple — The Way of the World — Confrontations at Carlton House — A Tumult of the Senses — Drink? Gambling? Opium? Women? — In Praise of Impatience — My Lady Greensleeves — The Colonel's Clever Contrivance — The Hanged Man — What Kind of Creature Is He? — A Visitor in the Night — Blackmail — A Rank Coward — Thank the Good Lord — A Fatal Flaw — The Bravest Man in London — A Summons from the Prince — Out of Bounds — All Things Low and Lubberly — Hiding from the Law — Will-o'-the-Wisp

I

What's in a Name?

This family has the curious distinction of employing a cook named Mrs. Cooke and a butler whose true surname is Butler. I wish I could add that our gardener is called Gardiner, but unfortunately his name is simply Hobbes. Mrs. Cooke has been with us since before I was born; but the hiring of our present butler took place when I was fifteen years of age, and I well remember the occasion.

Our previous butler, Winters, had died, in his sleep like an old dog, shortly before what would have been his eightieth birthday. I had known the dear old man all of my life. Near his end, he would occasionally call me "Miss Esmeralda" and Esmie "Miss Melissa"; likewise he mixed up "Mr. Eadward" and "Mr. Aelfred." The sad event of his death touched all of us deeply, but despite our grief, a replacement for him had to be found, and my parents were soon speaking with applicants for the position.

The best of them, who came highly recommended by an eminent family, was a man with the name of Butler. Papa and Mamma could find no flaw in him, save for that name. "It will never do," Papa explained to him. "We already have a cook named Cooke. That is bad enough. To have also a butler named Butler would border on absurdity. As a bishop, I must maintain a modicum of dignity and decorum in my house. That is already difficult with a pair of fifteen-year-old twins dashing about and getting into mischief. What did your previous master call you?"

"Butler, your lordship."

Papa grunted. "I own that it is a good English name, and I once knew a vicar named Butler. But what if his name had been Vickers? He would have been known as Vicar Vickers — and been the butt of laughter. As would I, had my surname been Bishop."

"Yes, your lordship."

"What is your Christian name?" asked Mamma.

"My mother was a devoutly religious woman, ma'am, and her greatest pleasure was reading Scripture. All of her children received Biblical names . . ."

"Splendid," said Papa. "What could be more suitable for a bishop's house? And what is that name, my good man?"

"Arphaxad."

"What?!"

"The third son of Shem, your lordship. Genesis, Ten, twenty-two."

"I know the sons of Shem," Papa responded, appalled. "They are Alam, Asshur, Lud, and Aram, in addition to the son after whom you are called. Intending no disrespect to your mother, why could she have not called you after one of the others?"

"She gave those names to my brothers, your lordship."

"One can not have a butler with the name Arphaxad," said Papa. "Would you object to being called by your middle name?"

"Not at all, your lordship. It is Ambrose."

"But that is *my* name! Imagine the confusion in this house if my wife were to call for me, and *you* appeared. Or *vice versa*. Good Heavens, what a dilemma. Have you no suggestions, man?"

The unhappy applicant shrugged helplessly and replied, "I have only three names, your lordship, and you have disqualified them all."

As if suddenly inspired, Mamma asked him, "What was your mother's maiden name?"

His face lit up. "Ah," he said. "That, if I may say so, ma'am, is an excellent solution. I should be proud to answer to her name. It was Pope."

Papa frowned and shook his head. "No . . . it has papist associations . . ."

"Actually, your lordship, that is a contraction of her family's original name."

"And what was that?"

"Poope. A very old and honourable name."

"I dare say. But the members of my family can not go about the house saying 'Poope.' "

"I quite understand, your lordship."

Exasperated, Papa all but wailed: "Must we turn you away for such a grotesque reason? By all accounts, you are an extremely capable fellow. What an intolerable muddle!"

Mamma asked the applicant, "Have you ever experienced this same difficulty in your other situations?"

"No, ma'am. My other employers have been content to call me Butler. I believe that it amused them. Only once, many years ago, did my name create a problem. My master — an eccentric, scholarly gentleman of antiquarian tastes — preferred the obsolete term 'steward,' which I believe now is largely confined to naval use. 'It has a fine old grandeur to it,' he said, and added that he detested the 'new-fangled' word 'butler.' You can imagine, ma'am, how annoyed he was on learning that my very name was that detested word. As a consequence, he never addressed me by my name: he always called me 'steward.' "

"I have it!" said Papa. "We shall call you Stewart. Do you find that agreeable?"

"I expect that I shall grow accustomed to it, your lordship."

And so he has.

I once asked our footman, Blodgett, if his ambition was to become a butler. Blodgett is quite a handsome young man in his dashing livery, with well-turned calves in snowy-white hose. He had replied: "Ah, no, Miss, that's not for me. Mr. Stewart earns more, to be sure, but I don't fancy that responsibility. Besides, my livery is more catchin' to the eye, so to speak. The young ladies, they do love it so." And he had actually winked at me! — but not in a disrespectful way, else I should have reported him.

In addition to Stewart, Blodgett, Tuttle, Hobbes the gardener, Garrett the groom, Mrs. Cooke, Abigail, Alice, and Annie (my, Mamma's, and Esmie's maids), we employ the customary assortment of kitchen-maids, scullery-maids, laundry-maids, and so on — but these come and go like the tides, either through marriage or dismissal for incompetency and sloth. The reason that we make do with a staff of such minimum strength is Papa's feeling that it would be unseemly for a clergyman, even a bishop, to live in ostentatious luxury.

II

A Vile Bounder

Some weeks after Mr. Summerfield had returned to Suffolk, I was alone in the music-room, running through some scales on my clarinet and playing a little Mozart, when Stewart informed me that a certain Mr. Heathman had called, asking to speak to me.

"I do not think that I am acquainted with anybody of that name," I said. "Did he state his business?"

"No, Miss. Shall I send him away?"

"That's all right, Stewart. Shew him into the drawing-room."

As soon as I walked into the drawing-room, I immediately recognised my caller as the young gooseberry-eyed foreman of Mr. Summerfield's brewery. "Good morning, Mr. Heathman," I said.

He proffered a quick bob of a bow, and somewhat deferentially asked, "I am not an inconvenience causing?"

"Not at all," I assured him, surprised at his foreign accent, and realising that I had not heard him speak at the brewery. "Won't you sit down?"

He sat, gingerly, on the very edge of one of our Sheraton chairs, as if he were afraid of breaking it. "I have for you this from Herr Vilfrid," he said, handing me a small, flat parcel.

I unwrapped it, to discover a set of fine handkerchiefs, in white lace, embroidered with my initials. There was a note, too:

"My dear Miss Worthing, —

"I ordered these made up before leaving London, and have instructed my faithful John Heathman to pick them up from the shop and deliver them to you. I hope that this insignificant, though sincere, offering of friendship will not impress you as impudent. I should have preferred to deliver it myself, but I have been detained on affairs of business here in Suffolk, and will not return to London as soon as I had expected. I also want you to know that I anticipate that return with a marked degree of anticipation. More than that *truly* would be impudence to say.

"I remain, until then,
"Your obedient
"Wilfrid Summerfield"

My heart was beating faster — how silly of it, I thought. My face felt suddenly warm. "Thank you, Mr. Heathman," I said. "I do not think that Mr. Summerfield's note requires an answer, but if you will be writing to him, I hope you will say that I thank him for the gift and that I hope for an early and successful conclusion of the business that keeps him in Suffolk."

A smile flickered across my visitor's face, dying as quickly as it had been born. *"Ja,* Miss Vorting," he said, brushing the lock of straight dark hair from his forehead. "It is not, I think, business that is in Suffolk keeping him."

"Oh? Then what is it that detains him there?"

Mr. Heathman replied, "It is, I think — how is it in your *Englisch?* — his *Verlobter."*

I shook my head. "I'm afraid I don't understand . . ."

He shrugged, and rose to leave. *"Ach,* it is not of importance. *Auf Wiedersehen, Fräulein."*

"Good day, Mr. Heathman. And thank you for bringing me this gift." I rang for Stewart, who shewed him out.

Later, at dinner, I asked my father: "Papa, you speak some German, do you not?"

"A few words," he said. "I am much more learned in Latin, Greek, and Hebrew. I acquired my little German from Mr. Handel, who was a guest in my father's house many times, over many years, when I was a boy. He would come to dinner and play his music for us, and teach me some simple terms in his native tongue. The mind retains such things tenaciously, when one is taught at an early age. I was seventeen when he died. Just a week before, we had seen him at a performance of *Messiah* at Covent Garden. It was to be his last appearance in public. The story goes that the King — that was old George the Second — was closeted with some members of his government when the news of Handel's death was whispered in his ear by a servant. He was much moved, and he rose to his feet and dismissed the meeting, saying, 'My lords; gentlemen; we have just learned that the great and good Mr. Handel has left our employ — to serve a higher Prince.' The King himself died the following year."

"You have told us that story many times, Ambrose," Mamma pointed out.

"Perhaps I have," he said, "but it is a touching story, and deserves to be told again and again. Mr. Handel was indeed great and good. I liked him tremendously. We shall not see his like again so soon." Papa turned to me. "But what were you saying, Melissa?"

"I only wondered, Papa, if you know the meaning of a German word, *Verlobter?*"

Papa's eyes closed in concentration. "I think that it means 'prohibited' or 'illicit.' That is to say, 'forbidden.' "

I could make no sense of that, in the context of Mr. Heathman's use of the word; but I said, "I see. Thank you, Papa."

"Where did you encounter the word?" he asked.

"In conversation. I can not remember with whom."

We continued eating, in silence, until Papa said: "No. I was mistaken. The word for 'prohibited' is *verboten.*" He closed his eyes again. *"Verlobter, Verlobter* . . . if I am not again mistaken, it is used in referring to one's betrothed, as we might say *'fiancée.'* "

I felt my face go icy-cold, and knew that I looked pale, for Mamma said, "Melissa, are you not well?"

I forced myself to reply: "I am perfectly well, Mamma, but I have no appetite. May I be excused, please?"

"Yes, of course you may, but —"

I got up from my chair and quickly walked to the door of the dining-room, as Papa said to the rest of the family: "Did I ever tell you that I was born on the very *day* on which *Messiah* was first given? The performance was a charity concert in Dublin, on the thirteenth of April, 1742 . . ."

Upstairs, I threw myself on my bed and wept in despair.

O duplicitous Mr. Summerfield! — that was my silent wail. To express such interest in me, to send me gifts, to say how eagerly you anticipate your return . . . and, through all that, to be courting another, indeed *engaged* to another, to be paying your attentions to your infernal *Verlobter,* damn her! And damn you, too, you provincial bumpkin, you perfidious brewer! Oh, how I loathe and detest the unspeakable smell of beer!

I had heard of such two-faced behaviour in men — dallying with women in the town whilst married or affianced to another in the country — but I had thought of such creatures as oily rakes of Cholmondeley-Cockburn's kidney, their lewdness fairly reeking from them. It did not seem possible that a person of Mr. Summerfield's upright and manly demeanour could be such a vile and reprehensible bounder.

And what did he think *me?* A demi-rep? A wagtail? I, the daughter of a bishop?

Oh, I railed in my inward rage, if only you were not so damnably handsome!

III

A Man Made of Moonbeams

That night, I had one of the strangest experiences of my life.

Customarily, I am a sound sleeper; from the time that my head touches my pillow to the moment when Abigail opens the blinds, I do not awake. But somewhat past one o'clock during that night, due perhaps to my unhappy state of mind, I woke up — or thought that I did (a remark which will become clearer soon). Goaded by an unaccountable restlessness, I put on my dressing-gown and slippers, and left my bedroom, walking out onto the landing. The whole house was very quiet, and there was not even a sound of carriages in the street outside. And yet I found myself listening — for what, I did not know.

Soon, I heard a voice, very faint, speaking just a few syllables which I could not understand. It was a female voice; and as I walked on tip-toe closer to Esmie's door — her rooms are next mine — I realised that the voice was hers. I smiled, assuming that she was having a dream and talking in her sleep. It was a pleasant dream, I surmised, for the tone of her voice was serene.

But as I turned to walk back to my own room, the character of her voice underwent a change. There was distress in it, and I could make out the words: "No . . . no . . . please don't . . ."

What is worse than being trapped in an ugly dream, with no-one near by to arouse you from it? I decided to awaken her gently from the nightmare, and so I carefully, quietly, opened her door, walked through her sitting-room and into her bedroom.

The room was drenched in moonlight, and the sight that stunned my eyes was like an etching in silver: Esmie was sitting up in bed, embracing a man who sat at her side. He seemed, himself, to be made of moonbeams, a creature of all soft and silvery radiance, and this quality sent a tremor up my spine even though I knew that his gossamer aspect was an illusion, compounded of silence and moon glow and the lateness of the hour and my own half-sleeping state.

"No," moaned Esmie, "please don't go . . ."

"I must," he whispered.

"Will you come again?"

"If I can. But even if I can not, you will come to me."

I blinked — and in that instant, the man was gone, like a candle flame snuffed out. Esmie sank back onto her pillow and was soon breathing in the deep, regular rhythm of sleep. I returned to my own room, climbed back into bed, and was soon asleep, too.

When Abigail opened the blinds in the morning, I immediately recognised that encounter for what it was: a dream. I had not awakened during the night; I had not walked out upon the landing and looked in upon Esmie. I had dreamt the whole thing.

Mamma and Esmie were my only breakfast companions, for Papa had already left the house on an early obligation, and Freddy, who had been out till all hours, was still asleep. I was wondering whether I should speak of my dream — and had decided against it — when Esmie spoke:

"I had the most curious dream last night," she said.

Mamma responded: "Oh? What was it, pray?"

"I dreamt that, as I lay there in my bed, my husband came to me . . ."

"Oh, my poor dear . . ." Mamma reached over and touched her hand.

"It was as if he had not died. He spoke to me, and kissed me, and in every way it was as if he were alive again."

I could not speak. I felt frozen to my chair.

Mamma said, kindly, "How sad, my poor Esmie."

"It was not at all sad, Mamma," replied my sister, "until he began to take his leave. I begged him to stay, but he said that he could not. I asked him if he would come to me again, and he said, 'If I can. But even if I can not, you will come to me.' "

I felt faint; and took a long, deep breath.

"And I *will* go to him — will I not, Mamma? — when life is over?"

"Yes, of course you will, my dear."

"It was a sweet dream. I should like to dream it every night." Then Esmie resumed eating.

Later, alone in my sitting-room, I asked myself what I had seen. Had the force of Esmie's dream been so strong that it had leapt the gap from her sleeping brain to mine, aided by the bond of sisterhood and love? Had I, in some uncanny way, shared her dream?

Or had neither of us dreamt at all? Did I truly awake in the night's small hours, and look in upon her, and see her in the arms of her husband's spirit?

IV

Enter Olivia

Jane Austen, her brother, and her sister-in-law presented themselves here on a Thursday afternoon not long after. By that time, the identity of the anonymous author of *Sense and Sensibility* had become the most open of secrets, and her name was on everybody's lips. The poet Mr. Walter Scott was also our guest. The two writers expressed admiration of each other's work:

"Your *Marmion,* Mr. Scott, and your *Lay of the Last Minstrel,"* Jane said, "have afforded me marvellous pleasure. And then, as if they were not enough, last year you gave us *The Lady of the Lake.* Its passages have imprinted themselves upon my mind —

'In listening mood she seemed to stand,
The guardian Naiad of the strand.' —

Now beautiful! It makes me wish that I were a poet."

"Have a care, Miss Austen," said Mr. Scott, "lest you turn my head with your gracious compliments. If I may be permitted to quote from the *Last Minstrel:*

'. . . For ne'er
Was flattery lost on poet's ear:
A simple race! they waste their toil
For the vain tribute of a smile.' "

(In my own humble judgment, a poet who would rhyme "ne'er" with "ear" and "toil" with "smile" — all in the space of four short lines — was somewhat lacking. Be that as it may, he went on speaking to Jane.)

"If I may say so, dear lady, for you to wish to be a poet, when you write such superior prose, is like a nightingale wishing to be a lark. Oh, I own that the big heroic strain I can do myself like anybody now going, but your exquisite touch, which renders ordinary commonplace things and characters interesting from the truth of the description and the sentiment — ah, that is denied me."

"The narrative force of your poems," she rejoined, "is as powerful as any novelist's. Do you think that you will turn your hand to novel-writing one day?"

"I think not, Miss Austen," he replied. "I tried to write a few chapters some years ago, but abandoned the project. I leave all that to you. But tell me: will you always be content with the wit and irony that you have displayed in your first book, superb as those elements may be? Will you not favour us, in future, with a serious romance?"

Jane laughed. "Bless you, I could no more write a serious romance than an epic poem. I could do so only to save my life. And even then, if it were made an indispensable condition that I must keep it up and never relax into laughing at myself or at other people, I am sure I should be sent to the gallows before I had finished the first chapter! No, I must keep to my own style and go on in my own way."

"So must we all," agreed Mr. Scott.

Jane said to me, "I so very much wanted to see Mrs. Siddons in a play — but she is ill, and can not appear. Such a disappointment. I have heard a rumour that she will retire soon; if not this year, then next. Do you think that it can be true, Melissa?"

"I have been given to understand," I replied, "that she is older than she appears to be."

"My brother took me to see an English version of *Tartuffe*. I dearly love comedies — what others now in the town can you commend to me?"

"The artful farce at the Proteus has been well received," I said — a statement that sent Freddy into a fit of coughing.

"Drink some tea, Aelfred," said Mamma, whilst I pounded him on the back.

Freddy had been playing at the Proteus every night, and contriving a wide variety of excuses for being out. Thus he went on postponing the day when he would have to reveal the fact of his new profession to our parents. He was billed as "Mr. Frederick Thingrow," a simple anagram of Worthing.

In the midst of Freedy's coughing, Stewart announced the arrival of Mr. Wilfrid Summerfield, and that person strode briskly into the drawing-room, exuding rural health and vigour.

"You are quite browned by the sun, Mr. Summerfield," said Mamma in greeting.

"We have enjoyed fine, open weather in Suffolk," he replied.

A bit later, when the rest of the company were discussing the works of Mr. Scott and Miss Austen, he drew me aside and handed me another small gift, wrapped in paper. "A little remembrancer," he said, "to keep me in your mind. I should like to think that you might place it next your bed, so that it would be the last thing you see upon retiring, and the first thing upon awaking."

I tore off the wrapping, and saw the gift to be an exquisite little figurine of a shepherd, done in Staffordshire porcelain. At another time, or from another hand, it might have delighted me. He added: "I'm not a shepherd, but I could find none of a brewer. If you think of this chap as standing in a summer field, however . . ."

"Very clever," I said coolly, "but I do not think that I should accept it."

He studied my eyes. "I sense that there is something awry here. I think that you do not welcome my presence."

"Oh, you may come and go as you please, Mr. Summerfield. I only wonder at what your *Verlobter* would say, if she were to see you handing me gifts."

"My — ?"

"Your future bride."

"I am hopelessly at sea, Miss Worthing — you speak in riddles."

"So amusing, riddles, are they not? Here is one for you: What is it that flirts in the town and courts in the country?"

"I am sure I do not know."

"A brother of the bung, Mr. Summerfield. That is to say, a brewer. More tea?"

"Thank you, no. Am I to understand that you believe me to be promised in marriage to some lady in the country?"

"Your faithful Mr. Heathman told me so."

"John? Ah . . . I begin to see . . ."

"Then it is true? Or did he lie?"

"No, he did not lie. I expect that he meant Olivia Fairchild."

"My compliments to Miss Fairchild, when next you see her, and my wishes for great happiness in her married life."

Mr. Summerfield took the cup from my hand and set it down. "We can not speak of this here," he said. "Tell me when we may be alone."

"Sir, I am shocked. Alone? What would Miss Fairchild say?"

"The devil take Miss Fairchild. Meet me across the river in Vauxhall Gardens to-night, at nine, near the orchestra pavilion. Bring your brother as protector, if you like."

"My brother is otherwise engaged."

"Then bring your sister, your mother, his lordship himself,

the lot of them! But meet me. I *must* talk to you, and have an end of this business."

"I can not promise to be there," I told him, coldly.

"*I* shall be there, in any case," he snapped, "and if you have not the good sense to meet me, then I will think you a silly girl."

We could say no more, so we drew apart and joined the other guests.

V

In the Dark Walk

Accompanied by Esmie, I took a hackney-coach across the bridge to Vauxhall Gardens that night. The lamps in the Gardens provided brilliant illumination, everywhere save in the so-called Dark Walk, where young gallants pursued squalling, squealing ladies who should have known better.

In the pavilion, the musicians were playing that charming *Nachtmusik* of Mozart's. I soon espied Mr. Summerfield, near the pavilion, pacing back and forth, restlessly. We approached him, and he bowed to us, saying:

"Good evening, Mrs. Cooper, Miss Worthing. I suggest that we sit in one of the supper-boxes there in the arbours, where we can order custards . . ."

Esmie said, firmly: "Mr. Summerfield, let us put aside pretence. I admire the music of Mozart, and should be glad to stop here and listen, without the necessity of making aimless conversation. I shall do so for a quarter of an hour, whilst you and my sister go off and say what you have to say to each other, and then return."

"Thank you, Mrs. Cooper," he said. "You are a tactful woman."

"And not a foolish one," said Esmie. "A quarter of an hour, and not one minute longer."

He nodded, and then led me away. Soon, we found ourselves in the Dark Walk, away from the bright lamps and the music. We had exchanged not a word. Now, he said:

"John Heathman did not lie. He told you what he thought to be true. I was, until recently, affianced to Miss Olivia Fairchild, whose family's ancestral house neighbours ours in Suffolk. That arrangement, however, has been broken off. It had been broken off even before I met you at your brother Eadward's house."

I thought carefully before I asked, "By 'broken off,' am I to take it that you jilted the lady?"

He sighed. "No. If there was any jilting done, it was Miss Fairchild who jilted me."

"For what cause?"

"Sufficient — by her lights."

"Had she fallen in love with another gentleman?"

"Not to my knowledge."

"Had she reason to be displeased by some misconduct of yours?"

"No."

"Then . . . ?"

He stopped walking. A giggling couple skittered past us in the dark, like beetles. "May we sit upon this bench?" he asked.

The bench was barely visible in the dark. "If you like," I said. It was damp, and he wiped it dry with his handkerchief. We sat down.

He said: "Miss Fairchild's family, and perhaps Miss Fairchild herself, formed a haughty dislike of the Summerfields."

"A dislike of your family; not only you?"

"My mother is exempt from their disfavour, I dare say."

"In other words," I said, "they do not relish the idea of being related to brewers."

He smiled. "Or brothers of the bung, as I once heard brewers called." I was thankful for the dark, else he had seen me colouring. "Yes," he said, "it is that sort of thing, more or less. The Fairchilds are a very old Suffolk family, you see."

"And you are truly not engaged to be married?"

"Truly. But John could not have known, so he is blameless."

"Were you very much in love with Miss Fairchild?"

He hesitated before replying. "I thought that I was. She *is* a pretty thing. But I can tell you, Miss Worthing, and I ask you to believe me, that I did not know the emotion of real love until now. What I felt for Olivia was like a sputtering candle, compared to the conflagration that consumes me at this moment."

"I think that we had best change the course of this conversation," I said quickly, "and begin to walk back to the orchestra pavilion. My sister will be waiting for us."

"Very well," he said, as we rose from the bench.

Walking back, I was determined to talk of less inflammatory matters, so I said, "Your Mr. Heathman is a German?"

"An Austrian," he replied.

"But surely John Heathman is not an Austrian name?"

"His name was Johann Hiedler, a name which does not exactly translate into 'heath man,' but comes close to it. He is from Spital, a small village in the Waldviertel region of Austria. My father and his have known each other for years; and, whilst Father and I were visiting the Waldviertel last summer on business, Father asked Martin — John's father — if the lad could come work for us in England. We needed a good man here in the new London plant, you see. John is quite young — only just nineteen — but he knows his beer, worked for a small local brewery there. They do a good product, partly because of the excellent water of the Kamp River near by. Well, of course, his mother, Anna, did not want him to go — you know what mothers are — but Martin looked on it as a splendid opportunity for his son, and Johann himself was keen. So there you have the tedious story of why a young chap with the very English name of John Heathman his verbs at the ends of his sentences is putting."

I laughed. "Yes, it *is* rather tedious, at that! Do you have any brothers?"

"I have one brother, Hodge — Roger, that is."

"He is the younger?"

"The elder. And he will inherit the bulk of father's estate, including our vast new house in Suffolk. But the business — save for a generous share of the profits, which Roger will always receive — will be mine. Roger has no liking for business, no head for it, he is a bookish chap whose greatest love is the library he is collecting in our house. I love him very much, but he could never manage the brewery, and he knows this better than anybody."

"Do you have any sisters?"

"Two, one of them married. There were two other boys, as well, but they died in infancy."

"Is your brother married?"

"I do not think that Hodge shall ever marry. His interests do not appear to lie in that direction. And so the responsibility for carrying on the name of Summerfield rests entirely with me. That is why my father was eager for me to marry Olivia. As he points out, time does not stand still — *Eheu fugaces,* and all that. I shall be thirty-three this year."

"Heavens! How ancient!"

"You may laugh, but many men a decade younger than I are already husbands."

"And younger than that," I said. "My brother Freddy's friend Percy is the age of your Mr. Heathman, and yet he has been recently married. Still: 'Ripeness is all,' Mr. Summerfield."

"I beg your pardon?"

"Shakespeare."

"Ah. To be sure."

The musicians were playing "Drink to Me Only with Thine Eyes" when we returned to the pavilion and my waiting sister.

That night, I put the little Staffordshire shepherd on the table next my bed, as Mr. Summerfield had bidden me do.

VI

Lord Byron's Curse

Freddy had now become so popular in his portrayal of Reggie Rakehell that people were flocking to the Proteus just to see the new young actor, Mr. Thingrow. His employer, wise in the ways of the theatre, took advantage of the favour that

Freddy enjoyed with the public, by decreeing that Freddy should speak the prologue in his stead. To this end, he provided my brother with some new lines, to precede the original verses.

Esmie and I, eager to see Freddy in his new eminence, contrived to pay the Proteus a second visit, and did so; this time on the pretext of attending a party. We did not lie — we did attend the party, but we left it in time to go to the theatre.

The party was given by Mr. Samuel Rogers, the banker and poet, at No. 22 St. James's Place. His house, though small, is filled with the most beautiful of paintings and *objets d'art*.

Lord Byron, whom we had met before through Mr. Brummel, arrived shortly before our departure for the theatre, sweeping breathlessly into the dining-room with that curiously attractive limp. His face was drawn, and he appeared older than his twenty-three years. Perhaps it was the toll of his long sojourn in foreign climes.

"I am sorry to be late," he said in apology to our host, "but I am just come from the House, where I made what the press will doubtless call 'an impassioned oration.' "

"Advocating what?"

"Advocating nothing, my dear Rogers. *Opposing* a Bill that [asks the death penalty for smashing looms in mills, as these Luddites, which they call themselves, have been doing in the North."]*

I asked him: "Was your speech effective, do you think, my lord?"

"It was *affecting,* dear lady, because it was so well written and delivered, and one *hopes* that it will also be effective." His handsome face clouded. "One hopes. One always hopes."

Mr. Rogers offered him the most tempting variety of dishes and the choicest vintages, but he declined them all. "Only a few biscuits, if you please, and a glass of soda-water."

"My dear fellow," said Mr. Rogers, "I fear that we have no such things in the house. Shall I send out for them?"

* Water damage having completely obliterated this passage, I have taken the considerable liberty of inserting this reference to a later speech made by Byron in the House of Lords. The Bill he opposed was passed, despite his efforts, and many Luddites were hanged. — R. R.

"No, no. A confounded nuisance, this stomach of mine. Just some of those mashed potatoes, then. And a little vinegar, if it's to be had."

Sinking into a chair next to mine, he sighed and said, "Life can be devilish hard, Miss Worthing. 'When sorrows come, they come not single spies, but in battalions.' I am but lately returned to England, and what do I find awaiting me here? Death, on every side. My dear mother, dead of a thundering apoplexy. When I heard of her attack, I rushed to Newstead to be with her, but she was already dead when I arrived. I did not feel much affection for her whilst she lived, I confess, but when I saw her lying there, cold and still, and knew that I should never again hear her voice or feel her soft hand upon my brow, I wished to lie down beside her and die, too. I realised in that moment that I'd had but one true friend in all the world, and now she had gone."

His voice faltered; then he went on: "Oh, I have other friends, to be sure — but 'had' is the more appropriate word, for whilst my mother was stretched out dead before me, I received word that my friend Matthews had drowned in the Cam. Two other friends, Wingfield and my dear Edleston, died just this past May. And I did not even know of it until I had landed on this shore."

My heart went out to him. "Those indeed are cruel blows, my lord. Please know that you have my sympathy."

"You are most kind."

"But, in a time of such trial, is not your gift a source of solace to you?"

"You refer, I suppose, to my curse: writing," he said. "It is an affliction, like this foot of mine. A man born with such a 'gift' must needs carry it with him everywhere. It is a fierce itch, a festering sore, a hump on the back, a withered arm, a freakish growth that sets him apart from other, happier, men, denying him the comforts they enjoy, troubling his sleep, disturbing his appetite, souring his affections, a source not of solace but of pain. A writer writes, Miss Worthing, not because he wishes to, but because he is hopelessly, helplessly driven to it, as a moth to a flame, a degenerate to his vice, or an addicted wretch to his blessèd, accursèd opium. And yet, there is something in what you say, perhaps: because, like opium, the act of writing cancels the world and makes the writer oblivious of everything save the passages that stream from his pen. But call it not solace, lady. Call it a venomous drug; and call its user a slave to it."

Then, seeing me prepare to leave with Esmie, he said, *"Partite? Crudele!* I had hoped that we might dance the minuet."

"I have promised to meet my brother," I explained. "Besides, I am more partial to the waltz. Do you not think that it will soon displace the minuet?"

"Let us hope that it does not, Miss Worthing," he replied, "for, in my judgment, the waltz encourages wantonness."

In our coach, on the way to the theatre, I said to Esmie, "Wantonness! He is hardly in a position to condemn it in others. They say that he has taken liberties with his own sister!"

"It's his foot," said Esmie.

"I *beg* your pardon?"

"The waltz is too difficult for him, I expect, with that deformed foot of his. She's only his half-sister, at any rate."

We arrived at the Proteus and were settled in our box just in time.

VII

Chum's Last Tragedy

The spectators cheered Freddy as he stepped out before the curtains in Reggie's foppish finery. So famous was he now that he was greeted with roaring approbation even before he opened his mouth; but open it he did, to speak the revised prologue:

> "Thin-grow am I, and thinner still may grow,
> If you deny affection for our show.
> So pity take on Reggie Rakehell's flaws,
> And treat us not to pissing, but ahaws —
> I mean to say, not *hissing,* but *applause!* . . ."

Tumultuous laughter billowed from Freddy's public. Needless for me to add, *that* ribald metathesis was not uttered in error, but had been written and planned by Cholmondeley-Cockburn. The remainder of the prologue, and indeed of the entire play, was relished by the audience. At the end, Freddy received the loudest and longest shouts of approval.

In the family coach on the way home, my sister asked him, "Is not your popularity resented by Mr. Chum? You have put him quite in the shade, and actor-managers are not known for being self-effacing."

"Chum's an odd chap in many ways," said Freddy, "and there's a great deal about him that one can not admire, I suppose. But I'll say this for him: whatsoever is best for the show is to his liking. 'The play's the thing' is what he says. I rather think it may not always have been so. I have heard that when he was younger, he was puffed up with self-importance, and put himself forward in unseemly ways. It may have been that disastrous *Macbeth* of his, some years ago, that made him modify his behaviour."

"Macbeth?" I said. "I thought him to be only a comedian."

"His beginnings were in tragedy," Freddy replied. "In point of fact . . ." Freddy rapped with his stick and called up to Tuttle: "Stop here at this tea-room." As Tuttle brought the coach to a halt in front of DeWitt's tea-room, Freddy said to us, "I want you to meet old Carruthers. He plays the part of Sir Malcolm Malfeasance in our play, and he's here every night after the show. He should be here already, because he appears only in the first act, and his paint is off and most of his costume is changed even before the curtain calls. He can tell you the story better than I. Besides, I could do with a bit of coffee and some cakes, and I expect that you could, too."

Inside the tea-room, Freddy looked about, and soon discovered his fellow-player, sitting alone at a table, reading a newspaper and sipping coffee. "Hi! Basil!" Freddy called.

Mr. Carruthers looked up from his paper and beckoned us over. Introductions were quickly exchanged, and Freddy ordered coffee and cakes all round.

"I started to tell my sisters the story of Chum's downfall in *Macbeth,"* said Freddy, "but you can tell it better than anybody."

Basil Carruthers laughed. "It must be over a quarter of a century ago. Dear Chum is my oldest friend. He and I were young actors, and we'd been engaged by the manager of a provincial theatre to play in *Macbeth;* Chum in the title *rôle,* I as Macduff. Shockingly low wages. Well, it was a wretched, misbegotten affair from the very first act. The Banquo was tipsy, and in Scene Three, when he was required to address the Witches:

> 'If you can look into the seeds of time,
> And say which grain will grow and which will not,
> Speak then to me, who neither beg nor fear
> Your favours nor your hate'

— he said:

> 'Speak then to me, who neither hate nor hear
> Your beggars nor your fate.'

Absolute nonsense, of course. And it rattled Chum, who, just a few lines later, bungled his words —

> 'By Sinel's death I know I am Thane of Glamis'

into:

> 'By Glamis' death I know I am Thane of Sinel.'

In the last scene of that act, Lady Macbeth came a cropper in those powerful lines about the milking babe:

> '. . . I have given suck, and know
> How tender 'tis to love the babe that milks me:
> I would, while it was smiling in my face,
> Have pluck'd my nipple from his boneless gums,
> And dash'd the brains out . . .'

What she said was not 'boneless gums,' but 'gumless bones.' Nobody seemed to notice, a sorry comment on the audience. Later, however, in the banquet scene, the silent ghost of Banquo — by this time *very* drunk — was unable to stifle an unusually resonant belch. That *was* noticed. So was his 'Excuse me,' which made matters only worse. Is it any wonder, ladies, that *Macbeth* is considered to be a bad-luck play? Still, those mishaps were as nothing when measured against what Chum later did, deliberately."

"Deliberately?" Esmie asked.

"Oh, yes, Mrs. Cooper. As you may know, *Macbeth* is the Bard's shortest tragedy, so Chum decided to amplify his part by writing a great number of extra lines for himself — after first taking care *not* to seek the approval of the manager. What he did, exactly, was to bloat up that familiar couplet —

'I will not be afraid of death and bane
Till Birnam Forest come to Dunsinane'

— into a rant of no less than seventy-five lines, composed in *terza rima*."

"Why that Dantean form?" I asked.

A shrug was his reply. He went on: "If seventy-five lines does not seem long to you as Shakespearean speeches go, I pray you remember that, of Macbeth's other speeches, 'Is this a dagger' is only thirty-two lines in length, 'If it were done' but twenty-eight, and 'To-morrow and to-morrow and to-morrow' a scant ten.

"Imagine our surprise when, during the progress of Act Five, the third scene thereof, Chum, instead of uttering the two lines that Shakespeare had written for him, droned the following:

'I will not be afraid of death and bane
Nor hostile forces seeking to destroy,
Till Birnam Wood attacks high Dunsinane.
Begone, therefore, dull care and sour annoy!
Let me prepare my heart for all content
And open it to floods of warming joy.
Through all my days I will be pleasure-bent,
Letting myself dispel all gouts of gloom,
Heedless of ill that hated foes have sent,
Defying dark and dismal drones of doom
That trait'rous fools delight to daily tell.
Now will I fill with columbine each room,
Making a Paradise of this my Hell,
Turning despair to glee of ev'ry kind,
Disdaining to ring Death's lugubrious knell,
Seeking, with certain faith that I will find,
Serenity and *bliss!* for *this!,* my soul,
Sweet gentle love and placid peace of mind,
My shatter'd self restorèd and made whole,
My spirit freed of all its deadly dark
That hitherto had taken such a toll
That it had made my life so shrill and stark . . .' "

"But that is the most awful verse!" I exclaimed.

"Indeed it is, Miss Worthing," Mr. Carruthers agreed, "and it is, therefore, not surprising that, at that juncture, the manager walked from the theatre in a daze, to the nearest alehouse, and there methodically drank himself into a state of unconsciousness. In the mean time, Chum rolled on:

'No more shall I be prey to restless nights
And wretched dreams of devil-dogs that bark,
Murdering all my cherishèd delights
In such a way design'd to drive me mad
By shewing to my mind such horrid sights,
So deeply and so dangerously bad,
That I would choose to be both cold and dead
Than so severely sorrowful and sad.'

"Here, taking advantage of Chum's pause for breath, the actor who played the Doctor quickly slipped in his line — 'Were I from Dunsinane away and clear, profit again should hardly draw me here' — and left the stage. Macbeth was required to exit with the Doctor, clearing the stage for the next scene, Country near Birnam Wood; but Chum was only halfway through his speech, and he rattled on like a stage-coach whilst I, as Macduff, and Malcolm, Old Siward, his Son, Menteith, Caithness, Angus, Lennox, Ross, and a dozen Marching Soldiers were left waiting in the wings:

'With all these myriad cares upon my head,
How shall I ever be calm and serene?
How sleep or eat my bitter daily bread
Or sip my soup from silver deep tureen
Until this curse from off my soul is lifted?' "

Other customers of the tea-room had gathered round our table to hear Mr. Carruthers's story. "Now Chum cupped his hand to his ear, as if listening, and bellowed on:

'Still do I hear that mournful piercing keen
Of widow'd women. How their cries are sifted
Through years and tears of faithful married life
With which they and their spouses then were gifted,
Now turned to doleful agony and strife

That frosts all human hearts with horrid chill
And cancels all the warmth of ev'ry wife,
Transforming them to cisterns of sore ill,
Repositories dire of dim dismay,
Making them yearn to curse and claw and kill!'

"I assure you, ladies, that Chum's fellow-actors had long since shared those widows' desires to curse and claw and kill. But still he went on, undeterred:

'Oh, how I rue that maledicted day
When first I coveted the kingly crown
And yearn'd but to possess the royal sway
And to enjoy high fame and wide renown
Throughout the limits of the Scottish land —
For by this coveting I was cast down,
Ay, to damnation, by mine own fell hand!
None but myself to censure or to blame,
Admonish, scold, or harshly reprimand —
Unless it be my diabolic dame,
Whose counsels overcame my tender heart
And urg'd me to achieve that dreadful fame
By cunning use of each deceptive art
That LUCIFER doth willingly provide
To blacken and pollute each single part
Of Man's eternal soul, that he may hide
Nowhere, and noplace find that blessèd peace
Without which it were better he had died.' "

I asked, "Why did not the manager order the curtains to be closed on him?"

"You forget, Miss Worthing," replied Mr. Carruthers, "that the manager was lying stupefied in an ale-house. And so, Chum was free to declaim the remaining lines of his doggerel:

'O Heaven! Grant, I beg Thee, sweet surcease
From pungent pangs of most deservèd guilt,
And let me have of life another lease
By which a better man may yet be built,
Lest my despair lead me to take this blade
And plunge it in my heart up to the hilt.
Is this the mercy Thou hast past display'd?

Dost Thou take back, stern God, life-giving breath?
Dost Thou stand by and see my mind decay'd,
And laugh to see me stagger to my death?
Take pity on this creature Thou hast made,
And pray redeem the soul of poor Macbeth!'

"Chum attempted to defend his interpolation by citing the examples of Garrick, Cibber, and other actors who 'improved' Shakespeare; but to no avail — he was dismissed. And that, if I am not mistaken, was Chum's last appearance in tragedy. The Lady Macbeth of that company, Matilda Frobisher, fell in love with him despite — or possibly because of — his outrageous act, and hounded him to the altar. He is married to her still. She is the lady who sings comic songs before the start of our play."

Mr. Carruthers, reaching into his coat for his pocket-book, said, "I received an interesting press notice, as a result of my appearance in that same *Macbeth.*" Carefully, I might say tenderly, he extracted from his pocket-book a newspaper cutting so old and worn that it was little more than lace-work. He passed it across the table to me, and I read aloud the underscored passage:

" 'As Macduff, Mr. Basil Carruthers gave what is surely the fullest portrayal of that character which I have ever seen.' Why, what a lovely notice!" I added.

"Yes, is it not?" he agreed, taking back the cutting and placing it inside his pocket-book again. "But there is a somewhat less lovely — and amusing — epilogue to it. I sought out the theatrical critic of that provincial paper in order to thank him for his kind words. A dour, unpleasant man, he was. 'The damned printer made a mistake,' he told me. 'Drunk again, more than likely. Substituted an *f* for a *d.* I did *not* write "fullest" — I wrote *"dullest!"* ' " Mr. Carruthers laughed at this anecdote, told at his own expense. Then he shook his head dolefully and added:

"The worst part of that appalling farrago was what happened after the seventy-fifth and final line of Chum's awful stuff had been delivered. The spectators, to their everlasting shame, gave him a standing ovation."

"Perhaps they only wanted to stretch their legs," said Freddy.

After we had taken our leave of Mr. Carruthers and had departed the tea-room — Freddy having paid for the old actor's coffee and cakes — Esmie said, "It is a wonder to me that Mr. Carruthers can remember that long oration."*

"Well, he *is* an actor, after all," said Freddy. "And it's been well worth his while to remember it — I understand that he has been dining out on that story for the past twenty-five years."

VIII

The Lost Cripple

"You look chap-fallen to-day, Mr. Brummel," I said to the Beau during one of our Thursdays not long after. "Are you a victim of unrequited love?"

He responded with a thin smile. "I have seen a verse satire in circulation which puts forward the proposition that 'love is a mere empty bubble' and 'not worth half the trouble,' or something of the sort. I must own that I agree with that sentiment."

I believe that he does. Although gossip abounds in our set, I have never yet heard any lady's name mentioned as one of his amorous conquests. Even Harriette Wilson, that vindictive courtesan, who has used every means to besmirch his reputation, has not been able to call him a debaucher of women. Some say that her hatred of him stems from the fact that he is the only man of the fashionable set whom she has not succeeded in getting into her bed. On the other hand, I have never heard any rumours to the effect that he — plays at back gammon, as Freddy might call it. I think that he is simply

* We might say the same of Melissa. I have no explanation, other than: (a) she obviously must have had an unusually retentive memory in order to write this chronicle in such detail; or (b) she may have reconstructed much of the pseudo-Shakespearean speech. — R. R.

indifferent to my sex, as well as to his own, and is too much in love with his own appearance in the looking-glass ever to be in love with anybody other than himself.

"Then why do you seem so gloomy?" I asked him.

"Alas," he said with a sigh, "I have lost my lucky cripple."

I knew him to mean that he had lost a "crook," or sixpence, a coin that has won its nicknames by reason of its being so often bent by much use.

"But surely you are not a superstitious gentleman?"

"I was never of a superstitious turn of mind," he admitted, "until the day I saw that cripple on the pavement and picked it up. Five o'clock of a summer morning it was, Miss Worthing, some years ago. I'd been at the gaming-tables all night, and I'd had a run of deuced bad luck. Kept on playing, hoping to get a bit of my own back, but Fortune was set against me. By morning, we were all of us nearly knee-deep in cards, I can tell you!"

"Why that?" I asked.

"A pack of cards is used for only one deal," he explained, "and then is thrown on the floor, and a new pack opened. I can see that you have never been inside a gaming-house."

"Indeed I have *not.*"

"Well, I quit that place at five, stript of my last penny, and feeling confoundedly low. So low, in fact, that my head was hanging and my shoulders bent as if I'd spent the day crouching in Little Ease . . ."

(He referred to that dark little cell in Guildhall, too small in all its dimensions for even a lad to stand up straight, sit, or lie down in, where the city chamberlain once was wont to confine disorderly apprentices, keeping them locked up there for as many hours or days as the extent of their unruliness dictated.)

"As I walked along in that drooping way," Mr. Brummel went on, "with my eyes fixed upon the ground, what did I see, there on the pavement at my feet, but this cripple. I bent down and swooped it up — then I turned right around, walked back into the gaming-house, threw that battered sixpence upon the table, and played another hand. And another. And another. And yet another — winning every one of them! I won back all that I had lost, and more!"

"How fortunate!" I cried.

"Indeed it was," Mr. Brummel agreed, "and I think you can understand why, ever since that day, I looked on that bent old coin as lucky."

"Oh, yes."

"For years thereafter, I wore it hanging from my watch-chain. Last week, the chain broke, so I kept the cripple in my waistcoat pocket until such time as I could get the chain mended."

"And you spent it!" I divined.

"Exactly, Miss Worthing. Gave it to a hackney-coachman by mistake. Oh, I have advertised for it, but to no avail. No doubt that rascal Rothschild, or some of his set, got hold of it."

"Why do you say that, Mr. Brummel?"

"These infernal Israelites all hate me," he replied.

"But why?"

"They see, in me, the kind of gentleman they try to ape, in vain. They grind me by their usury in their damned Jerusalem Chambers. They seek to ruin me. Shylocks, every man jack of them."

"Poor Mr. Brummel. But perhaps your coin will turn up?"

"Oh, I hope so, Miss Worthing, but I fear that it will not. I fear it is gone for ever. And with it has gone my luck."

"Surely not!"

But he smiled sadly, and held out his cup to Esmie, who had been doing the honours of pouring that afternoon.

After filling his cup, she said, "So close in this room to-day. I feel suffocated. I think I shall step out into the garden for a breath of fresh air."

She did so; and I, excusing myself to our guests, followed after her, fearing that she might be feeling faint again.

"Esmie, are you ill?"

She shook her head. "A little air is all that I require," she said. "It is so smoky there inside."

As before, I could not think what she meant. The weather was too warm for a fire, and none of the gentlemen had been smoking. I began to fear that she suffered from some ailment of the lungs that caused her to be short of breath.

"Esmie," I said, "it is not in the least smoky inside the house."

She smiled. "Perhaps it is those 'dark Satanic mills' of Mr. Blake's," she said.

"You are being playful and naughty now," I told her, "for we have no such mills near by, spewing out their smoke. I think we should send word to Mr. Cargrave to call here and look you over."

"No, no," she assured me, "I have no need of his tappings and proddings. I feel quite myself again now."

"Then do come back inside," I pleaded. "I fear that you may have offended Mr. Brummel by your hasty leaving."

"Terrible man," said Esmie.

"Silly, perhaps," I rejoined. "Vain. A ne'er-do-well. But amusing — and surely not terrible?"

Esmie kissed my cheek. Her lips were cold. "No doubt you are right. I am, likely, in that time of life when women go a bit awry in their minds. But it will pass. Let us go inside again, before the plum-cake is all gone."

When we returned to the drawing-room, Mr. Brummel was a model of solicitude. "I do hope that you are feeling better, Mrs. Cooper?"

"Yes, thank you, Mr. Brummel. Much better. And I must tell you I am sorry that you have lost your lucky sixpence. I do not entirely disbelieve in such-like tokens and omens. They are, perhaps, signs, signals, messages from the invisible world — if we could but understand them."

Mr. Brummel favoured her with an indulgent smile. "Do *you*, perhaps, understand them, Mrs. Cooper, and can you tell me what meaning lies behind my loss of that coin?"

"I am no seer, Mr. Brummel. Anything I may tell you is only that which you may find in your Bible."

"I am bound to say — as much as I regret to do so under a bishop's roof — that the Bible is not part of my daily reading," replied Mr. Brummel. "Precisely where in those sacred pages should I seek?"

"In the Old Testament," Esmie advised him, "the Bible of the Jews. The one hundred forty-sixth psalm, third verse."

Later, after our guests had left, I consulted that verse of that psalm. It read: "Put not your trust in princes."

IX

The Way of the World

I have written little of my elder brother, Teddy, and his wife, Luisa. Perhaps this is the time to do so.

Teddy has a distinct talent for architecture, but to my way of thinking, he lacks sufficient push; without which, talent is like a musket-ball without a charge of powder. Either is ineffective without the other: lacking powder to propel it, the musket-ball never leaves the musket; without a ball, mere powder alone does no more than flash in the pan, making a great noise, "sound and fury, signifying nothing." In either case, the result is the same — or, rather, the lack of result: the target is not hit.

Luisa is a woman of considerable push. She neglects no opportunity to put him forward into society and force him to meet influential people. Teddy is shy; she is bold. He is modest; she is shamelessly immodest when praising the talents of her spouse. This element of her character does not render her particularly attractive; but I do not criticise her, for I know that she is just what Teddy needs in a wife.

Earlier this year, when Mr. Summerfield's attentions to me were beginning to be apparent, Luisa said to me, with a bitter shake of her head: "If only you had known him before, Melissa."

"Why do you say that?"

"Is it not obvious to you? If you had known him then, I am certain that you could have persuaded him to overrule his father in the matter of the Suffolk house. James Wyatt, indeed! He can not hold a candle to Eadward! My blood boils when I think that he was passed over for Wyatt."

"And yet, Luisa," I said, "if you are suggesting that I might have used Mr. Summerfield's affection for me to sway a matter of business, I must tell you that I should never have done so, even if I had known him at the time."

She looked at me with surprise. "Do you not love your brother?" she asked me.

"Of course I do."

"Do you not wish him to succeed?"

"Yes!"

An unfeigned confusion emanated from her face. "Then I do not understand you, Melissa," she said. "Let me ask if you know the name of the Regent's favourite architect."

"Everybody knows that," I replied. "It is Mr. John Nash."

"Quite right. And what everybody also knows is that Mr. Nash has a wife, Mary Anne, the good-looking daughter of a coal merchant. It is common knowledge that in the Prince's younger days, when his affections fluttered betwixt and between Mrs. Fitzherbert and Lady Jersey and 'Perdita' Robinson, not a few pretty young ladies of the middle class were quietly led up the back stairs at Carlton House to serve his pleasure. One of these was Mary Anne Bradley, later to become Mrs. Nash. Are you so innocent as to believe it coincidence that Nash is now favoured with His Royal Highness's custom, and that he and his wife are now blest with a town house in Dover Street, to say nothing of a grand castellated residence at East Cowes in the Isle of Wight?"

"If what you say is true," I responded, "then it is no better than prostitution."

"Or princely gratitude," replied Luisa, "or simple payment for past services rendered. Whatever you choose to call it, my dear *belle-sœur,* it happens to be no more and no less than the way of the world; the world in which we live. There is no other, and we must make the best of it."

"Making the best of this world," I said, "is not nearly so good as making this world better." And I must own that those words sounded priggish, even to my ears.

"Idealism," she said, sneeringly.

That same evening, as she and Teddy sat at our dinner-table, Luisa said to Papa, during the soup course: "The word is out that the Prince is giving a grand reception at Carlton House next week."

"Oh?" mumbled Papa. "I had not heard of it."

"It is the talk of the town," Luisa went on. "Everybody will be invited." With a sigh, she added, "Everybody except Eadward and me. We have not received an invitation."

"Nor have we," said Mamma. "But one must not take offence at that."

"But you could have been invited, if you had wished to be," said Luisa; and, turning to Papa, added, "Or if Father had wished to be."

"That is just it," said Papa. "I do not wish to be."

"You must pardon me, Father Worthing, but you do not think enough of your wife's wishes. I am sure that she would much admire to attend such a reception."

Teddy, who was embarrassed, said, "Luisa, please —"

Mamma said, "The bishop knows my wishes far better than do you, my dear Luisa, if you will excuse me for saying so."

My sister-in-law persisted: "That is all very well, but what about Eadward?"

"What *about* him?" asked Papa, puzzled.

"Attendance at such a grand convocation would do him a world of good in his profession. He would meet all sorts of notable people, and make invaluable alliances. And if he were to play his hand wisely — who knows? — he might even succeed in replacing John Nash in the affections of the Regent."

"Nash is a very skilfull archi——" Teddy began to say, but his wife interrupted him:

"Oh, yes, to be sure! And so is Wyatt, to hear you speak of him. And Hardwick, who will probably build the chapel at St. John's Wood *and* the parish church of St. Marylebone, as well! Why should not those plums be yours? You are, after all, a bishop's son: what man is better suited to build churches and chapels?"

She turned to Papa again, and said, "Father Worthing, you are in a position to help Eadward no end."

"In what way?" Papa asked.

"You know the Prince. He respects you. He has been a guest in this house, at this table. Eadward told me so."

"That was some years ago . . ." said Papa.

"No matter," said Luisa. "You could procure for us an invitation to Carlton House."

Papa temporised. "I am not so sure of that, Luisa. As a bishop, it is not my place to —"

She abruptly turned away from him and addressed Freddy: "Aelfred, Beau Brummel is a friend of yours."

"Yes," said Freddy.

"And he is an intimate of the Prince. If you were to put a word in Mr. Brummel's ear . . ."

Freddy shook his head. "There is a coolness, these days, between George and the Prince. I doubt that George himself will be invited to next week's reception."

Not to be deterred, Luisa spoke to Papa again. "Then it is up to you, Father. And there is not much time to be wasted."

Papa sighed. "As you wish," he said. "I will send word to the Prince to-morrow morning."

Luisa smiled. "There! That's settled!" And she fell to the fish course with good appetite.

Later in the evening, when I was alone for a moment with her, I asked, "How far, precisely, would you go to increase Teddy's eminence in his profession?"

Luisa looked at me. "If you mean what I assume that you mean," she said, "I fear that I am too thin for the Regent's taste. He prefers his women to be more buxom. Like you, in fact. But if he *were* to seek my favours, I tell you with all my heart that I would do anything to advance the man who is the father of my children." Her eyes froze. *"Anything."*

X

Confrontations at Carlton House

Papa was as good as his word, and not long after, two invitations went out from Carlton House: one to Teddy and Luisa; the other to Papa and his family.

"I have no liking for this affair," Papa said to Mamma on the evening of the reception. "But I *must* attend, after soliciting an invitation as I was forced to do. Our daughter-in-law is a determined woman, Penelope. *Too* determined for my taste. She has made me go beyond the bounds of good behaviour."

"Don't fuss, Ambrose," said Mamma, playfully rapping him on the head with her fan. "I find that I am quite eager to go. So are our children."

He sniffed. "That is not surprising in persons who prefer Margate to London. But I suppose we must all make sacrifices for our children. There is a spider that I have read of, whose last act in life is to make herself into a feast for the infant spiders who swarm over her body, eating her flesh until she is dead . . ."

"Heavens, Ambrose! What a disgusting comparison! Carlton House will not be *that* repulsive, I feel sure!"

It was, in fact, resplendent.

Carlton House, of course, is the very centre of the fashionable world. It was an exhilarating experience when Tuttle drove the episcopal carriage past the Horse Guards stationed at the four corners of that world — that is to say, Pall Mall, St. James's Street, Piccadilly, and St. James's Square — and then even more exhilarating to enter the palace itself.

Its decorations are magnificent, if florid: gold tassels, bright red velvet, white ostrich plumes everywhere; dark shining ebony and bold gleaming bronze; and all of this reflected into infinity in tall pier-glasses.

A liveried lackey with a sonorous, far-reaching voice announced us sumptuously: "His Lordship, the Right Reverend Ambrose Worthing, Bishop of Hans Town, and Mrs. Worthing. Mrs. Balthasar Cooper. Miss Melissa Worthing. Mr. Aelfred Worthing."

His Royal Highness personally greeted us. "How good of you to favour us with your presence, your lordship," he said, expansively. "We see too little of you here. And your good wife: Madam, I am honoured. This lady, I am sure, is Mrs. Cooper: you are most welcome. And here are the twins: Melissa, is it not? And Freddy, you young scamp, how are you? The colour has returned to your cheeks since that morning at Newgate, eh? Splendid! Splendid! I wish Wellington were here — have you good people met him? — he's deuced fine company — but he is still in Spain, or is it Portugal? Ah well, it's all one. I invited his wife, Kitty, to this reception, thinking to lift her spirits, but she is too downcast by his long absence. *C'est la guerre,* what? These wars with the French are *too* tiresome. Come in, dear friends, come in . . ."

Teddy and Luisa were nowhere to be seen in that throng as yet, and I surmised that Luisa was planning a dramatically late entrance; but Lord Byron was there ("Perhaps to-night we are fated to dance the minuet, Miss Worthing?"), and so were the Austens (Henry and Eliza only, Jane having returned to the country). I recognised John Nash, as well, and his wife, who was still an attractive woman. And the Sheridans were on hand, too. But not Mr. Brummel.

It was Mr. Sheridan who, espying me and Esmie through the crowd of people, waved us over and introduced us to some friends of his. "I should like you to meet Mr. and Mrs. Royce," he said. "They are in from the country and are stopping with us at Bruton Street." Bows and curtseys were exchanged. "Royce is the son of an old friend," Mr. Sheridan explained, "and the lucky young cove has had the good taste to capture this pretty creature as his bride."

Mrs. Royce was indeed very pretty, and very pregnant. About six months so, I judged. Her complexion had the clear, glowing look of women in that condition. "I hope that you are enjoying the season here in London," I said to her.

"Oh, it's ever so exciting!" she replied, with simple sincerity. "If only I were not so" — she glanced with meaning at her swollen middle — "I should enjoy it even more. It is so much more interesting than Suffolk, Miss Worth—— or may I call you Melissa?"

"Of course you may. And your name is . . . ?"

"Olivia," she replied.

I smiled, but my mind was turning rapidly. Olivia, and from Suffolk? Well, doubtless there was an ample supply of pretty Olivias in Suffolk. Still . . .

"And what was your maiden name, Olivia?" I asked her.

"Fairchild," she said.

I continued to smile, although my mind was frowning. So here is the little baggage, I said to myself, who threw over Mr. Summerfield: she lost no time in finding a replacement. Some other small worm of vexation was beginning to bore its way into my thoughts, but I had no opportunity to examine it because, at that moment, a group of men entered the room, laughing noisily and drawing all eyes to them.

They were Mr. Brummel, with his companions, Mr. Henry Pierrepoint and Lord Alvanley. All of them obviously had been drinking: their faces were flushed, their eyes shone, and their voices were a trifle too loud.

The Prince graciously walked toward them, with the hand

of friendship extended. "Alvanley, my dear fellow. And Pierrepoint: so good to see you again." He shook their hands, and drew those two men into the company whilst chatting and laughing with them; but he did not as much as acknowledge Mr. Brummel's presence: he neither spoke to him nor looked at him, and he certainly did not take him by the hand.

Everybody noted the Prince's insult. Mr. Brummel now stood alone, his face no longer flushed, but white. I felt that I had to do something, so I stepped forward quickly and spoke to him:

"Mr. Brummel, I am glad to see you. I was hoping that you would be here."

"Good evening, Miss Worthing," he said quietly. "I am here on Lord Alvanley's coat-tails, so to speak, for he was invited. I was not."

Near us, we could hear Lord Alvanley saying to the Prince, "Pierrepoint and I had a damned good run of luck at Watier's to-night, Your Highness, so we decided to throw a celebration at the Argyle Rooms — but we simply had to come by Carlton House first and see you."

Mr. Brummel whispered through clenched teeth to me: "He cut me directly. Did you see him? Our porcine Prince cut *me.*"

"Please do not upset yourself, Mr. Brummel," I advised him.

Freddy joined us. "Forget it, George. Come and have a bit of this poached salmon. It's first-rate."

But Mr. Brummel did not budge from the spot. He was softly seething. "The greasy tub of lard," he said in a low voice.

"I *told* you that you'd criticise his figure once too often," Freddy said.

"We were drinking together the other day at Brooks's," said Mr. Brummel, "in a private room. I asked him if he would kindly ring the bell to summon the wine-steward to bring us another bottle. It was not as if he hadn't done so many times before. If there had been others in the room, I should not have asked him to do it; but we were quite alone; and he was simply closer to the bell: it was at his elbow. But he looked at me more coldly than anybody has ever looked at me in my life. 'I do not ring bells,' he said, 'when there is a valet in the room to do it for me.' An allusion to my ancestry, do you see. I could have struck the swine in that moment. Perhaps I shall do so now . . ."

He began to step forward, but my brother took hold of his arm.

"Let go of me, Freddy."

Now, Lord Byron quickly limped over to us and seized his other arm, whispering into his ear, "George! I beg of you! Don't make yourself more of an ass than you already are!"

Mr. Brummel turned slowly to Byron and said, "Thank you, my gracious lord, for that kind appraisal. And I will thank you, also, to remove your hand from my sleeve. This French cloth wrinkles so easily. You too, Freddy. Both of you, *let go!"*

They unhanded him, and he tugged at his sleeves, then flicked an imaginary speck of lint from his cuff. Drawing himself up to his full height, he walked stiffly forward, stopping a few feet away from the chattering, laughing group of Lord Alvanley, Mr. Pierrepoint, and the Prince.

"Alvanley," he said, at an ordinary conversational level.

Due, perhaps, to the press of people and the general buzz of voices, Lord Alvanley did not hear him — or pretended that he did not hear him.

Mr. Brummel was seen to suck a deep supply of breath into his lungs. And then, in a voice that cut through the room like a broadsword, he called out:

"Alvanley! Who's your fat friend?"

It was as if a deep and sudden spell had descended upon the room, petrifying everybody into statues, muffling all sounds into silence, stopping time, congealing the blood in every vein. Transfixed, we stood rooted thus for an hour — or so it seemed. It was probably no longer than five or six seconds. Then somebody cleared his throat; another set down a punch cup with a tinkle; still another giggled nervously; the spell lifted; and life began to flow again. The orchestra struck up the minuet from *Don Giovanni*.

Mr. Brummel turned and strode, in no haste, out of the room.

And at that particularly inauspicious moment, the lackey announced the arrival of two new guests: "Mr. and Mrs. Eadward Worthing."

Poor Luisa. The dramatic entrance that she had so carefully calculated for its maximum effect was completely flat.

(By the way, I *did* dance the minuet with Lord Byron.)

XI

A Tumult of the Senses

The following day, Mr. Summerfield returned to London, and called on us. He was invited to dine, and accepted with pleasure. The meal and the attendant conversation went smoothly and unremarkably; and, after the savoury, I asked Papa's permission to shew our guest the collection of Bibles in the library. Nobody was deceived, of course — all knew that I simply wanted some private words with him — but he had made such a favourable impression upon my parents as a trustworthy gentleman that permission was not withheld.

In the library, after shewing Mr. Summerfield a few of the more amusing errata, I continued to chatter of Biblical matters. "Of course, you are familiar with the passage that tells us that a rich man will have more trouble entering Heaven than a camel passing through a needle's eye . . ."

He smiled. "Are you telling me that I must give all that I have to the poor?"

"No," I replied, "I only wish to pass on to you an interesting comment of my father's upon that passage."

"I am relieved," he said, with an exaggerated sigh, "for I fear that a suit made of sackcloth would ill become me."

"Papa says that, considering that the Greek for 'camel' bears a striking resemblance to the Greek for 'rope' it is likely that 'rope' was the true and original meaning. And do you not think it to be an earthier, less outlandish, and altogether better image?"

"Oh, to be sure." He took my hand. "But I do not think that you brought me in here to talk of ropes and camels."

"No, I did not." I withdrew my hand from his. "I brought you here to talk of Olivia Fairchild."

"Olivia again? I thought we had settled all that."

"One or two questions more, if you have no objection?"

"No — but I would rather talk of you. That is, of you and me." He tried to take my hand again, but I resisted.

"How long is it," I began, but hesitated, for I knew that I was embarking on a hazardous course of enquiry.

"I beg your pardon? How long is what?"

"How long is it since your engagement with Miss Fairchild was broken off?"

"Oh, a very long time," he replied. "Three months, at least, perhaps four."

"Do you know that she is now married?"

"Yes, to a chap by the name of Royce. Decent enough fellow. Good family. Old Suffolk stock. But how do *you* know that she is married?"

"I met her last night at Carlton House."

"*Did* you, indeed! And did the two of you discuss me?"

"We had more interesting subjects to discuss."

"I am downcast."

"Such as her pregnancy."

Mr. Summerfield, with a rather too studied display of *insouciance,* strolled over to the table and leafed idly through the 1572 edition of Archbishop Parker's Bible, which still lay open there. He appeared to be studying the picture of Leda and the swan at the opening of the Book of Hebrews. "Pregnancy?" he said, casually, after a moment. "Royce has lost no time, then. Well, Scripture tells us to be fruitful and multiply, I believe, does it not? Replenish the earth, and all that?"

I walked over to him and closed the Archbishop's Bible. "She must have married Mr. Royce quite soon after her engagement to you was broken off," I said.

"It would appear so."

"She has been married, then, no longer than four months, possibly less."

He nodded, and said nothing.

"But," I continued, "she is at least six months pregnant."

"Come, Miss Worthing," he responded with a light smile, "do you condemn the lady? 'Judge not, that you be not judged.' "

"You need not cite Scripture to a bishop's daughter, Mr.

Summerfield," I said sharply. "And I was not judging *her* so much as I was judging *you.*"

"Me?"

He made me furious. "Do not *act,* sir. I happen to know good acting from bad, and I can tell you that your portrayal of surprise and innocence is most lamentably unconvincing. The child in that young woman's womb was conceived when you and she were still engaged. It was planted there by you, was it not?"

"Miss Worthing, I —"

I spoke firmly: "Only one thing is required of you, Mr. Summerfield: the truth."

"And that is precisely what I can not give you!" he retorted. "No man could do so. Not even a husband, in these times, can be certain that a child of his wife's was engendered by him or by one of the lady's other admirers."

"Then you *did* have to do with Olivia."

"Miss Worthing, such things are not fit subjects for —"

"Did you lie with her, sir?!"

"Well — *yes,* damn it!" he blurted out. "We were engaged — and I'm a man, after all — and the little vixen was asking for it!"

"Was she asking for it from every man in Suffolk? Do you accuse her of a general wantonness?"

He shook his head. "No," he said softly. "She was a virgin when — when I —"

"Then the child *is* yours."

He nodded, and turned away from me. "I expect it is." He turned back to me. "But I swear that I knew nothing of it until just now, when you told me. And, damn it, I *wanted* to marry her! It was *she* who broke the engagement, she and her fine old Suffolk family! As for the child . . . I am truly sorry that this thing happened . . . it is most unfortunate . . . but I will not hold myself guilty of anything, save that one moment of foolish passion and — and carelessness."

"Thank you, Mr. Summerfield," I said. "I have no more questions to put to you."

"I have one to put to *you,*" he rejoined. "Will you marry me?"

I inhaled sharply. "You . . . you do not believe in employing subtlety," I said.

"Damn subtlety."

"Or tact."

"Damn tact."

"You can not expect me to —"

"I expect you to say either 'Yes' or 'No' before we leave this library. If 'No,' you shall never see me again. If 'Yes' —"

His arms encircled me, and I was pressed to his body. Feigning indignation, I said, "You take what you please, I see!"

"Indeed I do, and I usually please what I take."

"You dare to —"

But his lips were on mine, first lightly and tenderly, then crushingly, and soon he was tipping the velvet, as Freddy would say, and I was dissolving like sugar in hot tea and returning his caresses. Through my frock and undergarments, through his trousers, through all those thicknesses of fabric, I felt the powerful iron thrust of him. I was frightened, and pleased, and confused. I was giddy with the tumult of my senses.

When finally he released me, I fairly staggered to the library door, and tried to call out, but I had no voice. I breathed deeply, and tried again, and this time my voice was like the chirp of a little sparrow as I peeped:

"Papa? Mamma?"

They heard me, however, and appeared from the drawing-room, whither they had gone after dinner.

"Did you call us, Melissa?" Papa asked.

"Yes," I said, breathlessly. "Mr. Summerfield has . . . he has . . ."

"What is it, child?"

"Mr. Summerfield has . . . something he wishes to ask you, Papa."

XII

Drink? Gambling? Opium? Women?

"In that case," said Papa, "I suggest that you repair, with your mother, to the drawing-room, and leave me to speak with him here in the library."

Mamma and I did as he asked. Later, the conversation between the two men was related to me by both of them, in separate, but not disparate, reports:

"Well, sir," said Papa, closing the library door. "Will you smoke a cigar?"

"Not at the moment, your lordship, thank you. Later, perhaps."

"Very well. The floor is yours, then." Both men sat down.

"I'll come straight to the point, sir. I love Melissa. She returns that feeling. I wish to ask you for her hand in marriage."

"Yes, quite," said Papa. "But you must tell me something about yourself, Mr. Summerfield. We scarcely know you."

"I'm thirty-three. Although I am not the elder of my father's living sons, I will inherit his business, for reasons that I have already explained to Melissa. And, even while he is alive, I will manage that business and reap most of the profits. My father will soon retire."

"Go on."

"There is not much more to be said, your lordship. I'm Church of England, as are all of my family. My mother was formerly Phoebe Fanshaw, of the Suffolk Fanshaws. Her money will be divided equally amongst her children on her death. It is a considerable sum. The interest alone . . ."

"Yes, yes," said Papa, "your solvency is readily apparent, and we need not dwell upon the details of it until later. Tell me where you and my daughter would live, if you were to marry her: in Suffolk?"

"No, sir, in London."

Papa grunted approval. "Tell me something else, Summerfield. This brewery of yours, here in Southwark. Might there be a position in it — I speak of a responsible position, of course, and well paid — for a young man? I allude to my son."

"Teddy?"

"No, Aelfred."

"Well, your lordship, I can not say —"

"He needs occupation, you see. He's a bit of a layabout. He has no interest in preparing for holy orders. No visible talent for anything, such as his brother's architectural gifts. But if you might take him under your wing, as it were, teach him the brewery business, perhaps even make him your second-in-command . . ."

"I'm sure that something could be arranged, your lordship."

"Good, good. Now tell me this, and we can come to an end: have you any vices? Drink? Gambling? Opium? Women?"

"I am very partial, indeed, to *one* young lady, your lordship. I drink very little, gamble seldom, and take no opium. I am rather fond of horses and dogs. And children, of course."

Suddenly, Papa asked, "I hope you are no Whig?"

"Oh, *no,* sir," my suitor replied, as if offended by the question. "Our family are staunch Tories."

Papa was relieved to hear that. "The Prince of Wales was a Tory until he became Regent," he said, "and now he is a Whig. One can not place confidence in such a turncoat. However, you appear to be a most acceptable young man — if appearances do not deceive. My elder daughter's marriage . . ." Papa shook his head. "A bad business. The fellow was a gypsy, you know. Half-gypsy, he said. Touched with the tar-brush, in any case. Well, he's gone now, poor devil. *De mortuis nil nisi bonum.*" Papa rose from his chair. "Shall we join the ladies, and tell them the good news?"

Wilfrid — for it was about this time that I began to use his Christian name — was overjoyed. "By all means!" he responded with a broad smile. "But before we do, perhaps I may have —"

"That cigar?"

"I would prefer — with your lordship's permission — a large whisky."

"So would I, my boy." And Papa rang for Stewart.

XIII

In Praise of Impatience

On the following evening, Wilfrid and I were permitted to venture across the river to Vauxhall Gardens, unaccompanied, but with strict instructions to stay out of the Dark Walk. I was dressed modestly but becomingly in a new frock of forest-green satin, buttoned up to the neck, not cut low in what Papa calls "the licentious fashion of to-day."

We sat in a supper-box, eating syllabubs laced with wine, and listening to the musicians play a *pot-pourri* of airs from Weber's new opera, *Abu Hassan,* which was presented this year in Munich.

"Melissa," he said.

"Yes?"

"Nothing. Just Melissa. It is such a pleasure to pronounce your Christian name. I was growing dreadfully tired of 'Miss Worthing.' "

"And I of 'Mr. Summerfield' . . . Wilfrid."

"It is enchanting simply to sit here with you. Heaven must be like this, do you not think?"

"The syllabubs there surely can not be any better," I replied, "for these are delicious. Do you know what my brother says about this place?"

"Teddy?"

"Freddy. He says that he imagines Sodom and Gomorrah to have been somewhat like Vauxhall Gardens and Margate. Jolly places, where one might have had a good time. He thinks it rather awful of God to have smitten them down."

Wilfrid laughed. "Your twin brother sounds a delightful fellow. I should like to know him better."

"You shall. You shall know all my family. And you shall love them all. Papa, for example: he is not such a stick as you may think him, for all that he is a bishop. He can be quite amusing — on the very subject of Sodom and Gomorrah, in fact."

"A difficult subject in which to find amusement, I should think, particularly for a bishop."

"He was recounting to us, not long ago, that passage in the Bible where Abraham bargains with the Lord about the destruction of Sodom, asking Him if He will destroy it if there are fifty righteous people within the city. Before the conversation is finished, Abraham has succeeded in Jewing down the Lord from fifty to ten!" I laughed, remembering how amusingly Papa had related the story. Then, recalling a less pleasant outcome of that evening, I added: "But the story upset my sister, for some unaccountable reason. She rebuked Papa, merely because he said how shrewd and cunning the Jews are, and have always been, ever since Abraham. And that is no more than the truth, is it not?"

"The people of that race," replied Wilfrid, "have often shewn skill in many matters, including business. I expect that your sister's discomfiture may have had something to do with the fact that her husband was a member of another old and wandering race which is looked upon with distrust by the English."

"I think that you are right," I said. "And Mr. Cooper was such a fine, brave gentleman. I liked him very much. And my poor dear sister will love him for ever."

"As I will love you," he said. "For ever and ever! Melissa, when may we be married?"

"Wilfrid," I replied, "you must not be impatient."

"I can be nothing else," he said stoutly. "A patient lover is a gelding, a milksop, and I am neither."

"Oh, I *know* you to be no gelding, Wilfrid," I rejoined, in oblique reference to Olivia Royce's condition, as well as to that marvellous construction that had erected itself miraculously in my father's library the day before. "And yet patience," I added primly, "is a virtue."

"It is a virtue in all things save in love," he declared. "In love, patience is a fault. It is cold. It insults the beloved. It casts doubt upon the lover's protestations of love, and questions their sincerity."

"Eloquent words, Wilfrid," I said, clapping my hands in

mock applause. "Did you utter them to Olivia, just before you took her maidenhead?"

"I swear to you that I have never spoken them to any woman before. My impatience is an earnest of my love for you, Melissa. Do not condemn it. Be glad of it." He took my hands in his.

"I am," I said feelingly. "Oh, Wilfrid, I am!"

"I can not wait for our wedding night," he said.

"You must."

"Yes, I know that I must. But it is a torment for me. That is why I wish you and your father to set the date soon. Oh, how I will love you, Melissa! I will *fill* you with love. I will fill you with children!"

I coloured at such talk, and turned my burning face away from him. My voice was husky when I said, "It is a torment for me, as well, Wilfrid. I love you so! I will try to persuade Papa to marry us soon."

He kissed my hands.

XIV

My Lady Greensleeves

"We must return," I told him.

"So soon?"

"My parents will begin to worry."

I rose from my chair and left the supper-box. Wilfrid followed, offering his arm. I placed my hand upon it, and we walked together, sedately for a while; then more warmly, as I slipped my arm through his; then warmer still, as his arm encircled my waist. Far behind us now, the musicians in the orchestra pavilion were playing "Greensleeves," one of my favourite airs.

Before I was aware of it, we had entered the forbidden territory of the Dark Walk. "Wilfrid," I said, "my parents expressly —"

"Even your parents were young once," he murmured. "They know that lovers require a few moments away from other eyes. What harm is there in a kiss?" His lips brushed my cheek.

I smiled, and shook my head in sweet, resigned exasperation. "You are incorrigible, my love, and any parents who trust you are fools. Surely Mr. and Mrs. Fairchild trusted you alone with their daughter, and what was the consequence?"

He instantly removed his arm from my waist and stepped away. "Do you throw that up to me again? Will the name of Fairchild haunt me the rest of my days?"

"Wilfrid, I am sorry." He said nothing. "Please say that you forgive me."

"How can I forgive you, when *I* am not forgiven for my one mistake; when, like some creditor, you thrust Olivia in my face like a promissory note every time I turn to you?"

His back was towards me: I encircled him with my arms and pressed my cheek against the broad spread of his shoulders. "I will never speak her name again, as long as I live."

He turned round and embraced me and kissed me long and lovingly. Our arms about each other, we strolled deeper into the Dark Walk. The music from the orchestra pavilion was almost inaudible now, like a melody heard in a dream; and, although no voices sang with the instruments, the magic of the night and the intoxicating effect of my emotions caused me almost to hear that song's familiar words . . .

Greensleeves is all my joy,
Greensleeves is my delight;
Greensleeves is my heart of gold,
And who but my lady Greensleeves? . . .

The meagre light of the quarter-moon afforded scarcely enough illumination for us to keep our feet on the path. Wilfrid kissed me again, fleetingly on the cheek, and it was like being brushed by a butterfly's wing. "Let us sit down for a moment," he said.

"Is there a bench? I can not see . . ."

"Here on the grass."

"But . . ."

"It is soft and warm, and the dew is not yet upon it." Using the gentlest of pressures, he pulled me down to the grass. "There. Is it not comfortable here?" He kissed me again, on the lips. I felt as if my bones had turned to water.

"Somebody may see us," I said.

"There is nobody else here."

"I am sure that I heard a sound in the trees."

"A bird. A cat. The wind. Do you love me?"

"Oh, *yes!*"

"If you could but know the agony that plagues me," he said. "The most diabolical fiends of the torture chamber can not have devised a punishment more cruel than this. What are racks and thumb-screws, thirst or starvation, to the pain a man feels when he loves a woman to distraction, when his blood reaches out for her — and she is denied him?"

"Wilfrid," I whispered, "I feel it, too . . ."

"You think that you do, my sweet love, but when a woman speaks of love's pain, she is speaking in metaphor. When a man speaks of it, when I speak of it, I speak of actual, literal pain, physical pain; my flesh *aches* for you!"

"A woman aches for her man, too, my dear. We are not airy phantoms made of poetry. The blood flows in my veins as hotly as in yours. My bosom yearns for you, Wilfrid; it aches for your hands . . ."

I took his hands and placed them on my breasts. Even through the satin, those strong hands of his were very Heaven to my flesh. They gripped me, kneaded me, and I gasped with the pleasure of their touch.

"This infernal frock . . ." he whispered, as he clumsily attempted to unfasten the buttons at my throat.

"Fumble-fingers," I murmured teasingly, and swiftly unfastened the buttons myself. His hands slid under my frock to my waiting breasts, and the lovely shock of his cold rough palms sent a tremor of exquisite delight rippling through me, all the way down to the tips of my toes, which wriggled now of their own volition inside my shoes.

"Dear God," he said in a hoarse voice, "so sweet, so warm, so soft you are, so silky-soft and yet so firm. So fragrant. So delicious . . ."

His lips were pressed to me now, like those of an infant, and I came near to swooning as I knew at last the truth of those lines — *I have given suck, and know how tender 'tis to love the babe that milks me . . .*

I sighed with pleasure; he groaned with pain. The poor dear man was in such anguish! My frantic fingers now worked away at his own fastenings, and soon I had released from its hiding place that instrument of torture that should have been the fountain-head of joy and love. *A royal sceptre,* Esmie had called it, and indeed it was much like. *Worship and revere it,* she had said, *press it to your lips . . .*

Hence, even as he had rendered loving lip-service to me, so now I did the like to him, playing him as I might play my clarinet, delicately holding the shaft of the instrument in my fingers whilst I moistened its beak with my mouth's waters, eliciting from him soft, dark, low melodious moans that were sweeter than any music to my ears; *abolishing pride* as Esmie had bade me do; *bestowing myself upon him without hindrance; no part of me denying him; no pleasure or caress gainsaying him. Shame, modesty, restraint I cast aside,* even as she had done, and *willingly, ardently, wheresoever he chose to spend himself, I received him there with welcome.* And if, when he had put his lips to me like a milking babe, no milk had come, as of course it could not, the same did not obtain when I returned his loving kiss in complementary devotion; for now a flood of richness was pumped into my mouth, as thick as thickest cream; and lest I turn my face away and cut his pleasure short too soon, he locked his hands behind my head and kept them here until his final shuddering spasm and deep cry of love and triumph. The dear rich whey of his love, the very stuff of life itself, rolled smoothly down my throat and, so to speak, into the most profound and hidden corners of my being.

" 'Her lips suck forth my soul,' " he whispered.

"I beg your pardon?"

"Christopher Marlowe," he said.

"Ah. To be sure."

Without another word, we fastened our clothing, rose from the grass, brushed ourselves off as best we could, and, arms tenderly round one another, made our way slowly out of the Dark Walk.

It was some time before he spoke again. "I love you and worship you," he said softly. "You are Venus, you are Aphrodite, you are the goddess of love."

"I am only a woman, Wilfrid."

"The queen of women, then. And I am your obedient subject."

Esmie had been right: the mighty king, with his royal sceptre, was now the humble servitor, meek and worshipful.

After a moment, he said, in a more conversational tone, "How lucky that you happen to be wearing a green frock."

"Why lucky?"

"Grass stains will not be seen on it," he explained.

"Ah yes, how fortunate," I agreed; for, of course, I could not tell him that I had chosen the colour for that very reason.

XV

The Colonel's Clever Contrivance

I would not wish to give out the impression that Wilfrid was the first man to have courted me. Before him, there were a goodly few, some of them titled gentlemen, of this and other countries.

The Viscount Wellington himself, Arthur Wellesley, once sought my favours, shortly before he married Kitty Pakenham. An Irish peer, Lord Francis Nolan, pressed his suit most ardently — but in vain, for he was a devout Roman Catholic, and Papa strenuously opposed him. The periwig-pated Chevalier Henri d'Hibou, who had but narrowly escaped the guillotine's chop as a hated aristo, was decorously persistent, and assured Papa that, even though he had once been a seminarian, he would gladly convert to the Anglican faith for my sake. Count Janku of Grzegorz-Stefanski, a puckish Polonian, was perhaps the most charming of them; the most obnoxious, the snivelling Marchese Orlando di Gazza-Silone; and the most deliciously frightening was Baron Hermann von Steinkopf, whose head was indeed as smooth and as hairless as a stone, and who peered at me lewdly through a single glass that greatly magnified his eye. There were others, as well, not all of them titled, most of them stimulatingly attractive; but —

until Wilfrid — none whom I had wished to marry.

Wilfrid now became a frequent guest at our house when he was in London. I could not understand his flutterings to and fro London and Suffolk, and I beseeched him to remove entirely to this town as soon as possible.

"I shall," he promised me, "but details of business make it necessary for me to flutter, as you call it, one or two times more. Now, then: have you broached the matter of our wedding date with your father?"

I sighed. "Yes, Wilfrid."

"Well?"

"He is partial to our marrying in December."

"December!" His face fell. "That is a lifetime away! How can I endure it? How can *you?* Why December?"

"Haste in marriage, Papa says, is fodder for gossips."

"Damn the gossips! If no child is born in the first nine or ten months, what does the date of the wedding matter? I shall perish, Melissa; I shall surely perish!" He shook his head and paced back and forth in our garden, where this conversation took place. "Or, if I do not perish, I shall go quite mad with craving. Perhaps, if I could get me a few of the Colonel's articles . . . but no, no, you would not . . . no, it is out of the question . . ."

"What is out of the question? I 'would not' what? And who is this colonel?"

Wilfrid turned to me, put his hands on my shoulders, and looked steadily into my eyes. "Melissa," he said, "if there were a way for us to love each other properly and fully, without the fear of your becoming . . ."

"What are you trying to say, Wilfrid?"

"There happen to be certain clever contrivances made of dried sheep-gut — a bit like those oil-skin cases that are used for holding regimental colours, only much smaller. Sheaths, you see, very thin and delicate. Men wear them. I have never availed myself of them — perhaps I should have, when Olivia and I — well, be that as it may, I have heard them well spoken of. They were invented by a certain Colonel Cundum, I understand, and in his honour they are called by his name . . ."

"For Heaven's sake, what are you talking about?"

"Years ago, they were sold by a Mrs. Philips, they say, at the Green Cannister in Half-Moon Street, in the Strand. She made a fortune, they were so popular. But that was long ago, and I expect that she has gone to her reward. No doubt your brother Freddy knows of them, and can tell me how I may put myself in the way of them . . . but no, it wouldn't do to consult your own brother about this . . . quite improper . . ."

"Stop *chattering,*" I said, "and tell me plainly what you mean. You say that men wear them. How?"

He shrugged. "Well, I assume that one simply pulls the deuced thing on like a stocking . . ."

"They are worn on the *feet?*"

"No, no, of course not. On the — well, you know — on a man's — that is to say, when he's aroused —"

"Do you refer, *Mr. Summerfield,* to the Horn of Plenty?"

He nodded.

"And you have the presumption to suggest that you should purchase such a — a — Conduit, or Conundrum, or whatever they are called — and pull it like a stocking over your — and then to — to — Wilfrid Summerfield, you should be ashamed! It is against Nature, against God. What manner of woman do you take me to be — one of the short-heeled wenches who move out like bats in the dusk of the evening and call out to men in Covent Garden? Do you truly think that I would allow you to put a thing like that into my body?"

He had a hang-dog look as he said, "I am truly sorry . . ."

"And well you should be, you naughty, *naughty* man! I do not think that I want to marry you, after all."

"Do not say that, Melissa!"

"You can be quite disgusting, you know."

"You did not think me disgusting the other night, in the Dark Walk . . ."

"You did not offer me a sheep-gut stocking!"

He glanced surreptitiously at the windows of our house to make sure that nobody was watching us there in the garden; then he took me in his arms. "Melissa, Melissa, please do not be angry. It was my impatience speaking. I will never raise the subject again."

"Something *else* is being raised," I said pointedly, as he held me pressed tight against his body.

"Ah, you can not blame me for that chap's ups and downs," said Wilfrid. "I am not responsible for him. He is his own master, and follows his own whims. Won't listen to me. The very devil of a fellow, he is. But rather loveable, for all that, don't you agree?"

"No, I do not," I said. "He is the opposite of loveable. He is selfish and arrogant."

Still holding me tightly, Wilfrid drew me behind a hedge, where we were completely hidden from all eyes. He has a pretty gift for mimickry, and he spoke now in the solemn manner of a barrister:

"May it please you, m'lud; gentlemen of the jury. I ask you to look at my client. Is he now the stiff, arrogant creature my gifted colleague has depicted him as being? Or is he, rather, a shrunken shadow of himself — dejected, repentant, his head hanging? Look at him — yes, *you,* milady — and tell me if he has not suffered enough? Deny, if you can, that he is a pathetic, empty thing. Hold out your heart to him — and your helping hand. See how your smallest smile, your merest mote of encouragement brings the rosy blushes to his face. See how your kindness causes him to hold his head high again, how your generosity restores to him that manly sinew that was hitherto his pride, and makes of him an upright fellow once more. Bestow upon his dewy brow that Kiss of Life which will send carmine currents of confidence coursing through his veins . . ."

"No, Wilfrid," I said. "Not here."

XVI

The Hanged Man

Esmie was dealing out her precious *tarot* cards at the large table in the library when Wilfrid and I returned from the garden. She swept them all together again into a pack when she saw us, and handed the pack to Wilfrid. "These may interest you, Mr. Summerfield," she said. "They are by way of being a legacy from my late husband."

Wilfrid looked through them, one by one, saying, "They are very beautiful." Half-way through the pack, he stopped at one card, as if studying it, and even turned it upside down to study it more closely. Esmie and I, from our point of view, could see only the back of the card, not its face, and yet Esmie said:

"Is it The Hanged Man?"

"Why, yes," replied Wilfrid, surprised. He placed the card, face up, on the table. It shewed a man hanging by one foot from a gibbet. With a smile, he said, "Does this mean that I am a candidate for the noose?"

"No, m'lud," said Esmie, returning his smile. (Esmie's sense of humour is inexplicable to me: why she should have addressed Wilfrid as if he were a peer, I do not know. It was typical, however, of her strange notion of wit.) "No, The Hanged Man has no prophetic meaning by itself. It is in combination with other cards that it becomes revealing."

"How did you know that I was looking at this particular card?" he asked her. "A trick of some kind? Are the cards marked?"

She shook her head. "It is a curious thing: hand a pack of *tarot* cards to a person and ask him to look through them, and he will almost always stop at The Hanged Man, and usually turn it this way and that. It is a card of profound meaning, but all of that meaning is hidden, as if by a veil. Some call it the card of martyrdom; others say that it is the card of duty."

"And what do you call it, Mrs. Cooper?"

"I call it what my husband called it — the card of the universe."

"I fear that your meaning is rather over my head," said Wilfrid.

"The whole history of Man's higher nature is buried in this symbol," Esmie declared. "When one brings one's self to accept that simple truth, then one receives certain understandings, images of the great awakening that awaits us . . . but I expect that I am becoming tiresome," she added, apologetically.

"Not at all!" Wilfrid assured her. "I find the subject fascinating — provided that you do not prophesy the gallows for me!"

"I prophesy nothing, Mr. Summerfield. Of course, one can not rule out a meaning when a person stops and scrutinises The Hanged Man, as you did. But what that meaning may be, it is impossible to say. Perhaps some friend or associate of yours is destined for the gallows; who can tell?" She smiled strangely at Wilfrid. "Are you acquainted with members of the criminal class, Your Majesty?"

Wilfrid was obviously puzzled by that odd form of address, and his laughter was therefore strained as he replied, "One or two who cheat at cards, perhaps, but nothing more villainous than that."

Esmie gathered up the *tarot,* saying, "That is one thing about these cards. One can not cheat with them. One can elicit from them only the truth." Turning to me, and in a brighter tone of voice, she said, "Is it not time for luncheon? I am feeling quite peckish."

"So am I," said Wilfrid. "What's on the bill of fare to-day?"

I said, "I believe that Mrs. Cooke is doing steak-and-kidney pie."

"One of my favourites!" Wilfrid pronounced it. "Good English provender! No foreign airs about it."

Later, after Wilfrid had left (he was stopping at Pulteney's Hotel), I said to Esmie, "What a contrary person you are. Why do you tease Wilfrid with 'Your Majesty' and 'm'lud'? I am sure that he was quite confused by it."

"Did I say those things?" she responded. "Perhaps I did. "Ah, well, I expect that I'm going a bit silly, Lissa. You must make allowances for your odd old sister."

"I shall do no such thing," I told her, "for you are neither odd nor old. But you do have the most curious sense of humour."

"And your Mr. Summerfield has a secret," she said. "More than one, it may be."

"What do you mean? What sort of secrets?"

"I can not tell you," Esmie replied, "because I do not know. But there is something — or some things — about your young man that he is keeping hidden."

XVII

What Kind of Creature Is He?

How absolutely infuriating of Esmie to have said that, and then refuse to say more. I felt quite cross with her, but no matter how often I brought up the subject, she insisted that she had told me all that she knew.

And yet I was certain that she was holding something back.

Why had she called Wilfrid "m'lud"? *Was* it silliness? If he had been a pompous man, full of airs, then her form of address might have been mockery — but Wilfrid was a very straightforward person; nothing nose-in-the-air about him.

And then to call him "Your Majesty"! What an absurd thing to have done!

Had she somehow got it into her head that Wilfrid was of aristocratic, even noble, birth? An illegitimate son of royalty, perhaps? Had her foolish *tarot* cards seemed, to her mind, to have revealed something of that nature to her? How absolutely ridiculous.

Wilfrid, she said, was keeping something about himself hidden; perhaps more than one thing. Could she have meant Olivia's child? — but that was not hidden; not hidden from me, at least. Did he have another bastard hidden away somewhere; *several?*

Was he heavily, ruinously, in debt? He had told Papa that he seldom gambled, but perhaps he had not told the truth. He *had* made that remark to Esmie, about knowing people who cheat at cards. Was that statement mere japery, or was it true? If true, how could he have known about their cheating if he had not played with them?

Was he the slave of opium, like Mr. Coleridge and so many others? He had assured Papa that he was not. Truth or falsehood?

In the supper-box at Vauxhall Gardens, when I asked him

if he had used his persuasive words on the theme of impatience to relieve Olivia of her hymen, he replied: "I swear to you that I have never spoken them to any woman before." Why "to any *woman*"? Why not "to anybody" or simply "never spoken them before"? Is it possible, I asked myself, that he may have spoken those seductive words to a man? Did he play at back gammon, and did his lust reach out to both sexes?

Why had Esmie asked him if he was associated with criminals? Why had she suggested that some friend or other may have been destined for the hangman?

I betook myself to Esmie's sitting-room that night. She was already in her night-gown, and preparing to go to bed. "Esmie," I said sternly, "you have heaped coals of fire upon my head."

"My *dear:* how so?"

"You have poisoned me with doubts about Wilfrid. I have been going over and over in my mind what you have said about him. About his secrets . . ." And I recounted to her all of my suspicions of hidden bastards, debt, drugs, and the rest, not even excluding the nagging fear that he might be a sodomite or an associate of villains.

"Lissa," she said to me soothingly, "a man may have secrets, but they need not be guilty secrets. Some secrets are benign."

"Then why should they be secrets?"

"Need everything about a man be common knowledge? Think of Freddy's secret. Is it malignant or shameful? Not in the least. One day, when the climate is right, he will tell our parents about his acting. In the same way, Mr. Summerfield will one day reveal his secrets to you, no doubt."

"One day!" I shouted. "And, in the mean time, I am set upon the rack and torn apart by suspicions. And *you,* dear sister, are my torturer! The hand that turns the crank is *yours!*"

My eyes streaming tears of anger, I turned to run from her sitting-room, but Esmie stood in front of her door and would not let me leave. "Be patient, I beseech you," she said.

I was in no humour to hear more discourse on patience and impatience. "Stand aside," I said. But she did not move. "Let me pass!"

"Not until you tell me that you do not hate me."

Her words softened my anger. "How could I ever hate you, dear Esmie?" We embraced; both of us were weeping now; our tears mingled on each other's cheeks.

Thus I was calmed, and at length returned to my own rooms, where I was soon undressed and into bed. But sleep did not come quickly or easily, for those same doubts and questions kept spinning round and round like fiery Catherine-wheels in my brain:

What kind of creature is he? What manner of man am I pledged to marry?

XVIII

A Visitor in the Night

The first thing I did on the following morning was to put on my slippers and dressing-gown and go into my sitting-room, where I sat at my desk and rapidly wrote this letter:

"My dear Wilfrid, —

"I write to you in considerable distress of mind, and only you can relieve me of it.

"My sister, as I need not tell you, is a strange lady, full of eccentric conceits. I love her dearly, but she can be vexatious some times. Yesterday, after you left, she told me that you are a man with secrets. She did not tell me what those secrets are, because, as she said, she does not know. They need not be guilty secrets, she added, but would not, or could not, say more.

"I will not tell you what loathly suspicions about you robbed me of sleep last night. They do me no credit, and you would think less of me were I to divulge them to you. But, Wilfrid my dearest, I do not like to think that my sister's mind has become unhinged. If you do have secrets, will you not tell me of them? Do I not have a right to share them, whatever they may be? I love you so much that nothing you have done, nothing you may be, can ever destroy that love. Do not hide anything from me, I beg of you, for anything that you may tell me will be better than this terrible, gnawing torture of not-knowing. Answer me at once, by letter or in person; and in that way ease the troubled heart of —

"Your own
"Melissa"

I sent for Blodgett, the footman, handed him the letter, and directed him to deliver it to Wilfrid at Pulteney's Hotel.

"Shall I wait for an answer, Miss?"

"Yes."

He left, with a strut of his beautiful calves. I washed and dressed, but had no appetite for breakfast. Before long — although it seemed like an eternity — Blodgett returned, came up to my sitting-room, and handed me a letter.

Although I had given Wilfrid the choice of replying either in writing or in person, I had hoped that he would deem this matter to be of sufficient importance to justify an immediate visit. Still, I said to myself, perhaps his letter was merely a note to assure me that he would call on me in an hour or so.

But when I took the letter from Blodgett's hand, I recognised my own writing on its cover.

"This is my own letter, Blodgett," I said.

"Yes, Miss," he replied. "The porter at Pulteney's told me that Mr. Summerfield had left."

"If he had left the hotel, then —"

"Left London, Miss."

Left London! Without a word to me? He had planned to stop another week in London, at the very least! What was he playing at?

Blodgett continued: "Very early this mornin', it was. More like the middle of the night. In the company of a gentleman — well, a man, anyway — who'd come to him 'with some urgency,' the porter said, and awakened him."

"What sort of man?"

Blodgett shrugged. "Hard to tell, Miss. Not from these parts, though. North Country accent. And nervous he was, the porter said."

"Thank you, Blodgett. That will be all."

I broke the seal of my letter; read it again; considered sending it by the post to Suffolk; then tore it into pieces.

I refused to believe ill of Wilfrid. That messenger may have come to tell him of sickness or death in his family; perhaps his father. Or of some industrial crisis that needed his decisive presence in the Suffolk branch of the business.

And yet I asked myself: do the people of Suffolk speak with a *North* Country accent?

XIX

Blackmail

Late one morning soon after, Stewart interrupted my clarinet practise to say that there was a lady who had called and wished to see me. "A Miss Wilson," he added.

"Wilson? I know nobody of that name. Are you sure that she wishes to see me, and not my sister or my mother?"

"Actually, Miss," he said, "she asked for Mr. Aelfred, and when I told her that he was not in, she asked to see one of his sisters. Mrs. Cooper has gone shopping with your mother, and so . . ."

"Very well, Stewart. I will see her in the drawing-room."

"Begging your pardon, Miss, but his lordship is meeting there, at the moment, with some gentlemen of the clergy."

"In the library, then."

"Yes, Miss."

When I walked into the library, a few minutes later, I saw a woman of indeterminate age, pretty in a rather coarse way, richly but gaudily dressed, and with enough paint on her face to project her features to the farthest row of a theatre. These aspects, in combination with her having called on Freddy, suggested to me that she was probably a member of Chum's company, and therefore one of Freddy's fair colleagues. She was staring at the rendering of Leda and the swan in Archbishop Parker's Bible, which still lay open on the table.

"Naughty Bibles you have in a bishop's house," she said, by way of greeting.

I made no response to that remark. "Miss Wilson?" I said. "I am Aelfred's sister Melissa."

She smiled insolently. "His twin sister, I think? I've heard him speak of you, and I can see him in your face. You're almost as pretty as he is."

I disliked her manner. Coldly, I said, "You are most kind."

"I have been even kinder to Freddy," she said, in an offensively insinuating tone.

"Indeed. And why should that be of interest to me?"

"Because I mean to be kind to you, as well. To your whole family, in point of fact."

"Perhaps you would do better to speak to my brother, after all," I said, and turned to ring for Stewart to shew her out.

"No, you'll do, dearie," she said, "seeing that he isn't here. Just tell him that I require a hundred pounds of him, by to-morrow morning."

"A hundred pounds! That is a great deal of money."

"I have a great deal of expenses, don't I? He knows all about that. Tell him there's no need to deliver it himself, unless he's so inclined. A messenger will do very well."

Anger flamed through me. "Why should he —"

"Ah," she said, laughing slyly, "you wouldn't *really* want to be knowing, would you? Dear Freddy's peccadilloes? Just relay my message to him, little girl, and I'll be obliged to you."

Suddenly, the library doors burst open and Freddy sprang into the room. "Damn it, Harriette!" he said, seething. "What the devil brings you here?"

"Business," she replied. "Your sister has been given the necessary details."

Freddy turned to me. "Has this trollop been offending you with stories about me?"

"Tut, tut, Freddy!" she said. "Language, language!"

"She only asked me to tell you —" I began to reply, but Miss Wilson cut in rudely:

"To tell you to send me a hundred quid by to-morrow morning."

"And why," said Freddy calmly, "should I do any such a thing?"

"Because if you do not . . ." She looked in my direction.

"But you don't wish your dear twin to hear the rest of this, I'll warrant."

"Speak plainly," he said. "I have no secrets from her."

"Perhaps not," she rejoined with a snigger. "But no doubt you have some secrets from your father. Suppose, my dear Freddy, that I were to tell *him* the astonishing sight that met my eyes last night?"

"Get to the point."

"Why, I was shocked!" she said. "And I think you are well enough familiar with me to know that I am not very easily shocked. But there was I, with some friends of mine, at the Proteus Theatre, watching a play. Quite a jolly play, too, if rather ribald. It was the final performance — I hadn't had an opportunity to see it before; but I had heard a good deal about it, and I must tell you that I wouldn't have missed it for the crown bloody jewels. For whom should I see upon the stage below, strutting about in paint and making a display of himself, but a certain young man of my intimate acquaintance who thought to hide himself behind the name of Thingrow? A young man who is, in truth, a son of a bishop?"

Freddy smiled grimly. "I see. And I can buy your silence for a hundred pounds?"

"That will suffice for the nonce," she replied.

"What if I were to tell you that I don't have that sum?"

"Then I should tell you to *get* it, Master Thingrow!" she snarled. "Borrow it from the Jews. Sell the family silver. Steal it, for all I care!"

"Will you not have mercy on me?" said Freddy.

"Why should I?"

"Will you not take fifty pounds, then?"

"A hundred, or I tell the bishop all!"

"Very well," said Freddy with a sigh, "I'll pay you . . ."

She smiled triumphantly. "There's a good boy."

He reached into his pocket and drew out a ha'penny. "I'll pay you *this!*" he cried, flinging the coin at her feet. "And *this,* as well!" Quickly, he stepped forward and slapped her twice across the face. "Do you want more, you blackmailing bitch? Shall I bid our coachman fetch me his horse-switch? Shall I flog the clothes off your whore's back?"

She was trembling with rage and fear. "Very well, Freddy-boy," she said in a shaking voice. "I shall go to a journalist-friend of mine. I shall tell him the true identity of the public's darling, Mr. Thingrow. He will write a leading article. By the day after to-morrow, all of London will know your secret. Including his pious lordship, your Papa!"

She swept out of the room and out of the house, slamming every door through which she passed.

The library was dreadfully silent. Quietly, I asked Freddy: "Is she . . . *the* Harriette Wilson?"

He nodded. "The same," he replied, through tight lips. "The same whore and blackmailer who has tried to sully the reputations of Brummel, Alvanley, Ponsonby, and I don't know how many other men. She's a despicable reptile, and I curse the day I met her. But she may go to hell! And she may publish what she likes about my stage activities, because to-morrow . . . to-morrow I shall tell Papa myself."

XX

A Rank Coward

The Dandy's Deception having enjoyed so much success, it was decided by Cholmondeley-Cockburn to follow it with a hardy comedy staple, Oliver Goldsmith's *She Stoops to Conquer*. The company had been rehearsing it during the day-time, whilst performing *The Dandy* by night; and the first presentation was to take place on the night of the day following Harriette Wilson's visit. Freddy, as if fulfilling a happy omen, would play young Charles Marlow, that same, shy, stammering character by whom he had won over Mrs. Siddons. It is one of my favourite comedies (I prefer it even to those of Mr. Sheridan's, although I have never told *him* that), and I was eager to see it. The fumbling, tongue-tied aspect of Marlow's character would lend itself perfectly, I saw, to "Mr. Thingrow's" now famously hilarious speciality. I had helped Freddy commit his part to memory.

At breakfast, next day, Freddy calmly said to Papa and Mamma: "If you have nothing better to do this evening, I should like you to be my guests at the Proteus Theatre."

"How considerate of you, Aelfred," said Mamma. "What is the programme?"

"She Stoops to Conquer."

Papa chuckled. "A most amusing piece. Your mother and I saw its first performance. Do you remember, Penelope? At Covent Garden. The ides of March, it was, 1773, the year after I was consecrated. I fairly split my sides with laughing. After the play, we met Goldsmith, through his friend Dr. Johnson. I was already an admirer of his novel, *The Vicar of Wakefield,* of course, and to meet the man himself was an honour. He died a year later, more's the pity. Yes, I should like to see that play again: thank you, my boy."

"Of course, Esmie and Mel are invited, as well," Freddy added.

"Splendid," said Papa. "Then it shall be a family occasion."

In more ways than you know, I said to myself; and, after breakfast, I got Freddy alone and scolded him:

"Do you intend me and Esmie to brave the full brunt of Papa's wrath when he sees you on that stage to-night? You should have told him the whole truth then and there, at breakfast!"

"How could I? He would have choked on his bacon!"

"Then tell him *now,* for he has finished his bacon."

"Mel, be reasonable. To-night, I will tell him that I have an appointment and that I will meet all of you at the theatre. A box has been reserved in the name of Worthing — you will all march right in and be seated. I deliberately waited until we were shewing a respected classic. Later, after the play, I will join you and we'll all ride home together in the family carriage. What could be simpler?"

"Telling him now: that would be *much* simpler!"

"But don't you see how much better it will be for *him* to learn the truth at the same time as he admires my qualities as an actor? I shall be superb as Marlow. And the excitement of the theatre, the approval of the audience, his own liking of the play itself . . . these things will melt him down, as it were, soften him, and prepare him for my appearance. I don't come upon the stage until the second scene. Papa will have the whole of the first scene to mellow him . . ."

"Oh, *very* well," I said. "But I think that you are being a coward."

"Of course I am," he snapped, flippantly, but I could see that I had hurt him. "I've always been a coward, haven't I? Flashed my hash at that hanging, and disgraced myself in front of the Prince. Couldn't approach old Chum without you waiting outside and lending me courage. That's why I balked at the notion of going into the Army. Oh, I'm a coward, right enough, and thank you very much for reminding me of it."

"Fweddikins, I did not mean —"

"But you did, you know. And you were right. I'm a coward: a *rank* coward, as they say, because I positively stink with fear whenever I'm faced with something that requires a bit of manly fortitude. I always manage to persuade someone else to face those things for me, or to hold my hand. I'm not a *man;* I've long known that; I'm a baby — you've told me so often enough."

"Freddy, my *dear* —"

"Moreover," he said, "I must admit that you're right about the play to-night. It would have put you and Esmie in a false position. Papa — when he recovers from his apoplexy! — will demand to know if you and she had any knowledge of my acting. You will either be forced to lie to our father — which is something I have no right to ask you to do — or you will tell him the truth, and he will rebuke you for plotting intrigues and deceptions with me."

"If he asks," I declared, "I shall tell him the truth gladly — and I shall tell him, too, that I am proud of you. And I am, Freddy, believe me that I *am!*" I squeezed him in my arms and kissed him.

"Good old girl," he said, and smiled. "But it's no good, I'm afraid. I must tell him now."

"Are you sure?"

He nodded. Then he gripped my hand for good luck, and walked straight to the door of Papa's study. As he lifted his hand to knock, I asked him, "Shall I come in with you?"

"No. I must do this myself. After all, I reached my majority several years ago . . . grown older without growing up. High time I *did* grow up, what?"

He knocked; we heard Papa bid him enter; he opened the door and went in. But I caught the door before it was fully closed, and shamelessly listened at it, as it stood ajar.

"Yes, Aelfred, what is it?" I heard Papa ask.

"I have . . . something to discuss with you, Papa," said Freddy.

"Capital. I have been meaning to speak to you, as well."

"It concerns . . . well, sir, you see . . ."

"Out with it, my boy."

"It is in regard to employment — *my* employment, that is to say . . ."

"Good! You could not have chosen a subject more pleasing to my ears."

"I own that I have been idle, Papa. And I know that you would have preferred me to prepare for holy orders. But I have given the matter considerable thought —"

"So have I, Aelfred, and I have good news for you."

"You have . . . news for *me?"*

"I have spoken to Melissa's young man, Mr. Summerfield, and he has agreed to find you a position of authority and responsibility in his business."

I could feel Freddy's surprise in the second of silence that followed Papa's pronouncement. Then, in a choked voice, Freddy spoke again:

"In his — you mean the *brewery?"*

"Why, yes, of course. You and he will soon be brothers-in-law, as you are well aware."

"Yes, I know, but —"

"You like Summerfield, do you not?"

"Yes, but —"

"You like beer, I think?"

"Yes —"

"Well, then! The problem of your employment is solved, is it not?"

Freddy's voice was small when he replied, "Yes, Papa."

"Then it's all settled. I must say that I am feeling very happy. Your brother has been well-situated for some time now, both in business and in family life. Your twin sister will soon be married. Your elder sister . . . well, that is all water under the bridge, and it was God's will. And now you stand in the prospect of gainful employment and useful occupation.

Splendid! But now, my boy, I have a large amount of work to get through, so if you will excuse me . . . ? We shall all have a fine time at the theatre to-night, shan't we?"

"Oh, yes, indeed," said Freddy, as he left Papa's study and closed the door behind him. Seeing me standing there, he said, "You heard?"

I nodded, unable to speak.

Freddy's voice was tight: "I would have told him, I *swear* I would have — but the pompous old bagpipe never gave me the chance!"

And he rushed out of the house.

XXI

Thank the Good Lord

Freddy did not return to the house for either luncheon or dinner. It fell upon *me* to tell Papa of his "appointment" and to say that Freddy would join us at the theatre.

In the evening, Tuttle drove the four of us to the Proteus. A box was reserved in our name, just as Freddy had promised. Mamma and Papa were in fine fettle, anticipating an evening of great enjoyment: only Esmie and I were apprehensive, fearing the vulcanic eruption that we knew must come.

Our apprehension was not diverted by the usual comic songs, for Mrs. Chum, the customary singer of those songs, having a large part in the play itself and being required to appear immediately upon the parting of the curtains, was not available for musical services. So Esmie and I simply sat there and stewed in our ever-increasing anxiety, pretending to be interested in the crowd below and in the occupiers of the other boxes.

I soon saw, three boxes to our left, Mr. Brummel — sitting alone. It struck me that I had never before seen him thus, without companions. He seemed to be forlorn, and I begged Papa: "May I ask him to join us?"

Papa sniffed. Mamma said, "The poor gentleman. Please Ambrose."

"Oh, very well, if you must."

I left our box and walked round to his. As I entered it, he heard the opening of the door, and turned to me. "Ah, Miss Worthing," he said, rising. "Your brother will be trying his wings in a new part to-night."

"Yes, indeed. Will you not join us in our box, Mr. Brummel? We would be glad of your company." (Here I must confess that I had an additional motive in asking him over to our box: Papa would be less inclined to rage in his presence.)

"You are kind," said Mr. Brummel. "But no, I would be an intruder."

"You would not, I assure you. Come, sir, you must not sit alone."

"On the contrary, it seems that I must. I am in Coventry, you see, after that evening at Carlton House. I may go so far as to say that I am in disgrace. I invited several of my whilom friends to share my box here to-night, but not one of them accepted. Some pleaded other engagements. Others did not reply at all. To be seen with me, apparently, would put them in bad odour with His Royal Thighness, the Prince of *Whales* — spelt with an *h.*"

"They are no true friends if they desert you at such a time. All the more reason for you to join *us,* who remain your friends."

He smiled wanly. "Bless you, dear lady, but I prefer to be alone to-night. I could not bear to make conversation, or to wear false grins."

"You must not be downcast, Mr. Brummel. You are guilty of nothing shameful. Impulsive, perhaps, but no more than that."

He sighed. "And yet the word has gone out, Miss Worthing. All of my creditors have learnt that I am *persona non grata,* and now they are like hounds at my heels. My tailor, my glove-maker, my wine-merchant, the lot of them, baying most fiercely. And, needless to say, the money-lenders, hungry for a pound of my flesh. Why, they flock outside the door of my lodgings as if it were the portal of a synagogue!" He permitted himself a pallid witticism: "Perhaps it is a *Solomonic* judgment upon me, eh?"

"Are you sure that you will not join us?" I asked again.

He shook his head. "I am most grateful for your concern, Miss Worthing, but I am better alone. No doubt the play will cheer me up." He took my hand and kissed it gallantly; then a ray of true feeling shone through a chink in his cold armour, tears glistened in his eyes, and he said, "You are the dearest young lady in all of this town." Sighing again, he added, "If only I had not lost my lucky cripple!" He bowed deeply to me as I left his box.

When I returned to our own box, Papa said, "Where is Aelfred? The play is about to start."

"I expect that he will appear soon," I replied, with literal truth.

Papa shook his head in resigned disapproval, muttering, "Unreliable, undependable, unpunctual . . ." as the curtains opened upon the play's first scene, the old-fashioned country house of Mr. Hardcastle. Applause greeted the entrance of the Hardcastles, played by Mr. and Mrs. Cholmondeley-Cockburn.

"I vow, Mr. Hardcastle," said she, "you're very particular. Is there a creature in the whole country but ourselves that does not take a trip to town now and then, to rub off the rust a little?"

"Ay," he replied, "and bring back vanity and affectation to last them the whole year . . ."

The first scene went off very well, and was warmly applauded at its conclusion. Papa looked about our box. "Still not here? Where can the boy have got to?"

When the curtains parted again, this time on a rural alehouse and its rowdy patrons, I began to be uneasy, for I knew this to be the scene in which young Marlow — that is, Freddy — was to make his entrance. And, before too many moments had passed, enter he did, in the company of another young actor, playing his friend Hastings.

Mamma, peering through her opera-glasses, recognised Freddy at once, and turned to me with silent amazement on her face. I shrugged with mute eloquence, and both of us turned our eyes towards Papa. He did not respond to Freddy's entrance. I gave thanks for his Johnsonian near-sightedness; but as I did so, I was stricken by a new fear. While Goldsmith's play is a blameless entertainment entirely fit for a bishop's viewing, what ribaldries might not Freddy perpetrate upon its chaste dialogue?

My heart was pounding as he spoke his first line:

"What a tedious, uncomfortable day have we had of it! We were told it was but forty miles across the country, and we have come above threescore!"

I breathed a sigh of relief. He might have worked carminative emendation upon that innocent "forty" — but he did not. My relief was not long-lived, however, when I remembered a particular point of the play: that Marlow's stammering came upon him only when addressing young women of his own class. When addressing serving-wenches, or men of any class, his speech was flawless. With what improper syllables would Freddy blemish the text in the scenes ahead?

My mind conjured up pictures of Papa purpling with righteousness and indignation at the like of "farts and arses" or "bend over my cunt" — even if he did not know that it was his son who uttered the indecencies. I wished that I had brought some hartshorn to the theatre in my bag, the which to revive him withal.

But I need not have worried. Freddy played the part without emendation of any kind. The play is so good, and he was so good in it, that no "improvements" were required. Skilfull writing and acting were sufficient to elicit an ovation from the public.

The press of the crowd was great, and our egress from the theatre therefore slow. Freddy was already waiting for us outside in our coach by the time we reached it. He was dressed in his own clothes again, and he had washed the paint from his face.

"Ah, Aelfred!" said Papa, as we climbed in.

Freddy responded nervously: "What did you . . . think of the play, Papa?"

"I enjoyed every minute of it. Goldsmith's gifts have not lost their lustre in these three, almost four, decades since the play's first performance. As his friend Dr. Johnson said, it borders upon farce, but it is so artful, the dialogue so quick and gay, and the incidents so well prepared, as not to seem improbable. And," Papa added, "I thank the good Lord for one thing . . ." He drew out his handkerchief and blew his nose.

"What is that?" Freddy asked.

"That you will never have to accept that position in the brewery. It would not have suited you." Papa rapped and called to our coachman: "Tuttle!"

"Home, your lordship?"

"In due course. But first, take us to a good tea-room. I feel like celebrating."

XXII

A Fatal Flaw

The tea-room whither we repaired was DeWitt's, that same establishment where we had heard Mr. Basil Carruthers' tale of the disastrous *Macbeth.* Mr. Carruthers was, as usual, already there, and was invited to join us. The proprietor, Mr. DeWitt himself, hovered solicitously about our table, impressed by the presence of a bishop, no doubt. Referring to him, Mr. Carruthers said, "Have you met our host?" and presented him to us. He was a short, portly man, with a ruddy face, a jovial manner, and a wig atop his bald dome.

When he spoke, it was in hearty theatrical tones as rich and fruity as Burgundy wine, so I was not surprised when Mr. Carruthers told us, "Paul was himself an actor in by-gone days."

Mr. DeWitt chuckled deeply and nodded. "Bottom in the *Dream,* the grave-digger in *Hamlet,* the porter in the Scottish play, things of that kidney." (I noted that, like many another person of the theatre, he avoided naming the bad-luck play, *Macbeth,* much as the Jews are said traditionally to avoid uttering the ancient Hebrew name of God, for fear of thunderous reprisals.) "I have found more stability in my present occupation," Mr. DeWitt continued, "as well as more tea and cakes." He proudly patted his paunch. Papa insisted that he join us.

Soon, the place was filled with customers: amongst them, the Cholmondeley-Cockburns and the Sheridans, all of whom were pressed to join us also. Papa said, "Do you know, Mr. Sheridan, that we have with us at this table a new and brilliant actor?"

"I do, indeed, your lordship," said Dick Sheridan, smiling across the table at Freddy, "for I saw him to-night at the Proteus. Congratulations, you young devil!" Turning to Cholmondeley-Cockburn, he added, "And congratulations to you, as well, Chum, on snaring him for your company."

"I know a good thing when I see it, Dick," he replied, then playfully pinched his plump wife, saying, "Do I not, Matilda? Eh?" The lady blushed like a young bride, and I could see that she still loved her philandering husband.

"But, Aelfred," said Mamma, "what is all this 'Frederick Thingrow' nonsense? I should prefer to see AELFRED WORTHING on those placards, in letters a yard high!"

It was now Freddy's turn to blush. He replied, "When I began with the company, I didn't know whether I would be a success or a failure, so I thought it best not to use the family name . . ."

"And now it's too late to change," said Chum. "The public know him and love him as Freddy Thingrow."

Papa nodded, albeit with regret. "It would have been pleasant to have a Worthing on the stage. When I was quite young, before I prepared for holy orders, I harboured fancies of . . ." His voice trailed off, wistfully.

"You, Papa?" said Freddy. "How odd: Kemble told me that if he had his life to live over again, he would continue his clerical studies and perhaps to-day be a bishop, like you."

"Kemble said that?"

"He did." Turning to the rest of us, Freddy added, "He told me all about the riots at his theatre two years ago, as well. Of course, I had already known about them." Freddy proceeded to recount Mr. Kemble's version of the riot story, in a full-blown parody of the Kemble manner, which was much appreciated by all present.

When he had finished, Mr. DeWitt, in his rumbling voice,

said, "That's Kemble's side of it, and it's all very well, but it's not the whole story. The truth of it is that the public were grumbling at the rebuilt Covent Garden even before the new prices were announced. It was built too quickly, at a hand-gallop, without check or superintendence, and the result was — and is — a dismal edifice, more like a barn than a theatre. And Kemble, moreover, tried to pack too many customers into it. The old popular galleries he reduced in size to make room for twenty-six private boxes. Now, you know as well as I that the private staircases and entrances of those boxes would surely attract — and did, in fact, attract — ladies of no extraordinary repute, and made the place commodious for their corrupt designs. His price rise — why, that was but the straw on the camel's back. And, if that were not enough, it had got out that Kemble had engaged an Italian soprano at a fee of seventy-five pounds a night — a *night,* mind you! Actors — even former actors like myself — bristled at that, I can tell you!"

"Have a care, Paul," said Chum, "lest you give young Thingrow ideas. He is already squeezing me dry. Why, he has even thumb-screwed me into giving him one per cent of the profits!"

"One and a half," Freddy reminded him. Turning to Papa, he said, "Did you ever do any acting at all, Papa, even in an amateur connexion?"

Papa, stirring cream into his coffee, replied, "I acted a great deal at school, and often recited poems and Shakespearean speeches at private gatherings. My father knew Dr. Johnson somewhat, as I have often told you, and Johnson knew Garrick, and so I met Garrick at our house. I recited the prologue to *Romeo and Juliet* on that occasion — you know, 'Two households, both alike in dignity' — and Garrick said, upon learning that I was destined for the clergy, 'The pulpit's gain is the stage's loss.' Perhaps he was being merely courteous, but I have always preferred to think otherwise. Still, my acting had a curious flaw that possibly would have held me back had I pursued it as a profession."

"A flaw, Papa?" asked Esmie.

"A minor flaw, but fatal in its effects. It is best illustrated by an example. At school, I was playing in a drama by — oh,

I can not remember the author — and I was required to convince a lady of my love for her, over her insistence that I never permitted her to enter my thoughts. 'I think about you for hours — I swear I do!' That was my line. But, in the presentation of the play, I said, 'I swear about you for hours — I think I do!' You may well imagine the spectators' response. If it had been a farce, it might have been acceptable, but in a drama of serious intention . . ."

I looked across the table at Freddy and caught his eye. The sins of the fathers!

XXIII

The Bravest Man in London

Early in the morning of the following day, as I was on my way to breakfast, I saw Freddy enter the house, holding under his arm a large, rolled sheet of paper.

"Heavens," I said, "have you been out and abroad already?"

He nodded, handing his hat and stick to Stewart, but keeping the roll of paper. "Come up to my sitting-room," he said.

I followed him into his room. "I have been to see Harriette Wilson," he told me.

"Freddy! You haven't!" I said, scoldingly.

"My visit wasn't social," he assured me. "I began thinking, last night, of what Chum said: that it was too late for me to use my true name on the stage because the public knew me as Thingrow. And I decided that I disagreed with him. Papa and Mamma would be delighted to see my name on placards and broadsheets; and Harriette would, in any case, make certain that all of London knew my identity — so why not hang for a sheep instead of for a lamb? I went to see Chum and persuaded him to have new placards printed for to-night's performance. He began to grumble about the expense, until I told him about Harriette's threat and said, 'Why shouldn't we profit from it?'

"He grasped the point at once. 'My boy, you're a genius,' he said. 'Her scribbler-friend, thinking to ruin you, will in actuality be providing you with a priceless form of gratis advertisement! His article will be read this morning by thousands — and they will swarm to the Proteus to-night, their money in their fists, to see the notorious bishop's son on the stage. And, by God, we shall be ready for them!'

"We went directly to the printer, who printed new placards in a great rush, and I carried away one of the proofs. Then I took me straightway to Harriette's, where I awakened the lazy lady-bird from her slumbers.

"She cursed me, and then she laughed. 'Well, well, well!' she said. 'If it isn't the famous Mr. Thingrow, idol of the London stage. To what may I attribute the great honour of this visit? Come here to apologise, have you? Come here to fall on your knees and lick my feet and beg my forgiveness?' She kicked off her slippers and extended her feet to me, wriggling her toes. 'Well, you may lick my *arse!*' She turned her back, bent over, hitched up her night-dress, and shewed me her plump posteriors. 'You may lick it from now till Christmas, young fellow-me-lad, and it will do you no good. My friend's article is written and on the press — and probably on the streets by now.' She covered her hind quarters again. 'Crawl and whimper as you may, but it's too late for repentance. Your secret is *out!*'

" 'So it is,' I said. 'Placards like this one will be outside the theatre — and all over town — to-night.' I shewed it to her."

Freddy unrolled the placard in his hand and triumphantly displayed it to me. It was truly a magnificent proclamation, set forth in a variety of shapes and sizes of type, couched in theatrical hyperbole, and decorated with an attractive engraving of a stage scene which, although I think it did not represent a scene from the specific play being announced, was probably the closest approximation in the printer's shop, and at least was not so far afield as a depiction of Leda and the swan. Best of all, Freddy's true name was writ large. With a thrill, I read the tall black words:

Cholmondeley-Cockburn's

PROTEUS

Theatre takes Pride in Presenting

Mr. Aelfred

WORTHING

☞(Formerly "Frederick Thingrow")☜

In His Unprecedentedly Successful

Portrayal Of MARLOW in

Mr. Goldsmith's Immortal Lampoon,

She Stoops to Conquer,

Which* will be Performed every Evening until further Notice Along with a *Phantasmagoria* of Other *Entertainments

"Oh, Freddy!" I cried with delight. "How wonderful!"

Freddy smiled proudly. "Harriette didn't think it wonderful. Her face fell. She snarled at me: 'This is a trick! You had this single placard printed, thinking to hoodwink me!'

" 'Believe that if you wish,' I told her, 'but soon you'll see them on every wall and hoarding. Some may be up already, I'll wager. I came here, you see, not to beg, but to thank you. Your friend's article will do me no end of good.'

" 'I'll have him stop it!' she screamed. 'I'll send word to him at once!'

" 'A bit late for that, don't you think?' I reminded her. 'As you've said, it's probably on the streets by now.'

"She grew worried, then. 'He'll kill me,' she said.

" 'Your journalist-friend?'

" 'He'll say I've made a fool of him. But I didn't mean to! His editor will storm and rage at *him,* and perhaps discharge him, into the bargain. He'll come here, demanding that I give him his money back —'

" 'He paid you for the information?'

" 'Ten quid,' she said. 'And I've spent all of it — I don't have as much as a farthing left . . .'

"I took out ten pounds and placed them on her table. 'A small price for such excellent advertisement,' I said.

" 'You have a good heart, Freddy, you always did,' she said. 'But he'll beat me. He'll thrash me to within an inch of my life!'

" 'Nobody will beat you. I'll go to him and tell him that if he dares to lay a —'

"There was a pounding at her door. A man's voice shouted, 'Harriette! Open this door, you filthy bawd!'

" 'There he is!' Harriette cried. 'He's found out already! He'll kill me!'

" 'No, he won't,' I assured her. 'What's his name?'

" 'Rankwort.'

"Outside, Rankwort shouted, 'Open it this instant, damn you, or I'll smash it down!'

"I opened the door. 'Come in,' I said. He was a sallow, unpleasant-looking cove with a runny nose.

" 'Who the devil are *you?*' he said.

" 'Aelfred Worthing. I believe I am the subject of an article of yours.'

" 'Then *you're* the swine who put her up to it!' He pushed his way into the house. 'I'll deal with you after I teach *her* a lesson she shan't forget!'

" 'I think not,' I said. 'I think you will not lay a finger on her, or on me, and that you will leave his house and never return. Never, do you understand? Not . . . ever.'

" 'Oh?' he said, with a sneer. 'And who or what is going to *make* me, Mr. Son-of-a-Bloody-Bishop?'

" 'Who?' I said. 'That honour will be mine. What? This stick in my hand. It's only fair to tell you that, not a fortnight ago, when a certain scurvy dog who called himself a gentleman insulted a lady in my presence, I took this same stick to him and beat him about the head and shoulders so severely that he has not been out of his house since that occasion. He is nursing his bruises . . . and his broken bones.'

"Harriette's journalist-friend backed away from me, looking very frightened. I asked him, 'How much did you pay her?'

" 'Five pounds,' he said.

"I picked up the money from the table and gave him half of it. 'There you are, sir. Refunded in full. Now get out of here.' He left the house quickly. I threw the remaining five pounds at Harriette's feet, and then I left, too."

"Is it true," I asked, "about you having beaten a man with your stick?"

"Good Lord, no!" Freddy replied. "I'd be terrified out of my wits to do a thing like that. I'm a coward. The trick, you see, is to find a cove who's even more cowardly than one's self."

I crushed him fiercely in my arms and kissed him. "You are no coward," I said firmly. "You are the bravest man in the world."

"Well," he drawled, "in London, perhaps. Shall we go down to breakfast? My nose informs me that Mrs. Cooke has made livers and bacon."

XXIV

A Summons from the Prince

After breakfast, Stewart handed me the items that had arrived for me in the morning post: two letters and a small parcel. One of the letters was a charming note from Jane Austen, saying how much she had enjoyed my company whilst in London, and thanking me for suggesting the title of her next book. "I am even now revising the draught, and I think that you will find it much improved when you read it in its published form. You will be amongst the very first of my friends to receive a copy."

The other letter was from Wilfrid. It was quite short:

"My dear Melissa, —

"I am sorry to have quit London in such haste. I had not even time to write you a message. Urgency compelled me to leave at once, and compels me to cut short this all-too-brief letter. Until I see you again, and I pray that it be soon,

"I remain,

"Your worshipful and loving

"Wilfrid"

The parcel that had come in the post was plainly wrapped. I tore off the wrapping and found a small jewel-case. Consumed by curiosity, I opened it to discover, inside, a necklace of glittering gems! Awed by the unique beauty of the piece, I lifted it reverently from its case and examined it closely.

The stones were seven in number, strung on a chain of gold, and each of them was different. I recognised, at once, an emerald, a sapphire, and an amethyst. The others I did not immediately identify. The central stone was truly unusual: an elegantly carved piece of amber — with a tiny fly embedded in it! What an oddity to be used in a necklace!

Had Wilfrid sent it? In apology, perhaps, for deserting me so suddenly? Now I saw a folded sheet of paper that had been hidden under the necklace. Quickly smoothing it out, I saw to my considerable surprise that it bore the crest of the Prince of Wales. On it was written:

"My dear Miss Worthing, —

"The trinket here enclosed is offered in gratitude for a service it is hoped that you will find within your power to render to the state, as regards a literary matter. I should deem it an honour if you were to call at Carlton House this afternoon at two o'clock, when a carriage will be provided to transport you here. The precise nature of the service will be then explained. In the mean time, you will perhaps appreciate an explication of this bauble:

"On a recent occasion, one described you, without the slightest disrespectful intention, as a pretty little fly. It was, no doubt, an unfortunate comparison. By way of reparation, the centre-stone of this necklace contains a little fly which is preserved for ever in your honour. If you will take the trouble to examine all the seven stones from left to right, you will discover (and, it is hoped, will be amused by) their precise order: *m*alachite, *e*merald, *l*apis-lazuli; then the central *i*nsect; followed by *s*apphire, *s*atin spar, and *a*methyst. To put it differently, *m-e-l-i-s-s-a*.

"Until two o'clock,

"I am, dear lady,
"With great truth,
"Very sincerely yours,
"George P."

My name in gems! Such a charming conceit! And so subtle: if the Prince had not explained it to me, I wonder if ever I should have puzzled it out?

But in what kind of literary matter did he require my help? Being neither a writer nor a scholar, I could not think what it might be. In a state of high anticipation, I spent the remainder of the morning dressing for my audience with the Prince. It goes without saying that I wore the lovely necklace.

When Mamma saw it on me, and noted that I was about to leave the house, she expressed astonishment. By way of elucidation, I handed her the Prince's letter.

"Extraordinary!" she declared. Peering at the stones, she

carefully recited: "Malachite . . . emerald . . . lapis-lazuli . . . amber . . ."

"No, Mamma: not *a* for amber; *i* for insect."

"Yes, to be sure: *i . . . s . . . s . . . a. Melissa.* How very clever. That is, indeed, an unusual gift. And this literary matter . . . ?"

I shrugged. "I am completely in the dark," I told her. "But I will become enlightened at two o'clock."

Stewart approached and said, "The carriage from Carlton House has arrived, Miss."

XXV

Out of Bounds

As I rode to Carlton House in His Royal Highness's carriage, I revelled in the new freedom I enjoyed as a woman engaged to be married. Before my betrothal to Wilfrid, I would have felt obliged to obtain my parents' permission even to obey the Prince's charming command; but ever since my engagement, there had been a tacit understanding that I was my own mistress. It was invigorating.

Upon entering Carlton House, I was asked to wait in a room with gilt chairs, inlaid tables, and couches covered in velvet. Full-length paintings hung on the walls: they depicted the Georges I, II, and III, as well as the Regent himself, who, some time in the probably near future, would almost surely become Number IV.

As I waited, I heard muffled voices behind a small side-door. One, which may have been that of Mr. Perceval, the Prime Minister, was praising Wellington's victories in the north, by which I assumed was meant the north of Portugal. The unmistakable voice of His Royal Highness roared in response: "Damn the north! And damn the south! And damn Wellington! The question is, how am I to be rid of this damned Princess?" — by which I assumed was meant his wife, the Princess of Wales.

A moment later, that side-door opened, and the Prince walked into the room. He exuded graciousness and courtesy: "Miss Worthing, so good of you to come. I hope you are well? And your parents?"

"Yes, Your Royal Highness, we are all in excellent health; and my parents extend their loyal felicitations."

"Splendid. Refreshments have been ordered and will soon be here. I am positively famished!" Indicating the paintings, he permitted himself a small pleasantry: "I see that you have already met my family?"

"They form an imposing gallery, Your Highness."

"Pray let us sit down, Miss Worthing, over here . . ." As he led me towards the velvet couches, he took note of the necklace at my throat, and said, "Ah! You like it, then?"

"Indeed I do, sir, and admire the cleverness of it; but I fear that I will not be deserving of such an ingenious and costly gift."

"Tut! Permit me to be the judge of that, dear lady."

Servants now brought in tea, wine, cakes, tarts, meats, fish, and other fare. The Prince and I seated ourselves on separate couches, with a table between us. After we had been served with our choices, he dismissed the servants and said, "I have a special purpose in meeting you in this room, Miss Worthing. This 'imposing gallery,' as you call it, has bearing upon the matter I wish to speak to you about."

"A literary matter, you said?"

"Quite. Try a little of this Westphalia ham . . ."

"No, thank you, Your Highness. I am content with the lobster and the sweetbreads."

He speared the rose-pink meat with his own fork and popped it into his mouth, chewing ecstatically. "My God, I love food," he said fervently. "But, as to this literary matter . . . I must confess to you that I first approached Lord Byron in this connexion, but he told me that he was far too busy with a long poem that he has been writing for the past two years or more. Something about a child, called Howard, or Harold, I believe, but no matter. I had in mind an epic poem, you see, about all the Georges — all the men you see looking down upon us from these walls — with possibly symbolic references to *Saint* George, slaying the dragon and all that. But when Byron declined it, I began to think of it in the form of a romance, a novel, or perhaps a series of novels . . . and that is why I am turning to you."

"But, Your Highness, I am not a novelist!"

"Aha," he said with a wink. "Nothing escapes my attention. You are an intimate friend of a new novelist whose first effort I admire very much: Miss Austen. Is that not true?"

"Yes, it is, and in fact I had a letter from her only this morning . . ."

"The rumour is that you have been of invaluable assistance to her in the writing of the book that now occupies her."

"I only suggested a title, Your Highness."

"Nevertheless, she respects your judgment. She listens to you. I ask of you, Miss Worthing, only that you put a word in her ear. Describe to her — when you answer her latest letter, perhaps — the project that I have mentioned. Speak of it glowingly, not forgetting to include an allusion to St. George. Whet her appetite for this grand literary monument. Will you do it, Miss Worthing? Speaking of appetite, this is an absolutely *heavenly* cherry tart. I beg you to take a slice of it."

"Thank you, Your Highness. It looks delicious. Yes, I will be happy to write to Miss Austen on this matter. But there is one thing that I must tell you . . ."

"And what is that?"

I swallowed a large bite of the cherry tart, washed it down with tea, and said, "I am not sanguine about her reception of the idea."

"Why not, pray?" Finishing his slice of tart, he helped himself to a second portion of ham.

"I am sure that she will be honoured to know that she is in your thoughts, sir; and will be grateful for the opportunity held out to her; but I have heard her speak about the writing of serious romances, and she has said that she could no more write one than she could write an epic poem. If she can not laugh at her characters, she says, she can not write at all."

The Prince looked doleful. "But she is a lady of great gifts. Surely those gifts can be turned in any direction she so wills?"

"I can only say, Your Highness, that I will write to her — this very day, in fact — and put it to her in the most enthusiastic terms of which I am capable."

"Thank you, dear lady. That is all I ask. And now: what may I do for you, in return?"

"Oh, Your Highness, it is a privilege to render you this small service, and no return is necessary. Besides, this beautiful necklace . . ."

"A trifle," he said, dismissing the necklace with a wave of his plump hand, the fingers of which were like little articulated sausages. "Surely there is *some*thing I can do for you."

"Not for me, Your Highness, but . . . perhaps for my brother."

"Freddy?"

"Teddy. That is to say, Eadward. The architect."

"Ah yes, to be sure . . ."

"I know that Your Royal Highness looks upon the work of Mr. Nash with great favour. But if you could also —"

"Say no more," he cut in, holding up a hand. "Mr. Nash has more work than he can conveniently execute. We have always need of other good men in that line. I will speak to my people."

"Thank you, Your Highness."

He reached across the table, took my hand, and held it. "If you truly wish to thank me," he said, "you will call me George."

I dared not remove my hand from his, but I said, "Oh, sir, I could not possibly do that."

"Why not? It would please me."

"It would be altogether too familiar, too lacking in respect."

"Not at all. Do you know that there are some ladies who call me Georgy-Peorgy?"

"How naughty of them!"

"Not in the least. I enjoy it. It is true that I am a Royal Prince; true that, one day, I will be King. But I am also a man . . ." He moved from his couch to mine, never letting go my hand. "A man like other men, with feelings, with warm blood, with tender affections, my dear young lady . . ."

"I am sure that you are, Your Highness," I allowed, trying, but failing, to move away from his great oleaginous mass.

"I am not made of wood, Melissa — may I call you that? —

and it is no secret that the Princess of Wales and I are not on good terms. We never were. She is repugnant to me. And I to her, for some reason. I should never have married her, but I had no choice. A prince is a kind of slave, you know, flogged this way and that by reasons of state. Our marriage is an unnatural union: we are first cousins. I have never loved her; that I swear to you. And when a man does not love his wife, where may he turn for that sweet solace that is the God-given right of all men? All men, Melissa, even princes."

His grip relaxed for a moment; I slipped my hand out of his, and moved quickly to the other couch. Instantly, he arose and joined me there. Now his arm was about my waist. His face was flushed, and he looked as rosy as the ham which he had just eaten. "Do I ask so much, dear lady?" he said in a plaintive tone. "It would be such a little thing to you, and such an overwhelming joy to me. You women have us in your power, you know. With a word, a kiss, a caress, you can transport us to Paradise; or you can deny us those blessings and consign us to the miseries of Perdition."

I moved away again, rising from the couch and putting the food-laden table between us. "Your Highness must surely know many ladies who are glad to be of comfort."

"None like you, Melissa," he said, slowly circling the table and growing ever closer to me as he spoke. "None with your beauty, your youth; those eyes that melt a man's bones; those lips, sweeter and more red than the cherries in this tart . . ."

The Prince was fiercely aroused; his blood was high; that part which Wilfrid called the very devil of a fellow, which followed its own whims, was following those whims now, and was asserting itself unmistakably under His Highness's princely raiment.

He is a swift and agile man, for all his flesh, and before I knew it, he had one hand upon my bosom and the other on my hinder part, parenthesising me, so to speak, both fore and aft. "Ah!" he groaned in rapture, his eyes rolling up inside his head. "These two pairs of lovely twins! These four divine rotundities! How dear they are!"

His own rotundities were as full as any woman's, I thought, as I pluckt off his hands and, stepping back, said, "I beg Your Highness not to pursue this course . . ."

"It is my size, is it not?" he said peevishly. "But what can

I do? I *must* eat. Am I a pauper or a monk, that I am required to waste away to a shadow? Other men guzzle food till it falls out of their ears, and still they stay slender as straws; whereas I but *think* of a joint of meat or a cup of chocolate, and my waistcoat buttons pop like champagne corks! I *hate* this ugly, bloated body in which I am entrapped. I avoid the sight of it when I undress. I would like to disown it, to cast it from me, but I am chained to it like a prisoner to his ball of iron. I know full well that I am one large monstrous deformity. If I were deformed in other ways — a club foot, a hump on my back — I would be pitied. But this deformity of mine is an object of ridicule and derision. No one pities me. They all mock me. Ah, Miss Worthing, if your shining eyes could but look *past* this unseemly mountain of blubber, these awful quivering rolls of jelly, these doughy dugs, this globular paunch, these vast pulpy posteriors, they would see a wand-like boy, 'a delicate and tender prince,' with a loving heart that is bruised by the slightest rebuff."

His words, gushing from such a deep well-spring of anguish, moved me. "You are built to heroic proportions," I assured him, "like Jove or Thor, like the Samson of Rubens, but there is something that I must tell Your Highness . . ."

"George! Call me George! Call me Georgy-Peorgy!" he pleaded.

"*Listen* to me," I insisted.

"I do, Melissa! I hang upon every word that issues from those cherry lips!" His bulk loomed forward again.

"Your Highness — George — what you do not know about me — what you could not possibly know because it was not true when last we met — is that I am engaged to be married."

Instantly, he stopped advancing. It was as if I had flung a jug of cold water in his face. "Engaged?" he said.

I nodded.

"To be married?"

"Yes, Your Highness."

"Are you speaking the truth?"

"Believe me that I am, sir. I am engaged to a Suffolk gentleman, Mr. Wilfrid Summerfield."

With deep sincerity and calm, the Prince said, "He is favoured above all men. I beg your pardon, Miss Worthing.

Had I known, I would not have behaved in this manner. The pursuit of a woman who is engaged to another is not the occupation of a gentleman. Please forgive me."

"There is nothing to forgive."

"Thank you. You are generous and understanding. And you need not think that I will forget about your brother. I have made a promise to you, and I will keep it. His fortunes will improve, and he will prosper."

"Your Highness is a noble prince. I will not forget my promise, either. I will write to Miss Austen to-day."

"I am obliged to you." He took my hand, this time most decorously and ceremoniously, and kissed it with much gallantry. "Please be sure to inform me when the wedding shall take place so that I may have the honour of sending a gift to you and your husband, whom I hope to meet one day . . . just as I hope to renew *our* acquaintance, Miss Worthing, after your marriage." His smile was roguish as he escorted me sedately to the door. "For, although engaged girls be out of bounds for gentlemen," he said, "married ladies are another matter. Quite another matter entirely."

XXVI

All Things Low and Lubberly

Gluttonous pig! — rooting with your thick, blunt snout for truffles in our deeps and damps. Mindless mole! — burrowing sightlessly in the musty dark, tunnelling the cellar where love's sweet wine is stored. Butting goat! — charging blindly with your hard, unyielding head. Slithering snake! — waiting, coiled, then striking with unblinking aim. Steely swordfish! Sly mosquito! All you prodding, poking, pushing, puncturing, penetrating bravoes of the animal kingdom! — you do I invoke in metaphor to apostrophise that dumb, relentless, stubborn part, that other-self, that secret eminence, that incubus, that hornèd devil, that power behind the throne of mind that turns the man away from sense and prudence, decency, from lofty bright ideals of art, philosophy, and faith, and sends him crawling through the mud and ordure.

My Wilfrid is a good man; the Regent is a prince of royal blood; yet even they become as grunting, drooling, panting beasts whenever it may please their pig, their mole, their goat, their snake to so transform them. Surely the Creator is in love with baseness, for He takes delight in all that is lubberly and low.

Some times, God help me, so do I. For when I look back, my senses cooled, upon that night in the Dark Walk, for instance, I shudder with revulsion at the unspeakably gross act that I performed, and I groan with shame to think of it. Can anything be more vile than that? more degraded? more depraved? Can the wretched, wriggling, writhing services of whores be worse? Can the ghastly abominations of Sodom and Gomorrah have been more loathsome? Can dignity and decorum dwell alongside such disgusting stuff within a woman's heart?

And yet, in those resplendent moments with my Wilfrid, all that now seems shocking, all that now appalls me, was bathed in poetry and golden light. That bestial act of slime and spittle, which would have horrified me had I witnessed others doing it, was transfigured into something ethereal.

When it was over, when the hot glare of passion had dimmed to a soft glow, when sense once more had conquered the senses, I vowed that I would never do it again. But I expect that I will — and if there is worse, I expect that I will do that, too, whatever it may be, with hearty appetite.

XXVII

Hiding from the Law

I had intended to write to Jane Austen immediately upon returning home from Carlton House, but when I arrived, Stewart informed me that Mr. Heathman had called, and was waiting for me in the drawing-room. I went in at once.

He gave me that quick bobbing bow of his, mumbled a deferential "Miss Vorting," and handed me a note. I opened it and read:

"Melissa, —

"Please come at once. I long to see you. John will take you to me.

"Wilfrid"

I looked up at John Heathman. "He is here in London?"

"*Ja.*"

"At Pulteney's Hotel?"

"*Nein,* at the brewery he is waiting."

"Very well. Let us go, then."

As we left the house, I told Stewart that I might not be home in time for tea.

John drove Wilfrid's hired stanhope straight to Southwark. During the ride, I wondered at the curtness and urgency of Wilfrid's note. Why did he wish me to meet him at the brewery? Why did he not simply come round to our house? As my future husband, surely he knew that he was welcome there at any time? With every passing day, Wilfrid had been becoming less and less the straightforward honest business man I had first thought him to be, until now he was a figure cloaked in mystery, a man with secrets, of sudden departures and reappearances. But to-day, I told myself, I will know all.

(Not *quite* all, as it turned out . . .)

John drove round to the rear of the brewery, and brought the horses to a halt at what appeared to be a small, deserted shed. He helped me out of the carriage, then knocked on the door of the shed, opened it a bit, and said something in German. From within, I heard Wilfrid's voice reply, "*Ja, ja, mein Freund, sehr gut! Danke schön.*" John motioned for me to enter; I did; and he closed the door, remaining outside. I smelled a pungent odour of liniment and other unctions.

"Wilfrid! What on earth?! . . ." I exclaimed, for I saw him, by the light of a single oil-lamp, lying on a narrow cot, his right arm slung in a scarf, and a dressing on his head. I rushed to his side. There was an ugly bruise on his forehead, and his left eye was swollen shut. "My dear! You've been hurt!" I cried.

"Not seriously," he said, "and I am much improved by the sight of your dear face."

"What has happened?"

"I'm a bit thirsty. Will you pass me that flask of water?"

I took the flask from the rude bench on which it stood, and held it to his lips. He sipped from it for several moments.

"Ah, that's better. Thank you, my dear."

"But why do you lie here, in this dreary shed? Come home with me at once! We will send for Mr. Cargrave, the physician . . ."

He smiled and shook his head, then winced, for the movement had caused him pain. "No," he said, "that would never do. I must stay here until these bruises disappear and my arm is better. John will look after me well enough."

"For Heaven's sake, darling, tell me *why* you must remain in this place! You behave as if you are in hiding!"

"I am," he said, "and you must tell no one that I am here. Not your parents, nor your sister, *no one*. Please believe that there are good reasons for all of this — and, furthermore, please do not ask me to tell you anything else. For my sake, for your sake, for the sake of your family, and for the sake of many people whom you will never meet, it is best that you know nothing more."

I shook my head vehemently. "It is no good, Wilfrid. I am your wife-to-be. If you have a secret, I deserve to know it, I deserve to be brought into your confidence."

"Of course, you are right," he said with a sigh, "or would be right were the situation other than it is — if I were the only one in danger — but other people are involved . . ."

"Wilfrid," I demanded of him, "have you broken the law?"

"Yes," he replied, without hesitation.

"Have you done murder?"

"No."

"Are you a traitor to the King?"

"No."

"Have you swindled, embezzled, sold an adulterated product?"

"I have done none of those."

"Then what can you have done that is so grave, so heinous, that you must lie here in this filthy shed, beaten, injured . . . ?"

"I can not tell you."

"You must! I will not leave here until you do!"

He groaned. "Please do not add to my difficulties, Melissa. I can not, and I will not, tell you. Not now. Not ever. Or, if ever, only after many years have gone by and we are both of us very old parties, bent and grey, with a score of grandchildren. I will tell you only this: I have done nothing that is shameful. I regret my actions, yes, for they have led to fearful consequences which I could not have foreseen. But my intentions were good — Hell's paving-stones although they may have been — and my conscience, in that respect, is clear. When I reproach myself, it is for rashness, blindness, lack of foresight — not for infamous or unmanly acts." He licked his lips and asked for another drink of water.

After giving it him, I kissed his poor, bruised face, scratching my lips on the fierce bristles of his unshaven cheek. "Wilfrid," I said, "I can not leave you. I will stay with you until you are mended."

"No. Go home. John will take you."

"I refuse to go! I *will* stay!"

He sighed. "My dear, consider: if you were to not return to your house, your parents would become alarmed. They would ask questions of your butler. He would say that you had gone off with John. In no time, they would have traced you here — and found me. That must not happen."

I was in tears. "Very well, Wilfrid, I will go."

"And do *not* come back."

"May I not even visit you from time to time, until you are well?"

"Most certainly not. Give me your *word* that you will not. One visit is no matter, but repeated visits would draw attention to this place. I repeat that *nobody* must know. The most prudent of persons, meaning me no harm, could give me away by an incautious word. Even John, who tends me, knows nothing of my illegal activities: he hasn't a notion of what caused these injuries. He is as faithful and as unquestioning as a dog, but I must be guarded even with him. Do you understand?"

I nodded, but the nod turned into a shake of the head as I replied, "No, I do not understand, but I will do as you bid me. You have my word."

He gripped my hand. His palm was hot and dry. "Go now, my love. Wait for me. Pray for me."

I kissed him again, and walked to the door of the shed. "Melissa . . ." he said, faintly, from his cot. I turned around. "What a very strange necklace," he said. "I have not seen it before."

"No," I said. "It is new." I smiled. "A present . . . from an ardent admirer."

He rose on one elbow, his eyes blazing. "Who is he? I'll thrash him through the streets of London!"

I managed to summon up a laugh. "You could not thrash a sparrow, in your condition. And, besides, he is only a poor lonely wretch, twice my age, with crowds of companions but no friends. A fat old man with an awful wife. He is to be pitied. As for his name: well, all of us have our little secrets, Wilfrid. One day, perhaps, when we are old and grey . . ."

He smiled. "You're a devilish tease!" he said.

I blew him a kiss, opened the door of the shed, and left.

"No," I said to John Heathman, as he began to escort me towards the carriage. "Stay here with him. He should not be left alone. I will hire a hackney-coach in the street. Give him good care, John. If he is in need of anything, anything at all, send word to me. Do you understand?"

"*Ja,* Miss Vorting."

I found a hackney almost at once, and was soon home.

XXVIII

Will-o'-the-Wisp

I had, indeed, missed tea, so I went straight to my sitting-room until it was time for dinner.

My mind was awhirl. Wilfrid a law-breaker! How distressing that was to me. My future husband hiding in a dismal shed, battered and bruised. I could make neither head nor tail of it.

I rang for Abigail and bade her fetch water for my tub. The immersion in the hot water calmed me somewhat.

"Abigail, I hope that you have been a good girl of late."

"Why, yes, Miss."

"I mean, I hope that you have not allowed my brother to take liberties with you again."

"Oh, *no,* Miss. Not that he hasn't tried . . ."

"The rogue!"

"But I told him, I did, that my heart belonged to another. That made him respect me, you see. He's not a *bad* young gentleman."

"Is it true, about your heart belonging to another?"

"Yes, Miss." She giggled. "And all the rest o' me, as well!"

"Why, Abigail! Then you have *not* been a good girl, after all."

"Well, as to that, Miss, Mr. Stewart, he thinks I'm *very* good, indeed he does."

"Stewart?! *He* is your lover?"

"Of course, Miss. For years now. You never knew? Why, Miss, it's understood, in all the best houses, that the butler takes that privilege if he fancies a member of the female staff. Part of his perqs, you might say."

I shook my head in numb amazement.

After bathing, I put on my dressing-gown and sat at my desk to answer Jane's letter. I painted a bright picture of the "literary monument" proposed by the Prince; but could not help adding that, knowing her feelings about serious romances, I thought it not likely that she would accept the commission. I had come almost to the end of my letter, when Mamma tapped on my door and entered.

"Stewart told me that you had returned from Carlton House," she said. "Why did you not come to tea?"

"I took tea with His Royal Highness," I replied. "A very sumptuous tea. So I decided to bathe and rest before dinner."

"What is this literary matter he wished to speak to you about?"

I told her, adding that I was in the midst of carrying out the Regent's request.

She said, "Miss Austen would do well to take up the Prince's suggestion. I read that novel of hers, which you pressed upon me, and I think that she will do herself little good by continuing in that satirical vein. Such stuff may amuse and titillate for the moment, but it will not commend her to posterity. Charm, japery, and clever conversations do not wear well. Mockery, even gentle mockery such as hers, rubs the reader's fur the wrong way. If she has her eye on immortality — and what writer has not? — she would be well-advised to turn to things of more substance; and to deal with them responsibly and weightily and with respect, eschewing that caustic wit of hers."

"I shall tell her that you said so," I responded.

"No, you shall not," said Mamma. "I have no wish to offend the lady. That was a private comment, intended for only your ears." Looking closely at me, she added, "Are you upset, child? Surely not by what I said about Miss Austen?"

"No, of course not, Mamma."

"By something that the Prince said?"

"The Prince was charming, and very . . . warm. I am not upset, Mamma. I am merely tired. I'll have a lie-down before dinner, as soon as I finish writing this letter."

"Very well. Bring a good appetite with you to table. Mrs. Cooke is giving us roast pig with prune sauce. I think it was a reference to that dish in *She Stoops to Conquer* that caused your father to ask for it to-night. How that man loves his food!"

(He does, and has always done. Papa eats as much and as richly as the Prince, and yet — although he is no beanstalk — he is not in any sense obese. The poor Prince is right in feeling abused by his body and by those who blame *him* for its vastness. Nature is to blame; God, perhaps.)

When Mamma had left, I finished my letter to Jane. I then read over some letters from Wilfrid, which were lying in a drawer of my desk. The most recent of them was the one I had received in the post that same morning, apologising for having left town so suddenly. Examining its cover more closely than I had done before, I now saw that it had been posted not from Suffolk, but from Nottingham. The North Country.

I then unfolded an older letter, in which he had answered some questions of mine about the Luddites, those masked marauders who were going about by night, smashing looms and lace-frames in the textile mills of Nottingham, in retaliation and protest against the machines that had thrown them out of work. "Their name, about which you enquire," he had written, "is said to derive from the will-o'-the-wisp who directs their actions, a certain 'Ned Lud' or 'General Lud' or 'King Lud' of Sherwood Forest . . ."

I looked up from the letter and stared into the air. Then all those trips out of London, I realised, all that journeying to and fro, when he told me that he was tending to brewery matters in Suffolk . . . and Esmie unaccountably had called him "m'*lud*" as well as "Your Majesty" . . .

The letter fell from my hand.

"Good Heavens!" I cried aloud. *"Wilfrid is King Lud!"*

And, silently, I added: What is his other secret?

I learnt the shattering answer to that question all too soon.

BOOK THREE

Knave

Rumours of War — Prophecies, True and False — Wilfrid's Other Secret — The Enemy — A Singing in the Blood — Love Is an Imbecile — My Eye and Betty Martin — I Will Be Waiting — Torn Asunder — When a Christian Turns Rogue — An Intimate Examination — A Kind of Caul — A Skinful of Max — Return of the Rapist — Blood for Blood — From Darkness into Light — Murder Most Foul — Circumstantial Evidence — Warts and All — Nothing But the Truth — One of Life's Greatest Pleasures — A Servitor of Satan — Whore of Babylon! — Hodge Shall Not Be Shot — All the Jews Must Go to Prison — The Bachelor and the Widow — Rankwort Redux — Swear It in the Name of God! — A Horrible Suspicion — Hateful, Hateful Woman! — Only Love — Move the Stars to Mercy — A Great Lesson — Married Life — Dark Satanic Mills — All for the Best

I

Rumours of War

Foolish ninny! If only I had not given my word to stay away from Wilfrid's hidey-hole!

That was my first thought upon awaking the next morning. For I yearned to rush to him, to hold him in my arms and comfort him, to sit by his side all day and all night, every day and every night, until he was fully recovered from the injuries he had received.

Perhaps I could send Blodgett with a hamper of food? — but no, Wilfrid would be furious if I divulged his whereabouts to anybody. I could not even send him a loving message, a few tender words.

"The will-o'-the-wisp who directs their actions . . ." It was himself he had described in that earlier letter — a *Will*-o'-the-wisp, indeed; Will for Wilfrid — not his Radical friend Will Cobbett, as once, fleetingly, I had suspected.

I read again that letter in which he had answered my questions about the Luddites. In one passage, he had written: "To their credit, the Luddites never have shed blood in their riots; and yet one of the mill-owners, Mr. Horsfall, is threatening to instruct soldiers to fire upon them, should they attack his mill again. Let us pray that it will not come to that."

It seemed likely, now, that it *would* come to that. Soldiers would discharge their muskets into the ranks of those rioters; in retaliation, the Luddites would vent their wrath not only on machines, but on flesh and blood, as well; legislation would be passed to suppress them and punish them by hanging — and all of Wilfrid's humanitarian visions would be shattered.

Moreover, if the authorities were ever to learn that he had been the instigator of their first riots, then he, too, would almost surely be brought to trial — and probably to the gallows! I hoped that his true name had never been known to his followers. Perhaps they knew him only as Lud. I fervently hoped so.

I called to mind the time when Mr. Brummel had been ordered to Manchester with the 10th Hussars to suppress a riot in the cotton mills there; and how he had resigned his commission, rather than go. When asked if he had been in sympathy with the mill-workers, he had given a flippant answer about his horror of being exiled to a provincial town. We had all laughed at that reply, for it had been so characteristic of the scornful Beau; but I wondered, at this later time, and in light of Wilfrid's own sympathy with mill-workers, if Mr. Brummel had not been hiding his own finer feelings behind a mask of indifference? For, in his set, sentiment and concern for the lower orders is looked upon as one of the less seemly aberrations. He had given a beggar a shilling when asked for only a ha'penny, and then made excuses for his generosity by the ridiculous claim that he had never owned so small a coin. Perhaps Mr. Brummel was a better man than any of us knew; and perhaps some "better" men were less meritorious than he.

As for Wilfrid, there was nothing for it but to put him out of my mind — a monumental, indeed an impossible, task. Cast out my beloved Wilfrid from my thoughts? Put aside my future husband as I might put aside a book, marking the place with a ribbon so that I might pick it up again where I had left off reading? Can a woman leave off loving, and pick it up again where she left off, giving no thought to her lover in the interim? And yet that is what I had been bidden to do. That is what I had given my word to do. Wait. Wait and pray. That had been Wilfrid's command.

Not many days after I had visited him, Teddy and Luisa were our guests for dinner. Teddy was in good spirits. Beaming across the table at me, he said, "I can not tell you how happy I am that you are engaged to be married to my friend

Summerfield. He is an excellent fellow in every way, and a fine match."

"I agree with you," I said, smiling to cover the anxiety I continued to feel over Wilfrid's situation.

"And," Teddy went on, "I am no less gratified at our brother's remarkable success. Freddy, everywhere I go, I am asked if I am, by any chance, related to the famous Aelfred Worthing — and I am proud to answer 'Yes.' "

Freddy grinned shyly. "Bit of a turnabout," he said. "They used to ask me if I was related to the architect chap."

Teddy laughed. "Touching on my own work: I, too, have some good news to impart. Or perhaps you should tell it, Luisa? After all, it was your doing."

Luisa replied, "It was your father's doing."

"Eh?" grunted Papa, looking up from his soup.

"Yes, Father Worthing," she said, "it was you who got us that invitation to Carlton House, and provided Teddy with the opportunity to know the Prince."

"Actually," said Teddy, "I spoke hardly two words to him all that evening, and I had come away thinking that he had taken no notice of me."

"But he had," said Luisa, "for Eadward has been asked to design some of the additions and improvements that the Prince wishes to be made on Carlton House."

"And word of that has got about," Teddy added, "so that I am besieged by clients of quality. More than I can accept."

"How wonderful," I said, trying very hard not to look or sound like the cat who ate the canary. "And all because of a little invitation."

Papa declared, "I can take no credit for it, Eadward. This very enterprising lady whom you are proud to call your wife must be crowned with that laurel. It was she who suggested — I may say insisted — that I obtain the invitation for you." He raised his wine-glass. "Let us, therefore, toast her. To Luisa, who is my favourite daughter-in-law — and *not* merely because she is my only one!"

All of us laughed at Papa's little pleasantry.

Mamma said, "I always knew, Eadward, that it was only a matter of time before you would receive the wider recognition you deserve."

"Thank you, Mamma."

"But matters of time can be accelerated," said Luisa, "and often should be. Our lives are short. We must make the most of the brief span that has been allotted us."

"And yet," said Esmie, who had been silent till now, "I have come to feel that, however we may plot and scheme and try to sculpture our lives, we can never escape the plans that have been made for us by Destiny. Success, failure, happiness, unhappiness: those will come, or will not come, despite our efforts."

Luisa ignored Esmie. Exuding self-satisfaction, she asked me, "Where is Mr. Summerfield, Melissa? I had hoped to find him here to-night."

I was prepared for such a question, and I lied without effort: "He is in Suffolk, attending to matters of business, but he will return to London before long."

"I am glad to hear it," she said. "He will prove to be an important connexion for Eadward in the years ahead. Of course, they are already friends — long before *you* knew him — and, in point of fact, you have Eadward to thank for bringing the two of you together — but when he becomes a member of this family, the connexion will then be even closer, and more useful."

Teddy was embarrassed. "But that is not the *only* reason Luisa is glad of the coming marriage. She likes Wilfrid; she rejoices with you and shares your happiness. Do you not, my dear?"

"Naturally," Luisa replied. "That goes without saying."

"Even things that go without saying," purred Mamma, "occasionally need to be said."

During the fish course, the talk turned to war and rumours of war. Our present conflict with Bonaparte, on the Iberian Peninsula, led Teddy to speak of our blockade of Europe. "It is causing no end of trouble with the neutral countries, you know. America, for one."

"Troublesome lot," muttered Papa.

"We may even be at war with America by next year," Teddy continued.

"Again?" Papa said. "It seems but yesterday that we were at war with them."

"It is a good deal longer ago than yesterday, Papa," I said.

"The Treaty of Paris took place three years before Freddy and I were born!"

"So it did," he said. "*Tempus fugit.* Why, I can even remember, as if it were but a fortnight ago, the change of calendar. I was ten years old. It caused no end of confusion. Everybody grumbled; swore they would not recognise it. But eventually we all grew used to it. The true confusion, of course, had been going on for centuries, ever since 1582, when the rest of Europe, or most of it, went over to Pope Gregory's system, but England stubbornly held on to the old Julian calendar. It made our dealings with the Continent confoundedly difficult — shipping schedules, dates of letters and bank draughts, all manner of things were always ten or eleven days out of joint. I remember going to bed on the first of September, 1752, and coming down to breakfast the next morning, and being told by my father that it was now the *fourteenth* of September. Something about an Act of Parliament. I was dumbfounded, until he explained it. I said: 'But what has happened to all the days in between, Papa? Where are the second, third, fourth, fifth, sixth, seventh, eighth, ninth, tenth, eleventh, twelfth, and thirteenth of September? Where have they *gone?*' He replied, 'To Heaven, Ambrose, where you will encounter them, many years hence, when you have gone to your reward.' "

We had all heard the story many times, but we did a good job of dissembling close interest. When he had finished, Freddy turned to our elder brother, saying, "Do you really think we'll be at war with America by next year?"

"That is what I hear, wherever I go."

"Bit of bad luck," said Freddy. "Chum has been thinking of taking the company to America next year, for a tour. I'd been rather hoping to go." He shook his head, dolefully.

Mamma said, "But you are so very subject to sea-sickness. Besides, surely the Americans do not go to plays? They are rough people who dress in buckskin and wear hats made of baboon fur."

"Raccoon, Mamma," said Esmie.

"Precisely. Even that Mr. Benjamin Frankland of theirs wore such a hat. I saw him in it, here in London."

"I thought they all went naked," I said, "save for head-dresses made of turkey feathers."

"Some of them are almost civilised," said Freddy, "and

attend the theatre. That's what Chum claims. But if war should break out, he'll be forced to call off our tour."

"I should hope so!" Mamma exclaimed. "Why, even if there is no war, what sort of fare would suit them? Pantomimes, that is all. Displays of juggling and tumbling. You are much better off here, Aelfred."

"I expect you're right, Mamma."

Changing the subject as the *entrée* arrived, I said, "I have heard that the Regent has slipt and hurt his ankle whilst attempting to teach the Highland fling to his daughter."

"Yes," added Freddy, "and the Duke of Cumberland —"

"Disagreeable man," murmured Mamma.

"The Duke of Cumberland, they say, remarked that the Prince's ailment is centered a deal *higher* than his ankle, and that a plaister on his *head* might be more to the point!"

"An unbrotherly comment," said Papa, "and very near to *lèse-majesté,* when one considers that the Prince reigns in his father's stead and will be our next King."

"Which is what Cumberland would *like* to be," I said, "and that is why he makes churlish remarks against the Prince. Thank God a man like that will never be King!"

"There is a remote chance that he could be," said Papa, "but between Cumberland and the crown there are a goodly few other royal dukes interposed . . . The family tree includes —"

"Speaking of trees," Mamma interrupted, "I have heard that the King is talking to them now. To trees, that is."

"Do they reply?" asked Freddy, grinning. "Perhaps they *bark* at him, what?"

Papa said, not too sternly, "He is a pitiable wreckage of the man he was, sick in mind and body, but he is still our Sovereign, Aelfred; he is the King who took my hands in his at my consecration; and at this table he commands our respect."

"Yes, Papa," said Freddy, meekly.

11

Prophecies, True and False

Later, after our guests had left, I asked Esmie what signs she may have seen about the rumoured war with America, either in her *tarot* cards or by other divination.

She shook her head. "These are political chess moves," she said, "and I seldom receive intimations about such things. Teddy's rumours are no doubt as reliable as any other information which we may hear on that subject. I dreamt last night that the ravens will leave the Tower in my lifetime.* But often my dreams are only dreams, and have no special significance."

"Have not those ravens inhabited the Tower of London since antiquity?" I responded. "And is there not a legend that warns us England will fall should they ever fly away?"

"I should not worry about it, Lissa," she said. "I assure you that *I* do not. The ravens may never leave; or, if they do, it may be only when I am a very old lady. And legends such as that need not be taken as if they are gospel. I, as you know, am by way of being attuned to certain mysteries and portents; but for that very reason I turn a sceptical eye towards all such claims. There is much chaff in them, and very little grain. Separating one from the other is difficult; often impossible."

Her face brightened. "But I think that I have had a happy foretelling recently," she said.

"Oh, let me hear of it!"

"I have had a strong premonition that Monsieur Mathieu's tunnel will be built, after all."

"The Channel tunnel?"

She nodded.

"How jolly!" I said. "Now Freddy will be able to visit the Continent without being so horribly afflicted with *mal-de-mer.*"

* See *Princess Pamela,* 15 June. — R. R.

Nine years ago, Albert Mathieu, a French mining-engineer, presented Bonaparte with a proposal to link Britain and France by means of a tunnel, or tunnels, under the English Channel. The tunnels, each approximately twelve miles in length, together would reach from Dover to Calais. They would rise from the surface and be joined on a man-made island to be built in mid-Channel, upon the underwater formation called the Varne Bank. On that island, the men and horses employed in the hauling of wagons and carriages through the tunnels would be able to stop and rest, and enjoy a breath of fresh air before continuing on their journeys. The tunnels would not be completely airless, of course, for they would be ventilated by a system of pipes protruding out of the water. Gas-lamps would provide illumination.

Mathieu's plans were exhibited at the Palais de Luxembourg, and stimulated enormous interest; for, thanks to the Peace of Amiens, there was a period of tranquillity between our two countries. Our late parliamentarian Mr. Charles James Fox pronounced the idea to be "one of the great enterprises we can now undertake together." But Prime Minister Pitt had other ideas; as did Bonaparte; we were at war with France again within two years; and dreams of the Channel tunnel were abandoned.

"When will the great undertaking be completed, Esmie?" I asked.

"That I can not tell," she replied, "but I feel confident that you and I will see it come to pass."*

"I am eager to have it do so," I said.

Of course, Esmie's visions are somewhat unreliable. Her seeming knowledge of King Lud's identity notwithstanding — and I must stress *seeming* — she is often visited by mere nonsense, such as non-existent smoke, or that fair on the frozen Thames; and her new seeings of ravens and tunnels, I told myself, could be of that kidney.

I continued to be troubled in my mind about Wilfrid. My sister had seemed to be so right about one of his secrets, now revealed to me. But I thirsted to know what other secret he may have been withholding from me.

* Wrong. For more about the Channel tunnel, see the Afterword at the end of this volume. — R. R.

The unwelcome quenching of that thirst was granted me the very next day.

III

Wilfrid's Other Secret

For, on the following morning — less than a week after I had seen Wilfrid in that shed — John Heathman called and handed me a letter from him. I ripped it open eagerly and read it·

"My dear Melissa, —

"John must go out to buy provisions, so I am seizing this opportunity to dash off a note which he can hand to you.

"First, I must say how much I miss you and long to be with you. Then, I must apologise for the awkward and false position that I have forced you to assume, all because of my rash actions. Finally, I must tell you that I will not hold binding our engagement to be married, should you wish to cancel that agreement. I can fully understand, in light of what you have but recently learnt about me, that you may no longer wish to have me as your husband. But, whatever your decision may be, please know that you will always have the love of

"Your devoted
"Wilfrid"

I looked up at John and asked, "How is he?"

"He is still not *gut,* but he is being *besser,* I think."

"Thank God for that. Does he need anything? Food, wine, ointments?"

"Nein, nein, danke. At the shops I am *alles* buying."

"Can you wait whilst I write him a note?" He appeared to be hesitant. "A very *short* note?" I added. He nodded.

I immediately sat down at the drawing-room desk and wrote as rapidly as I could:

'My darling Wilfrid, —

"But perhaps I should address you as 'My foolish Wilfrid,'

for you are speaking nonsense when you ask if I wish to cancel our engagement. Nothing that you have done could ever compel me to do that. Say no more on the subject, I pray you.

"John tells me that you are better, but still not completely well. Take good care of yourself, my dear love, for I am as a woman dead, until that day when you will take me in your arms and bring me to life again. God grant that it be soon!

"Your own
"Melissa"

I folded the note and sealed it with a gobbet of Papa's red wax. After rising from the desk and handing the note to John, I felt so grateful to the faithful go-between that I was reluctant to let him leave without shewing him some sign of friendship and regard. "Will you not stay a few moments more, and take some tea?" I asked.

"Ach, nein, danke," he replied.

"I understand. You do not like to leave him alone for too long."

"Ja."

"I want you to know, John, that I am grateful for the good care that you are giving Mr. Summerfield. Your fidelity to him is so commendable that I almost wish to call you Fidelio — after the title of the opera, you know." John seemed not to understand this reference. "By Mr. Beethoven," I added. "I saw its first performance in Vienna, some six years ago, with my parents and my sister, at the Theater an der Wien. But perhaps, like my brother Freddy, you are no lover of the opera?" He shook his head. "Mr. Summerfield has told me that *you* are from Austria," I went on. He nodded. "And that your father and his have known each other for a very long time."

"Ja, since they were *Kinder,"* he replied.

"How pleasant," I said, "and how unusual for your father to have been the childhood friend of an English boy."

"Ein Engländer?" He seemed puzzled. *"Wer? Der Alte?"*

"Yes, the . . . old man. The elder Mr. Summerfield."

John smiled crookedly and pushed the hair off his forehead. "But always his name is not Summerfield being, *nicht wahr?"*

"Not Summerfield?" Now it was my turn to be puzzled. "What was it, then, if it was not always Summerfield?"

"Sommerfeld," replied John.

"Sommerfeld! Do you mean to tell me that *he* is an Austrian, too?"

"Nein!" he retorted, almost vehemently. "He is from *Österreich* coming, but . . ." He struggled with the language. *"Ich bin* . . . I am *österreichisch, und mein Vater,* he also is *österreichisch* being, but Herr Sommerfeld is *jüdisch* being, *verstehen?"*

"I beg your pardon. I don't quite . . ."

"Ein Jude he is being. He is — *ach,* how is it said in the *Englisch?* — he is a Jew."

IV

The Enemy

The word exploded upon me like a bomb.

"What . . . what did you say?"

"I said he is a Jew, *Fräulein."*

"Surely you are mistaken. The Summerfields are a Christian family."

"Ach, ja," he rejoined, with the hint of a conspiratorial smile, "he *now* a Christian is, but always it was not so."

"I can not believe you," I said.

He shrugged. "I am the *Wahrheit* telling you . . . the truth. But it is not of importance." He turned to leave.

"John," I said. He waited for me to continue. But I shook my head. "Nothing. Please tend to Mr. Summerfield's needs . . ."

"Jawohl, Miss Vorting."

He left. I stood numbed, unable to deal with what he had told me. Wilfrid's father a Jew? Could it be possible? Wilfrid himself half a Jew? I thought of everything Papa had said about that outcast race: killers of our Lord, perpetual aliens in the world, allies of the Antichrist, professed enemies of Christianity and Christians . . .

I felt dizzy, and I could not breathe. I staggered to the nearest chair and collapsed upon it. I summoned the face of Wilfrid to my mind. I saw it clearly, for what seemed to be the first time: the large, arched nose; the full lips; the brilliant brown eyes. Not an English face at all; a foreign face; sensual, strange, exotic, conjuring up blinding visions of hot sand and hotter sun; a face that belonged under a skull-cap; the face of a Jew.

I saw his thick lips part, and heard a stream of Hebrew gibberish pour from his mouth. I saw him with a shawl over his shoulders, rocking back and forth in a synagogue, praying to the vengeful God of Israel, not humbly, on his knees, like a Christian, but arrogantly, on his feet, like a Jew. I saw him as an oily usurer, hunched in his Jerusalem Chamber in 'Change Alley, lending money to English gentlemen, gloating and grinning and rubbing his hands together, like Mr. Kemble as Shylock: "Vell den, id now abpears you neet mine helb 'Shylogg, ve vould haff moneys . . .' "

I was afraid that I would faint. I ran to the windows and threw them open, breathing deeply. Reason returned to me John Heathman had lied: it was as simple as that. He had concocted it. But how *much* had he concocted? Only the part about Wilfrid's father being a Jew? Surely Sommerfeld might be the name of a Gentile Austrian, and not necessarily that of a Jew? And it satisfactorily explained how those two men could have known each other since boyhood: a thing that had given me wonder.

But if only *that* much were true, why had Wilfrid kept it from me? The mere changing of a name, the Anglicising of a name, is not a sinful secret. Wilfrid had told me of John's original name, after all, and had not blinked an eye — nor should he have done so. And everybody knows that Mr. Frederick Albert Winsor, the industrialist who is determined to replace all of our oil-lamps with gas-lamps, was born Friedrich Albrecht Winzer in Germany. The great musician of Papa's youth, Georg Friedrich Händel, was known here as plain George Frederick Handel, pronounced "handle," but his birthname was no mystery. Why should a similar change, from Sommerfeld to Summerfield, be veiled in subterfuge?

Because, I told myself with swelling resentment, Wilfrid's father was not simply an Austrian (and not Austrian at all, by John Heathman's fastidious lights), but an Austrian *Jew*. It was the only answer as much as I was loth to accept it. A:

Jew, he could not be naturalised; so he had changed his name and his religion, converting to the Church of England. I was repelled by the deceit of it; I despised the crass Jewish cynicism.

And this was the family into which I would marry!

"No," I said aloud; then silently continued: I shall never marry him. I shall throw him over, for the same reason that Olivia Fairchild did so: not because he is a brewer, but because he is a Jew.

For now I was certain that she had broken off their engagement for that cause and no other. Who could blame her? I would follow her example. Papa would support and defend me. None of our friends would rebuke me. On the contrary, they would rebuke Wilfrid for deceptively trying to worm his way into a Christian family, a bishop's family, in order to plant his Jewish seed in my English womb and raise a hook-nosed tribe of grasping little Isaacs and Rebeccas . . .

But what if no part of it were true? What if every word of John's had been a lie?

And yet: *why* should he have lied?

As I stood at the window, I could see him outside, climbing upon the driver's seat of the stanhope. It was starting to rain. On an impulse, I called out to him: "John! Wait!" He looked in my direction, saw me, and nodded.

I ran out of the drawing-room, and out of the house, into the rain, stopping for neither hat nor wrap, and climbed into the stanhope, saying, "I am going with you."

"Nein, Fräulein, das ist verboten!"

"Do as you're told, damn you!"

"Ja, Miss Vorting," he said, obediently. The carriage pulled away from the kerb with a creak and a hoof-clatter.

And *now* (I said to myself), Mr. Wilfrid Summerfield or Sommerfeld or whatever your true name may be, let us see you wriggle your Jewish way out of *this!*

V

A Singing in the Blood

As the carriage plunged, splashing, through the rain-pelted streets, I thought bitterly of a sentence in Wilfrid's latest letter, the one which John had delivered to me just minutes before: "I can fully understand, in light of what you have but recently learnt about me, that you may no longer wish to have me as your husband."

How true! — but for a reason entirely different from that to which he had referred. His great-hearted concern for the poor, his noble if ill-considered rabble-rousing — these had not made him a lesser man in my eyes. *Had not,* but now, in light of yet another disclosure, *did:* for now I saw his actions to have been driven by a Jewish hatred for Christian England, by a diabolical desire to undermine our way of life, to throw our country into chaos and confusion.

I thought of his friendship with Radicals like William Cobbett, who looks upon pious religious tracts as no more than things to teach people to starve without making a noise. I called to mind his interest in the sacrilegious theories of Lamarck; and how, when I had expressed the hope that he was not a disbeliever, Wilfrid had replied that he was "Solid Church of England." Solid? Or as flimsy as gauze? Deception, deception!

The rain had abated somewhat by the time we reached the shed behind the brewery. I leapt out of the carriage and was at the door of the shed even before John. I flung open the door in a fury.

"Melissa?" said Wilfrid from his cot. "Why have you come here? Did I not tell you —"

"I am not your servant," I snapped, "that I must obey your every command. You are not my lord and master, and will *never* be, Mr. Whatever-Your-Name-Is!"

His left arm was still slung in a scarf, but the eye that had been swollen shut was now open, and his bruises had begun to fade. The growth of dark beard on his face was thicker, and that, together with his luminous large eyes and other features, made him look such a Jew!

John had entered, directly behind me, and was saying apologetically to his master, "Herr Vilfrid, the *Fräulein,* I could not stop her . . ."

"That's all right, John, I don't blame you. Please wait outside." John left the shed. "Now then, Melissa, what on earth is all this about?"

"It is about Wilfrid the Deceiver," I replied. "And I do *not* refer to your King Lud mask —" He began to speak, but I waved aside his words, saying, "Yes, yes, I have pieced that together, so there need be no more pretence between us on that subject. Nor do I refer to Mrs. Royce's child, which you have explained. I refer to the greatest of all your deceptions, the biggest of all your lies, the guiltiest secret in a life pocked with secrets! I refer to the fact that you are nothing more than a Jew!"

He sighed. "Ah. I see."

"Then it is true?"

" ' "What is truth?" said jesting Pilate . . .' "

"Do not quote specimens of *English* literature to me, Mr. *Zzzzzommerfelt!"* I shouted, giving the name the most foreign sound I could summon. "Quote extracts from the Kabbalah or the Talmud, if you wish, or some other *Hebrew* classic, but do not persist in this masquerade as an English gentleman!"

He smiled sadly. "But I *am* an English gentleman."

"You are not a Jew?"

"I have been a Christian all my life."

"Your name is not Sommerfeld?"

"Not now nor ever."

"And your father . . . ?"

"Before we discuss my father," said Wilfrid, "shall we finish our examination of his son? Please sit down, Melissa. That chair is a bit rickety, but I expect that it will not collapse under you."

Somewhat reluctantly, I calmed myself and sat down.

"That's better," he said. "How beautiful you look, even by the light of that poor lamp, with the sparkles of rain in your hair . . ."

"Have done with honeyed words," I said. "I'm surfeited with them."

"Very well," he said. "No honeyed words. Simple facts. You ask if I am a Jew. I must answer that question with another question: What *is* a Jew? And I will endeavour to answer, by asking still more questions, and replying to them, after the manner of a catechism. Is a Jew one who worships according to the Jewish faith? Yes. Does a Jew accept Jesus Christ as the promised Messiah? No. Does he, rather, still await the coming of that Messiah? Yes. Does a Jew eat only what is called a 'kosher' diet, eschewing pork and certain other foods, in obedience to Mosaic law? Yes.

"But I, Melissa, pray in a Christian church, to that one God Who is shared by both Christians and Jews. I recognise Jesus as my Saviour and the true Messiah. My favourite dish is roast pig — I could do with a slice or two of it now, in fact! I know not one word of Hebrew — whereas I dare say that your father is deeply learned in the language. As for my name, it never has been anything other than Summerfield — Wilfrid Noah Summerfield — the name I was given in baptism, by a vicar of the Church of England, soon after I was born. Noah was my paternal grandfather's name. My father was his first son, and I am my father's fourth son, just as Lud was the fourth son of the first son of Noah — rather complicated, but you will see how I came to choose the name Lud for my clandestine activities. It struck me as most devilish clever at the time."

"Do not attempt to change the subject," I said. "Get back to your father. Is he an Englishman? Was he born with the name Barnaby Summerfield?"

"He was born in Austria," Wilfrid replied, "as Baruch Aron Sommerfeld."

"Then he *is* a —"

"Was. My father *was* a Jew. He has been a Christian for a very long time — for far longer, in fact, than he was ever a Jew. He is now quite an elderly man; and he became a Christian before he married my mother . . . my very English mother, I might add, whose lineage could probably be traced back to the time of King Egbert, at *least*. According to Jewish law, I am not a Jew because my mother is not a Jewess, no matter what my father may be. If it were the other way round — if *she* were Jewish and he not — I would be recognized as a Jew by Jewish law."

"These technicalities are not to the point," I said, impatiently.

"Right you are," said Wilfrid. "I will add that the only Jewish insignia which my father suffered his sons to wear, like a secret badge hidden under our clothing, was conferred upon us in infancy by the venerable Rabbi, Chaim Levinsohn, in an ancient ceremony, a ritual which Christ himself experienced in *his* infancy, but which in our modern world has been abandoned by Christians and limited to Jewish and Moslem boys, almost exclusively. In other words, if you will forgive the indelicacy, I am circumcised — as you, my dear, have very good reason to know."

My face went hot with sudden blushing.

"My father's name," Wilfrid concluded, "was Anglicised quite legally, by deed poll, when he came to this country as a very young man, about the time that he converted to the Christian faith."

"In other words," I said crisply, "he doffed one faith and donned another, like a changing of coats, for the sake of expediency."

"The royal families of Europe, my dear, have been doing the same for centuries, dropping the Protestant faith and taking up the Roman, or *vice versa,* for the sake of expediency — to bring about advantageous marriages and political alliances. You call it expediency; I call it survival. What does it matter, Melissa? — there is but one God."

None of his methodical marshalling of facts and logic had the desired effect upon me. I responded to it by telling him: "Papa says, 'Once a Jew, for ever a Jew.' "

"In great part, he is right," Wilfrid said.

I was surprised. "Do you, then, agree with Papa when he says that it takes more than a splash of baptismal water to wash away the stain of Jewishness?"

Wilfrid shrugged. "I object to the word 'stain,' " he said. "I would prefer the word 'glory.' But yes: I agree that a splash of water will not eradicate a long and great tradition. A belief in Jesus — no matter how devout — will not destroy a Jew's pride in being descended from the seed of Abraham and Moses and David."

He had been half-sitting, supported on one elbow, but now, tiring, he fell into a supine position again, his eyes closed. A long, soft exhalation of breath escaped his nostrils. When he resumed speaking, with eyes still closed, his voice was little more than a whisper:

"For there is more to a Jew than religion, language, diet," he said. "Something more than race, too. There is a singing in his blood, an ancient song of rejoicing and despair that he hears every hour of every day, whether he wishes to hear it or not. It is the song the Psalmist sang. 'By the rivers of Babylon, there we sat down, yea, we wept, when we remembered Zion . . . If I forget thee, O Jerusalem . . . if I do not remember thee . . .' " He opened his eyes. "A Jew can not ever stop being a Jew, no matter what he eats, what language he speaks, what faith he embraces. In that sense, your father is right. And in that sense, my father is still a Jew, will be a Jew to the day he dies, and — God willing — will remain a Jew for all eternity."

He smiled. "I like to think that he will enjoy long conversations, in Heaven, with all the most illustrious of his fellow-Jews, including that radical young rabbi of Nazareth. Perhaps all those Jews will wave their hands about up there and shrug excessively and pull their beards and clap both palms to their cheeks and wag their heads from side to side, as English actors do when they are playing in *The Merchant of Venice* or *The Jew of Malta*. Do you think so?"

I could see that he was trying to charm me — and, indeed, he could be the very devil of a charmer — but I was having none of it. I arose from the chair and said, coldly:

"What dialogues your father may conduct in Heaven, and with whom, is no concern of mine. You have admitted that he is a Jew. That means that you are half a Jew. You hid this from me, as you hid other things. Perhaps I can not blame you for the deviousness and cunning of your race; possibly you can not help it; but I must tell you that I could never marry a member of that race, or bear his children . . ."

"Or love him?" He sat up again. "Can you look at me, Melissa, and say that you do not love me?"

"I will say only one thing more to you, and then I hope never to speak to you again: Good-bye."

I walked quickly to the door of the shed. "Melissa!" he

cried. But I did not turn back to him. I opened the door and left. From inside the shed, I heard him cry again, "Melissa!"

It had stopped raining. John offered to take me home, and I accepted, for I had come away without any money, and I could not hire a hackney-coach.

All the way back to my house, I held back the tears that ached to gush forth. I was determined not to weep in front of John. And yet, with all my soul I longed to weep — for I could *not* look at Wilfrid and tell him that I did not love him. How could I possibly have done that when I loved him desperately, shamelessly, hungrily; when I loved him more than anyone or anything in the world?

VI

Love Is an Imbecile

I was far too upset to join my family at the dinner-table, so I went directly to my rooms, sending word that I was indisposed and would not be dining. Then I threw myself upon my bed and gave myself fully to the luxury of weeping. I felt as if my life were over. I had rejected so many other suitors — titled gentlemen! — and saved my affections for this man, this paragon of love and epitome of respectability; who was now revealed to be the impregnator of at least one unmarried girl; and the revolutionary leader of a band of lawless marauders; and, worst of all, a Jew!

To think that *I,* not Kitty Pakenham, might now be Wellington's wife! To think of such excellent matches as Lord Nolan, Chevalier d'Hibou, Count Grzegorz-Stefanski, Baron von Steinkopf: all of whom I had rebuffed! True, the first three of those were papists, but at least they were Christians, and all of them would have become Church of England gladly, had I accepted them. Even the egregious Marchese di Gazza-Silone would have been preferable to a wily Jew who passed himself off as a country gentleman of old established family!

So reasoned my brain; but my heart said: You loved not a

single one of them, Melissa — nor have you loved any other of the gentlemen with whom you have carried on flirtations: Shelley, Byron, Brummel, the lot. You have loved only one man in all of your life, and that man is a son of the Jew, Baruch Sommerfeld.

Then "love" is an imbecile, Reason replied; a drooling, babbling creature best shut away lest it do harm. "Love" is a thing to be shunned lest it destroy us — therefore, have nothing more to do with it, Melissa. Avoid it, spurn it, scorn it, cut it dead. For "love" will scourge you and shame you and lead you to nought but infamy and scandal, humiliation and disgrace. "Love" comes too easily and goes too swiftly. Could you not "love" your handsome young footman with the well-turned calves, and could not the two of you rut like beasts and call that rutting "love"? Cast this monstrous "love" out of your life, my girl, and be the happier and cleaner for it.

I was resolved to listen to that voice of Reason. What had love ever done for me? It had caused my present tears. It had led me to commit disgraceful indecencies on the grass in Vauxhall Gardens.

What had love done for my sister? It had given her a few months of joy, and then left her a pining widow. Better had she never loved at all!

I would remain a single woman, I told myself. I would model myself after my friend Jane. I would write satirical romances, perhaps, mocking love; or compose music — the repertory for solo clarinet was sparse, and could do with augmenting.

As for providing my parents with grandchildren, Teddy already had done yeoman service in that office, and no doubt would do so again, many times. Freddy, I guessed, would not remain unmarried for ever, and would spawn his own brood. Moreover, those grandchildren would carry the Worthing name, not the name and blood of Jew or gypsy.

It was *good* that Esmie's child had died at birth! — such was the fierce and sinful cry of my pain. Why should our dear Papa be forced to have the squalling brats of swarthy gypsies and oily Jews thrust upon his lap to dandle? What had that good man, that man of God, ever done to deserve such descendants? Why had he been cursed with wayward daughters who gave themselves shamelessly to cunning foreign charmers?

No "Mrs." ever would pollute my name, I vowed. I would remain what I always had been: Miss Melissa Worthing, respectable spinster of Hans Town. Thus I would live out my life, and thus I would die: a virgin, an avoider of men, and men's deceptions, and men's filthy desires. No, sir, I would say to all vile males who might seek my favour: I have no need of you, I can do very well without you, I am quite content as I am, thank you very much, you dirty creature.

I thought of the Prince and his importunate wheezing advances; I thought of Cholmondeley-Cockburn and his leering proposals; I thought of Percy Shelley and his offensive crucified Venus; I thought of Wilfrid and his circumcised sceptre — and all of them were transformed into beasts in my mind.

Beasts of the jungle, slavering and snorting, but dressed in exquisite clothes by fashionable London tailors. How ridiculous they were! Swine in silk! Dogs in buttoned boots — foam-flecked tongues lolling out of their fetid mouths, sniffing and licking every passing bitch!

I was well rid of them.

VII

My Eye and Betty Martin

The next morning, at breakfast, I made my announcement:

"I have decided that I will not marry Mr. Summerfield, after all," I said.

"What???" responded Papa, Mamma, and Freddy, in chorus. Esmie said nothing.

"When did you reach this decision?" Papa demanded to know.

"Yesterday."

"And what is the cause of it?"

"He and I simply are not suited to one another."

"Absurd!" Papa declared. "You and he are admirably suited. He is an excellent match, of good family, with fine prospects."

"And you love him," said Mamma. "You love him and he loves you — one can see it in your faces when you are together."

"Be that as it may," I said, "I will not marry him, and there's an end to it."

"My dear," said Mamma, "did you quarrel?"

"We had some words."

Papa said, "By way of the post? He is not in London."

"He has returned. I saw him yesterday and told him that I would never marry him."

Mamma said, "Some words . . . You had a lovers' tiff, then."

"It is more serious than that," I told her.

"It always seems so, my dear," she said, "but these things, which appear so large at the time, never fail to pass. Do you think that your father and I did not have lovers' quarrels before we were married?"

"I would not call them quarrels, Penelope," said Papa. "That sounds so common. They were discussions, debates, if you will, in which I — by reason of my superior education and intellect — happened always to be right, and you to be wrong."

"Yes, Ambrose," said Mamma. "Melissa, tell us: is there another man?"

"No, Mamma. And there never will be. I shall, from this day forward, no longer encourage suitors. I am decided to remain a spinster for the rest of my life."

Freddy muttered, "Confounded waste, if you ask me. A prime article like you."

"A what?" asked Papa.

"A beautiful young lady," Freddy explained, "of lively and agreeable disposition."

"And so you are," Papa said to me. "I concur with your brother that it would be a waste to spend your life in spinsterhood."

"Nevertheless, Papa, that is my decision."

"See here, young woman —"

But Mamma calmed the storm: "Ambrose, I pray you finish your eggs and kidneys. We can talk about this matter privately, after breakfast. I am sure that it is nothing more than what I have said, a lovers' quarrel, and we shall be able to work out a sensible solution together. Let us say no more of this now lest it interfere with our digestions."

Later, Freddy took me aside and said, "Wilfrid looked to be a decent enough cove, to my way of thinking. What the deuce is all this about, then?"

"It is just as I said, Freddy: we are not suited."

"Humbug," he retorted. "That's all my eye and Betty Martin. The two of you are as suited as a pair of turtle-doves, the way you coo and look cow-eyed at each other."

"Turtle-doves do not look cow-eyed," I informed him.

"Thank you very much; correction noted; but you know very well what I mean. Why, you and he are fairly champing at the bit to be leaping into the jolly old nuptial bed; I've seen you! And please don't scold me for mixing equine and human metaphors, Dr. Know-All." Suddenly he slapped his forehead. "Here!" he exclaimed. "I know what the trouble is!"

"Do you indeed."

Freddy laughed. "Of course! The cheeky devil has made advances, hasn't he? Been a bit too familiar with you — that's it, isn't it?"

"Whether it is or it isn't, it is no business of yours," I said sharply.

"I'll be blowed if it ain't!"

"Please do not speak vulgarly. It is a silly affectation."

"Dear me! What a cultured lydy we 'ave 'ere! Lips all pressed together; standing up stiff and straight as if a poker were stuck up your arse . . ."

"You're vile!"

"Vile, am I? Now see here, sister mine: when have we not told each other everything? Whether you like it or not, I am bloody well *making* it my business. If Wilfrid has been a mite too forward for your taste, slap his wrist if you like, but don't throw him over. I mean to say, he's a man, isn't he? And you're a damned luscious wench. Why, it wouldn't be natural if he could keep his hands off you. Don't jilt the poor beggar for that."

I sighed and shook my head. "Fweddikins, I assure you, such a thing is not my cause for breaking the engagement. It is something quite, *quite* different. All I will tell you is that he is not the person I'd thought him to be. He pretends to be something that he is not. I wish to say no more on this subject."

"All right, Mel, suit yourself," he rejoined. "But that's no reason to turn a sour face on *all* members of the male sex. If you do, you'll regret it. I've said it, and I'll say it again: it would be a confounded waste; a waste of a damned fine, warm, loving, passionate filly. A prime article if ever I saw one."

VIII

I Will Be Waiting

Mamma came to me in my rooms a bit later, determined to talk sense to me.

"Your father is very upset about this, Melissa. You are a disappointment to him. All of us are so favourably impressed by Mr. Summerfield. He seems to leave nothing to be desired. Whatever you and he may have quarreled over is a trifle, I am sure; a speck of dust in the eye that feels like a mountain. Young people exaggerate everything. How can you be so contrary and give Papa such anguish?"

"He would be much *more* anguished, believe me, if I were to marry Mr. Summerfield. If Papa knew what *I* know about him, he would be the first to demand that I break off the engagement. I will say no more."

"You are a stubborn, wilful girl."

"I am sorry to have earned your censure."

"You are ungrateful and selfish. You give not a thought to your intended, nor to your father, nor to me, nor to your poor sister, who lies sick in her bed even now, because of your foolish behaviour."

"Esmie sick?" I rose from my chair. "I did not know. I shall go to her . . ."

"You shall not. I expressly asked her if she wished you to sit at her side, and she said, 'No, not Lissa. I would choke if she were to come into my bedroom.' "

"Choke? What a peculiar thing to say. What did she mean by it?"

Mamma shook her head. "I do not know. I asked her, 'Do you mean that Melissa disgusts you? That her behaviour makes your gorge rise?' She said:

" 'No . . . it is the smoke . . . she brings the smoke with her . . .' "

"That ridiculous smoke again!" I said, peevishly. "Her mind has left its moorings . . . I fear that she is quite mad."

"Yes, I am concerned for the state of her senses. I asked her if I should send word to Mr. Cargrave, but she said no. Still, if she does not improve by evening, I will do so. But, I pray you, do not go to her. In her present condition, who knows what harm you might do?"

"Very well, Mamma, I will stay away from her."

"Will you come down and speak to your father and allow him, with my help, to sort out this folly of yours, to save you from yourself?"

"No, Mamma, I have said my last word on that abhorrent subject."

She turned and walked to the door. "Children!" she cried out savagely. "I wish not one of you had ever been born!" She slammed my door as she left.

I, too, wished that I had never been born. I wished that I were dead. What had I to live for? A long span of loneliness stretched ahead of me. I would be a wrinkled old maid, unloved and unwanted. I would be simpering old Aunt Lissy to Teddy's children and to the brood that Freddy would sire. The female part of me would become as dry and brittle as a pressed flower; my blooming breasts, that men fairly slavered to fondle and kiss, would become withered dugs, unsucked by babes or lovers; I would yearn and pine and hanker for the attentions of men, and in my yearning would no doubt befoul myself with solitary fingerings or worse: I might even, in the depths of my lonely depravity, avail myself of some device such as Freddy once told me is used by ladies of Lombardy to pass the time and who call the vile thing therefore *passatempo* and sometimes *diletto,* their word for delight, shrunken to *dildo* by our ignorant English bawds . . .

If that was the level to which I would sink, then so be it, I vowed. Better *that,* than to have anything more to do with men.

At the point when my thoughts had reached that nadir of

despair and degradation, Stewart knocked on the door of my sitting-room, and entered. (Disgusting creature, swiving Abigail as part of his perqs!) He handed me a letter that had arrived by the afternoon post. The direction on its cover was written in an unfamiliar hand, so I set it aside, being in no humour at that moment to read letters from strangers.

I decided to change my clothes, so I began to remove them, and when I was completely naked, I stood before my tall pier-glass and appraised my body from head to foot. Alabaster skin; breasts like ripe fruits trembling on the vine; gently rounded belly, punctuated by the shadow of the navel; curly thicket; firm long smooth thighs; dimpled knees; delicately curved calves, tapering to fragile ankles, high-arched feet, ten tiny toes like a row of perfectly matched gems. Yes, Freddy was right: I was a prime article, and no mistake.

"Ah, bella signorina, Melissa mia," the Marchese di Gazza-Silone had moaned, "eef-a you would be-a my wife, my Marchessa, I would kees-a you from-a your leetle peenk nose to your leetle peenk toes — and *tutti* in-a-between . . . all-a the day, all-a the night!"

No doubt he would have, but his kisses would have seemed like those of a lizard; whereas, such kisses from Wilfrid . . . a ripple of pleasure went through my nude body. I turned away from my nakedness in the pier-glass and put on my dressing-gown.

Overcome by a lethargy, a heaviness of the senses, I stretched myself out upon my bed, suddenly and mortally tired. My hand crept under my dressing-gown and toyed with my private floss. I sank into a doze, wherein I drifted or floated on a warm sea, half-way between sleeping and waking. Phantom images blossomed beautifully before my closed eyes, then disappeared. Colours and scents and musical sounds eddied past me, into me, through me. Wilfrid appeared, opened my dressing-gown as if he were unwrapping a packet of *bonbons,* and left no part of me untouched by his hands, his lips. I melted into a pool of sweetness, like a strawberry ice in the sun.

When I awoke, some twenty minutes later, I saw again the letter I had set aside. Feeling little curiosity about its contents, I desultorily opened it and read these surprising words written in a hand I did not recognise:

"Mellisa mine —

"In the dark Walk to night at our Place I will be waiting.

"W"

Immediately, I was overwhelmed with concern for him. He had, obviously, taken a turn for the worse — his wounds had perhaps become infected — and in his pathetic weakness and possible delirium of fever, his mind was so distraught that he could not even spell my name correctly; and the strong bold hand that I had come to know from prior letters was not itself, either, but a poor scrawl.

Then I became alarmed: he was in no condition to venture out into the night air, all the way to Vauxhall Gardens! And why was he risking discovery thus, after all his admonitions about seclusion and secrecy?

Foolish, reckless, brave, *dear* Wilfrid! He was doing it for love, all for love, for love of me! Even after I had said such foul things to him, insulted his race, called him a devious Jew. Oh, my lovely, darling Jew! my Solomon! my David! my singer of psalms! What can I do, king of my heart, but obey your rash command? . . . thus ran the burthen of my boiling thoughts.

And so, after dinner, I changed into my green satin frock and betook myself over the bridge to Vauxhall Gardens.

IX

Torn Asunder

The Dark Walk is aptly named, because of the absence of lamps along its way. Moreover, that night there was no moon, rendering the path veritably like ink. That was good, from Wilfrid's standpoint, but the journey from his Southwark shed, across the river to Vauxhall, surely would expose him to many eyes? I told myself, as I stepped carefully along the Dark Walk, thatt it was his powerful love for me, mingled with the fancies of fever, that had been distilled into his mad daring.

His reference to "our place" surely could have meant no other than the spot where we had lain together in the grass, that night when he had called me his goddesss of love. No other place had been so consecrated as to be called ours. In the blackness of this night, it was only with extreme difficulty that I found what I thought — what I hoped — to be "our place."

Having found it, I stood and waited for him. The heady arboreal scent of the surrounding foliage acted upon me like a rare and soporific incense. It was very quiet: I could faintly hear the musicians in the orchestra pavilion playing the first movement of Beethoven's Pastoral Symphony, *allegro ma non troppo,* described by him as "The awakening of cheerful feelings on arriving in the country." It was pleasant to stand there, hearing those distant strains of music, awaiting my lover; but I quivered with a tremor of apprehension, too, because of his wounds and illness, his need for furtive movement.

Perhaps he would not come. Perhaps he had scrawled that note in a fit of fever, and then had forgotten about it when the fever had passed. Perhaps he was too ill to rise from his cot. Perhaps he had been captured on the way. Perhaps he was dead.

I stifled such morbid speculations and resolved to wait patiently for him, no matter how long it might take. A chill breeze moved in from the river, and I rippled with the cold.

I was filled with humiliation for things I had said to Wilfrid in the past, there in those very Gardens, sitting with him in a supper-box, eating syllabubs. I had laughed about Abraham "Jewing down" the Lord. What a thorn that phrase must have been in his heart! What a cruel, bigoted girl he must have thought me, even then. And yet he had not rebuked me. In his wisdom, he had known that I'd spoken from benighted custom, fashion, ignorance; from a lifetime spent in a house where his father's people were, by a high-ranking man of God, considered to be outcasts, outlaws, allies of the Antichrist, professed enemies of Christianity, haters and killers of Christ. O Wilfrid, I begged silently, can you forgive me?

I *felt,* rather than heard, somebody behind me, midst the trees. "Wilfrid?" I said softly. Then that somebody stepped closer, and I could hear his foot as it trod upon the grass.

"Wilfrid?" I said again, as I felt his body's warmth, and felt his breath on the back of my neck. His arms encircled me from behind, and I felt his lips pressed to the soft skin under my ear. It was in that same moment that I smelt the odour of gin — and divined the knowledge that it had been not only great love and fever delirium that had made him reckless and distorted his handwriting, but Blue Ruin as well. "Gin is evil stuff," he had said once, but now, in his physical pain and distress of mind, denied the comforts that I could offer him, he had been driven to the evil stuff in search of solace. I did not care. Drunk or sober, I adored him.

"My dear love," I said, turning to him. He kissed me fiercely, and ran his hands up and down my body. When he removed his lips from mine, I said, "You are too ill to be here. Let me take you back." He did not reply, but I could sense that he had shaken his head. "If you wish to be alone with me — and it is my wish, too, Wilfrid — why may we not be together in that shed of yours, with John Heathman standing guard outside?"

He seemed almost to bristle at this suggestion, for his body stiffened; but then he chuckled and kissed me again. For one fugitive moment, the fearful thought occurred to me that this man might not be Wilfrid at all, but a stranger, a lurker waiting in the dark for *any* passing woman; that I had come to the wrong place, and that Wilfrid was even now awaiting me elsewhere. "Wilfrid?" I said, anxiously.

Instantly, I was reassured, for he chuckled again and whispered, "Bishop's daughter." The words, although slurred and thickened (no doubt by the gin), confirmed that I was not a stranger to him even in that pitch blackness; that he had been waiting for me, specifically for *me,* the bishop's daughter.

"Brewer's son," I playfully replied.

He laughed softly. The soft laugh continued as he drew me down upon the grass. It did not stop as he roughly lifted my skirts and pulled at my under-garments. "Wilfrid!" I said, reprovingly. "No! Not like this!"

That soft, low laugh turned chilling as it went on and on, never varying, like that of a madman. Gin was evil stuff, indeed, to so distort a man's nature! He was atop me then, and when I reached down to protect myself, I felt the hard unyielding length of his lust against my palm. I caught that thing and tried to push it away from my body, but he seized both of my hands and held them in a grip so cruel that I thought the bones would break, pressing them down into the ground, spread-eagling me as in a wrestler's hold.

I felt the delicate petals of my privities being parted by that awful ram's horn. I cried out, "Wilfrid! No! Please do not!" He continued to laugh in that soft mad way. The relentless shaft invaded my body — I screamed in pain — my maidenhood was torn asunder — it seemed as if my whole body were being torn asunder, and my soul, as well — I despaired — I called upon God to save me from this horror — but still the beast astride me laughed and thrust and pumped without mercy, without tenderness, without love.

"Bishop's daughter," he whispered again in a cloud of disgusting gin; and now I knew the reason for the repeated phrase. Even through my pain, my terror, my humiliation, I knew that his vile act, neither love nor true honest lust, was nothing more than an expression of contempt for a Christian virgin, the daughter of a bishop of Christ; it was the act of a Jew, spitting upon the Cross, defiling Jesus, paying me back for what I'd said to him in that shed.

"Bish——" he started to say again, but in the very midst of the word, he gasped as he spent himself inside me.

Then he rolled his weight off me, rose to his feet, and, laughing again, ran away, into the trees.

X

When a Christian Turns Rogue

Ravaged, weeping, bleeding, in pain, I lay sprawled on the grass, my legs grotesquely apart, my skirt over my face, my under-garments down about my ankles. What an exquisite refinement of the torture it was, I thought bitterly, that Wilfrid deliberately should have chosen to rape me so contemptuously in this place where I had first offered him my love. What a fine, delicious, cruel, Jewish irony!

My hat and one of my shoes had come off: I searched in the dark, on my hands and knees in the grass, until I found them. I struggled to my feet and put my clothes in order as best I could. Then I made my way out of the Dark Walk, some times stumbling against benches. The act of walking was painful to me, for Wilfrid had not been gentle in his violation. I could feel a warm thin trickle of blood making its slow way down my inner thigh.

As I approached the lighted part of the Gardens, my one fear was that I might be seen by somebody who knew me. Head down, I hurried, despite my pain. I was surprised to hear that the orchestra were just beginning to play the second movement of the Pastoral Symphony, *andante molto moto,* the scene at the brook. Far less time had elapsed than I had thought. The serene music of that movement had no soothing effect upon me: rather, it formed a contradictory counterpoint to the turmoil of my feelings.

I walked faster, head still down, my face averted from the eyes of others, until I quite literally bumped into a man. "Excuse me, sir," I murmured, and started to hurry on my way again; but he spoke, in a familiar voice:

"Miss Worthing?"

I looked up at him. He tipped his hat and bowed.

"Why, Mr. Brummel," I said, flustered, "I did not recognise you . . ."

"Little wonder, scurrying along the path as you were, your gaze fixed upon the ground. Will you join me in a fruit punch?"

"No, thank you."

"A custard, perhaps?"

"No . . . I must be on my way . . ."

He peered more closely at me. "Are you unwell, Miss Worthing?"

"I am quite all right, thank you, Mr. Brummel, but I am expected at home, and —"

"Surely you are not here in the Gardens alone?"

"Yes, I am."

"You have no escort?"

"No."

"Then you must permit me to see you safely across the river and to your door."

"Pray do not trouble yourself."

"It is no trouble, but a duty — a pleasurable duty, to be sure — and I would be no gentleman if I did not insist that you allow me to accompany you."

I gave in to him; and, in truth, I felt need of some support. "You are most kind," I said, and took the arm that he offered me.

As we walked, he said, "I fear that you *are* unwell, Miss Worthing. You seem weak, and you are deucedly pale."

"A momentary indisposition, that is all."

"I expect you have caught a chill. There is an unseasonable cool breeze off the river. But, that aside, it is a most pleasant evening, is it not? And that lovely Mozart music they are playing in the pavilion is perfectly enchanting."

"Beethoven," I said.

"Really. Ah well, I have no ear, if truth be known. As I once told Byron, I can barely distinguish between 'God Save the Weasel' and 'Pop Goes the King.' "

I had heard the joke before, and was in no temper for jesting in any case, but still I summoned a small semblance of courteous laughter.

"I have heard the good news of your engagement," he said. "Summerfield seems a splendid fellow. Dresses well for a rustic, too."

"Thank you, Mr. Brummel." I saw no need to tell him more on that subject. "And you," I asked, "have your problems been solved?"

"The Jews still are sniffing me out with their long noses," he replied, "but I hope to outwit them and survive."

"They are a persistent and pernicious people," I said, scarcely succeeding to disguise my bitterness.

"Indeed," he agreed with a sigh, "but I'll say this for the beggars: as bad as they are, there's always a Gentile to be found who is as bad or worse."

"I can not believe that," I said, feelingly.

"It is true, I'm afraid. There's a comedy of Dick Sheridan's, in which a Jewish pedlar tells his son that Gentiles are worse than any Jew in the world, 'for when a Christian turns rogue, he will cheat his father, his mother, and what is worse, the devil himself.' "*

"But that is merely Mr. Sheridan's comedic reversal," I said. "It is like calling a bald man Curly-Top or a fat man Skin-and-Bones. The humour lies in the absurdity of saying something that is the opposite of the actuality."

"Perhaps you are right," Mr. Brummel replied, "and yet, many a truth is spoken in jest."

When, at last, we had reached my house, and Mr. Brummel had helped me out of the hackney-coach he had hired, I said, "I should like to invite you inside, but it is late, and I am feeling very tired, and my sister is not well . . . ."

"Tut, Miss Worthing, say no more. I hope that both you and Mrs. Cooper will soon improve. It was delightful to see you — unplanned meetings are often the best, are they not? — and I will bid you good night."

"Good night, Mr. Brummel, and thank you for your company."

"The pleasure, I assure you, was all mine." He tipped his hat and climbed back into the hackney.

I entered the house.

XI

An Intimate Examination

Rushing past Stewart towards the staircase, I tried to avoid his eyes, hoping to reach my rooms without seeing anybody else, whether a member of the family or of the staff, but he called out to me, "Miss Melissa —"

"I am in somewhat of a hurry, Stewart."

"Yes, Miss. I only wished to say that Mr. Cargrave is here, and is attending your sister."

**Moses and Shadrac, or, A Specimen of Jewish Education*, first performed at Drury Lane, 1784, but never published. The only known copy is a manuscript in the Larpent Collection at the Huntington Library, San Marino, California. — R. R.

"Has she taken a turn for the worse?"

"I do not think so, Miss, but your mother felt it best to send word to him and have him call by."

"Where is Mother, and the rest of the family?"

"Your mother is in Mrs. Cooper's bedroom, with Mr. Cargrave. His lordship is in his study. Mr. Aelfred, of course, is at the theatre."

"Thank you, Stewart. Please instruct Abigail to fetch water for my bath at once; and I should be obliged if you would ask Mr. Cargrave, when he is finished looking after my sister, to come see me in my rooms. I . . . I fell and scraped my knee. It is a trifling thing, but, as long as he is here, I should like him to look at it."

"Yes, Miss. I will tell him."

I reached my rooms without encountering anybody else, and quickly undressed, wrapping myself in my dressing-gown. Abigail followed soon after, with the water.

"Thank you, Abigail. That will be all."

"Don't you want me to help you, Miss?"

"No, I will manage by myself."

When she had left me alone, I threw off the dressing-gown and lowered myself slowly into the tub. I gave out a tiny cry of pain as the hot water touched my injured parts; but soon the bath had a beneficial and soothing effect upon me. The water turned pink with my blood.

I was out of the tub and into my dressing-gown by the time Mr. Cargrave tapped on my sitting-room door. I let him in.

"Good evening, Miss Worthing," the flaxen-haired young physician said with a smile. "What's all this about a scraped knee?"

"Tell me first about my sister. How is she?"

"Fit as a horse," he replied, "from the physical point of view, at least. I am less happy about these delusions from which she suffers. Smelling smoke where there is no smoke. Most peculiar. But it does not worry me overmuch. No doubt it is no more than the change of life, and will pass. Now then: let us look at that knee."

I sat upon my couch, and said, "Mr. Cargrave, will your examination of me be conducted in strictest confidence?"

He smiled again. "Such secrecy about a scratched knee?"

"It is not my knee. I wish you to examine, and treat if need be, a more intimate part."

"By that," he asked, "am I to take it that you mean —"

"Yes, that is precisely what I mean. But I must have your solemn word that you will say nothing of this to my mother or to any other member of my family."

He stroked his silky blond moustache. "Well, you are not a child. You reached your majority some few years since, and therefore have every right to private consultation."

"Thank you. I must ask you one thing more. Was my mother present when Stewart asked you to look at my knee?"

"No, she remained in your sister's room."

"Good," I said with relief. "Had it been otherwise, I should have been forced to ask you to lie to her and tell her some story about my knee."

"I am not averse to the occasional use of my imagination in a good cause, Miss Worthing. And now, if I have passed muster, may I ask you to lie back upon the couch and open your dressing-gown?"

"All the way?" I asked bashfully, as I lay back upon my couch.

"Only as far as that certain intimate part to which you have alluded," he replied, pulling a chair near the couch and sitting down.

I did as he bade me. His fingers were remarkably gentle as he probed and peered, but still I winced with pain.

"Forgive me," he said gently. "I will try not to hurt you again. This injury seems to have been quite recently washed."

"I have just stepped out of my bath."

"Good. That was wise," he said. "You will be happy to learn that the injury is superficial. You have already given it the best treatment. I can leave you an ointment which will soothe the discomfort and speed the healing. Other than that, my only advice is to avoid further activity for a time — in this intimate area."

I coloured deeply. "I intend to avoid it for the rest of my life!" I assured him.

"That was not my prescription," he said, "but you must do as you wish. May I ask you one or two questions, in my professional capacity?"

"If you must."

"I will endeavour to be delicate. Prior to this evening's episode, were you *intacta?*"

"Do you mean was I a virgin? Yes."

"Your partner: is he a friend of yours?"

"He was," I replied bitterly, "but now he is my enemy."

"I am not surprised. Rape is a nasty business, and any man who commits it deserves to be horsewhipped. I have no right, of course, to ask you his identity . . ."

"Nor would I tell you."

"Quite. But — although I assure you that this injury will heal very swiftly — there may be another complication in a few weeks' time. Possibly not; let us hope not; I think you know to what I refer."

"A complication? Do you mean an infection?"

"Your attacker," he said, "this friend who is now your enemy — could you ever find it in your heart to forgive him and welcome him as a friend again?"

"No! Never!" I said vehemently. "Why do you ask such a question?"

Mr. Cargrave replied, "I wished merely to ascertain if marriage with that man is completely out of the question."

"Yes. Completely. As is marriage with *any* man. Why on earth should I ever marry? Can you give me one reason?"

He said, "A husband — either your attacker or some other man — might be a convenient thing to have . . . if, a few weeks from now, you should find yourself to be with child."

XII

A Kind of Caul

"With child!" My hand flew to my mouth. "Merciful Heaven," I said, "I had forgotten about that!"

"Do not upset yourself, Miss Worthing," said Mr. Cargrave. "You may not have conceived to-night. The odds, in fact, are against it, even if the man . . . fulfilled himself, so to speak . . . while he was still . . . that is . . ."

"Even if he discharged his spunk inside me — is that what you mean to say?"

"Very concisely put."

"Thank you. He did."

"That is unfortunate, but not necessarily disastrous; for, as I have just said, the odds are against your having conceived, even if he — if he did what you have described so succinctly. May I ask if he approached you unprepared? — or was he, perhaps, wearing —"

"One of Colonel Cundum's sheep-gut sheaths? He was not."

This time it was Mr. Cargrave who coloured. "I see. Well, we must hope for the best. All may be well. Do not worry."

"I assure you that I *will* worry, Mr. Cargrave — until a sufficient passage of time dispels that worry."

He nodded. "Naturally," he said, and arose from his chair. "You may close your dressing-gown now, if you wish," he added.

Quickly, I did so.

He took a small phial of unction from his bag and placed it on the table next my couch. "I will leave this balm with you. Apply it every morning, and every night before retiring. If you have need of me, do not hesitate to send word." He smiled. "A skinned knee can be a bother, and may need further treatment."

"Thank you, Mr. Cargrave. I am grateful to you."

He closed his bag, and his smile faded. "As a physician," he said, "I am required to be disinterested, dispassionate, to display no emotion, make no moral observations. But when I look upon such youthful beauty as yours, and think of the reprehensible monster who would violate such beauty . . . by God, Miss Worthing, I would happily throttle such a man to death with these hands!"

He held his hands in the air, their fingers curled into menacing claws. Then he dropped his arms to his sides. "I apologise. That was not an ethical thing for a physician to say. Our mission is to save life, not to take it. But some men do not deserve to live. Still, that is not my province. That is what we have hangmen for."

"Rape is not a hanging offence," I reminded him.

"It should be," he replied. "In a just world, it would be." Smiling encouragement to me, he bowed and left my rooms.

As soon as he had closed the door, I sprang to my feet, strode furiously into my bedroom, picked up the Staffordshire shepherd from Wilfrid that stood on the table next my bed, and hurled it with fury against the wall, where it smashed into a hundred shards.

Pregnant?!

Crammed with his brat? That would be the ultimate indignity! Forced to carry his loathly spawn for nine months; to grow swollen and heavy and grotesque; to give it birth in pain and blood and tearing flesh; to *die,* perhaps, in bearing it; or, if I be not granted the mercy of death, to care for it, coo to it, hold it, rock it, kiss it, *love it?*

How could I — how could any woman — love a thing so foully engendered? A creature despicably conceived not in love but in brutality and hatred? What, suckle such a thing at my breast? Intolerable! I would, far rather, *pluck my nipple from its boneless gums and dash the brains out!*

Those awful words of Lady Macbeth's had hitherto seemed the most horrible thing a woman could contemplate or utter; a thought that could not ever be born in the mind of a human female, but only in the dark and soul-less brain of a she-devil. Now *I* had become such a she-devil, for the thought blazed with hellish force and satisfaction through my entire being.

Even hanging was far too mild a punishment for Wilfrid, or for any rapist. I longed to see done to him and to all other vile ravagers of women what the Duke of Cumberland said had been done to Damiens: flesh ripped off with red-hot pincers, molten lead poured into his orifices, then his body torn asunder by four horses — torn asunder as my flesh and spirit had been torn asunder in the Dark Walk! And even *more* should be done to him, my fiendish fancy declared: that weapon of his should be guillotined! *In a just world, it would be,* I told myself, in an echo of Mr. Cargrave's parting words.

I was too angry for tears. My eyes were dry with the cauterising heat of outrage. Yes, I said to myself: gladly could I take the knife myself, a paring knife from Mrs. Cooke's kitchen, and bend over him as he lay naked, chained to the torture-table, and slowly, painfully, bloodily re-circumcise him as he screamed in agony and begged for mercy . . .

My thoughts came to a sudden halt, like a whinnying horse sharply reined in.

Re-circumcise?

I remembered reaching out my hand to protect myself from the attacker crouched over me in the grass. I remembered touching him as I tried to push that horrid object away from my body. I clearly recalled the feel of it against my palm and fingers:

Its ruthless arrow-head — the mouth-piece of the clarinet, as it were — was not a naked beak: rather, it was covered by a protective hood, a sliding, retractable kind of caul, by which I do not mean an appurtenance of dried sheep-gut, but a thing of living skin. I thought of Freddy in the bath, when we were children . . .

And, as if a fork of lightning had flooded my mind with an instant's blaze of brilliance, I knew at once that the man who violated me was not circumcised . . . was not a Jew . . . was *not* Wilfrid!

XIII

A Skinful of Max

But if my violator was not Wilfrid, who *was* he?

Thoughts went rocketing and careening through my head: the man had been no stranger to me, no simple monster lying in wait for any woman who might pass his way. He had known who I was. He had called me "Bishop's daughter."

Moreover, he had known that I would be there, at that exact time, at that exact place in the Dark Walk. Whoever he was, it was *he* who had written the note. That was why the writing was so unlike Wilfrid's.

"Bishop's daughter" had been said with a kind of sneer, I now realised. Was it the sneer of an unbeliever? an atheist? a man like Percy Shelley? But Shelly was in Edinburgh . . . might be have returned to London?

Scurrying out of the Dark Walk, why, of all men, had I run into and nearly bowled over Mr. Brummel? Had it been no more than coincidence? or had it been the *second* time I had encountered him that evening?

He had been cool and immaculate — but he is *always* cool and immaculate; nobody has ever seen him in a fluster. He had been polite and solicitous — but might not that have been his disguise, as well as the ironical sauce to garnish his deed withal?

In the way of irony, was there another meaning to be read into the seemingly blameless words he had uttered as we parted, outside the door of this house? —

The pleasure, I assure you, was all mine.

And what of his remark, a moment before, that *unplanned meetings are often the best* — had that been a satirical reference to a meeting that had been all *too* planned by him? Why had he insisted that when a Christian turns rogue, he can be worse than any Jew — had that been a sly description of himself?

I had, until that moment, thought of Mr. Brummel not only as a friend and a gentleman, but as a person untouched by lust for woman or man. Had I been wrong in that assumption, and was his particular depravity an appetite for rape?

And yet, how could he — or *any* man other than Wilfrid, for the matter of that — have known about "our place" in the Dark Walk?

Had Wilfrid, in the bragging way of men, told others about our escapade in the grass? I could not believe that of him. And, even if he had, is it likely that he would have described the precise location?

Or: had we been seen together, that night? Had my rapist been peering at us from the shadows, as we lay bathed in moonlight?

I am sure that I heard a sound in the trees.

A bird. A cat. The wind.

The reek of gin: it was associated in my mind with people of the lower orders. Could it have been a servant? Blodgett, perhaps? He certainly had a fondness for the female sex. So had Stewart. But even the Prince Regent drinks gin, they say, oft-times laced with laudanum, to dull the pains of his high office and responsibility.

Had it been the Prince?

But now I was entertaining absurd fancies. True, he had pursued me round tables and couches in Carlton House; had put his hands upon me . . . but a prince of royal blood does not skulk about in public gardens on dark nights, raping women.

What, however, of a *duke* of royal blood? What of the Prince's profligate brother, the odious Duke of Cumberland? He had a fearful reputation, by reason of his violent temper, as well as his voracious sexual habits.

Brother, will you not present me to your charming friend?

That, my dear Ernest, would be like presenting a great spider to a pretty little fly.

Flies are disgusting creatures. I *would not compare you to one, Miss Worthing.*

Had it been that great spider who had ravaged me?

Despite the Duke's ill-repute, I was reluctant to think so. Who else might it have been?

Lord Byron? Mr. Lamb? Ridiculous. Mr. Cholmondeley-Cockburn? Assuredly not, for at the very time that I was being raped, he had been playing the part of Mr. Hardcastle on the stage of the Proteus Theatre.

I asked myself if it was possible that the words spoken by my attacker had not been "Bishop's daughter," after all? For, if they had *not* been, then the man might have been completely unknown to me, and I to him. What could *sound* like "Bishop's daughter" and yet be not those words at all? What words or combinations of words sounded like "daughter"? I went through the alphabet: *bought her, brought her, caught her, fought her, sought her, slaughter, taught her, thought her, water* . . .

"Bitch to the slaughter?" No. Too many syllables. "Wish I'd taught her?" Nonsense. "Dish of water?" That, too, made no sense — unless it was a specimen of the vulgar language, like "prime article." Could a pretty woman be known, in the streets, as a dish of water? Freddy would know. I would ask him.

I looked at my clock. Time had flown: it was already past

midnight. Freddy should have returned, but I had not heard him pass on the landing. Perhaps he had gone to DeWitt's with his friends. I decided to wait up for him

It was another half-hour before I heard his familiar step as he walked past my sitting-room. I rushed to the door and opened it. "Freddy?" I spoke quietly, so as not to waken the rest of the family.

"Oh, hullo, Mel, not abed yet?"

"Come in here for a moment. I want to ask you something."

He walked into my sitting-room. "What is it?" he asked, yawning. "I'm mortally tired."

"This will take no time at all. Is there a popular expression, 'dish of water,' referring to a woman?"

He shook his head. "Not that I've heard. And I think that I've heard 'em all. By the way, how's Esmie?"

"Fit as a horse, your friend Mr. Cargrave says."

"Good man, Cargrave. May I be excused now? I've had a long night of it. The play started almost an hour late. Carruthers had to take over the part of Hardcastle at the last moment, and we had to drum the lines into his head. As it was, he missed a few, but on the whole he got through it all right."

"Why did Mr. Carruthers have to play Hardcastle?" I asked.

"Old Chum was 'indisposed.' The truth of it is, he had a skinful of max."

"Max?"

"*You* know. Gin." He yawned again. "Good night, Mel. I'm for Bedfordshire." Yawning a third time, he left my room.

XIV

Return of the Rapist

So Cholmondeley-Cockburn could *not* be disqualified as my attacker! He had been provided with a perfect opportunity to slip out of the theatre unseen, *reeking of gin*.

However, does not gin, and do not other spirits, diminish a man's prowess in matters of venery? Perhaps Chum had not been truly tipsy, but had been dissembling — after all, he was an actor — and had merely gargled a mouthful of gin for the sake of its aroma?

Every man I *knew* was suspect, except Wilfrid — and, of course, Papa and my brothers — but, of them all, the most likely candidate was Chum, a man of notoriously lecherous bent, who had attempted to seduce me within a few seconds of the moment that he first clapped his eyes upon me.

There is a well-stocked apple-dumpling-shop inside that bodice, I'll be bound . . . Virgins do not interest me overmuch. They require too long a time in the breaking-in, and I am a busy man.

Not so long, really, I thought angrily: just a few minutes in the grass, less time than it takes to play the first movement of the Pastoral Symphony. Even a busy man like you, Mr. Chum, could accomplish it easily.

Ah, his bit of crackling, are you? Lucky young devil, he had said enviously, thinking Freddy to have been my lover. The more I thought about Chum, the more certain I became that he was the man who had attacked me. How could I prove it?

By his handwriting! I opened the drawer of my desk and found the note I thought to have been written by Wilfrid. I scanned it again. To what could I match it, however? I had never received a letter from Chum. And then, with a little cry of triumph, I espied a thick sheaf of manuscript in the drawer, under the stacks of letters and stationery. I pulled it out, laughing exultantly.

The Dandy's Deception,

OR,

An Exquisite Unmask'd

A COMEDY

by Humphrey Cholmondeley-Cockburn

So read the title page, in Chum's "own fair hand," as Freddy had told me. The manuscript had been hidden in my desk ever since the time when I had been secretly helping Freddy to commit his part to memory. I placed the play next to the note and compared the writing of them.

Even without turning to the first scene of the play, I could see that the two hands were markedly different. The note was written in a pinched and broken scrawl; the play was in a rolling, flamboyant script. Could drink have wrought so great a difference in a person's engrained custom of writing? Individual letters were different, as well: the *s*'s of "Dandy's," "Exquisite," and "Unmask'd" were identical to each other, but far from similar to the single *s* of the note's misspelled "Mellisa." The small second *d* in "Dandy" did not remotely resemble the note's small *d* in "dark." Neither *l* of "Cholmondeley" looked like any of the *l*'s in "Mellisa," "Walk," "Place," or "will." And there were other dissimilarities.

I read over the note again:

"Mellisa mine —

"In the dark Walk to night at our Place I will be waiting.

"W"

Chum could have misspelled my name in haste or nervousness, I suppose, but he was an educated man, with a good command of the language: would he have used a capital *W* in "Walk" but a small *d* in "dark," when the correct way is to use capital letters in both words, not only in the noun? Would he have used a capital *P* in "Place"? Such proliferation of capital letters went out of fashion early in the last century — in England, at any rate. Would Chum have spelt "to-night" as two separate words: "to night"? Would he have placed the verb, "waiting," at the end of the sentence? — it had such an awkward, backwards look to it.

I recalled the slurred and thickened sound of the words "Bishop's daughter" when spoken by my attacker. I had thought the thickening to have been caused by gin, but the true reason, I now told myself, may have been that he had not actually said "Bishop's daughter" at all, but its closely resemblant counterpart in his native tongue.

The man who had scrawled that note, asking me to meet him at a place to which undoubtedly he had followed Wilfrid on a prior occasion and had spied upon us from the trees; the man who had raped me —

I felt a cold draught through the silk of my dressing-gown. It was blowing into my sitting-room through the open door of my adjoining bedroom. I walked into the bedroom just as my attacker entered through the window.

XV

Blood for Blood

I tried to scream, but I could not summon up the slightest sound from my throat. I turned to run back into my sitting-room, but he bounded across the floor in a second, standing between me and the bedroom door. Now, never taking his eyes from me, he shut that door, thereby putting the two thick closed doors of my bedroom and sitting-room between me and the similarly closed rooms of the rest of the house. If I screamed, the sound would be so muffled that it was unlikely to be heard — particularly by sleeping people.

That chilling, low, incessant laugh was issuing from his parted lips. Those boiled-gooseberry eyes of his never left mine.

I managed to whisper, "What do you want, John?"

"In the dark," he said softly, "I think I am not seen. But I must be certain making."

I pretended to not understand him. "What do you mean? And why do you enter by way of the window? You know that you are always welcome here, through the front door."

He was not sure of me. His eyes narrowed as he tried to ascertain whether I was, as I pretended, unaware of the identity of my attacker, or merely simulating that unawareness.

I continued to speak: "I own that it is very late, but that is all the more reason not to climb through windows. What if you had been seen doing so? Why, you might have been apprehended as a burglar! Let me ring for the butler, and order you some brandy . . ."

He shook his head, frowning malignly. His voice was a low growl. "*Nein,* you are thinking me a fool. You *are* knowing! In the *morgen,* you are telling! My name you are telling, *nicht wahr?* To Herr Vilfrid, to *alles* you are telling . . ."

He began to move towards me, his large strong hands held out before him. "There in the dark it should have been, the killing. But I think I am not seen. 'Vilfrid,' you are saying. 'Brewer's son.' But I must be certain making, so I am coming here — and you are *knowing,* and you must be now *dying!"*

I began to step slowly aside, saying, "John, listen to me. No man has ever been hanged for raping a woman. But *murdering* a woman is another matter. I have seen such a man hanged. Have you? It is not a pleasant thing. It is not quick. It is slow, John. You will kick and twitch as you strangle in the noose. Your eyes will pop from your head. Your tongue will hang out of your mouth. Your face will blacken. And still you will be alive — until the hangman takes hold your ankles and pulls down on them till your neck breaks . . ."

My words had no effect upon him. He continued to advance towards me, hands extended. My eyes darted about, looking for a weapon, anything with which to strike out at him and defend myself. My fingers sought the porcelain shepherd on my night table — until I remembered that I had smashed it, and silently cursed my childish tantrum.

He lunged — and encircled my throat with his hands. His fingers were like an iron collar, swiftly tightening on my neck. I felt my windpipe being crushed. I tried to breathe, but could not. I began to sink to the floor, but still he did not let loose his grip upon me.

"Bischofs Tochter," he snarled with loathing. *"Du bist eine Hure! Du bist eine schamlose Hure!"* His hate-blasted face rippled before my eyes as I fought, in vain, for air. "In the grass I see what you are doing . . . you and Herr Vilfrid . . . you and the *Jude!* No lady would do such filth . . . only a *Hure!"*

My hands flailed in spasms, like flopping, gasping fish pulled from the water. I felt a sudden pain in my right palm — I had cut it on some sharp object that was lying on the floor. My fingers closed on that object — a jagged piece of the broken figurine. Seizing that piece, I struck out wildly at John's face with all my strength.

He screamed, let go my throat, and covered his left eye with his hand. *"Gott im Himmel!"* he cried. Blood oozed between his fingers. I struck again with the dagger of porcelain, this time sinking it deep into his other eye. As I withdrew my weapon, the eye came from its socket in a gush of blood and slime, dangling from his face on red strings.

He howled and reared backwards, stumbling against furniture, knocking over chairs and tables. Though blinded, he could feel the cool breeze blowing through the open window, and some beast-instinct sent him reeling towards that nearest means of escape, and through it, hurtling to the garden below, screaming in pain and rage as he fell.

Quickly I ran to the window, leant out of it, and looked down. The fall was a short one, and had been broken by hedges. He was already rising to his knees, then to his feet, and then he was running, staggering, both blood-drenched hands pressed to his face, tracing a crazed and crooked path as he ran, like a frothing dog, out of our garden, onto the street, into the engulfing night.

I looked down at my own blood-dripping hand. The sliver of porcelain, incarnadined with gore, was still gripped tightly in it. The little shepherd's head and shoulders formed a crude handle and hilt, and a jagged long appended piece of one arm served as the blade. I opened my fingers to drop the weapon to the floor, but it stuck horribly to my palm, glued there by the thick blood and other suetty matter. Shuddering, I shook my hand until the awful thing thumped down upon the carpet.

Not precisely the ancient Jewish justice of eye for eye, I told myself; but, rather, blood for blood. In the Dark Walk, he had violently gouged me until I'd screamed and bled; now I had done the same to him. I felt neither remorse nor triumph. I felt nothing.

Methodically, numbly, I washed the blood from my hands; soaked a handkerchief in water and cleaned more blood from my dressing-gown and carpet, then cleaned up all other blood spots I could find; wrapped the gory porcelain splinter in the handkerchief, together with the other pieces of the broken figurine, and threw them into the commode. Just as methodically, moving through all of this like a mindless clock-work doll, I closed and locked the window.

Then, those things done, I was overwhelmed by a black tidal wave, and collapsed to the floor in a faint.

XVI

From Darkness into Light

How long I lay there sprawled upon the carpet, I do not know. In that state of suspended life, that state resembling sleep yet which was not sleep, I was beset by visions or dreams, I know not what to call them; pictures let us say, but active pictures, scenes imbued with movement and strange life.

I saw a naked man, glinting light from every facet of his body like a great, animated diamond. He walked on clouds as if they were solid earth; and descended through roofs and ceilings as if they were as insubstantial as clouds.

He came unto a woman who was as naked and as beautiful as he, and so blinding-radiant that her face, like his, was too dazzling for me to see clearly. She opened her glowing arms to him, and they cleaved together in the act of love.

I felt no shame as I watched them in their slow and silent loving, for it was as if I saw the mating of seraphim, of purest spirit uncorrupted by flesh, with nothing of the animal about it: no sweating, grunting, panting labour; no seeping or dripping lubricity; no stains; only a gentle pulsation.

The shining goddess, when their sweet, sublime rite was done, addressed her numinous consort as Balthasar, saying that her sister was in dire case, indeed in hazard of her life.

This was already made plain to him, he gave her to know, but he was powerless to help her, being a creature of spirit.

And even you, my love, he added, have no more substance than a nimbus round the moon when you are in my arms thus, for the gross corporeal part of you lies asleep, whilst this beloved being I embrace, this dear one so exuberant, alive, and passionate, dwells on another plane for these few precious moments of my visit.

But I fear that she may die.

If it is to be that she must die to-night, replied her lover, then she will die; but what of that? Do you not know, have I not shewn you, that death is but a simple step from darkness into light? Life on this plane is not life at all, but a sentence in prison, the while we are loaded with heavy chains, locked within a cell of rough cold stone, breathing the foul miasma of a cistern.

And yet I must go to her.

In this state, he said, you can not be of help to her; but now I must take my leave of you, and when I am gone, this Self of yours that I hold and kiss will sink back into its slumbering carapace; and it may be that some delicate remembrance of your fear will linger, like a thread of incense, in your dreams . . .

"Lissa? Lissa?"

Esmie's voice was calling to me in the dark.

"Lissa, wake up." I felt a cool hand on my brow. I opened my eyes.

"Oh, thank God," said Esmie, who was kneeling beside me, clad only in her night-dress, without even dressing-gown or slippers. I was still stretched out upon the carpet, near my bedroom window.

"Speak to me, Lissa," she said.

"Esmie . . ."

"How do you feel?"

"Cold."

"Yes, your skin is like ice to the touch. Come, you must get into your bed. Can you stand up?"

"I . . . think so . . ."

With her help, I managed to climb into my bed. She drew the coverlet around me.

"What happened?"

"Nothing," I said, for I did not want to tell anybody about the rape, or the rapist's return.

"But you were lying on the floor."

"I felt faint, so I went over to the window to open it. I needed a breath of air. But before I could unlock it . . . everything became dark. I suppose I must have swooned."

"Do you feel ill?"

"Not at all. Just very tired. Will you sit here until I fall asleep?"

"Of course. Shall I blow out the candles?"

"No."

"Very well. Now close your eyes."

I did, but soon opened them again and asked her, "Esmie? How does it happen that you have come to my bedroom at this hour? Did I cry out? Did I waken you?"

"Perhaps you did," she replied. "And yet, if you *had* cried out behind these closed doors, I do not think that I could have heard you in my sleep."

"Then . . . why . . ."

She shook her head. "I do not know. I awoke suddenly, and thought: Lissa is in danger. So I sprang from my bed and ran to your room, and there you were on the floor. For a moment, I thought that you were dead, and I almost screamed. But then I saw that you were breathing."

"Breathing . . ." I said. "Speaking of that, does not your nearness to me suffocate you with smoke? Mamma said —"

"No," she replied flatly. "That fancy of mine has departed as mysteriously as it came upon me."

"Ah, good. I am so glad."

I closed my eyes again, and soon I was fast asleep.

XVII

Murder Most Foul

I spent the entirety of the following day in my bed, recovering from the powerful series of physical and emotional buffetings that I had undergone. I told Mamma that it was my time of the month — and, in point of fact, it was close enough to that time that she did not question it. The bruises on my throat, from John Heathman's fingers, were quite faint, I was happy to see, and they were easily covered by a bit of powder. The pain of the other injury inflicted by him earlier that evening subsided rapidly, helped by Mr. Cargrave's ointment. I speak of the fleshly pain only; for the anguish of my mind caused by that rape took far longer to subside, and may never entirely disappear.

The day after that, I received by the morning post a rather bulky letter from Wilfrid. Removing its cover, I saw that another letter from him was inside, in yet another cover, somewhat rumpled and stained, and this was wrapped in a short note:

"My dear Melissa, —

"A terrible thing has happened. The body of a friend of mine has been discovered on a bank of the Thames, foully murdered. You knew him, too: young John Heathman. He had been killed in a particularly brutal fashion, by the gouging out of his eyes, so viciously that the violence done to his brain, and the severe loss of blood, caused his death. He was faithful and loyal to me, and I shall miss him sorely. Now it is my painful duty to write to his parents in Austria, and tell them the news. He was not even twenty. Who could have done such a thing, and why? . . ."

John Heathman dead! Killed by my hand! I was shocked, but not saddened. The man had been a vile rapist and a would-be murderer: a few moments more, and *I* would have been the corpse. Nor had he been "faithful and loyal" to Wilfrid: he had hated him and his father for being Jews, and felt no gratitude for the opportunity generously presented him by the elder Mr. Summerfield. He resented the very love that Wilfrid and I felt for each other, and sought by several means to rend us apart: first, by "accidentally" mentioning Wilfrid's *Verlobter;* and, when that did not have the desired effect, by telling me that Wilfrid was a Jew. Finally, pretending to be Wilfrid, and fired by the false courage of gin, he had raped me. He had been a loathsome knave, devoured by envy and hatred, bent on destroying the happiness — and even the lives — of others. I could not mourn his death or regret my killing of him. But was it necessary to tell Wilfrid any of this? Would it not be best to remain silent about it all?

I returned to his note:

"I had given John a letter to post to you, but the poor fellow never had the opportunity to do so. It was only by the finding of it in his pocket, in fact, that the authorities, seeing the brewery's name and mine on the cover, traced him to me and learnt his identity. That letter is enclosed herein. I entreat you to read it.

"In truth,
"Wilfrid"

Quickly, I tore open the older letter and read it:

"My dear Melissa, —

"I know that you have said you wish never to see me again, but I can not let you go out of my life without asking you to let me have one more meeting with you.

"In your note — which has just been handed to me by John, after your cruel departure — you said I spoke nonsense when I asked if you wished to cancel our engagement. 'Nothing that you have done could ever compel me to do that,' you wrote.

"Nothing that I have done? — and yet you will break off with me because of something that I *am;* something over which I have no control; something, moreover, that is no shame, but a source of pride to me — albeit a secret pride, a secret made necessary and forced upon me by English bigotry.

"I can not bring myself to think that you are no better than Olivia; that you are as stupid, as shallow, and as heartless as she and her family. Write to me, at the brewery, I beg of you, and tell me when and where we may meet and talk. If you wish me not to come to your house, I will meet you anywhere else that you may say.

"I remain
"Your ever-loving
"Wilfrid"

I reached for my pen — but set it down again. I would not write to him. I would go to him, at once. I rang for Stewart, and told him to instruct Tuttle to have the coach readied for me immediately. Pausing only to dab some Cologne water behind my ears and to put on my hat, I fairly ran downstairs and out of the house, into the waiting coach. The weather was uncomfortably close and humid.

"To the shops, Miss?" Tuttle asked.

"No: to the Summerfield brewery in Southwark."

"Yes, Miss."

When we reached the brewery, I told Tuttle to drive to the shed in the rear. But when I opened the door of the shed, I found it to be empty. Climbing into the coach again, I told Tuttle, "Go round to the front."

As I entered the main offices of the brewery, I reasoned that Wilfrid's absence from the shed was a good sign: it meant that he had sufficiently recovered to vacate that sordid hovel.

Wilfrid's stern, be-spectacled clerk, seeing me enter, walked up to me and asked, "May I be of help to you, Miss?"

"I wish to speak to Mr. Summerfield."

"I am Mr. Summerfield's clerk," he said, "but I am afraid that —"

A man appeared from an inner office — well dressed, of pleasant features and fair complexion, in early middle age. He addressed the clerk: "What is it, Cavendish?"

"This lady says that she wishes to see Mr. Summerfield, sir."

Turning to me, the man said, "Will you step into this office, please? I am Mr. Summerfield."

XVIII

Circumstantial Evidence

"I beg your pardon?" I said.

"And whom do I have the pleasure of addressing?" he asked, not unkindly.

"My name is Melissa Worthing."

"Ah, yes," he said, with a gentle smile. "Please come this way," he added, leading me towards the door of Wilfrid's office. To the clerk, he said, "Cavendish, I will receive no callers whilst Miss Worthing is with me."

"Yes, Mr. Summerfield."

(Was this the latest of Wilfrid's secrets? — that his name was neither Summerfield nor Sommerfeld? — that he was not fish nor fowl nor good red herring, but an imposter, a confidence trickster?)

Inside the office, the man who called himself Mr. Summerfield bade me sit down. He sat behind a large desk. "This is Wilfrid's office, of course, not mine," he said. "I happened to be in London to buy books, and he asked me to look after matters in his absence. Your visit is most opportune, for I had intended to call on *you* this morning, at his request. I am his brother, Roger."

"You do not look like him," I said with suspicion.

He laughed lightly. "That is true. I resemble Father, and Wilfrid is the image of our mother." How odd, I thought: for Roger's small nose, blue eyes, and other features gave him a more Gentile appearance than Wilfrid; and yet it was their father, not their mother, who was Jewish. "Have you visited this office before?" he asked.

"Yes, once," I said. "Please tell me —"

"It is rather bare, is it not?" he remarked, looking about the place. "I some times chide my brother by calling his tastes monastic — although, in truth, I am more monkish than he; and yet, if it were mine, I should have it decorated richly. However, that is neither here nor there, for I am but a temporary occupant and will be enjoying these premises only until he returns." His face clouded. "If he returns."

"Where *is* he, for the love of God?" I almost shouted.

"Forgive me. You do not know, of course. I am sorry to tell you that he is in Newgate Prison."

"What?!"

He nodded. "On a charge of murder."

'Murder! Whom is he suspected of —" But, needless to say, I could guess.

"A lad named John Heathman, who worked for him," he replied. "The fellow was found shockingly butchered. As I understand it, some scrap or other of brewery stationery was found upon the body, and this led the authorities here. Wilfrid was able to identity the cadaver, and no more was said at the time, but on the following day, the authorities returned and took Wilfrid in charge, accusing *him* of doing the deed."

"But why?"

Roger Summerfield spread his hands in a gesture of helplessness. "When the officers came here to interview Wilfrid, they found him not in his office, but in a *shed* at the rear. I don't know why he should have been there. He also appeared to have been recently in a fight. He was bruised and cut. It looked very much as if he were in hiding. They reasoned — not without cause, I must admit — that he and Heathman had fought, that Wilfrid had mortally wounded his opponent, that Heathman had fled and died on a riverbank, and that Wilfrid, terrified of the consequences of his act, had hidden in that shed. Wilfrid, of course, denies all of this."

"Naturally. He is innocent."

"I should like to believe that," Roger replied, "and I will do all that I can to help him. But he can offer no defence. When he is asked how he received his injuries, he tells a story about being set upon by bandits late at night in the street. Why did he not report the incident? He has no satisfactory answer. Why was he hiding in the shed? 'It is my shed, and it is my business,' he says — a reply that does not inspire belief in his innocence."

"*I* believe in his innocence," I said.

He smiled. "You are understandably biased on his behalf, Miss Worthing."

"Are not *you* so biased, as his brother?"

"I love him," he replied, "but I can not swallow his makeshift story of street bandits; and I can not, for the very life of me, understand why he was in that shed! Something is rotten in the state of Denmark."

"And yet," I insisted, "we must stand behind him."

"Of course we must," he agreed, "and we will. All the resources of the family will stand behind him. Our solicitor will engage the very best barrister."

"My father is a peer and a clergyman," I pointed out. "Our family are well known to the Prince Regent, and my elder brother is one of his architects. My twin brother is a famous actor. I am affianced to Wilfrid. Surely all of these considerations must carry weight."

"I think that they do and they will," he said. "We can only pray that they will carry weight sufficient enough to *out*weigh the evidence that is being marshalled against him."

"That evidence, so called, is merely circumstantial," I reminded him.

"Men have been hanged on such evidence," he responded.

"Do not say that!"

"I am sorry, Miss Worthing."

"Call me Melissa, I pray you. I shall soon be your sister-in-law. And, if I may, I will call you Hodge."

He winced slightly. "Please do not," he requested. "I have always disliked Wilfrid's nickname for me. Dr. Johnson had a cat named Hodge. But I do beseech you to call me Roger."

"Very well, Roger," I replied. "And now I will tell you that I do not merely think or hope that Wilfrid did not kill John Heathman. I *know* that he did not."

He smiled indulgently, as at a child. "And how could you possibly know that?"

"Because —"

I intended to say "Because *I* killed him," but I thought: What would the authorities make of my wild tale? Raped by Heathman in Vauxhall Gardens; then accosted by him again in my bedroom; faced by strangulation at his hands; defending myself with a bit of broken porcelain . . . I could not even shew them the pieces of the figurine or the bloody handkerchief, for the chamber-maid had emptied the commode. Would it not be thought that I was making up a fantastic story to save my lover, my husband-to-be? Was not the false evidence against him far more believable than the truth I could offer? Hiding in a shed, nursing bruises and cuts . . . everything was arsey-varsey! . . . would Wilfrid escape punishment as the leader of the Luddites, which he was, only to be hanged as a murderer, which he was not?

"Yes, Melissa?" said Roger. "Because . . . ?"

"Because," I replied, "Wilfrid was with me, in my bedroom, all of that night."

XIX

Warts and All

"Is this true?" Roger demanded of me.

"I am prepared to swear to it."

A smile of crafty amusement crinkled his eyes, and for the first time he reminded me very much of Wilfrid. "I note that you do not answer my question," he said, "but let that pass. Have you considered the consequences of such a statement? The shame, the scandal, not only for yourself, but for your family, as well? You, the daughter of a bishop . . ."

"Precisely because I *am* the daughter of a bishop," I said, "they will tend to believe me. A bishop's daughter has much more to lose by such an admission than another woman."

He nodded. "You have a point. But they may still take into account your love for him, and dismiss your confession for that reason. Could you, if pressed, prove that Wilfrid had been with you?"

"Perhaps not," I replied, "but I could provide evidence as circumstantial and forceful as theirs, if need be."

"What kind of evidence?"

"If I must, I will tell that to the proper authorities, at the proper time."

"Of course," said Roger. "Do you know, I am beginning to become encouraged, Miss Wor—— Melissa. I see a ray of hope. Nor do I think that your reputation need be blemished by your disclosure. It may be possible for your testimony to be heard privately *in camera* by a judge. The barrister will try to arrange that. He will no doubt mention your father's high ecclesiastical office, my own family's prominence, your delicate position as an unmarried lady of good background. He will appeal to the gallantry of the judge, as well as to his sense of propriety, and so on. It is often an advantage to be well connected. It is unjust, it is unfair, but it is damned convenient."

"I like your plan, Roger," I said. "Let us proceed at once to carry it out."

He got up from behind Wilfrid's desk and paced the room, scratching his head. "First, a rehearsal is in order. Let us pretend that I am the judge. You are sitting in his chamber. You have already told him that Wilfrid could not have killed Heathman because he was with you. Now I — the judge — say to you: What proof do you offer, Miss Worthing?"

I hesitated, not sure what I should reveal to this stranger; but a rehearsal was certainly a good idea; and, besides, I had taken an immediate liking to Wilfrid's brother; and so I said:

"I can offer you the testimony of a physician, who examined me after Wilfrid Summerfield had taken my maidenhead, and who asked if the man who did it was a friend of mine. He will testify that I said he *had* been a friend but was now an enemy. That remark, sir, was merely the result of a passing anger. Wilfrid, my betrothed, had been driven by such a hunger of desire that he had taken me stormily, recklessly, overcome as he was by ardour. Perhaps the fault was partly mine, for inflaming him. He did me some minor injury, even, in the rash blindness of his frenzy. The physician called the injury superficial and gave me an ointment for it. My anger with Wilfrid subsided quickly, for he was very contrite and begged my forgiveness."

Still playing the part of the judge, Roger asked, "Did this physician examine you in his consulting rooms?"

"No, in my house. My sitting-room."

"Not in your bedroom? That would seem to be the customary and more convenient place for such an examination."

"Wilfrid was still in my bed."

"Was the physician aware of that?"

"No, sir."

"Then he can not swear to it."

"No, but I can, and I will."

"My dear young lady," said Roger in stern mummery, "am I expected to believe that you sent for a physician immediately upon completing an act of venery?"

"No, sir. The physician can confirm that he was already in our house that night, treating my sister for a minor complaint. I knew this, and because I was bleeding and in pain . . ."

(I prayed that the staff would not be questioned, for Stewart had seen me entering the house. That was the weakest link in my chain of lies.)

"Yes, yes. Continue," said Roger.

"That is all."

Roger frowned, in his *rôle* of judge. "All? It is flimsy stuff. Perhaps you *were* with a man that night — but how am I to know that the man was Summerfield? Can you describe any identifying feature of his body — any wart or mole or other thing in a place ordinarily concealed by his clothing?"

"Pardon me, Roger," I said, slipping out of our rehearsal for a moment. "Is a judge likely to ask such a question?"

"He may," Roger replied casually. "If you were able to tell him that Wilfrid has, let us say, a large diamond-shaped mole on his left inner thigh, and they were to examine their prisoner and find such a mole, it would surely help to corroborate your story."

I retorted, "Even if Wilfrid has such a mole, would I necessarily have seen it? Do lovers customarily make love with all the candles ablaze? Does a woman examine her man with a magnifying glass from head to foot? You said it would help to corroborate my story. Why do you call it a 'story,' not testimony? I believe that you think me to be lying, and that your question about moles and warts was meant to satisfy *you,* Roger, not our imaginary judge."

He smiled. "You have caught me out," he said. "I confess that the rough, inconsiderate brute that you describe does not sound to me like my brother. And yet I want to believe, for his sake, that you are telling the truth. To tell lies to a judge would not be wise: he will not be a stupid man, and he will try to trick you into betraying yourself, if you lie to him. Yes, Melissa: before you face the judge, and even before you face the barrister, I would feel much more at ease if I knew that your testimony were true. And so you must forgive me if I ask you again — not as a judge, but as Roger Summerfield — whether Wilfrid has any unusual birthmarks or scars or —"

"Scars?" I said. "The only scar I could discover, if it can be called that, is one similar to that which presumably could be found in exactly the same place on your own body, and on your father's: the scar of a simple surgical operation that is seldom, if ever, performed on Christian infants. Does that satisfy you, Roger?"

"It does," he replied. "And now, to bring our rehearsal to an end: Did anybody witness Wilfrid Summerfield entering your house and your bedroom that night?"

"Of course not, sir! He was very circumci—— circumspect. My father is a bishop, after all!"

"How did he, in fact, enter your bedroom?"

"By way of the window."

"The window!"

"Yes, sir. No doubt, if you were to examine our garden, you would find evidence of his entrance — and, more particularly, of his exit; for, as he left, just before dawn, he fell, somewhat damaging a hedge, as well as himself. He sustained some cuts and bruises from the fall."

"He told us that he received those injuries from street bandits."

"He was protecting my reputation; do you not see?" Then, falling into the part of supplicant, I histrionically concluded, "Oh, *please,* sir, do not tell my father, I beg of you!"

Roger laughed. "Very good, Melissa. I think that any English judge would be moved by chivalry, and by the credibility of your testimony, to believe you and to let the matter go no farther than his chamber. That, of course, leaves the question of Wilfrid hiding in the shed, but I do not think that the judge will place importance on that one point, if we satisfy him on the others."

"He was hiding in the shed," I suggested, "until his injuries healed. He did not wish to be asked questions about them — again because of my reputation."

Roger nodded. "Plausible," he said. Then he looked at me piercingly. "You *can,* if need be, produce that physician?"

"Yes," I assured him.

"Excellent." Roger looked at me again. "That business about your garden . . ."

"You can see the broken hedge for yourself."

He nodded. "Good. You know, I had not realised that my brother was such a lusty rascal. Climbing into bedroom windows! Really! And his rough treatment of you truly is inexcusable. Such conduct can not be condoned."

"I have forgiven him," I said, "and so must you."

"Well spoken. My brother has found a treasure in you, Melissa. I hope that he appreciates you. And now, we must pay a visit to the Summerfield solicitor, Mr. Barstow. He will engage a barrister, and you must hold another rehearsal for him."

"My coachman is waiting outside."

"Dismiss him. We will take a hackney."

"Why?"

"The fewer people who know your comings and goings today, the better. I am sure that your coachman is a trustworthy fellow, but . . ."

"I quite understand."

We left the brewery; I dismissed Tuttle; Roger hailed down a hackney-coach; and we were on our way.

XX

Nothing But the Truth

The following day, I went through another rehearsal for Mr. Lowell West, the barrister engaged for us by Mr. Barstow. The day after that, I was summoned to Mr. West's office in a great rush. Roger was already there.

Mr. West said, "We are in luck. I have found a judge, Sir Desmond St. Cloud, who has agreed to see us in" — he glanced at his watch — "three quarters of an hour. Come, we must hurry."

In the barrister's carriage, on the way to the obliging judge, Roger said, "I admire the despatch with which you have arranged this meeting, Mr. West."

"Sir Desmond will leave London on holiday to-morrow," said Mr. West, "so I pressed him on a 'now or never' basis. He owes me a favour, you see — I sponsored him for acceptance into my very excellent club, Almack's. Besides," he added, "he happens to be my brother-in-law."

Sir Desmond St. Cloud kept us waiting outside his chamber for over half an hour, but he apologised for this when he finally appeared.

"Pray pardon this delay," he said. "The city chamberlain required my assistance in explaining to Princess Caroline that, on no account, could her lady-in-waiting be confined in Little Ease for a week, stark naked if you please, because she had offended Her Highness in some trifling way. Perhaps it is the custom in her native Germany — I do not know — but we do not lock up ladies of quality in that manner here. Please step into my chamber, Miss Worthing, Mr. West. And, Mr. Summerfield, you will oblige me by waiting here."

I need not recount our entire meeting with Sir Desmond, for the proceedings went very much as I had rehearsed them, save for insignificant differences in sequence and choice of words, various repetitions of Sir Desmond's (no doubt to catch me out in lies), and things of that nature. I was not asked for a catalogue of Wilfrid's warts and scars.

"Miss Worthing," Sir Desmond said, near the conclusion of the interview, "I hope that you are aware that there are certain clouded points in your testimony."

"Do you mean untruths, sir?" I asked, sharply.

"That is not what I said. I merely meant that one or two points can not be proved, and we have only your word for them. Mr. Summerfield lying in your bed whilst you were being examined in your sitting-room, for example. The physician can attest to the examination, perhaps, but not to the presence of Mr. Summerfield, or indeed of anybody, in the adjoining bedroom. Then there is the matter of Mr. Summerfield's leaving your house just before dawn. He may have left much earlier than that, immediately after his episode with you, falling upon that hedge it may be, but nonetheless in plenty of time to kill John Heathman. In fact, Miss Worthing, if you were so angry with him because of his rough use of you that you told the physician Mr. Summerfield had become your enemy, is it likely that you would have permitted him to tarry there in your bed, in amorous dalliance, until dawn?"

I cast down my eyes, tried to summon a blush, and coyly replied, "A woman's anger can be dispelled by her lover's caresses . . . Surely you know that, Sir Desmond?"

He sighed, and nodded.

"And surely you know two other things, my dear Desmond," added Mr. West.

"What two other things?"

"First: that Wilfrid Summerfield is not required to prove his innocence; the law is required to prove his guilt. Second: that the 'clouded points' you speak of are small indeed when measured against the great gaping chasms in that patchwork of so-called evidence against him. Do you have a motive? No. Do you have any reason to suspect that there may have been hostility between the two men? You have not. On the contrary, everybody will tell you that Wilfrid Summerfield cherished John Heathman as if he were a brother."

"That remains to be seen," said Sir Desmond, solemnly. He turned to me. "I will now require of you the name of your physician and where he may be found." He dipped his pen in his inkpot and prepared to take down the information.

I said, "His name is Julian Cargrave —"

"Cargrave?" Sir Desmond looked up from his pen-point. "Young fellow? Blond hair? Moustache?"

"Why, yes, sir. Do you know him?"

"He saved my grandson's life. Surely you remember, Lowell?" Mr. West nodded. Sir Desmond went on: "The boy was suffering from a severe case of putrid throat.* He could not breathe. My daughter had given him up for dead. She was hysterical. Victims of that disease often die on the seventh day. On the sixth day, when all hope seemed lost, my son-in-law called in young Cargrave. He took one look at the child and said, 'I suppose that my predecessor has been giving him emetics and purges?' The reply was yes. 'Then the wonder is that he's not already dead,' Cargrave said. 'The poor lad's body is almost depleted of fluid.' Well, the long and the short of it is that he pulled the boy through. I do not know how he did it, but my grandson is alive to-day. Yes, Miss Worthing, indeed I do know Mr. Cargrave." He put down his pen, and did not write the name.

"I will speak a word in one or two ears," he said. "I have small doubt that Wilfrid Summerfield will be out of gaol and breathing the fresh air again before the sun has set. As for that broken hedge beneath your window: it happens that I live not far from your house in Hans Town. If, to-night after my dinner, I pass your garden during my evening stroll, and stop to admire the foliage, no doubt I will be satisfied, and your right reverend father need not be troubled by official callers."

Mr. West and I rose from our chairs.

"I thank you from the bottom of my heart, Sir Desmond," I said. "May I ask one thing more of you?"

"What is it?"

"I desire you to say nothing to Wilfrid of our meeting. It would embarrass him to know that I spoke of such things."

"I quite understand. He will be told no more than that the charge against him has been dismissed."

*Diphtheria. The modern term was coined fifteen years later, in 1826, by Pierre Bretonneau. — R. R.

"May God bless you," I said.

"May He bless you, as well, Miss Worthing. You are exceptional. I know it was no easy task for a young lady to come here and speak to me of such delicate matters."

"I spoke nothing but the truth," I lied.

"And the truth will set him free," said Sir Desmond.

XXI

One of Life's Greatest Pleasures

Roger was waiting for us anxiously when we left Sir Desmond's *sanctum sanctorum.* His eyes searched my face. I winked at him and smiled. We thanked Mr. West, and he took his leave. Soon, sitting in a hackney-coach, I recounted the entire meeting to Roger.

"I am very glad," he said when I had finished. "Was the old gentleman very frightening?"

"Not half so frightening as you were, as the mock-judge," I assured him. A moment later, I added, "Roger, will you do me a great favour?"

"Anything," he declared.

"You will be waiting at Newgate for Wilfrid when he is released, will you not?"

"Yes."

"Will you, please, say nothing to him of my testimony; and will you say nothing to suggest that you know about his window escapade?"

Roger did not respond immediately. When he did, he said, "I think he should be made aware of your generosity in coming forward with such intimate details. You are too self-effacing in desiring that your sacrifice be kept secret from him. In addition, as his elder brother, I believe I should have some stern words with him about his brutal behaviour towards a tender young lady."

Heaven forbid! If Wilfrid were told of my ruptured

maidenhead and medical examination, he would demand that I reveal the true culprit's name, and all would be lost. I said:

"Please honour my wishes in this, Roger. Say nothing to him about these matters. Let him believe that he has been released because the Crown's evidence was too flimsy."

"Very well," he said, with an air of reluctance.

"Splendid! And now, I require refreshment after our labours in this stifling weather. Let us celebrate by taking tea. Where shall we go?"

"I do not know London very well," he replied. "You choose."

"DeWitt's."

As we walked into DeWitt's, what should I see in a far corner — gleaming like a great red beacon-light — but the nose of Mr. Cholmondeley-Cockburn; and, attached to it, the gentleman himself, drinking tea in the company of a young woman with enormous round eyes and enormous round breasts, the size of melons. The entire northern hemispheres of the latter features were exposed, in all their rosy amplitude, by her low-cut frock. Chum seemed not in the slightest degree embarrassed to be found there with her.

"Ah, Miss Worthing!" he boomed. "Well met, dear lady, well met!" He arose, bowed, and said, "May I present Miss Hermione Hotchkiss —"

" 'Itchcock," she piped.

"Indeed. An ardent aspirant of the Thespian arts, for whom I have great plans and greater expectations."

"I am sure that you have," I said. "This is Mr. Roger Summerfield, my brother-in-law-to-be. Roger, this is —"

With infinite aplomb, Roger interrupted me: "The noted Cholmondeley-Cockburn requires no introduction. I saw you in the provinces once, a number of years ago, as Macbeth. The performance was an unforgettable experience. A great pleasure to meet you, sir. And you, Miss Hickock."

" 'Itchcock."

I said, "I am happy to see that you have recovered from your recent indisposition, Mr. Chum."

He lowered his eyes in an attitude of profound repentance. "You see before you the most contrite creature in the world,

Miss Worthing. How does the Bard say it, in *Othello?* — 'O God! that men should put an enemy in their mouths to steal away their brains!' Henceforth, *this*" — he held up the teacup — "will be my only potation."

He then took a snuff-box from his waistcoat pocket, offered it to Roger, me, and Miss Hitchcock (we all declined), and carefully inserted a pinch of the pungent brown powder into each of his cavernous nostrils. There followed a moment of suspended activity and expectation, a kind of calm before the storm, as he waited, with parted lips and half-closed, glazing eyes, for the desired results; then he whipped a large handkerchief from his pocket, held it to his face, and sneezed explosively, three times in succession.

"Bless you," I said.

"Ah-h-h-h," he said, beaming with satisfaction as he put away the handkerchief. "Thank you, Miss Worthing. I have always averred that a proper, resounding sneeze is one of life's greatest pleasures. Almost as good as a fuck."

When Roger and I had been seated at another table by our genial boniface, Mr. DeWitt himself, and we had ordered a sumptuous tea, I asked my future brother-in-law:

"Roger, *does* Wilfrid, in fact, have a large, diamond-shaped mole on his left inner thigh?"

"No," he replied, "but I do. I admit that I was trying to entrap you by mentioning it."

"If I had said, 'Now that you remind me of it, I *do* recall that curious mole of Wilfrid's,' you would have known that I was lying."

"Yes. But as you did not, and as you knew of The Summerfield Scar, I was convinced that you were telling the truth."

" ' "What is truth?" said jesting Pilate . . .' "

"What? Ah yes, Francis Bacon." Roger glanced about the tea-room. "Why did you choose this place, Melissa?" he asked.

"I like it."

"But it appears to be a haven for actors."

"So it is," I said. "And I feel that I have become one of their number."

"Oh?" he responded, puzzled. "Ah, I see! Because of your brother's connexion to the theatre."

I glowed with an inward, invisible smile; but I said no more than "Yes, of course."

XXII

A Servitor of Satan

After tea, in another hackney-coach on the way back to Hans Town, I said, "Roger, when you see Wilfrid at Newgate as he is discharged, please convey to him a request from me . . ."

"What is it?"

"Say that he would oblige me by shaving off that fearsome dark stubble he grew in the shed, before he appears with you at our house to-night for dinner. Tell him that Melissa prefers him smooth of cheek."

Roger laughed. "I will gladly convey that message."

"And will you convey one other message?"

"Of course."

"Tell him that I love him very much."

"I will, but I am sure that he already knows that. It goes without saying."

"Even things that go without saying," I replied in words of Mamma's, "occasionally need to be said."

Roger seized my hand. "By God, Melissa!" he declared in a rush of feeling. "If I were the marrying kind, I would steal you away from Wilfrid and carry you off!"

"I should find it difficult to resist you, I think. But why are you *not* the marrying kind?"

"That side of life," he said — somewhat wistfully, I thought — "has never interested me. I think I should have been happy as a monk, provided that I had plenty of books to read and care for."

"And yet I think that you do not hate women."

"How could I, when the dearest person I have ever known is a woman?"

"Your mother."

He nodded. "And when a brave new friend of mine, whom

I admire more than I can say, is a woman?" he kissed my fingers as he said this.

I felt my eyes tingle. "I love you, Roger," I said. "We met only to-day, and yet I love you like a brother; not like a brother-in-law, but like a true brother, like my own dear Freddy."

"And you are as dear to me," he said, "as if you were one of my true sisters."

Blinking back tears, I sniffled and said, "Please ask the coachman to stop at the next turning. I will get out and walk the rest of the way to my house. I do not want anybody to see you until to-night, when you arrive with Wilfrid."

"A clean-shaven Wilfrid," he said, with a smile, and called out: "Coachman, stop here!" Roger leapt out and helped me down. "Until to-night," he said, tipping his hat.

When I entered the house, I sought out Mamma, who was in the drawing-room. "So there you are," she said. "Where have you been all the day?"

"Taking tea with Wilfrid and his brother, who is in London."

"Wilfrid? Then . . ."

"Yes, Mamma," I said, bending to kiss ner cheek, "we have had a reconciliation."

"Thank Heaven! Your father will be so relieved."

"I should like to tell him. Is he in his study?"

"No, he is ordaining a new deacon. But he will be home long before dinner."

"Speaking of dinner, I have invited Wilfrid and his brother to our table to-night."

"Good. It is time that we met other members of the Summerfield family. I'll inform Mrs. Cooke."

I said, "I am going to lie down for a while. I am quite worn out."

"I dare say it is the weather," remarked Mamma. "It is so humid." She embraced me. "I am happy that you have come to your senses," she said.

Upstairs in my bedroom, after undressing, I opened my window to catch any breeze this humid day might afford. I looked at the table next my bed, and at the empty space where the little shepherd once stood. I regretted its loss, for it was Wilfrid's gift to me, and I had smashed it in a foolish fit. Still, if I had not smashed it, I would not have had a sharp weapon with which to defend my life. If Wilfrid had not given it me, I might be dead instead of John Heathman. How strange are the workings of Fate!

But what would I tell Wilfrid if, one day, he should ask me what became of the figurine? I should have to say that one of the maids knocked it over and broke it whilst dusting.

So many lies! Each lie leading to another. A scraped knee. A lie to Mamma about taking to my bed because of my monthly courses. A lie to Esmie, when she discovered me in a swoon on my bedroom floor. A pack of lies told to Roger and Mr. West and Sir Desmond. Another lie to Mamma about tea with Wilfrid that very afternoon. More lies to follow, if necessary, about the vanished figurine; and suppressions, if not outright lies, about the true reason for Wilfrid's release from prison.

And what lie would I tell him on our wedding night, when he would discover that I was not the virgin he thought me to be? Was it possible that he would not notice? Could I deceive him by some trick, some dissembling?

Damn you, John Heathman! But for you, I would have no cause for lying. But for you, I would never have known of Wilfrid's connexion with Olivia Fairchild, and be ruefully aware of his child in her womb. But for you, I might have lived my whole life without knowing that his father was a Jew; nor would I have said those cruel, cutting things to him. But for you, I would be still a maiden, and could proffer that maidenhood to my husband, as a gift, on our nuptial bed. But for *you,* miscreant knave! But for *you,* evil Serpent in what had been the Eden of my life!

Surely you were a servitor of Satan, a member of the community of Hell; and of a certainty your black soul has returned thither, and you are even now prostrate on your knees in the smoke and flames before your hornèd master's throne; and he is commending you and saying, with a snigger, "Well wrought, my son; a tidy little mischief thou has worked, and I'll reward thee, as I promised, most magnanimously — with a clear cool drop of water on thy crusted tongue, once in every million years!"

XXIII

Whore of Babylon!

When Papa returned from the ordination ceremony over which he had been officiating, he knocked on my bedroom door, entered, and sat on my bed next to me. I was already half-awake, having enjoyed a restful, dreamless nap.

"Your mother tells me that you have tidings of comfort and joy to impart," he said puckishly, and took my hand.

"Yes, Papa. Did she tell you what they are?"

"No, but I can guess. Have you and Wilfrid patched up your differences?"

"Yes, we have."

"Splendid. My prayers have been answered."

"He and his brother will join us for dinner."

"I shall be pleased to see them." He kissed me on the forehead, and left my room.

I had almost told him of Wilfrid's ancestry, but had not the courage to do so. I dreaded his response to such a disclosure. Was it necessary that he know? Even if I could find the courage to tell him, had I the right, without first discussing it with Wilfrid? Life had become so peaceful once more, so pleasant, after that fearful turmoil: I had no desire to roil the waters again. I closed my eyes and silently asked God for guidance.

He, Whose eyes see all, the Jews' Lord God Jehovah and mine; He, Who cleaved unto a Jewish maiden to sire His only begotten Son; He, from Whom no heart may hide its secrets: He would tell me what to do.

I felt someone sit on the bed next to me. Papa again? I opened my eyes, and looked directly into the mocking smirk of that blackmailing trollop, Harriette Wilson.

"What are you doing here?" I demanded of her. "How did you get in?"

"Never you mind, dearie," she said.

"Get out!"

"Don't take that tone with *me,* my girl," she snarled. "I've come bearing a gift for you. A bonny little *i* to replace the *i* in that necklace Georgy-Peorgy gave you, that filthy fly in amber."

"How do you know of that necklace?"

"There's not much that goes on in London I don't know about. Would you like to see the *i*, my dear?"

"I want no gifts from you."

"Tut, tut, such manners! Here, I'll shew it you . . ." She unfolded a lace handkerchief (one of *mine*, from Wilfrid, with the initials M.W. embroidered upon it!) and thrust its contents before my face, saying, "Here's the *i* — isn't it pretty?"

It was a *human* eye. Bits of blood and gore still clung to it. I turned my face away, shuddering.

"You'll be ever so interested, I'm sure," she said, "in hearing how I came to have it. I happened to be walking past your house t'other night, quite late it was, and what should I see but this howling fellow come tumbling out your bedroom window! — that very window over there, the one I climbed through just now. Careless of you to leave it open like that. He fell to the ground, and I thought he was dead; but he got up again and ran off, his hands clapped over his face. But something of his dropped into the street as he ran away. A button, I thought, or p'raps a jewel . . . so I picked it up in a handkerchief . . . and here it is."

"Take it away!"

"Don't you want it, lovey?" she said, sneering. "I'll let you have it cheap. A hundred pounds."

"Get out of here!"

"A hundred pounds, or I go to the authorities with this little morsel and tell them who killed John Heathman!" She dangled the eye in front of my face by its red strings.

My bedroom door flew open. Papa stood there in the doorway, dressed in his full episcopal regalia: robes, mitre, pectoral cross, pastoral staff. He pointed the staff at Harriette Wilson and roared:

"Whore of Babylon! Get thee hence! Begone!"

Screaming as if branded with hot irons, she leapt from my bed and went hurtling out my open window . . .

"Melissa?"

"Yes, Papa . . ."

I opened my eyes. It was Mamma standing over me, not Papa.

"Wake up, Melissa," she said. "You have less than an hour to dress before our dinner guests arrive."

"Guests . . . ?"

"Wilfrid and his brother. Mercy, you are such a sleepy-head."

"Oh . . . yes . . . thank you, Mamma."

She left the room, and I arose from my bed and splashed cold water on my face to dispel the vestiges of the dream that still clung to my mind like strands of ghastly cobweb.

I turned to my bedroom window. It was, as I had left it, wide open to admit any breeze that might be passing on this stifling day. I walked over and closed it, vowing never again to open it as long as I lived in this house.

Then I dressed and went downstairs to await the arrival of our guests.

XXIV

Hodge Shall Not Be Shot

As soon as Wilfrid and Roger handed their hats and sticks to Stewart, I immediately took Wilfrid's arm and spirited him off to the alcove for a private word.

"Oh, my darling," I said, kissing him ferociously.

"You look delectable," he murmured. "You could be served up on a plate as the sweet after dinner, and I would gladly eat you, every part of you, starting with these delicious little ears . . . ."

"Shhh . . . Stewart may hear you."

"Let him."

"You are looking ever so much better than you looked the last time I saw you. No more bruises or cuts — and I see that your broken arm has mended."

"It was only a sprain. It's still a bit stiff." He stroked his clean-shaven jaw. "Hodge gave me your message, and you will be pleased to note that I no longer resemble an Old Testament patriarch."

I looked downward, shamefaced. "Please do not mock me, Wilfrid. I am so dreadfully sorry for those horrid things I said to you. Can you ever forgive me?"

"You were forgiven in the very moment that you uttered them."

I warned him to say nothing to my family about his brief imprisonment. He assured me that both he and Roger would be silent on the subject; adding, "There will be nothing in the press about it — Hodge exerted great influence in that regard."

"Influence?"

"A polite word meaning threats and bribes. Do not be deceived by my brother's gentleness. He is as hard as nails under that bland exterior."

When we had been seated in the dining-room and Papa had spoken the grace, the conversation amongst us was lively and varied. Freddy told a number of theatrical anecdotes; and Papa supplied amusing stories of clerical life.

Mamma asked Roger, "You are in London on business, Mr. Summerfield? — I may call you that without fear of confusion with your brother, for he is now known as Wilfrid to all of us."

"Business of a kind, Mrs. Worthing, although I am not a man of affairs, as Wilfrid is. I am buying books for the library of our new house in Suffolk."

"The 'ancestral mansion,' " Wilfrid put in, satirically.

Roger said, "The next generation of Summerfields — including your children, Wilfrid — will call it so without sarcasm."

"I dare say they will, Hodge."

"Wilfrid," I said, eager to change the subject, "Roger does not like to be called Hodge."

"Really? First I've heard of it."

"He says," I went on, "that it reminds him of Dr. Johnson's cat."

Papa looked up. "Yes, of course!" he said. "I never met the animal myself, but Boswell writes of it. Dr. Johnson was telling somebody about the lamentable condition of a certain unnamed young gentleman: 'Sir, when I heard of him last, he was running about town shooting cats.' Then he added, in what Boswell calls a kindly reverie: 'But Hodge shan't be shot; no, no, Hodge shall not be shot.' "

"You have got the quotation verbatim, your lordship," Roger said admiringly.

"See here, Hodge," said Wilfrid, "do you really object to that name?"

"It is hardly a matter of great importance."

"But you call me Willikins, and I've never objected."

"I have not called you Willikins for well over twenty years."

"True. And, now that it has been drawn to my attention, I will from this day forward calling you nothing other than Roger."

"Thank you. I will appreciate that."

"Goodness!" I said. "I hope I have not started a family quarrel."

"Not at all," Roger assured me. "On the contrary, you have removed a thorn from my side. A very small thorn, I grant you." Turning towards Esmie, he said, "I am given to understand, Mrs. Cooper, that you are a remarkably gifted player of the harpsichord."

Mamma said, "She does it proud."

"What composers do you favour?" Roger asked Esmie.

"Haydn and Mozart," she replied, "although I am fond of many others, as well."

"They are my favourite composers, too," said Roger. "Will you play for us after dinner?"

"If you wish, Mr. Summerfield. And my sister can join in, on her clarinet."

"Uh-oh," said Freddy, "that's done it. They'll play your ears off, Roger."

"My ears will be honoured."

"Don't say you weren't warned."

"Mr. Summerfield," interjected Papa, "of what mind are you in regard to Mr. Handel?"

"He is the greatest of English composers, in my judgment; greater even than Purcell. And I reiterate 'English,' for, although he was born in Germany, he made our country his, and his most monumental works were written here. *Messiah,* for example."

"I am glad to hear you say that," Papa responded. "You

will be interested to know that I was born on the very *day* that *Messiah* was first performed. It was in Dublin — not my birth; the performance — and the occasion was a concert for the benefit of charity . . ."

Later, in the drawing-room, Esmie and I played some duets. It was obvious to me that Roger was consumed with admiration for my sister. It was the most pleasant evening I had spent for a very long time, and to see Wilfrid again — to see him, moreover, in a state of health once more — was heavenly. My fears for the future were shut away and forgotten during those happy hours.

XXV

All the Jews Must Go to Prison

The days and weeks that followed were happy, too, for Wilfrid visited us frequently, often with Roger, coming to tea or dinner. On one such day, when the weather was particularly fine, Wilfrid suggested that the Summerfield sons and Worthing daughters all go for a ride together in his stanhope. Mamma had also been invited, but she declined, saying, "You young people should have some time to yourselves." Freddy was rehearsing a new play during the afternoons. Papa was occupied with episcopal duties.

But the carriage party ended up being a party of two — Wilfrid and I — for Roger expressed a wish to stay behind and speak privately with Esmie. So the two of us went off.

"Wilfrid," I said, after some other talk, "I think I now know all that I care to know about your association with the Luddites, but I worry about those who know more than I and who may betray you. For instance, who was that man with the North Country accent who came to see you at the hotel in the dead of night?"

"Ben Trumbull? He's a good friend. Completely trustworthy. But how do you know of him?"

I told him.

"Ben was simply acting as a messenger," said Wilfrid. "He came to tell me of trouble brewing. Unrest. Threats of impending violence. 'They'll hearken to you, Squire,' he said. He always calls me that. 'What I say to 'em goes for nowt. If they'll hearken to anybody, they'll hearken to you.'

"At first, I told him that I would not go. 'Things have got out of hand,' I said. 'They have grown bigger than I ever anticipated. They will *not* listen to me any more.'

"But Ben said, 'Damn it! You must at least *try,* man! Come up and say summat to 'em. You owe us that much! It was *you* who started it all.'

" 'Yes,' I had to admit. 'It was I. But what this thing has become is none of my making, Ben. One act! That was all I ever suggested, all I ever advocated — one act of symbolic protest. A cry of outrage, to redress wrongs, to relieve the sufferings of innocents.'

" 'That's all very well,' said Ben, 'but you can't back out now, Squire, for all your fine talk. If the hot-heads amongst us aren't stopped, this thing will spread. Already, look you, they're talking about reaching out to Yorkshire, Lancashire, Derbyshire, Leicestershire . . . and you know that it can have only one end. Blood will be spilt. Lives will be lost — by musket-fire and by the noose of Jack Ketch an' all!'

"And so I went away with him, to the north, to the barn where they were meeting. I talked. I shouted. I pleaded. I begged. But it was no good. They would not listen. They were on fire with rage — rage at injustice — and who could blame them? They were starving. Their children were starving, crying out with hunger. 'We watch our bairns grow thinner day by day,' they said.

" 'Put your trust in God!' I told them; and one of them came back with: 'That we have, lad! And look where it's got us!'

"I tried to stop them by force. I stood in front of the doors. 'You shall not pass,' I said, 'unless you beat me senseless first!'

" 'We will!' their new leader replied. 'And kill you an' all, if we have to!' But I stood my ground, for I did not think that they would hurt me . . ."

Wilfrid smiled ruefully. "I under-estimated their anger, their disappointment in me, their impatience with anybody who would talk reason. I fought with them. As it is, I was lucky. I came away with my life, and just a few scratches . . ."

He closed his eyes. "They will die," he whispered. "They will be shot and hanged, just as Ben said. And all because of me. Because I goaded them, and led them, and fanned the spark of their despair into a flame. Yes: they will die. And I will live." He gave a short, grim bark of a laugh. "There's justice! There's the fruit of high ideals! Gallows-fruit, dangling in the hemp!"

I kissed him, unconcerned that I could be seen doing so by people passing us in other carriages. "There is one thing I still do not understand," I said. "Why should you, a rich man, a respected man of business, mix with such people?"

He returned my kiss. "Perhaps because I want to get into Heaven with somewhat less difficulty than a camel — or, as you say, a rope — passing through a needle's eye. Oh, I don't really know, my dear. I am a traitor to my class, I expect. I only know that I was torn this way and that by my feelings. I felt like two men, split down the middle. My heart went out to those starving folk; I made their anguish mine; and I rallied them. But I was a fool, meddling in matters in which I had no right to intrude. And for the rest of my days I will live with the guilt of what I have done, the lives I have recklessly endangered . . ."

"You must not blame yourself for seeking to help your fellow-man," I said, kissing him again. "Let us say no more about it, *ever.*" He gripped my hand.

I deftly changed the subject: "Wilfrid, I can not think what to tell Papa about your . . . your ancestry. I do not like to hide things from him; and yet I dread what will happen when he knows. I will be guided by your wishes in this."

He kissed my hand. "I was about to say that I will be guided by *yours*. If you fear his response, perhaps it is best to say nothing at this time."

"But you are proud of your heritage — will I not offend you by keeping it a secret?"

"My dear," he said, "the most shameful thing about me is that I have been keeping it a secret all of my life. I have never *felt* like a Jew. I see those bearded old fellows in 'Change Alley and what-not, in their funny skull-caps, and I ask myself: Am I a member of that race? I know that I am, and yet for many years I denied it, even to myself.

"Some of my closest friends detest the Jews — how can I tell them that I am one? Cobbett, for example, whom I visited in his gaol cell not long ago: he is the very best of fellows, and we share certain political beliefs, as well; but when it comes to any mention of my father's people, he is transformed into a rabid bigot. 'Why do you dislike them so much?' I asked him once.

"He said, "I dislike them for the same reasons that our forefathers did so. I dislike them as insolent ruffians who mock at our religion. I dislike them as people who never *work* as you and I do and as our fathers did; wretches who live by trickery and usury.' Never work! No man ever worked harder than my father did all his life! But Cobbett went on: 'Why, there is something hateful in the very nature of those ceremonies which they have the infamy to call religious. Their whole lives are spent in getting at money somehow or other. They are everywhere the friends of political corruption and the enemies of political freedom.'

"I said to him, 'But there are good and bad chaps in all races, are there not?'

"He replied, 'There are good and bad Englishmen, yes, Wilfrid, but there are only *bad* Jews.'

"Well, what could I say? I suppose I should have got to my feet and told him, '*I* am a Jew.' Knocked him to the floor. But I didn't; I couldn't; I hadn't the courage. It would have cost me a friend."

"Is such a friend worth keeping?" I said.

"Perhaps not. But, damn it, I *like* Will Cobbett. He is an excellent man in so many ways. He has this one flaw in his character, but we all have flaws, have we not? God knows that *I* am not a paragon of all the virtues. Dare I condemn him? Dare I judge him? What gives me that right?"

I shook my head in perplexity. "I wish I were wiser and could advise you," I said. "It is a very difficult question."

"As schoolboys," Wilfrid went on, "Hodge — I mean Roger — and I often would hear the other boys tell jokes about Jews. Roger would turn and walk away from such conversations, but I would stay, you see."

"He retreated, but you would stay and fight."

"No," Wilfrid replied, his voice faint with shame. "I would stay and *join in.* I wanted so very much to be one of them that I would laugh at their jokes, and even tell a few. I said to myself: Why should I fight for the Jews? I am an English lad. Roger may seem to you less virile than I, but the opposite is true. He would not be part of such jokes. He walked away, but he was not retreating when he did so; he was protesting.

"I wonder if you can imagine how it felt," Wilfrid continued, "when all the boys would rush out of chapel on Easter Sunday, bawling out that sing-song ditty —

Christ is risen, Christ is risen,
All the Jews must go to prison . . .

They sing it still, you know. You may hear it at any school. Oh, I grant that it is not part of the curriculum; they do not sing it *in* the chapel. But the masters do not stop them."

"Poor little boy," I said, of the child Wilfrid I never knew. "How terrible it must have been for you to hear them sing that."

"How terrible to hear *myself* sing it," he said. "Can you picture what it was like, in the school baths, trying to keep the other boys from seeing our privities? I remember a time when one boy, Merlyngton Major it was, saw Roger in the nude and said, 'Look, Summerfield's lost part of his family pride!' The other boys laughed. 'Damned if you don't look like a Jew,' Merlyngton added.

" 'I'm Church of England, just as you are,' Roger replied, 'but what if I were not?'

"Merlyngton said, 'Then I'd teach you not to sluice your filthy skin in a Christian bath-house.'

"Roger retorted, 'You would teach me *nothing,* Merlyngton, because you are a stupid buggering horse's arse.' Merlyngton Major struck him, of course, and soon both boys were rolling about, naked as monkeys, on the bath-house floor. Roger came away with a bloody nose, but he gave as good as he got; better, in fact, for Merlyngton lost two of his teeth." Wilfrid smiled, remembering the scene. "I was proud of Roger that day," he said. "I wish I could be as proud of myself."

I squeezed his hand, but did not know what to say to him.

"A peculiar irony," he added, "is that Merlyngton, who now sits in the House of Lords, has become rather a good friend of mine, and has been helpful to me in the way of business. Of course, he doesn't know that I am a Jew." Wilfrid smiled bitterly. "Half a dozen years ago and a bit, when that fever broke out in Gibraltar, he wrote an anonymous letter to the *St. James's Chronicle*. He shewed it me before he posted it. The letter blamed the fever on the filthy habits of the Jews. The only scolding I gave him was to say 'If you really believed that, old chap, you would have signed your name.' "

When we returned to the house, we joined Mamma in the drawing-room for tea. "Where are Esmie and Roger?" I asked. "Oh, there they are — I can see them out in the garden. Shall I call them in to tea?"

"No," said Mamma. "I believe that Roger is making a very serious offer to your sister."

XXVI

The Bachelor and the Widow

Esmie later recounted to me her meeting with Roger in the garden. They spoke first of literary and musical matters, but soon the conversation grew less impersonal.

"Mrs. Cooper," he said, "I think I need fear no contradiction if I say that you and I have a great deal in common. We like the same books, the same music. We are neither of us in first youth, and yet we are far from old, and we have many years ahead of us, God willing. We live without partners: you, because you were tragically widowed; I, because I have never met a woman whom I wanted to marry — until now. Have I spoken too boldly? Do I offend you?"

"You do not, Mr. Summerfield," Esmie replied. "I am not a green girl, and do not swoon at the mention of marriage."

"Then I am encouraged to go on and say that I think you are a lady of uncommon intelligence and grace. I am by nature shy; but in your company I become voluble and forward. I find you warm and amiable and responsive. I will even say delightful. Do I dare to think that you find some of those qualities in me?"

"I find many of them in you."

"You have no idea how much your words cheer me, Mrs. Cooper."

"And yet, sir," said Esmie, "all of these qualities and shared interests need not, necessarily, recommend marriage. They are, perhaps, the foundation of a friendship."

Roger said, "What is marriage, dear lady, but simply the best and closest of friendships? What are married partners but the dearest and truest of friends?"

"They are all of that," she agreed, "but they are also much more — or they should be."

Roger ignored that and said, "Please permit me to put a question to you which I have no right to ask: Is there another?"

"Another?"

"Another suitor. Another man in your life."

Esmie hesitated before replying. "Not . . . precisely. Not a suitor. Not even a man, really. The memory of a man."

"Your late husband."

"Yes."

Roger said, "I admire that loyalty in you, Mrs. Cooper. But it is not good to dwell in the recollections of past years. You must live in the present."

"I do, Mr. Summerfield."

"Not sufficiently, if I may say so. My dear Mrs. Cooper, we could have such an agreeable life together. We could travel to all the capitals of Europe, to all the most glorious sights of Man and Nature; to the best museums and theatres and opera-houses. We would enjoy each other's company and conversation so very much! And we could simply sit by our fire on winter nights, you playing your harpsichord, I reading poetry to you. Is that not an idyllic picture?"

Esmie replied, "You have left one thing out of your idyl, Mr. Summerfield. You have said nothing of love."

"Then let me repair that fault by assuring you that I am filled with a profound affection for you, as well as a most sincere respect."

"A profound affection is not love," said Esmie.

"Surely you quibble over words, Mrs. Cooper? If 'affection' displeases you, then believe me when I say that I love you."

"As you would love a sister."

"A dear and cherished sister; a sister highly valued and utterly admired."

"But do you love me, Mr. Summerfield, with that love which one is forbidden to feel for one's sister?"

Roger chose his words with care. "I will not attempt to deceive you," he said. "That love of which you speak is a thing I have never felt for any woman. I do not feel it for you. But is that thing all of life, Mrs. Cooper? Is it not but a few minutes' fever, which leaves all the rest of the day to fill up with other, perhaps better and nobler, pursuits? Can that little animal-fit compare to the sublime paintings of Leonardo, the sonnets of Shakespeare, the symphonies of Mozart, the marbles of Michael Angelo? Such things live for ever; the heat of the flesh cools quickly."

"Without that heat," Esmie replied, "there would *be* no paintings, no poems, no music, no marbles. It is that heat which kindles the imagination of the artist, infuses him with divine warmth, makes his talent blaze. It is true that its fleshly expression lasts but a few minutes; but its glow lasts all the day, lighting the dark corners of the heart and soul. True, it can cool and it can die; but it leaves behind a soft and gentle radiance that nurtures and sustains, soothes and comforts and solaces for the length of a lifetime and, God grant, beyond. You ask if it is all of life. Yes, it is, Mr. Summerfield. It is the palette of brilliant colours without which life is an insipid sketch; and I could never consider marriage with a man who could not provide it — no matter how fine, how dear, how sweet a man he might be."

Esmie told me that it was many moments before Roger spoke again. "I stand humbled before you," he said at last. "I have offered you an empty vessel, when you deserve a chalice overflowing with wine."

"Not an empty vessel, Roger," she said. "Let us say that it is filled with good, honest, quenching stuff from the Summerfield brewery: the hearty ale of friendship; of lifelong friendship, I hope."

"It is my hope, as well . . . Esmeralda," he said; and, soon after, escorted her inside to tea.

XXVII

Rankwort Redux

Soon after that occasion, I paid a visit to Wilfrid at his office in the brewery. "Roger calls this place monastic," I said.

Wilfrid laughed. "Dear Hodge: he wants me to hang pictures all over the walls, and what-not. But this is a seat of business, not a home or a museum. My brother is the man of culture in our family, and he is happy directing the decoration of The Ancestral Mansion. After all, it will be his one day — why should he not?"

"Where shall *we* live, Wilfrid, after we are married?"

"They are putting up some fine-looking houses in Mayfair," he said. "Perhaps we might have a look at one or two of them to-day?"

"I should love that."

Cavendish opened the door, poked in his head, and said, "Sir, there is a Mr. Simeon Rankwort in the outer office. He has not an appointment, but he is pressing to see you."

"What sort of fellow is he, Cavendish?"

"He says that he is a journalist, sir."

"Then by all means shew him in!" said Wilfrid, expansively. "The brewery could do with a big puff in the press."

"Yes, sir." The clerk withdrew.

The name Rankwort had a familiar sound to me, but I did not immediately make the proper connexion. Cavendish ushered in the journalist a moment later. He wore a tall hat perched precariously on the back of his head. He was pale; the tip of his nose was pink and perpetually moist. His gloves were none too clean.

"Sit down, Mr. Rankwort," said Wilfrid.

"I am obliged to you," said the journalist, sitting down and crossing his spindly legs.

"May I present my *fiancée,* Miss Worthing."

"How-de-do, Miss," he said, doing a kind of bow from his sitting position, not bothering to remove his silly hat. "The right reverend's daughter, I believe? And sister to the first comedian of the Proteus?"

"You are well informed, Mr. Rankwort," I said.

"Ah, well, you see, Miss, that's my business."

Wilfrid said, "And how may I help you?"

Rankwort scratched his nose and sniffed. "I'm writing an article on a certain subject," he said, "and require confirmation from you of a few details."

"Very well," said Wilfrid, "fire away."

In a conspiratorial wheeze, Rankwort said, "The details are of a somewhat delicate nature, sir, and I feel reluctant, in the presence of the young lady . . . do you grasp my meaning, sir?"

"No, I do not. You may speak right out before Miss Worthing." He smiled at me. "She knows all of my most shameful secrets."

"In that case, sir," said Rankwort, "I will mention the name Ben Trumbull. Nottingham chap?"

Wilfrid's face clouded. "I see," he said.

"I thought you would," Rankwort remarked. "Ben's in a bad way, you know, in the matter of finances, and I've been able to pass him the odd fiver now and again . . ."

"Good of you," Wilfrid said coldly.

"He's been able to return the favour by making me privy to certain information . . ."

That is when I remembered when I had heard the name of Rankwort before. I said, "You often pass the odd fiver for information, do you not?"

He shrugged. "I may do."

"To prostitutes like Harriette Wilson, for instance," I continued.

"Your brother told you, did he? That shankerous whore bilked me!"

Wilfrid cut in: "I suggest that you moderate your language in front of my *fiancée,* Rankwort."

"As you like, but it was *she* first mentioned prostitutes."

"Get back to Ben Trumbull."

"With pleasure." Rankwort settled himself more comfortably into his chair. "Well, then: I was in Nottingham recently, for my paper, sending back despatches about the Luddites' activities. I bought Trumbull a pint of ale, and he told me a story that I could hardly believe. It's a story that could be published under such a heading as: *A Jacobin Brewer. Industrialist Incites Workers to Smash Mill Machines.* Catchy, wouldn't you say?"

"I'm sure that such an article would make your name in Grub Street," Wilfrid replied.

Rankwort nodded. "It would, indeed, were I to write it. But I don't look for glory, Mr. Summerfield. Not for me the bubble reputation. I am willing to sacrifice my professional advancement — even fame, it may be — for a consideration."

"How much?"

"Well, sir, I don't mind telling you that I'm partial to a certain amount of security. Rather than name some single sum, I was hoping that you and I could reach an agreement, a kind of salary or annuity, to be paid into my account periodically — on the first of every month, shall we say?"

Wilfrid replied, "That arrangement holds no interest for me."

"Quarterly, then? I'm not particular."

"I did not make myself clear. I meant to say: I reject your kind offer *in toto*. You may write your article, if you wish."

"I will," Rankwort said harshly. "Oh, I will, indeed!"

"If you do," said Wilfrid, "and if you mention my name, or by *innuendo* suggest my identity, you and your paper will be sued for libel. Down to the last farthing. I will break you, Rankwort, and chop you up into feed for my kennels."

Rankwort snarled, "You don't frighten me, Summerfield! Every word I write will be *true!*"

"And how will you prove that?"

"By the testimony of Ben Trumbull."

"He will swear to it in a court of law?"

"Yes."

"Why will he do that?"

"Because I've paid him!"

"The odd fiver?"

"And more!"

Wilfrid sighed sadly. "Poor Mr. Rankwort. I am afraid that you are an innocent." Wilfrid walked to the office door and opened it. "Cavendish: will you send in the foreman, please?"

Rankwort sneered. "Need your bully-boy to throw me out, do you? Not man enough to try it yourself."

"I wouldn't dream of throwing you out," said Wilfrid. "A man of business must avoid unpleasant notice in the public prints. *Beer Baron Flings Journalist Down Stairs. Penny-a-Liner Beaten to Pulp*. Not the sort of thing I'd want my customers to read. The stock-owners would raise the very devil of a row."

In a moment, a work-hardened man of about Wilfrid's age entered the office. Rankwort, seeing him, went even paler than he had been before, and cried, "What are *you* doing here?"

"I work here, sir," the foreman replied.

"Yes," Wilfrid said. "I recently lost my valued foreman because of his untimely death. In casting about for a good replacement, I thought of my old friend, here, and made him an offer. I think it was a very generous offer — would you say so, Ben?"

"That I would, Squire. I make more money here in a month than I did in half a year, up north in the mills — even in the days when there was steady employment to be got. And there's nowt to be got now."

"You're reasonably happy, then?"

"I am that. M' wife and bairns are happy, an' all."

"Now, Ben," said Wilfrid, "please listen very carefully. This gentleman is Mr. Simeon Rankwort. I want you to take a good long look at him. And I want you to tell me if you have ever seen him before?"

Ben shook his head. "No, I ain't ever seen him."

"You're a liar, Trumbull!" shouted Rankwort.

"Sorry, sir, but I ain't never seen you before this very minute."

Wilfrid asked, "You're certain of that, Ben? Not just hereabout in London. Think back to Nottingham. Did Mr. Rankwort every buy you a pint of ale and talk to you?"

"Never, Squire. Leastways, not as I can remember." He grinned. "Mind you, when I has a few pints under m' belt, I can bloody well forget m' own name." Then he apologised to me for his language: "Beggin' your pardon, Miss."

"Very well, Ben," said Wilfrid. "Thank you. I don't think we need keep you from your work any longer." Ben left the office, and Wilfrid turned to the disgruntled journalist. "I don't think we need keep *you* any longer, either, Mr. Rankwort. Allow me to bid you good day."

Rankwort left, seething.

Wilfrid explained to me: "Ben came to see me the day after he talked to Rankwort. Said he'd been drunk, frightened, worried about his wife and children. He begged my forgiveness. I offered him John's position. Worked out rather well, don't you think? And now, let us go look at those houses in Mayfair."

XXVIII

Swear It in the Name of God!

It could not have been more than five weeks after my terrible encounter with John Heathman in the Dark Walk that I awoke in the morning feeling most awfully sick to my stomach.

Nausea crawled over me like a gigantic worm as I lay there in my bed. When I sat up, thinking to better my condition, the horrid queasiness only grew worse. Then, springing in a rush of panic from my bed to the washing-basin near by, I vomited violently into it.

Had I eaten something the night before that had gone off? Or was the vomiting a sign of an approaching fever? I returned to my bed, weak and shaking, but I could not sleep again. I felt utterly miserable.

When Abigail came in to open the blinds, she saw — and surely smelt — the basinful of reeking slime. "Are you feelin' poorly, Miss?"

I nodded. "Something I ate, no doubt. Perhaps those sweetbreads." The very thought of them, of any food, made my gorge stir again.

"But all of the family had them same sweetbreads, Miss," she said. "Mister Aelfred had a double portion. Nobody else is sick."

"Take away the basin please. I can not bear the smell of it."

"Right away, Miss. You won't be comin' down to breakfast, I suppose?"

"No."

"May I bring you up a tray? A boiled egg? Tea and toast?"
"No."
"Very well, Miss." She left, taking the basin with her.
The moment she did so, I was seized by desperation. for the hideous nausea was sweeping over me again, and I had no basin! I lunged over the side of my bed, reached down under it, and pulled out the jordan. Fortunately, it was empty, for I had not got up during the night. I peered down into its ornamental china depths, looking into the face of Bonaparte that was painted there. Such pots were all the rage in London, expressing as they did a species of coarse patriotism. It had been a ribald gift from Freddy on my last birthday. I spewed a gush of acrid stuff into the Corsican's face, and sank back, trembling, upon my pillow. My whole body was covered with sweat, and my night-dress was sodden with it.
Esmie, still in her dressing-gown, came to me soon after. "Abigail tells me that you are unwell," she said.
"Perfectly ghastly."
She sat on my bed. "Open your night-dress," she said.
"Whatever for?"
Without waiting for me to do it, she began to unlace the strings of my night-dress, and had soon laid bare my bosom. She placed her hands on my breasts, and squeezing slightly. I gave a sharp little cry of pain.
"Do you always cry out like that when your breasts are squeezed so gently?"
"What a question!" I replied indignantly. "I am not in the custom of going about having my breasts squeezed!" But I knew that when Wilfrid not only had squeezed them, but also kneaded them and sucked them, much less gently than Esmie had handled them, I had not felt pain: only exquisite pleasure.
"They are quite hard to the touch," she said. "Here: feel them for yourself." She placed my own hands upon my breasts. It was true: they had always been firm, but this was a new kind of firmness — a hardness, just as Esmie had said. And they were *very* sensitive.
"Lissa, my dear," she said tenderly, "you must not be angry when I ask if you and Wilfrid have anticipated your wedding night?"
" 'Anticipated?' I anticipate it with the greatest joy, and I am sure that Wilfrid anticipates it no less eagerly."

"That was not my meaning. Have you and he ever . . . gone beyond the bounds of courtship?"

"Only once," I admitted, in a small voice.

"Once is enough," she said.

"Enough for what?"

She smiled. "My dear sister, you are pregnant."

"Preg——!!"

"Shhhhh." She put a finger to her lips. "You need not worry. It means only that the wedding will have to take place sooner than planned."

"But Wilfrid and I — we only —" With burning face, I told Esmie precisely what we had done in the grass that night. "I did not think that caresses of *that* kind would make me pregnant," I said in conclusion.

"They can not," Esmie assured me. "Wilfrid must have done more than that."

"He did *not!* I *swear* to you he did not!"

"Then who did?" she asked.

"Can you not be mistaken?"

She shook her head. "I have been through this myself, you know. The signs are unmistakable. I recognise them." She sighed. "What's more, Mamma — who has been through this many more times than I — will surely recognise them, too."

"Oh dear God . . ." I began to weep.

"Now, now, no more of that," she said, and kissed my forehead. Then she added, "My dear, do not try to protect Wilfrid by lying."

"It was not Wilfrid," I said. "It was . . . somebody else."

She winced as if slapped. "That *is* a great pity," she admitted. "And I must say that you surprise me. I had not thought you to be a promiscuous girl."

I shook my head dolefully. "I am not," I said. "I was forced."

"Good Heavens! Is that true?"

I nodded.

"Who is he?"

I groaned. "What does it matter?"

"It may matter a great deal. If I know Papa, he will insist that the man marry you."

"That is impossible."

"What will you say to Wilfrid? This condition of yours will

be obvious even to him in a few months' time. He will know that the child is not his, if you truly did no more than . . . blow his clarinet, as you put it."

I gave a little squeal of rage and pounded my fists against the bed. "Damn, damn, *damn!*" I cried. "Here I lie, pregnant *not* by Wilfrid, whilst *his* child . . . oh, never mind. What a hopeless muddle!"

"I understand why you will not marry the child's father. What he did to you made him so repugnant —"

"Repugnant, yes — the most repugnant creature ever born. And not alone for what he did to me. Evil. Destructive. Devilish. Besides — even if I loved him — marriage to him simply is not possible."

"He is already married: is that it?"

"No."

"Then —"

"He is *dead!*" I blurted out. "And I killed him!"

Seizing her shoulders in a cruel grip, I glared directly into her eyes. "But if you ever repeat that to a living soul — to Mamma, to Papa, to anybody — I will hate you for the rest of my life! Swear that you will keep silent!"

"Lissa, my poor dear . . ."

"Swear it!"

"Very well, I swear it," she said, in a resigned tone.

"Swear it in the Name of God!"

"I do so swear it," she said softly, "and I will do more, if it will comfort you: I swear it on the spirit of my dead husband."

I released her, and fell back upon my pillow. "Life!" I said venomously. "What awful muck it is!"

XXIX

A Horrible Suspicion

Wilfrid, who had always a standing invitation to tea, called that afternoon. But I kept to my room, and sent down word that I was too ill to see him. He sent back word that my illness gave him all the more reason to be at my side; but I was adamant. I understood from Esmie that he took tea with the family, and that he had shewn great concern over my health.

He returned on the following day, and the day after that, but still I would not see him. He scribbled a note which Stewart brought up to me:

"Melissa, —

"You are cruel to deny me your company. We will soon be man and wife, 'in sickness and in health,' so why may I not see you now? Have you had third-thoughts about marrying me? Is it because of my race? I will remain downstairs until you send me some word.

"Your devoted
"Wilfrid"

Taking my pen, I encircled his phrase "because of my race?" and wrote beside it in the margin of his note:

"No — not because of that or anything else about you. The fault is mine. I can not marry you."

I did not sign it, but merely folded it again and handed it to Stewart, who took it down to him.

Not many minutes later, Mamma walked into my sitting-room without knocking. "Explain yourself!" she insisted. "Wilfrid tells me that you have changed your mind yet *again,* and that you now say you can not marry him. Why in Heaven's name not? And as for being ill — you look perfectly well to me!"

It was true — my indisposition struck only in the early hours of the day; by afternoon, I always felt myself again. I knew that I could not keep my condition a secret from her any longer.

I said, "I am afraid that my illness attacks me only in the mornings, Mamma . . ."

"Ridiculous!"

"In fact, I believe that it is *called* morning-sickness."

She sat down abruptly on the nearest chair, all the wind knocked out of her. "Are you sure?"

"Ask Esmie. *She* is sure."

"Oh dear," said Mamma. Then, quickly recovering, she said, "What's done is done. No use weeping over spilt . . . well, never mind. Such things happen in the best of families. I will not scold you, Melissa. You and Wilfrid are human, and young, into the bargain. The two of you have made a mistake, but all is not lost."

"Wilfrid is not the father," I said flatly.

"What?"

"That is why I can not marry him, Mamma! I am pregnant with another man's child!"

"You never."

"It is true! God help me, I was taken against my will!"

Not surprisingly, her next question was: "Who is he?"

And that is when this tug-of-war with my parents began, with them demanding to know the name of the rapist, and I refusing to divulge it. What possible purpose would have been served by divulging it? John Heathman was dead and could not marry me. I would have refused to marry him even if he were alive.

Mamma left my room, gave out some story or other to Wilfrid, and, when Wilfrid had left, told Papa all. He immediately came up and said to me:

"It was Wilfrid Summerfield, was it not? You are foolishly trying to protect him."

"It was *not* Wilfrid, Papa. I swear it. But I will tell you nothing more."

"Why not? Why do you protect a foul rapist?"

"I have my reasons."

He talked to me for almost an hour. Near the end, he begged me to "desist in this stiff-necked behaviour. Break your silence. It is prideful and stubborn. I might indeed deem it sinful; or, if it is not an actual sin, then surely it is wayward and impious. It displeases me. It displeases God — to Whom you must pray on your knees for guidance. I have no doubt that He will command you to tell me all."

On the following day began his suspicions of Brummel, Byron, Shelley, Sheridan, Scott, the Prince Regent, *et alii;* but I need not repeat conversations I have set down earlier in these pages.

I have now told the whole story of the events that led me to my present state. I am at this time three months gone with child, and, although my condition has not yet begun to shew, my spirits are so cast down that I seldom leave the house.

In this interval of some weeks that followed my disclosure of the problem, Papa's insistence has somewhat abated, but from time to time he will again attempt to pry the rapist's name from my lips. Only to-day, for example, when he found himself alone with me for a moment in the drawing-room — Mamma having gone to consult with Mrs. Cooke about dinner — he said:

"Lamb . . ."

"No, Papa, I believe Mamma said that we are having roast beef for dinner to-night."

"I mean that Cockney scribbler. There's insanity in his family . . ."

"Mr. Charles Lamb?"

"Yes. I've seen the way he looks at women. Was it *he?"*

"Papa, will you never have done with these questions? I have told you that I will not play at this game."

"Game! It is no game to me, child," he said sternly.

"I am no longer a child . . . obviously."

"My dear, you must forgive my persistence: I believe you when you assure me that it was not Wilfrid Summerfield, for if it had been he, you surely would not have refused to marry him. But was it, perhaps, his brother . . . ?"

"Roger?" I laughed. "Roger is entirely free of carnal desires."

"Rubbish! He proposed marriage to your sister."

"And she rejected that proposal — for the very reason, by his own admission, that all he could offer was a *marriage blanc.* Having known a real marriage, Esmie was not attracted to such a bloodless arrangement."

Papa fidgeted in his chair. "Melissa," he murmured, "what I am about to say is very difficult for me to put into words. To call it indelicate would be to understate it a thousandfold. The thing of which I am about to speak is condemned and proscribed by every religion, every race, even by naked savages, even by the pagans of ancient times. But your stubborn refusal to reveal the man's name, your adamant determination to protect him, your insistence that marriage to him is, in your words, 'an absolute impossibility,' all this has spawned a horrible suspicion in my thoughts."

"Good Heavens!" I said. "You make it sound so ominous! Whatever can it be?"

Hesitantly, he said, "You and Aelfred, ever since you were babies, have always been inordinately affectionate with each other: you kiss, you embrace . . ."

I immediately arose and went to my father, sitting on the carpet at his knees. I took his hand. "Dear Papa," I said. "Poor dear Papa. I have caused you so much anguish! I have caused you to suspect even your own son. Therefore, I swear by Almighty God that it was *not* Freddy."

"Thank you," he whispered. "I am ashamed of my own suspicion. It has shewn me a side of my nature that I wish I had not seen."

Wilfrid, needless to say, has not returned since that day when I sent back his note; nor has he written. He is, I am sure, completely exasperated with me; and, knowing nothing of my predicament, probably thinks me the silliest girl he has ever had the misfortune to meet — sillier and shallower than even Olivia (who, by now, must have given birth to his child, albeit under the name of poor, unsuspecting Mr. Royce). Likely, Wilfrid has forgotten me and found another young lady. He may even be engaged to her. If so, I am glad. I wish him every happiness.

Oh, Wilfrid, how I love you!

XXX

Hateful, Hateful Woman!

I had intended to bring this chronicle to a close with that love declaration, for, having carried my account of past happenings all the way forward to the present, there seemed to be nothing further to write. To continue it as a diary, setting down the tiresome passing of my life from day to day, would be a dull and dreary duty for which I have no taste or inclination. For this reason, it has been a week and more since I have taken up my pen. I do so now only to record a thing that happened to-day.

Esmie came to me in my sitting-room and said, "Lissa, I must have a serious word with you."

"Oh, let us be serious, by all means," I replied, "lest I fall into the peril of overmuch gaiety and laughter."

She ignored my bitter attempt at wit, and continued: "I made a vow to you some three months since," she said. "I swore it in the Name of God and on the spirit of my husband. Do you remember?"

"Of course."

"Do you remember it *precisely?* For I do."

"Are we lawyers, Esmie, that we must be so exact?"

"I swore to you that I would never tell anybody that the man who raped you is dead, and that you killed him."

"Quite right. You may go to the top of the form."

"That is *all* I swore. I did *not* swear to tell nobody that you are with child."

"What does it matter? Everybody knows that. The whole family, all the servants, Mr. Cargrave . . . everybody."

"Not everybody," said Esmie. "Not Wilfrid."

I searched her face. "What do you mean?"

"I mean, my dear, that I broke no vow by going to see him to-day and telling him of your condition."

"You had no right!" I shouted.

"Perhaps not. But *he* has a right, as the man who loves you, to be told the reason that you refuse to marry him. It was cruel to keep him in the dark. It was dishonest."

"And what have you accomplished by your honesty?" I demanded. "What have you achieved, other than blabbing about my shame to yet another person? Did you think to bring him back to me? He will not marry a woman who is stuffed with another man's spawn! He could not bring himself to love such a loathly brat. He could not love *me* again, either, for I am no longer the unspoilt virgin that I was, but a plundered, damaged piece of goods. That upright sceptre of his would wilt like wax at the mere *thought* of another man's tool plunging into my quim and spewing his seed inside me. Oh, go *away*, Esmie! Leave me alone! I know that you were well-intended in what you did, but you had no right, and I am sorely vexed with you!"

"You like to speak of rights," said Esmie, "but *you* have no right to put thoughts into Wilfrid's mind. You have no right to say that he no longer loves you. You do him an injustice even to *think* that of him without proof. You must face him, Lissa."

I shook my head. "No, I can not go to him. You must not ask me to do such a thing."

"You need not go to him," she said gently. "He is here."

"In this house?"

"Just outside the door to this room."

I was appalled. "Dear God! Do not let him in! You *must* not! I can not face him! How *dare* you put me into such a distasteful position? You are a hateful, *hateful* woman!"

"I have risked your hatred in the best of causes. See him, my dear."

"I can not. I *will* not!"

"Do it, I beg of you, not for me, not for yourself. Do it for him."

"No."

"He deserves it, Lissa. He is a fine man. You hurt him very much when you broke off your engagement the first time. You hurt him again when you broke it a second time. You must see him. You must talk to him. You owe him that."

I picked up my mirror and examined my face. "I look a sight."

"You look beautiful. All women do when they are in your condition; but you are more beautiful than most."

"I am all swollen in the middle."

"Nonsense! Look at you: lissome as a nymph. You may *feel* swollen, but you will not begin to shew it for another month or even two."

"He can not love me, Esmie; he can *not.* What man could? It is unnatural to expect it of him."

"Let *him* tell you that."

"Another time. To-morrow, perhaps. I am unprepared; I am taken by surprise. Not now, Esmie. Please, not now."

"Now," she said.

I sighed, defeated. Almost imperceptibly, I nodded.

"Thank you," she whispered. She went to the door and opened it. "You may come in now, Wilfrid," she said.

XXXI

Only Love

My back was turned to the door. I heard it close. I waited. Then I heard his voice: "How are you, Melissa?"

Just that sound, the sound of his voice alone, without even seeing him, set every fibre of my flesh to humming! So shaken was I that I did not dare to turn and look at him, lest the sight of him cause me to break into tears.

"I am well, thank you," I said. My voice trembled. "And you?"

He walked slowly round in front of me, put his hand under my chin, and tilted my face upward. His beloved face looked down at me. "I am far from well," he replied in a sepulchral voice.

"Wilfrid, are you ill? What is wrong?" I said in a rush of concern.

Gravely, he said, "I am dying." I gasped! Then a crinkle appeared about his eyes — The Summerfield Crinkle, I had come to think it, for I had seen it in Roger's face, too — and he added: "Of a broken heart."

I said, "I have treated you abominably."

"No," he said, "somebody has treated *you* abominably. Why did you not tell me about it?"

"I was afraid. It was all so . . . confusing, so complicated . . ."

"And you will reveal the man's name to nobody? Not even to me?"

I shook my head. "What purpose would it serve?"

"Well," he replied, "for one thing, it would afford me the great pleasure of breaking every bone in his body."

"You would not be able to do that, even if I were to tell you his name."

"Is he so much bigger and stronger than I, then?"

"He has gone away."

"Quit London?"

"Quit England, never to return." (Not exactly a lie.) "Please, Wilfrid, may we say no more about him? I want to forget."

He took my hands. "As you wish. I will ask you only two more questions. If you answer both of them in the negative, my future will be bright. If you answer in the affirmative, I will know that nothing lies ahead for me but darkness and despair. Tell me, Melissa: have you stopped loving me?"

"Oh, *no,* my dearest!"

"Are you determined not to marry me?"

I did not know what to say. "How can I marry you, when I am carrying —"

"Simply answer my question, please. Are you steadfast in your decision to break our engagement?"

"Things have *changed,* Wilfrid!" I cried, walking away from him. "Decisions are no longer mine to make. That privilege has been revoked by the thing in my belly! *It* makes all the decisions now; *it* controls my destiny!"

"Not *it,*" he said softly. "Not a *thing.* A child."

"Whatever you call it," I said viciously, "the answer to your question is: no, *I* have not decided to break our engagement — *it* has!"

"A child," he repeated. "A child whom you will bear and love and nurture; whom I will love and raise as my own."

"Oh God, Wilfrid, why will you not shew some *anger?*" I cried. "You will raise another man's child as a Summerfield, whilst off in Suffolk *your* child is being raised as a Royce! Does not the thought of it drive you mad? It is beginning to drive *me* mad!"

"Things are not always what we would wish," he said. "When they are not, we must make the best of them, and work with what we have."

"Spare me your pale, pusillanimous platitudes!"

"You prefer me to shew anger," he said. "To whom should I direct that anger? To the unoffending child in your womb? To you, the innocent victim of a rapist? To the rapist, whose identity you will not reveal?"

"Life," I shot back at him. "Life should be the target for your anger."

He smiled indulgently, as if at a pouting child. "Do you remember your first visit to the brewery?" (Indeed I did, for that was the first time I laid eyes upon the author of my misfortune, John Heathman!) "I told you that a man makes his *own* life — into a paradise, a purgatory, or a hell, according to his taste, his will, and his opportunity."

"Yes, I remember," I said sulkily. "It started as a discussion of horses."

"Well, I see before me an *opportunity* to marry a girl who is very much to my *taste,* and by God I *will."*

"Prettily spoken."

"I am in a very hell of longing and unhappiness now, but I will hoist myself into Heaven on the train of your gown." He took hold my shoulders and looked straight into my eyes. "Another question, and this one you must answer in the affirmative: Will you marry me?"

I turned my face away. "Wilfrid, please . . ."

"Will you marry me, you contrary little baggage?!"

He shook me like a rag doll.

"Y—— yes . . ." I said.

He crushed me to his body and covered my mouth with his. Tearing away his lips at last, he growled, "Ah, God, how I want you, girl! Give thanks that I'm a decent chap, or I would take you here and now!"

"Yes," I said, in a voice all breath and whimper. "Yes, Wilfrid. Take me. Take me now."

"Do you mean it?"

"Now. Here. No more need for caution or waiting. I can *not* wait. I want you *now."*

He required no further urging. Lifting me in his strong arms, he carried me into my bedroom. Gently, he lowered me onto the bed. Tenderly, he unfastened and removed my frock and under-garments; plucked off my shoes and peeled off my stockings. Quickly he stripped away his own clothing and stood naked before me, tall and beautiful, his shoulders broad, his belly flat, his chest plated with an armour of muscle, his dear privity jutting out saucily and proudly, hard and smooth as marble. He joined me on the bed and awakened my body with kisses, with caresses, with every sweet and wicked fondling of his hands and lips, from my head to my toes, leaving no nook of me asleep. It were grotesque, I know, to carry musical similes too far; but if once I had played him like a clarinet, it may be said that now he, in a sense, played me as if I were an instrument lacking his sort of reed and mouthpiece, having no hard beak but only a modest little hole to which the artist cunningly must needs apply his mouth to coax it into charming concord: so I may say that Wilfrid blew me like a fife or transverse flute; and, just as the *timbre* of that latter may vary greatly from low, thick tones to brilliant and more penetrating ones, being an instrument of extreme agility when blown by players of extreme ability, and just as trills are possible on every note, and rapid reiterations of pitch may be executed by skilfull tonguing, so my beloved musician plied his art until I thought I could not endure another melodious moment of his playing.

And then at last he entered me, like a longship's prow sliding into harbour, smoothly, regally, victoriously, and there was no pain, no blood, no rending; only rapture, only joy, only pleasure keen and bright and high; only love.

XXXII

Move the Stars to Mercy

When we had dressed again and I had put my hair in order, we went downstairs together.

Mamma and Papa were in the drawing-room. They were not surprised to see Wilfrid: obviously, Esmie had told them that he was here.

Wilfrid spoke:

"Your lordship; Mrs. Worthing: I know all. I apologise most humbly and contritely for my inexcusable behaviour some three months past; my importunate, precipitate conduct towards your daughter. The only excuse I can offer you is the deep urgency of my love. I hope I may be forgiven. She is blameless, except in this: she never told me that she was with child. Her sister told me, only to-day."

Papa looked at him steadily. "Then you are the father?"

"Of course I am," Wilfrid replied.

"I have always thought so," said Papa.

Wilfrid continued: "I hope you will agree, your lordship, that Melissa and I must be married as soon as possible, not waiting till December."

"Even if you were married this very day," Papa growled, "my daughter's reputation would suffer; for a scant six months after the wedding, she would be delivered of a child."

"We could plead prematurity," I suggested.

Mamma shook her head. "A baby of eight months," she said, "or even seven, perhaps . . . but *six?* A healthy infant of full size? No, my dear, the prematurity would stand revealed for what it truly was: a prematurity not of birth, but of connubial congress."

She turned to Papa. "Ambrose," she said, "you are no ordinary man, no common father faced with this age-old problem. You are a spiritual peer of the realm. You are a member of the House of Lords. You are a right reverend bishop of the Church of England, fully consecrated, with powers put into your hands by the hands of His Royal Majesty, King George."

"What are you trying to say, Penelope?" asked Papa.

"Surely," she replied, "you can fiddle the date on the marriage documents?"

Papa was shocked. "Fiddle the — do you mean — do you dare to suggest that I — ???"

"Yes, I do suggest it," Mamma said firmly. "Come, Ambrose: it needs but a stroke of the episcopal pen. All you need do is choose a date three months — or four, or five — in the past, and write it down."

"You appal me, Madam! To abuse my privilege in such a way would be a vile offence against my office, my Church, my King, my God!"

"Would you rather be known, and laughed at, as the bishop whose own daughter went to the altar not a virgin but a fornicatress, untimely planted with the ripening fruit of her sin?"

"The sin was mine," Wilfrid reminded her.

"I wonder," Mamma said sharply. "But no matter. People will not believe that she was forced by her own intended. They will assume that she was your willing accomplice. Besides, Wilfrid, would you wear a placard reading, *She Is Blameless; The Sin Was Mine?*" Again she turned to Papa. "Ambrose?"

Papa looked suddenly ten years older. "What you propose

is distasteful and illegal," he said. "It even may be a form of sacrilege. Still, it might be done . . . but what of the marriage ceremony itself? A stroke of the pen will not set *that* back. It will have to take place in the world of hard reality, in the present."

Wilfrid spoke: "May I suggest, your lordship . . ."

"By all means!" roared Papa. "Suggest away! Make free! You are responsible for our predicament — why should you not suggest a solution?"

"I suggest a small private ceremony, here in this house, with your lordship presiding —"

"I would have done so in any case," said Papa, "even under happier and less irregular circumstances. Eadward was married in our house, as was Esmeralda. This modern notion of being married in the church itself is bizarre. That is hardly a suggestion at all."

"I was about to say," Wilfrid added, "that the guest-list might be limited to members of our immediate families. My parents and my brother. My sisters and brother-in-law, if they return from Switzerland in time. Melissa's sister and brothers. And her sister-in-law, of course."

"No," I said, "not Luisa. She would take a superior attitude towards me for the rest of her life. I do not want her to be present. That means Teddy must not be invited, either."

Mamma sighed. "And no reception," she said. "Such a pity. Mrs. Cooke will be disappointed. These grand occasions bring out the best in her. And there are so many people I'd planned to invite."

"Yes," I said sadly. "I wanted to invite the Austens, particularly Jane. And Mr. Brummel and Mr. Lamb and the Sheridans and the Cholmondeley-Cockburns and Mr. Carruthers and so many more. Even the Regent, perhaps. But there is no help for it."

"I'm afraid," said Papa, "that it will appear somewhat suspicious: to announce, as a *fait accompli,* a marriage that is claimed to have taken place a full season or more ago."

"It is the best that we can do," said Mamma. "If anybody should dare to indulge in *innuendo,* they will be faced with a suit for libel or slander, and the marriage document will be produced in evidence. No one will dare to defy the Church of England — is that not so, Ambrose?"

"If you say it, my dear," he replied.

I asked, "When may the wedding take place?"

Mamma decisively replied, "No later than one week hence. Are we agreed?" Everybody nodded. "Good. Then I suggest, Wilfrid, that you write to Suffolk at once, bidding your family to come here for — let us say 'a family meeting.' We can explain the rest of it when they arrive."

Although dry of eye through all of this, now tears rolled down my cheeks and I wailed, "I have not even been fitted for a wedding gown!"

"There, there," crooned Mamma, embracing me. "You will wear mine. After all, your sister did. A few alterations here and there, and it will fit you perfectly. And now that everything is settled, I think it only right that you two young people be told something. I must ask you never to tell it to a living soul, and most particularly not to Esmeralda. I am divulging it now, and *only* to the pair of you, because I think it may help you to feel somewhat less guilty and humiliated. It will confirm the undeniable fact that all of us are human. I think the bishop knows the matter to which I refer: do you not, Ambrose?"

Papa's eyes went wide. "You can not mean . . . ?"

"I will not tell it if you forbid me to," she assured him.

"I do forbid it! What can you be thinking of?"

"Of these two children. Oh, Ambrose, my dear, I entreat *you* to think of them, as well: to think of what solace it could bring to our dear daughter and our son-in-law. Perhaps you would prefer to tell it yourself?"

"You may be right," said Papa, resignedly. " 'He who is without sin among you . . .' and so on." He cleared his throat and said to me: "When your mother and I were married, my dear, we were both very young. She was only seventeen; I was twenty-four. And she was . . . that is to say . . . she was already some five or six weeks *enceinte* . . . with your sister . . . Esmeralda . . ."

Mamma added, "Your father was a *very* vigorous and impatient young man."

Papa blushed a deep shade of crimson.

Wilfrid returned to the hotel, and I went to bed.

Some time in the middle of the night, I awakened with the rhythms of a poem throbbing in my mind. It was the lovely sonnet that Papa had composed for Esmie's twenty-first birthday. I had long ago absorbed it into my memory, for I admired it so, but only now were its more cryptic passages made clear:

"The baby is delivered, sir; a girl,"
The midwife told me, and I felt a flood
Of pride to see a female child, a pearl
Begotten of my rash and hasty blood.
But how could I foresee the love in store,
The precious moments of your growing up,
The many cherished ways that you would pour
Such joy into my undeserving cup?
When mortal time comes to an end for me
And that Recording Angel weighs my worth,
Deciding what my punishment shall be,
Perhaps my small part in your blessèd birth
May move the stars for mercy to exhort,
And judge me guiltless in that highest Court.

XXXIII

A Great Lesson

One week later, to the day, the wedding took place in our house.

Roger and his parents, in response to the letter Wilfrid had written them, had arrived the day before from Suffolk. They had intended to join Wilfrid at Pulteney's Hotel, but Papa would not hear of it, and insisted that they stop with us in the episcopal residence, where there were rooms in plenty. (Wilfrid's sisters had not returned from their journey to Switzerland.)

There was a surprise in store for me when I met Wilfrid's

parents. His father, who had lost almost all trace of his Austrian accent during his many years in England, looked hardly like Wilfrid at all. He resembled Roger, having the same small nose, blue eyes, and rather thin lips. It was a face not in the least like what I have come to think of as the typical Jewish countenance. And yet I knew that this man had been born Baruch Sommerfeld, and was indeed a Jew.

The "Jewish" features which I thought I saw in Wilfrid's face I now saw again in his mother's! For there, in the face of the former Phoebe Fanshaw, daughter of a very old Suffolk family that could probably trace its lineage back to the first King of the Saxons, I saw the large, arched nose, the full lips, and the coffee-brown eyes of my Wilfrid. So much for glib and ignorant notions of so-called Jewish faces, I told myself. And, now that I came to think about it, did not many notable English gentlemen with not one drop of Jewish blood in their veins have prominent "Jewish" noses? — Wellington, for instance? I learnt a great lesson that day.

"My dear," Wilfrid's mother said to me with the most kindly of smiles, "both of my sons have described you as beautiful — but, even so, I was not prepared to see a young lady as lovely as you. Wilfrid is a fortunate man."

Wilfrid's father kissed my hand, then took me aside for a private word. "My daughter," he said, "I beg your forgiveness for the way you were treated by my rascally son. He has a good heart, but he is impetuous, and you must be firm with him in your married life. Do not let him bully you. If he should ever do so, come to *me*. I will deliver to him such a scolding!"

"Thank you," I said, and added in a whisper, "Papa Sommerfeld." I winked.

He winked back. "Wilfrid told you?"

I nodded.

"Your Papa: he knows?"

"We have not told him."

"It is perhaps better so. But please: you must call me Barnaby. It sounds so very English, yes? It is a form of Barnabas, you know. A great Jew of the tribe of Levi, who defended and supported that other great Jew, Saul of Tarsus — the man we call Paul — when other Christians mistrusted him."

I promised to call him Barnaby, and to go to him if Wilfrid should ever cause me trouble.

The ceremony was, of course, a simple one: stark, some might have called it. Esmie served as my only bridesmaid; Roger was Wilfrid's best man; Freddy gave me away. (Papa, of course, as officiating priest, could not do so. Teddy had done the same at Esmie's wedding.)

Papa spoke the beautiful words of the marriage service with that fine balance of churchly dignity and actor's eloquence I have always admired in him. Everything went smoothly, until he intoned these words:

"I require and charge you — as you will answer at the dreadful Day of Judgment, when the secrets of all hearts shall be disclosed — that if either of you do know any impediment why ye may not be lawfully joined together in matrimony, that ye confess it."

At that point, my knees shook under Mamma's white wedding gown. I felt as if I should say: I am a liar, Papa, and so is the man at my side. The child I now carry is not his, as we told you. All of us in this room are liars, for we knowingly are participating in an improper ceremony with fiddled documents and a pregnant bride who wears virgin white. We stand here covered in deceit and falsehood, and we dishonour this solemn sacrament.

Of course, I said none of this. Papa, after the customary pause, prepared to read the closing words of the service, the words that would bind me to Wilfrid as his lawful wife.

But at that moment Wilfrid spoke:

"My right reverend lord," he said, "I know of nothing that either your daughter or I would consider an impediment to our marriage. And yet I feel bound to tell you something that *you* may deem an impediment."

Papa was greatly surprised. "In all the years that I have performed this service," he said, "I have never known anybody actually to utter a response to those words. They had come to seem no more than an empty form. Speak if you must, then."

"All of my family," said Wilfrid, "are faithful members of the Church of England. But my father was not born to that faith."

Mrs. Summerfield, stepping forward, said, "Wilfrid, don't! That is ancient history."

"Please, Mother," said her son, "I must." Turning back to Papa, he continued: "My father is a convert, your lordship. He was born to the faith of Israel. Therefore, in some sense, he is — and I am — a Jew."

A silence fell upon us, not unlike the silence that had fallen upon Carlton House when Mr. Brummel had shouted, "Who's your fat friend?" In the present case, the silence was broken by a muttered "Uh-oh" from Freddy, a whispered "Oh dear" from Mamma, and a small, simple *"Oy"* from Wilfrid's father.

"I beg your pardon, Wilfrid," murmured Papa. "What did you say?"

"I said, your lordship, that I am a Jew."

Somewhat in a daze, Papa nodded. He inhaled an enormous chestful of air and let it out in a long sigh of resignation. "So was our Saviour, my boy," he said. "If there are no further disclosures, I will, with your permission, conclude the ceremony."

I think that Papa learnt a great lesson that day, too.

XXXIV

Married Life

The lesson had not been learnt on that single day of our wedding, however.

As Papa told me later, "Ever since the time that your sister censured me for my story of Abraham; ever since her abhorrence of me made her so ill that she took to her bed; ever since that day, I have prayed that my mind be opened, that the path to true Christianity be lighted for me. I have spent many hours in prayer, many hours in thought, many hours in reading deeply of my Bible. In those hours I have strengthened in my soul the ties that bind our faith to that of the Jews, that link our destiny with theirs; and I have come to understand — not only with my mind, which has always known it, but with my heart, with my blood and bones — that the Jews are our fathers, and the faith of Israel is the well-spring from which our faith derives its strength. What hurts a Jew hurts me, a Christian. What I deny to a Jew I deny to myself. I am an old man: I might have gone to my grave steeped in that sinful error — but God has been good, He has shewn me the light before it was too late, and He has impressed it forcefully upon me by bringing a son of Israel into my family. For that, and for my two daughters who were His instruments of enlightenment, I am filled with thanks."

The day after the marriage ceremony, Wilfrid and I sailed from England on our wedding trip. We spent it chiefly in Vienna, but we did not see quite as many operas by Mozart and Weber as we had planned, for much of our time was occupied in the privacy of our hotel rooms, affirming and re-affirming our love in that sweetest of all rituals. Whole days would pass when we would not step out of our rooms, never putting on our clothes, having all of our meals sent up to us from the hotel kitchen.

I believe we did every thing it is possible for a man and a woman to do together. I even rode St. George, which both of us thought to be quite jolly, and I intend to do it many more times before I am laid to rest; but whether it will ever result in the birth of a bishop, I can not say.

Before returning to England, we journeyed to the Waldviertel region — my father-in-law's homeland — and to the little town of Spital, where we paid a visit to John Heathman's parents.

I was intensely uncomfortable in their presence, for reasons on which I need not elaborate, but our stay was not long. Wilfrid spoke to them in German, and I understood almost nothing; but when Anna Maria wept and uttered the name "Johann," my heart went out to the grieving mother, and I had to stop myself from saying: He lives, Anna. His child — your grandchild — lives in my womb!

Upon our return to England, we moved into the house that Wilfrid had bought for us in Mayfair. There, on a stout new bed, we continued the re-affirmations of our love; and, as the weeks blossomed into months, we settled happily into married life.

In the evenings, after dinner, we would sit in the parlour, Wilfrid smoking his pipe, and talk of all manner of things. On one particular winter evening, when the warmth of the gently crackling fire provided a cheery contrast to the snow-storm that was roaring like a demon outside, I said to him, "Wilfrid, do you remember that journalist, Mr. Rankwort?"

"Disagreeable chap," said Wilfrid. "A swine, really. All blackmailers are swine."

"That is what I wanted to talk about," I said. "Were you not just as surely blackmailed by Ben Trumbull? He came to you, told you what he had revealed to Rankwort, and you bought him off with a highly paid position in your company. In return, he pretended not to recognise Rankwort, thus foiling Rankwort's scheme. Is that not simply another form of blackmail?"

Wilfrid drew on his pipe for a moment, then replied: "I think it comes down to a matter of intent. Rankwort's intent was plainly villainous. I believe Ben to have been sincerely contrite when he came to me and told all. He asked me for nothing. He wished only to know what he might do to repair the damage. I believe that he would have gladly killed Rankwort, had I asked him to do so. Besides, Ben is a friend of mine; and, seeing that he needed employment and poor John was gone, it made perfect sense to offer him the position of foreman. He's caught on rather well, in fact, and is doing a good job of work."

Wilfrid's answer satisfied me. On that same evening, I brought up the matter of his father's un-"Jewish" features. He smiled and responded, "I am the farthest thing from an authority on racial characteristics, but a few years ago I read a book by Isaac D'Israeli,* in which he brought forward the point that what we think of as the 'Jewish visage' is actually Spanish. The dark complexion, black eyes, long aquiline nose, and what-not were acquired by the Sephardim — that is, the Spanish Jews — during their long sojourn in the Iberian Peninsula. Father, on the other hand, is from Central Europe. He has the blue eyes and fair complexion of —"

Here, I cried out in surprise and sudden pain.

"What is it, Melissa? What on earth's the matter?"

* *Vaurien* (1797). The author was, of course, the father of Benjamin Disraeli. His racial theories, a Jewish friend of mine insists, are *narishkeit* (pure nonsense). — R. R.

I pressed a hand to my belly. "I think — I think it is — the child," I said.

"It can not be," he replied. "It is much too early. Scarcely six months . . ."

"And yet I fear that it is coming," I said, dread in my heart and in my voice.

"Good Lord," said Wilfrid, "what do you wish me to do?" The decisive man of business was flustered and helpless.

"I want to be with my mother and my sister. Please, Wilfrid, may we go to Hans Town at once?"

"Of course," he said, plainly relieved that I had made the decision. He rang for Paley, our coachman, and in less than a score of minutes we were driving through the swirling white of the snow to my father's house.

XXXV

Dark Satanic Mills

As soon as we arrived at the episcopal residence, Mamma installed me in my old bedroom and bed, and Papa sent word to Mr. Cargrave and a midwife.

The whole family stood round me as I lay in the bed: Wilfrid, Papa, Mamma, and Esmie. (Freddy was at the theatre.) I was terribly afraid. "Oh, Mamma," I whimpered, "it is going to be all right, is it not?"

"Of course it is!" she assured me. But Mamma is not a very good actress, and I could see that she was worried. "You must try to rest. Mr. Cargrave and the midwife will be here soon." Turning to Papa, she said, "Where *are* they?"

Papa replied, "Tuttle just returned from Cargrave's house. He is not at home; he is out attending to another delivery, with the midwife who customarily assists him on these occasions. Tuttle left word at his house to come here, and —"

Wilfrid said, "But surely there are other physicians and midwives! He may be hours on the other case!"

"I have already sent Tuttle out again to Eadward's house,"

Papa told him. "Luisa has been through this more than once, and will tell him the names of the physician and midwife whom she trusts." Savagely, he added, "There are bunglers in plenty to be had — we want nothing botched here!"

"This storm is no help," Wilfrid said fretfully. "Travel through the streets has slowed to a worm's crawl."

Esmie took charge. "Leave the room, all of you," she said. "This talk is doing Lissa no good. Yes, *you* go as well, Mamma, for you will only fuss. I will stay with her."

There was such command in her voice, and such sense in her words, that nobody resisted her. They all left the room, and Esmie sat beside me on the bed. She took my hand.

Outside, the wind blowing over the chimneys of the house made a low, hollow sound like the kind Freddy and I once made, as children, by blowing over the tops of empty wine bottles. But this sound was larger, darker, wilder, like the moaning of lost souls in Hell.

"Am I going to die?" I asked my sister.

"Not for many, many years; and when you do, it will not be in child-birth, for you will be a very old lady, far past the child-bearing years."

Through my tears, I gently mocked her: "Gypsy fortune-teller!"

She smiled. "Jew's doxy," she said.

I returned her smile, albeit quaveringly. "Are we not a pair?"

"We are, indeed, for we have both of us married fine, good, loving men; the best of men."

"And yet my child . . ." I said, turning away my face, "my child will not be his."

"All of your other children will be his," she reminded me. "And this child will be raised as his own." She placed the palm of her hand upon my swollen belly. She closed her eyes. "It is a male child within you, my sister," she said.

I was able to laugh a little, despite my fears. "Come, Esmie, how can you know any such a thing?"

"I feel the little emblem of his maleness."

"You mean his . . . ? Surely not!" I added, to myself: I wonder if Wilfrid will want the boy circumcised?

Esmie, her eyes still closed, now said, "I see that maleness, in time, itself generating another male child . . ."

I laughed again. "I am not yet a mother," I said, "and already you make me a grandmamma."

She paid no heed to my interruption. "I see — I see —"

Suddenly she broke off speaking, opened her eyes, and withdrew her hand from my body, turning her face from mine.

"Esmie, what is it?"

When she turned her face again in my direction, I saw that she had gone as white as milk. "Esmie," I said, distressed by the look of her, "what is wrong?"

"Smoke," she said.

I became cross with her. "Esmie, not that foolishness again!"

"Do you remember, Lissa, standing in our garden earlier this year, when I spoke of 'dark Satanic mills'?"

"Yes, yes," I said impatiently, "Blake's line, but —"

"I smell those mills again," she said in a low hoarse voice, as if she were choked.

"I wish you to leave," I said sharply. "You are no longer a comfort to me. I hate it when you are like this, when you behave as if your mind were crazed . . ."

The mournful groaning of the wind rose and fell.

Slowly and in a level tone, she said, "It were better, Lissa, it were better by far, that this child of yours not be born."

Angrily, I cried, "Likely it will not be! It is coming too early! And its chances of survival are even less, now that you are upsetting me! Go away!"

"Pray for his death," she whispered. "Beg the Almighty to strike him lifeless in your womb."

"Why? Because it is not Wilfrid's? A moment ago, you were saying . . ."

"Pray for his death," she repeated.

"I can not do that!"

"You must," she insisted. "The poisonous flower must be cut down in the bud."

"Esmie, you are frightening me," I said, my voice shaking.

She placed her palm again upon my belly. "Oh, sister," she said in an awful moan, "I see a horror greater than any the world has ever borne! I see it in the form of smoke — I see the horror billowing around your grandson like thick fumes — darkening the skies with filth and stench . . ."

Sleet began a brittle chatter against the windows.

"Stop this talk, I beseech you," I said.

"The smoke is flowing from ranks of chimneys — the chimneys of dark mills or factories — and your spawn, the son of your son, stands over them like a Colossus, his eyes as soul-less as boiled gooseberries —"

(How strange that she should have said that!)

"— like a hideous Colossus, directing the ceaseless day-and-night workings of those factories — and the smoke grows thicker and darker . . ."

"Please . . ." I begged of her.

"The smoke is spreading," she said with closed eyes. "It is choking the world . . ."

"You are making me ill!"

"Now I see, marching like troops of demons out of the mouth of Hell, the legions who follow him. I see their banners rippling in that smoke, and upon those banners I see a black and crooked sign, the antique fylfot, what some are wont to call *croix cramponnée* and others Cross of Thor — and your grandson's myrmidons hail him by his name; with stiffened arms and croaking cries of carrion birds they hail him, even as the weird sisters hailed the son of Sinel: *Hail!* they scream in their devil's tongue; and *Hail!* again those maddened multitudes extol him. I hear his name — not clear, but twisted through the rasp of clotted throats and through the smoke that never, never stops . . ."

A knife of agony drove a cry from my lips. Faintly, I said, "Esmie — call Mamma — I feel —" But so lost was she in sibylline frenzy that she could not hear me.

Her eyes opened wide at a new vision; a long, shuddering gasp stopped her voice; then she spoke again, starting in a whisper; but this whisper mounted, giving way to ever stronger, strident tones until, when she reached the end, she was screaming the words like a madwoman:

"Those factories that spew the smoke into the sky — I can see inside them now — *oh, God!* — inside them are rows upon rows of ovens — gigantic ovens —"

"Call Mamma . . . *please,* Esmie! . . ."

"And into the flames are being thrown — men and women — little children — by the thousands — hundreds of thousands — *millions!* I am peering into Hell itself! And through the smoke I see and hear those demons still, your grandson's votaries, roaring out his name — I hear it echo and resound across the moat of time that lies between us and the is-to-be — *Hail!* and *Hail!* again they cry — *Hail Hiedler! Hail Hiedler! Hail Hiedler!*"

A deafening drum-rattle of sleet assaulted the windows, as my sister, choking, gagging, coughing, suffocated by her visionary smoke, fell back, off the bed, onto the floor, in a faint.

"Esmie!"

I remember wondering, as again sharp pangs lanced my body, driving all else from my mind — wondering how in the name of all that is holy or unholy Esmie had discovered my deepest secret: the true name of my baby's father.

Then I plummeted into unconsciousness, too, beaten into it by pain's black bludgeon.

XXXVI

All for the Best

It has been a year or more since I have plucked this secret album from its hiding-place and written in its pages. When one's life is full and happy and busy, as mine has been, there is little need to spend precious hours scratching away with a pen. There are better things for a young wife to do: a husband, for instance, to love and please — and manage. I think that I manage him rather well, and without his being aware that I am managing him. I love him well, too, and please him greatly — as he does me.

There are dinners to give, and to attend. We are a popular and sociable young couple, and we move in the best society. Lord Byron calls here often; so do the Sheridans; the Austens are among our dearest friends — in particular, Jane, when she comes to town: she tells me that *Pride and Prejudice* is completed and will be published next year. We have been several times to grand receptions at Carlton House. Now that I am a married woman, the Regent has resumed his amatory pursuit of me; but I have been able to parry his thrusts without offending him — so far, at least.

We see Mr. Brummel, too, but I fear that he is in decline and is often morose. He speaks vaguely of removing to the Continent, "Paris, perhaps," some time in the indefinite future. Often he will say, with a sigh, "Oh, my dear friends — if only I could find again my lu[cky cri]pple!"

At Lady Heathcote's ball, earlier this year, Lady Caroline Lamb, sick with love for Byron, slashed her wrists with a broken wine-glass. Byron was not impressed by her display: he responded with a c[rooked s]mile.* I wonder if it can be true that she sends him clippings of her private hair through the post? The person I feel most sorry for is poor William Lamb, her husband. Needless to say, his mother, Lady Melbourne, strongly disapproves of her son's wife. When Caroline had rushed from the room after cutting her wrists, I heard her mother-in-law say, "I could not have believed it possible for anybody to carry absurdity to such a pitch."

In May, Mr. Spencer Perceval, who had been our Prime Minister since 1809, was murdered in the lobby of the House of Commons by a man named Bellingham. It seems that Bellingham had once been imprisoned in Russia, of all places, and the British representative there, Mr. Gower, had done nothing to help him; so when Bellingham returned to this country, he was determined to kill him. However, not being able to locate Mr. Gower, he contented himself with killing poor Mr. Perceval instead. I call *that* carrying absurdity to an unbelievable pitch.

The word "pitch" reminds me that, strange to tell, it appears that I have lost all interest in my clarinet. Perhaps it is because so many duties and other interests occupy me now; or perhaps it is because Esmie is not in this house to accompany me on the harpsichord. And yet I wonder: might not my clarinet have been, in some kind, a substitute for a thing heretofore lacking in my life? — that other, more beloved, clarinet, of which I have become an a[ccomplished virtuo]so?†

*Or "c[lever si]mile"? — R. R.

†Other possibilities: "an a[ddict who loves it] so," "an a[ctive advocate, al]so" . . . and there must be more. Readers who wish to suggest others may write to me in care of the publisher. — R. R.

Mrs. Siddons has retired from the stage, as was predicted. And (so tiresome) we are once again at war with the United States of America — as was also predicted. Freddy, thanks to this war, has not gone off to America, for which I am grateful, because I should have missed him sorely. "Just as well," I suppose, he said at dinner recently, "seeing that I am so damnably disposed to sea-sickness."

Cholmondeley-Cockburn, who, with his wife, was among our guests that evening, said, "I have crossed the Atlantic only once, in my youth, and I suffered greatly from that malady. Green, I was. A grizzled old jack-tar, seeing me in my affliction, shook his head in pity. 'By the look o' thee, lad,' he said, 'thou'lt never shite a seaman's turd.' And indeed I did not, for *a full nine days* of that wretched voyage! My guts were tied up in knots! But on the tenth day, when I sat upon the jakes, my prayers were answered, a miracle occurred, and I was delivered of a veritable prodigy that rolled unendingly from me until I thought that it would never stop. When at last I arose and looked down upon what I had wrought, I was amazed to see a long, firm, unbroken, perfect marvel, coiled up neatly like a sleeping snake, and black as ebony! I had a mind to mount it and preserve it as a curiosity for my mantelpiece, as men sometimes are wont to do with gall-stones of remarkable size. Alas, I failed to do so."

I did not appreciate such a story at my table, but Wilfrid laughed most heartily, as did Freddy, Mr. Carruthers, Mr. Charles Lamb, and a new friend just come to London, Mr. Hazlitt, all of whom also dined with us on that occasion. Freddy, as if in compensation for the loss of American audiences, gained fresh favour with his London public in another play from Chum's pen, *Farquhar the Artisan,* a farce based on the tempestuous life of the Seventeenth Century playwright; as well as in new stagings of Dick Sheridan's *The Rivals* and *The School for Scandal,* which happily brought coin into Mr. Sheridan's pocket, too. Teddy's professional fortunes also have continued to rise, and Luisa has presented him with another son.

On the subject of sons, it seems almost unnecessary to add that John Heathman's son, by reason of such extreme prematurity, was born dead. I did not think that this would distress me, considering the beastly circumstances of the baby's siring and my loathing of his hateful father; but a woman can not carry a child within her body for months, and bring it forth in painful travail, then feel nothing when all of it comes to naught and the poor blameless little creature never opens its eyes in this world. The sadness of that event made me disconsolate for some time; but gradually, and with my dear Wilfrid's help, I regained my former cheerfulness.

"God's will," Papa said of the baby's death; and, without putting any credence or significance to Esmie's incomprehensible ravings, I suppose it may have been for the best, at that. Who can tell? — perhaps *all* things are for the best in what Voltaire's Dr. Pangloss called this best of all possible worlds.

Afterword

Melissa's stillborn son is mentioned glancingly in the diary of her younger daughter, Pamela (see *Princess Pamela,* 3 January, 1837), who obviously had no knowledge of the child's true father. Before turning to stranger and weightier matters, I will round out Melissa's chronicle by tying up a few loose threads:

Some readers, noting that Olivia Fairchild, while carrying Wilfrid's baby, married a Suffolk man named Royce, and remembering my almost certain conviction, in the *Princess Pamela* Afterword, that Pamela's second husband was also a Suffolk man of that name, will ask if Pamela unknowingly may have married her own half brother. I can only say: I do not know, but it is a distinct likelihood.

Esmeralda's Channel tunnel, far from being completed in her and Melissa's lifetimes, as she predicted, has still not materialized, as of the year of the present volume's publication (1981). But interest in the project was revived as recently as 1979. Nor was this the first revival since Albert Mathieu's original 1802 proposal. In 1875–76, a French company took over seven thousand seabed soundings, in order to map out a tunnel route. Over three thousand samples of the seabed structure were drilled. The British began work in 1881, blasting a seven-foot shaft and boring two thousand feet through the Cliffs of Dover and under the sea. Meanwhile, the French were beginning to dig from Sangatte in the Pas des Calais. But by the early 1880s, British enthusiasm was cooled by the Duke of Cumberland (*not,* of course, the same one touched on briefly in the present book, and who figures significantly and sinisterly in *Princess Pamela*). As commander-in-chief of the Army, Cumberland wrote a massive memorandum condemning the proposed tunnel as a threat to British security, conjuring up visions of another Norman invasion, this time via underwater tube. His fears were echoed in our own century, when, shortly after World War II, Field Marshal Montgomery opposed the idea. It was to surface again in the 1960s, but was squelched when President De Gaulle vetoed British entry to the European Common Market; and in 1973, with Britain at last a member of the Common Market, the project was yet again revived, the British advancing 250 yards through the Dover Cliffs, near the site where the earlier attempt had been halted in 1883. In 1975, however, the Labour government cancelled the work, and an immense boring machine, costing British taxpayers roughly the equivalent of $700,000, was sold to a junk dealer for less than one-tenth that figure. In 1979, possibly as a vote of confidence in the Conservative government of Prime Minister Margaret Thatcher, Britain and France again agreed to study Mathieu's 1802 dream, this time as a single tunnel to be used exclusively by railway trains; but differences in the electrification systems of the two countries, as well as discrepancies between French and British traditions of bridge and tunnel clearance heights, posed technical problems not *necessarily* insurmountable.

The blackmailing courtesan, Harriette Wilson, having learned no lesson from her experience with Freddy, continued her extortionary ways: in 1824 her target was no less a figure than Wellington, whose contemptuous response has become a permanent part of our language: "Publish and be damned!"

A final word about the Luddites: The last and fiercest mass trial of Luddites took place at York two years after the time of this chronicle, in 1813, when over a dozen of them were hanged and many more sentenced to overseas transportation.

Nowhere in *Princess Pamela* is Wilfrid's exotic ancestry touched on, so we must assume that Pamela was never told her paternal grandfather's original name and religion. It is interesting to note, however, with appropriate hindsight, that Wilfrid casually and quite unnecessarily once made use of the word "rabbi" (*Princess Pamela,* 16 March), and when he sought to comfort Melissa as they both stood over the body of their dead daughter (8 May), he did not say, as well he might have said, "She is with Jesus," or ". . . with God," or "She has gone to a better place," or any number of similar pious clichés. The particular pious cliché that came to his lips in that first sharp moment of grief was "Our girl is in the bosom of Abraham."

Esmeralda's fevered vision of the future's smoke-belching camps (the culmination of prior smoke-sensings that had come upon her whenever she encountered strong manifestations of anti-Semitic feeling) cannot pass without comment. Esmie seems to have known what others have learned only through bitter historical experience. An epithet of contempt directed at a race or group will do little harm; it is no more than bad taste. But bad taste, as Stendhal reminded us, leads to crime; and cumulative contempt, persistently expressed, can create a climate conducive to lynching, torture, and genocide. The "harmless" Polish jokes of today are no less dangerous than the "harmless" Jewish jokes of the Nineteenth Century — which led inevitably to the dark Satanic mills of the Holocaust.

"The son of Sinel," mentioned *en passant* in Esmie's vision, is Macbeth, of course ("By Sinel's death I know I am Thane of Glamis" — *Macbeth,* I, iii). "Fylfot," *"croix cramponnée,"* and "Cross of Thor" are all synonyms for the swastika. If the ravisher of Melissa was that same Johann Georg Hiedler who was born in the Austrian village of Spital, near the Kamp River, in 1792, son of Martin Hiedler and Anna Maria Göschl, then he was the man supposed by many contemporary biographers, including Robert Payne, to have been the most likely candidate for the genealogical post of grandfather to our century's most Satanic figure (or third most, if one holds the opinion that the even more efficient Georgian and Hunanese slaughterers must vie for first and second places).

The name Hiedler is of dubious background, John Toland saying it may have been derived from a Moravian name, Hidlarček; Payne — somewhat farfetchedly, perhaps — citing Heide ("heath") and Heidjer ("heath man," hence "heathen" or "pagan") as its possible origins. Payne tells us that Johann Georg married a Hoheneich girl in 1823, but that she "vanishes from sight, and it is possible she died early in the marriage." Johann Georg "had the reputation of being a shiftless wanderer," and in 1836, having shiftlessly wandered to Strones, he is believed to have impregnated a middle-aged peasant woman. The following year, she gave birth out of wedlock to a boy, Alois, who, fifty-two years later and with the collaboration of his third wife, who was also his niece, spawned that infamous son. (Johann Georg dutifully married the mother of Alois, incidentally, although in no unseemly haste, for the wedding did not take place until 1842, when Alois was five.)

But both of Johann Georg's marriages, and the siring of Alois, would have been flatly impossible, given the recorded years of those events and the year of this chronicle, and assuming that Melissa wrote the truth. It is irresistible to speculate that if Melissa's violator indeed had been that Johann Georg, and if he died in 1811 without marrying, and if his only progeny was stillborn, the scroll of history might never have been stained with one of the darkest blots the world has ever known.

Our world, perhaps I should say, referring the reader to the Afterword of *Princess Pamela* and its reflections on quantum theory, breakdown of causality, and worlds of alternative possibility; for, to paraphrase words from the aforementioned *Macbeth,* who can tell which seeds of time took root, and which did not, in Melissa's world-next-door?

R. R.

To

THE UNKNOWN PARENTS

of my father

and to

his adoptive mother

FREDA RAESE RUSSELL

and to

my mother's parents

HENRY OTTO *and* EMMA BÜCHEL OTTO

this book is humbly dedicated